LOVE'S ORPHAN

J.C. WILSON

JWC

MAR 2019

Acknowledgements

I would like to thank my former students: Johanna, Mike, Jessica, Ryan, Brandon, Tina, Jacob, Charlie, and especially Erin. Your daily persistence in asking (begging) to read this manuscript, and your enthusiasm for the story when it was in its fledgling and utterly-deplorable state, encouraged me to finish something I had given up on. Thank you also to Catherine, who read through an early draft and further convinced me I had a story that someone besides myself might enjoy reading.

I also wish to thank my beautiful, patient, kind, and ever so supportive wife, Liz. Your tolerance of my countless days and nights staring into a glowing computer screen ("working on my book, baby") allowed me the time and space to finally cross the finish line.

Most importantly, I wish to thank my Lord and Savior, Jesus Christ. I can't imagine my life without Him in it. God's mercy and grace toward me is more than I can do justice to with mere words. It is my hope that those who read this book will find something in it that points them to Him and the ultimate meaning of life. Like Elsea, may you discover that regardless of the storms you are going through, our God is watching over you and is ready to answer the moment you call upon His name.

J.C. Wilson

Contents

CHAPTER ONE

Love Poems

Regensburg, Bavaria, 1251

The sentries bracketing the door slapped their chests in salute when the old man reached the top of the steps.

"Is the duke in his room?" he asked after catching his breath.

"Yes, Lord Savoyen," replied the guard nearest him. "He's not left all day."

Savoyen waved a hand, and they pushed open the door.

Duke Otto's bedchamber was as spacious as it was Spartan. A few oaken chairs and a too plain bed competed to fill the vastness between faded tapestries hiding the cold stone walls. The room was dark but for the far corner where the crackling flames from a recessed fireplace had carved out a small refuge of warmth and light.

Sitting before the blaze was a white-haired man cloaked in a blanket. He stirred himself at the sound of footsteps. "Is that you, Savoy?"

"Yes, Your Grace."

"Have you found them?"

"I am sorry, My Lord, but the patrols have nothing to report."

"Nothing?"

"Not even a rumor, My Lord, good or ill."

Otto pulled his blanket tighter and hunched closer to the flames. "My shoulders ache whenever it rains now," he grumbled. "The cold seeps into my very bones."

Savoyen stepped over to the wood box and tossed another log into the pit causing an explosion of sizzling sparks to fly up the chimney.

"How long has it been?" asked Otto.

"This is the sixth day since they were expected back, My Lord."

"Six days!" moaned the duke. "I feel some evil has befallen them, Savoy. What if I have lost them? What am I to do without my sons? How am I to live?"

"It is too soon to despair," replied a calmer Savoyen. "Perhaps they have merely gone deeper on their foray this time and are returning by a more difficult route."

"Or perhaps that witch has murdered them," lamented the skeptical Otto.

A soft knock interrupted Savoyen's reply. He went to the door and spoke in hushed tones with an unseen person in the hallway before returning to the duke.

"What is it?" asked Otto without looking up.

Savoyen came all the way back to the fire before answering softly, "She is dying, My Lord."

The duke spun around with a start. "What! So soon?"

"She is asking for you," added Savoyen.

Otto's only reply was to stare blankly past his shoulder.

Savoyen stepped closer and laid a hand on the back of his chair. "She will not last the night," he said with more urgency.

The tone in Savoyen's warning brought Otto around. He sprang from his chair and flung his blanket aside. "Bring me my robe!" he bellowed.

The two guards hurried to keep up with the old men as they flew down twisting stairways and bolted along dimly lit hallways stopping only when they came around a corner to a hidden alcove concealing a locked door. Savoyen pulled a key from his pocket and inserted it into the keyhole. There was a faint click, and the door swung open to reveal a set of stone steps spiraling down into darkness.

"The duke and I will proceed alone," he said, taking a lantern from one of the guards. "Remain here and make certain no one follows."

"Yes, Lord Savoyen," they answered in unison.

The stairs led to a seldom used tunnel that ended far beyond the castle walls. The discreet passage was always cold and wet, but tonight was worse. The frail light from Savoyen's lamp struggled to hold back the musty blackness as they crept along shoulder to shoulder.

Otto pulled up the collar of his robe. "Blast this dampness," he murmured.

When they reached another door at the tunnel's end, Savoyen hung the lamp on a corroded hook protruding from the wall. "Let us hope it is still burning when we return."

They labored to unstick an iron bar and then pulled together on the door which groaned on its rusted hinges. Dazed momentarily by the cold rain that assaulted them, they cinched up their robes, and ventured out into the night. Savoyen paused to look up at the trees swaying back and forth around them.

"Do you remember the way?" shouted Otto above the wind.

"I believe so," answered Savoyen.

A wending course through the trees brought them to a road, and they trotted along its muddy ruts with heads bowed against the rain. At last they came to a cluster of wood and thatch dwellings common to the peasants of the region. They stepped up to a home noticeably larger than its neighbors. The cracks around the doorframe glowed dimly from a light within. Savoyen knocked lightly three times.

The young girl who opened the door led them across the only room to an elderly woman sitting next to a narrow bed. The embers of a wood-starved fire smoldered in the fireplace, and a few candles sputtered on a nearby table. On the bed lay a woman not as old as Savoyen and Otto. The candlelight exaggerated her paleness, yet revealed a face of classic beauty. Her high cheekbones and full lips hinted at how striking she had been in her youth.

The seated woman offered Otto her stool. As she took his robe, she gave him a somber look and shook her head. He sat down and tenderly grasped the dying woman's hand.

She opened her eyes at his touch. "I knew you would come," she said faintly.

Otto raised her hand to his lips and softly kissed the backs of her fingers. The smile that blossomed on her face only added to her beauty.

"Is he home yet?" she asked with a hint of concern.

"Savoyen thinks they are merely returning by a more difficult route," he answered, trying hard to sound cheerful. "We expect him back any moment now."

"I gave him to Our Lord before he took his first breath," she said confidently, "and I know God will keep him safe. I only wish I could've spoken to him just once more." She turned her head to look him in the eyes. "Oh, my love, why wouldn't you let me tell him? I'll die tonight, and I've never told him the truth." Though these were words of reproach for Otto, her soft and sad voice carried no bitterness.

"Forgive me, Dana," he begged.

"You've nothing to be forgiven for, my darling, but..." Her bottom lip began to tremble and she stopped to regain her composure. "But he's all grown, and now I'm dying. You made me choose between you and my own son. A mother shouldn't have to make that choice, but I did for you. Please, my love, he deserves to know. I beg you to tell him."

Otto paused to glance up at a stone-faced Savoyen before answering. "I will, my dearest."

Her eyes opened wider, and she pulled his hand to her bosom. "Oh, promise me that you will," she pleaded. "Swear to me on my very soul before I leave this world."

"I will tell him," he promised, with his hand resting on her weakly beating heart, "and may God have mercy on me for what I have done."

"Thank you," she sighed, as she squeezed his hand tighter. "You don't know how much you've eased my mind." Looking into his dejected face she added, "Do not fault yourself, my love. You've done many wonderful things for me. Yes, many more things than a woman like me deserved."

"You know I do not like it when you speak that way," he scolded gently. "I wronged you most wickedly, Dana. You could have had the life you deserved if not for me."

"We both of us were wrong," she smiled, "but God has not laid our sins upon him. God's blessing is on his life, and that has given me a joy worth more to me than anything you think I've lost."

He laid his head on her shoulder.

"Do you remember how young we were?" she whispered, still clutching his hand to her heart. "We did love each other so very much, didn't we?"

"I have never loved anyone more," he whispered back.

"It was so long ago that sometimes I feel it was only a dream and never real," she said. "But it *was* real, wasn't it?"

"It is still real for me," he answered. He lifted his head and began to stroke her auburn hair which, though streaked with silver, was still long and lush. "Do you remember how I used to do this?"

"Yes, my love."

"Do you remember those silly poems I would write?" he asked, running his fingers through her hair. "You always let me read every line and pretended they were the most moving words you ever heard."

"I was never pretending. It flattered me to know you were thinking of me even when we were apart. Those memories are still precious."

Her breathing grew fainter, and she drifted off to sleep. Otto looked up at the old woman who mouthed, "She's getting worse."

Dana opened her eyes. "You were very kind to bring him to me, Lord Savoyen," she said clearly.

"You are welcome," he answered with a slight bow. "I regret I cannot do more."

"We must say goodbye now," she said, turning to Otto. "I've put you at great risk by asking you here, and you know you can't come back again."

At those words, he broke down. "Oh, Dana," he sobbed, "you are still young and beautiful, and I am old and withered. Why doesn't God take me instead?"

"Don't weep for me, my darling," she struggled to say. "I've had a good life: I was loved by a kind man who gave me a brave and wise son. Your promise was the only thing left to complete my happiness. I go to be with our Lord now. We'll meet again in His kingdom someday, and together we'll find the joy this life could never give us."

The duke sat up and wiped his eyes.

"Please go," she implored softly. "I don't want you to see me die."

He reached out and took her face in his hands. Looking into

her eyes for a long moment, he bent down and kissed her like he did when they were young. "Goodbye, my sweet Dana."

"God bless you, my love," were the last words he would hear her say in this life.

The duke followed Savoyen into the stinging rain, and they set out on the way they had come. They had gone only a short distance when Otto suddenly stopped and sank to the ground. Before Savoyen could react, the duke was on his hands and knees in the muddy road.

"Dana," he wailed as the rain fell harder, "my sweet Dana!"

Savoyen struggled in the slippery mud to lift his friend who continued his heart wrenching laments and refused to be consoled. Eventually able to coax him into standing, they staggered back down the road toward the forest. When they finally emerged from the tunnel where the sentries still stood vigil, Savoyen collapsed from exhaustion.

"Take hold of the duke!" he gasped.

The guards quickly grabbed him from either side. Back in his quarters, they helped strip his wet clothing while several anxious servants fussed over him until they got him into his night clothes and tucked into bed.

With the guards and servants gone, and Otto lying back on his pillows quietly sipping hot broth from a mug, Savoyen removed his own rain-soaked garments and spread them out on the hearth stones of the fireplace. He collapsed into Otto's high-backed chair with a sigh. As the steam rose up from his wet clothes, he let himself stare into the fire and was soon under the spell of its dancing flames.

"I should have married her, Savoy," interrupted Otto from his darkened corner.

"Then you would not be the Duke of Bavaria today," replied Savoyen coldly. "Coronets are not won by espousing pretty peasant maidens."

"Easy words for you," returned Otto. "I am the one who turned away the only happiness I ever knew. It is a hard thing to bear in my old age I tell you."

Savoyen turned in the chair to face the duke. "You are overcome with sorrow, my friend. It speaks well of the sincerity of your feelings for the woman, but do not forget that you did honorably by her. She never wanted for anything, and you brought the boy into this castle and made him a knight."

"But I made her lie to him," countered Otto. "I should have let her tell him the truth—or told him myself."

"We both know it was needful to conceal that truth, My Lord, and now more than ever that we are so close to the fulfillment of all our aspirations."

"Or so you keep telling me!" snapped the duke.

"The boy has lived contentedly in ignorance thus far," said Savoyen in a more soothing voice. "A brief season longer will cause him no harm."

Otto took a long sip from his mug. "A brief season for *you*," he mumbled beneath his breath.

CHAPTER TWO

Cunning and Capture

The Austrian frontier, six days earlier

A dozen weary knights rested their horses atop the spine of a barren ridge. The vapor from the panting animals lingered about them like a stubborn fog. Before them was a pine forest, behind, a vast swamp made more imposing by the approach of night.

"Charles, I disapprove of this scheme of yours," complained Prince John.

"We have no time to argue," answered Charles from beneath the scarlet tunic he was pulling down over his head. "Somehow, they know you are with us, and it is clear they will not relent until you are captured. Your safety is all that matters now."

"But this ploy has the stench of cowardice about it. I should wear my own shirt and fight to the death!"

Charles finished putting his arms through the sleeves. "Your Highness," he smiled wryly, "there is no shame in cunning."

Not appreciating the humor, the prince turned to the large man at his left. "William, I say we turn and charge these swine and punish them for their insolence!"

"Charles knows what he's doing, My Lord," William assured him. "We'll punish the insolent Austrians another day."

The lead rider of a company of knights suddenly cresting the ridge ended their debate. "Here they come!" exclaimed Charles. "Take the prince into the swamp before it is too late."

William wheeled his horse and led Prince John and four of

his knights down the backside of the hill toward the swamp. "I'll see you in Bavaria," he yelled over his shoulder before they disappeared beneath its trees.

Charles and the others trotted in the opposite direction for the pines. He looked back in time to see their pursuers turn in his direction. "It's working!" he shouted. "Let's get into these woods before they discover our ruse."

They spurred their horses deeper into the trees, but the fatigued animals could barely manage a canter. When Charles saw that they would soon be ridden down, he motioned for a halt. His men swung around to face their tormentors who came to a thundering stop before them under the pine boughs.

"Who dares harass the son of Duke Otto?" cried Charles across a small clearing that separated them.

"You know very well who we are, Prince John," yelled the black-haired leader.

Charles was stunned. Even in the failing light the leader was close enough to see his features and should have been able to tell he was not the prince. He decided to take advantage of this unexpected development. "I am on a diplomatic mission," he announced in a voice he hoped was princely enough, "and I demand you give way."

"Is trespassing and looting what you Bavarians call diplomacy these days? I declare you my prisoner. Now throw down your weapons or we will take them by force!"

"I insist you first release my men."

"Your men are no less guilty, and I expect Her Grace to make a proper example of them."

"The duke will not tolerate mistreatment of my personal guard!" answered Charles, doing his best to sound properly indignant.

"Ha! Maybe it is time that old man learned some toleration.

Look around you, Prince John—you have only seven swords against one hundred. The mouse should not squeak so loudly in the presence of the cat." He nodded his head slightly, and his men began spreading out to the left and right encircling the worn out Bavarians.

Charles turned in his saddle. "They believe I am the prince," he whispered to the men behind him. "Do as I do and you might yet escape."

He drew his sword and faced the knights now closing in around them. "Seven swords for seven dead men!" he cried before he led them forward in a charge.

Their sudden assault caught the Austrians by surprise, and they burst through a narrow gap in the ring.

"Get the prince, you fools!" shouted the leader. "I need him alive!"

Charles urged his men to scatter into the pines, but turned himself back to fight. Ignoring the other knights disappearing into the gathering dusk, they quickly had him surrounded. He spun his horse in a tight circle, slashing wildly with his sword, but his valiant stand ended ingloriously when they pulled him to the ground and bound him hand and foot.

The black-haired Austrian studied him from atop his horse. "I see you have left boyhood behind," he observed with a sneer, "but have grown none the wiser."

Lying on his back in the pine needles, Charles looked into the dark eyes of his captor. "I am at a disadvantage, Sir, as I do not know your name."

"Lord Eugene, at your service," he answered with an exaggerated bow that robbed it of any humility. "What an entertaining display of bravery, Your Highness. It is a pity your own people did not linger long enough to see it. In Austria, we expect our knights to sacrifice themselves for their nobles. It seems Prince John 'the Dim' has gotten it the wrong way around."

Before Charles could think of a witty response, Lord Eugene laughed loudly. "Get him ready to move," he ordered as he trotted away.

The Austrians rode single-file along the narrow trace of a road winding through the pines. Lord Eugene insisted on extra precautions against losing his valuable prize. Charles straddled his horse with his hands tied behind him, while a rider in front held his reins. Another rope passing below the belly of his horse bound his ankles together making it impossible for him to leap down.

The sun had set, and the twilight gave way to the first sliver of a waxing moon.

Charles was fidgeting in his saddle to alleviate some cramping, when Lord Eugene cantered up on his left.

"And how is our esteemed prisoner doing?" he asked. "I hope being strapped to the back of an animal like a sack of grain headed to market is not too disagreeable for a man of your celebrated refinement."

Charles thought it best to ignore the gibe. "Where are you taking me?"

"Fortune smiles upon you, young prince, for you will soon be the guest of the duchess herself: the ever-gracious Elsea Babenberg. I am sure that in the course of some pleasant conversation she will ask you to explain your presence in Austria."

"We were not in Austria when we were attacked," lied Charles.

Lord Eugene threw his head back in a forced laugh. "I admire your stubbornness, Prince John, I really do. Yet your sudden concern for the sanctity of the border lacks credulity. After all, according to my scouts, it is the third time this month you have raided our land."

"Then your scouts are mistaken," Charles smiled faintly, "it is the fourth time."

"Ah, if we are to speak of mistakes, then allow me to point out the folly in pillaging the estates of the good Baron Kirchenbetter two times in one week. I have been patrolling his district, and I thank you for stepping into my little trap."

"War has its risks," shrugged Charles.

"Who said anything about war?" asked Eugene. "Though greedy princes like your father cannot wait to make a meal of our little Austria, we are not yet at war. It is a point I imagine Her Grace will bring to your attention."

Bored with trading barbs with the pompous lord, and fearful of letting slip some comment that might give him away, Charles made no reply but to stare ahead at the long line of knights ambling through the trees.

Lord Eugene did not take the hint.

"Speaking of the duchess," he continued, "I believe it has been a number of years since you had the privilege of her company. You will find she has grown to be, shall we say, an *unusual* woman. Out of consideration for your youth, I pass on a few caveats to keep in mind when you meet. Consider it a courtesy of one noble to another."

He leaned back in his saddle, rubbing the short beard and moustache that encircled his mouth, and began. "First of all, though it will admittedly be difficult, you must not stare at her face. She is understandably sensitive about her ugliness." He let out a mournful sigh that Charles found unconvincing. "I really do not know which is worse, Prince John, to die from the pox or be left to live with its scars."

"That is a question only God can answer," replied an indifferent Charles.

"So, I take it you are a religious man. I am afraid you will find little in common with Her Grace in that regard. The duchess long ago gave up such quaint views."

"Is that all?"

"Only one more thing," said Eugene. "Her Grace, ironically, is somewhat lacking in the social graces." He leaned in and added in a lower tone, "Some would say *completely* lacking. I therefore strongly advise you against disagreements. As you will shortly discover, she does not well abide contrary opinions." He sat up and smiled at Charles as if expecting some gesture of appreciation.

Charles indulged himself in an unnecessarily protracted yawn.

A brief scowl flashed across Lord Eugene's face, and he urged his horse closer. "Prince John," he said with a false calmness, "I detect you do not fully appreciate the delicate nature of your circumstances. Perhaps this is due to your youth, or perhaps to your lack of a full portion of intelligence, but I dare say your attitude will change ere long." With that, he lashed his horse and galloped to the head of the line.

Feeling as if a noose had just been taken from around his neck, Charles let out a long exhale. He had not expected his hasty plan to actually succeed beyond a few minutes. How he had been able to fool this Lord Eugene fellow, up close and face to face, he could not explain, but certainly things would get worse when they reached Vienna. What would become of him once they discovered him for a fraud? As was his habit, he decided not to dwell on that unsettling thought for now. Instead, he comforted himself with the knowledge that each rhythmic stride of his horse brought William and the prince closer to safety.

Eventually the column left the woods and broke out into

more open country. The weak light from the moon mixed with the starlight of the cloudless sky to illumine the road before them. Scanning the heavens above, Charles soaked in the majesty of the constellations, and thanked God to be alive.

CHAPTER THREE

First Impressions

A metallic creaking awakened Charles with a start, and he sat up on his skimpy cot groaning from a sharp pain in his back. Two guards squeezed through the door of the cramped cell and informed him that Lord Eugene was on his way to escort him to the duchess. They had orders to make him presentable and did their best to brush the dust and dirt from his clothing. He used the comb they gave him to comb his long brown hair straight back.

Lord Eugene stuck his head inside the door. "I hope you had a pleasant sleep, Prince John. It helps to be well rested when meeting Her Grace."

"A blissful night," answered Charles, rubbing his lower back. "And these fine gentlemen would rival the best valets in all Bavaria."

The guards grinned widely at the compliment.

"Don't stand here gawking," barked Lord Eugene. "Notify the duchess I shall bring the prince momentarily."

With a guard at each elbow, Charles followed Lord Eugene through the confusing passageways of the castle interior until they reached a wide stone staircase spiraling up to a grand landing. Passing through two ornately carved doors, they entered a long hall lined with two rows of matching pillars that ran down the middle supporting the weight of a vaulted ceiling. The morn-

ing sun shone through a series of tall windows on the left. At the
far end, a shaft of light fell on an unassuming throne centered on
a low platform. A few servants waited discreetly in the shadows,
and several dozen knights and nobles were scattered about in
small groups talking quietly among themselves.

The low drone of conversations ceased abruptly as Lord
Eugene led Charles to the dais. Facing the empty throne, he
announced in a loud voice that startled the assembled courtiers,
"Your Grace, I present to you his royal person, Prince John of the
House of Wittelsbach of the Duchy of Bavaria."

All eyes turned toward a solitary figure gazing out one of the
windows. She wore a long-sleeve, faded blue tunic that hung
down to her knees. Her long dark hair was pulled back tightly
from her face and tied on top of her crownless head in a strange
sort of knot. With her riding boots, tight leggings, and wide
black belt she could have passed for a knight, albeit one of low
degree.

"She looks more man than woman," thought Charles.

The Duchess did not stir at Lord Eugene's booming announcement and continued to stare out the window. Charles wondered
if she had a problem with her hearing.

At last, she turned and held him in a prolonged glare. "So
this is the infamous Prince John," she said as she made her way
to the throne, "only son of the high and oh-so-righteous Duke
Otto the Illustrious. I must confess my disappointment, Lord
Eugene. Considering all the trouble he has caused us, I expected
you to bring me someone a little more imposing. Is this really the
man that took a month to capture?"

"Indeed, Your Grace," smiled Lord Eugene, "though their
combat skills could use refining, the Bavarians are quite adept at
evasion. I doubt the prince's companions have stopped running
even now."

The quip evoked some snickering from the nobles in the hall who had now migrated toward the dais.

Elsea stepped onto the platform and crossed the few strides to the throne. She sat down and studied Charles anew. "Tell me, Prince John," she asked calmly, "are all Bavarians born as thieves, or must your mothers *teach* you to steal?"

From the moment he came through the doors, Charles expected someone who knew the real Prince John to speak out and end his charade. It only now occurred to him that neither Elsea nor any of her nobles had seen the prince since he was a boy. Standing before the sarcastic duchess the thought crossed his mind to reveal himself and have a long laugh at her expense. He dismissed the impulse, however. "Your Grace," he said wryly, "I am thankful for my career as a thief if only because it has allowed me to meet *you*."

Elsea clapped her hands slowly in mock applause. "Why My Lords," she said looking around the hall, "it seems our visitor is not only a prince but a jester as well. Perhaps we can find him employment at our next banquet."

The room exploded in laughter.

Charles answered her insult with a slight nod and a faint smile.

The laughter died away, and when she got up from her throne to face him he could see she was no longer in the mood for humor.

"Prince John," she began tersely, "can you give me one reason why I should not declare war on your father before another sun rises?"

"Because a war with Bavaria would not be to your advantage," he replied casually.

"And I suppose it is out of concern for my advantage that your father has ordered these raids across my border. Maybe stealing my property is his way of revealing his tender feelings. I beg your pardon for my ingratitude."

Charles was still groping for a response when she continued.

"Do you think me a fool?" she shouted, pounding her palm with a fist. "Your father's ambitions are no secret. Any child can see he hopes to take advantage of our current distress to pluck my Austria like another flower for his foul bouquet. Well, he will find this flower has thorns and its aroma not so sweet. He will start by paying dearly for you. I will have a ransom of fifty thousand gold florins from him and not one penny less. I do not care if he has to tax every dainty Bavarian noble down to his undergarments to raise the money. He will bring it himself, kneel before me, and beg my forgiveness. Until he does, you will sit in this castle and rot!"

The final words of her tirade reverberated through the hall, and she shot him a piercing look that dared him to challenge her.

He saw that would be pointless. "As you wish, Your Grace. I am, after all, your humble prisoner."

"I see you fancy yourself chivalrous, Prince John," she said with a measure of composure returning. "I am sure there are those who appreciate it, but you will find such niceties wasted on me. I do not trust polite men."

"Forgive me," he answered without thinking, "but good manners was something else my mother taught me as a child, and I have not been able to break myself of the habit."

"What? Do I detect a clever tongue? Could it be the reports of your slow wits are less than credible?"

"Perhaps the reports of Her Grace's shortcomings are false as well," he shot back.

Elsea leapt off the platform and strode towards him with eyes ablaze. She stopped an arm's length before him, and he could now see the blemishes left behind by the disease that all but killed her. Her jaw tightened, and he steadied himself for another rant.

Instead, she took a step back. "It is fortunate for you," she informed him calmly, "that you are worth nothing to me dead." With that she turned her back on him and headed for a door behind her throne. On her way out she said to Lord Eugene over her shoulder, "Do what you must to keep our clever-rob-ber-prince alive."

Charles dropped down onto the thin bag of straw covering the wooden slab that was his cot. A narrow beam of light from a tiny window high above allowed him to survey his scant accommodations. Except for a pitcher of water next to a quarter loaf of stale black bread, nothing had changed since the night he arrived.

"Well, at least they didn't forget breakfast."

Hoping to soften the hard bread, he dipped it into the pitcher before biting off a corner. While he chewed, he could not keep himself from laughing out loud as he considered the bizarre twist his effort to gain his friends a few extra minutes to escape had taken. Not only had he completely hoodwinked the Austrian lords, but the duchess was holding him for a ransom! He wished he could be there to hear the roars of laughter from Otto and Savoyen when they received her outrageous demand.

He stretched himself out on his lumpy bed and went over his encounter with the remarkable woman. Though her wardrobe was shocking and her demeanor caustic, she was not exactly the hydra-headed monster he had expected. A little too angry, perhaps, but who could blame her? She would be out of place among the ladies of Otto's court to be sure, but behind her sharp tongue he detected an intelligence that those frivolous and overly perfumed women would not understand.

He gnawed off another piece of bread, and tried to estimate how far William and the prince should have gotten by now. Distracting him from his calculations, however, was the angry face of Elsea floating through his mind like an apparition.

CHAPTER FOUR

The Trophy

Later that night the guards came to take Charles to dinner. This had nothing to do with any concern for his appetite. Elsea's brief reign as duchess had become noteworthy if only for its many disappointments. Snatching someone like Prince John of Bavaria was a remarkable accomplishment, and the most would be made of her symbolic victory over the renowned Duke Otto.

Lord Eugene led Charles into Elsea's great hall now transformed into a vast dining room packed to capacity with knights and nobles crowding around tables of every width and length. The dull roar of their conversations turned to cheers as Lord Eugene paraded his trophy through the hall. Not used to being the center of so much attention, Charles could not decide if his face should look humble or proud and so attempted a mixture of each.

Though many of the cheering men were prestigious in their own right, waiting at the table closest to the dais were the most powerful nobles in Austria. The white-haired Lord Raglan, Count of Hohenberg, sat across from a reserved Bishop Prochaska. At the far end of the table, the Barons Keinmeyer and Kirchenbetter leaned back in their chairs snickering over some private joke. Lord Eugene introduced Charles, and after the perfunctory greetings they gave him a seat between Keinmeyer and

Raglan. Lord Eugene sat opposite him, and only the chair at the head of the table remained empty.

With nothing else to do while they waited for the duchess, Charles took in the surroundings. The assembled guests, laughing and joking loudly with each other, occupied every bench and stool. Hundreds of burning lamps and candles, suspended from the ceiling or jutting out from the walls, filled the air with a smoky haze. Servant girls with heaping platters of food flowed in and out through two doorways and circulated among the tables. Alongside loaves of bread and wedges of cheese, they placed roasts of pork and venison, as well as whole chickens, ducks and geese. Pitchers of drink dotted the tabletops like trees towering over the plains of plenty. The excitement of the boisterous men increased with each new tray of victuals set before them.

The growling of his stomach reminded Charles he had eaten nothing more substantial than bread and water in three days. His eyes grew blurry from staring at the piles of steaming food, and he struggled against the temptation to begin the repast prematurely.

At last, a sentry came through another door and shouted over the cacophony of voices, "My Lords, Her Grace of the House of Babenberg, Elsea, Duchess of Austria!"

Everyone jumped to their feet as Elsea strode into the room trailed only by a young girl. Charles was surprised to see that, except for a pearl-lined golden circlet atop her head, she was dressed no differently than when he first met her that morning. A thunderous and sincere ovation filled the hall as she made her way to her place. Word that Elsea had captured the notable prince, only son of the aspiring Otto, would make the neighboring duchies envious indeed. The men in the room understood the importance of the moment, and they cheered and applauded as if trying to erase the frustration of the last four years. Shouts of, "Elsea the Great!" resonated off the stone walls for several minutes.

When Elsea reached the table, she paused near her chair and responded to the adulation with a few weak smiles. She looked pleased, but Charles sensed her satisfaction ran shallow, as if she distrusted this sudden outburst of enthusiasm. She took her seat which was the signal for her loyal guests to give their hands and voices a rest.

After Bishop Prochaska asked the blessing, the dining began and the noisy drone of conversation filled the hall again. Ignoring the efforts of his tablemates to converse with him, Charles stacked his plate high with food and attacked it like a fortress under siege.

Lord Raglan gave him a long look. "The prince eats like a starving man," he observed. "I trust you are seeing to the welfare of our distinguished guest, Lord Eugene."

Before Eugene could reply, Charles answered around a mouthful of roast pork, "On the contrary, Lord Raglan, I find Lord Eugene's stale bread most satisfying. That is, I am most satisfied when it is gone."

The joke elicited some honest laughter from his fellow diners. Lord Eugene did not join in.

Raglan turned to Elsea. "My Lady, do you not think we can provide the prince something more conducive to good health than stale bread?"

"Why Lord Raglan," she answered, "I hear the Bavarians these days are so starved for food that they have taken up thievery just to feed themselves. One would think they would be happy with bread of any kind." She looked down at Charles long enough for him to catch the sneer in her eye. "Nevertheless, Lord Eugene, the count is correct. Since the prince's value to me is in direct proportion to his health, you will see that his diet is improved upon."

"As you wish, Your Grace," replied Lord Eugene calmly. He and Charles stared at each other from across the table.

Charles had already made up his mind that he detested Lord Eugene. In his travels with Duke Otto and the prince, he discovered many of his kind haunting the ruling houses of Germany. They were always subtle and devious men skilled at giving silky praise or committing heinous murder as circumstances required. Charles never understood why the princes tolerated such men in their courts. As he returned Eugene's glare, he could not help feeling a mild thrill at having scored a tactical victory over him with his little barb.

"Prince John," said Raglan, breaking the silence at their table, "I have not seen your father in ten years. Please tell us how he is doing these days."

"The duke is as active as ever, My Lord," answered Charles after a quick swallow from his goblet. "He is still trying to breed the perfect horse, bring down the largest stag, and never misses a chance to go hawking."

"Ah yes," laughed Raglan, "he always did love his falcons. I remember the pair he took with him the year we campaigned in Italy with Emperor Frederick. That was before you were born. Does he ever speak of those days?"

"I have heard many accounts of his Italian adventures," smiled Charles. "The duke can be quite entertaining when he has an audience."

"Well, bravo for Duke Otto!" snapped Elsea. "It is refreshing to know that one of the wealthiest men in Germany, who nevertheless must steal my property, has so much time for leisure and frivolity. Tell me," she continued with growing agitation, "which of his quaint pastimes kept him from sending any condolences when my mother and brother died?"

Though taken aback by her unprovoked rudeness, Charles was not flustered. He realized that she was angry with Otto and not him. "Your Grace," he began in his most respectful voice, "as you know, I have no brother, and my mother is still alive. I cannot pretend to understand what it is like to lose someone so close, but it certainly must have been difficult. Please accept *my* condolences, belated as they are."

The other men at the table had stopped eating, and Charles sensed an uneasy anticipation. His soft answer seemed to have quieted her stormy spirit, however, and she simply frowned before returning to her food. Lord Raglan and Bishop Prochaska exchanged puzzled glances.

Elsea's outburst dampened the mood of the table for a time, but Baron Keinmeyer stepped in to rescue the flagging conversation. "Tell me, Prince John," he began a little too pompously, "are the serfs in Bavaria as slothful and discontented as they are in Austria? We seem to be overrun these days with ungrateful peasants with nothing better to do than foment discord and calls for freedom—as if they would know what to do with it anyway!"

"Lord Keinmeyer," replied Charles, as he lowered the hunk of cheese he had just put to his lips, "I believe that were it not for the ill treatment many so-called lords showed their serfs, very few of them would *want* to leave their manors. Nevertheless," he continued after popping the cheese into his mouth, "I am convinced that God has purposed men to be free, and freedom is not compatible with serfdom."

Keinmeyer's jaw hung slack, and he blinked his eyes several times. "Are the serfs not free to enjoy the land we let them work? Are they not free to live in the homes we let them build? Does protection in time of war mean so little? I cannot share your view, Prince John. The peasants are free from want and idleness, and they should be grateful for our generosity. Is that not so, Lord Kirchenbetter?"

"Yes, Prince John," agreed a condescending Kirchenbetter, "you would do well to listen to Baron Keinmeyer. He is older and possesses greater wisdom in these matters. As we all know, Almighty God desires every creature to enjoy his place in society. He created some to rule, but most to be ruled. It has always been this way."

"Lord Kirchenbetter," replied Charles, still chewing, "tradition seems a deceptive place to find God's will. The pagans of the Orient have worshipped idols since before our Savior was born. Does this mean we should as well?"

The conversation's new theological tone aroused Bishop Prochaska. A lifetime of service in the Church of Rome made him the only one at the table qualified to speak with authority on behalf of God. Laying aside his leg of duck, he sallied forth to clear up all confusion.

"My dear Prince," he began as if speaking to an errant altar boy, "one should ponder more carefully the mysteries of the Almighty. Do not look to the heathen world to find the will of God. It is clearly manifested to us, here, in the Christian world. He willed that there should be a sun to rule the day and a moon to rule the night. He willed that there should be kings," and quickly catching himself added, "and queens—to rule the earth. He willed that there should be lords to assist his chosen monarchs and that there should be peasants to serve the lords. It is not for us to question God's intentions, young Prince, but rather to humbly submit ourselves to his divine decrees." Bishop Prochaska finished his brilliant oration by rewarding himself with an extra-long drink from his cup.

Charles was not impressed. "I look not to the heathen for my inspiration, Your Excellency, but rather to the pages of Scripture. Our Lord taught us that to love our neighbor was the second greatest commandment. Are not the peasants our neighbors?"

Bishop Prochaska nearly choked on his swallow.

"Prince John," interjected Elsea, "the list of your talents grows by the hour. I see that to court jester we must now add theologian. Maybe your father should have sent you to a monastery. You might have made a better priest than a prince."

The men around him laughed politely.

Charles looked into Elsea's face and for the first time noticed her green eyes reflecting the light of the many lamps and candles. He could not decide if she had intended to offend him, or was merely trying to save him from another of Prochaska's sermons. Giving her the benefit of his doubt, he responded only with a broad smile before looking down at his plate.

By now, most of the guests had eaten their fill, and all attention was directed to the main door where entered a minstrel strumming on a stringed instrument accompanied by a pretty woman dancing gracefully. The duo wended their way between the tables regaling their audience with a repertoire of melancholy ballads alternating between the glorious triumphs of heroes long dead and the blissful rapture of requited love. The enchanted men quaffed their drinks in silence, and many grew teary eyed. Charles occasionally looked over at Elsea and several times caught her yawning.

The musicians finished with an embellished bow before the head table amidst a deafening applause. After they were ushered from the hall, and the ovation died down, lord after lord began rising to present what they believed were moving toasts worthy of the occasion.

Baron Keinmeyer stood first and held up his mug. "To our

esteemed Duchess," he said in a voice that boomed through the hall, "may her reign outlast that of all her enemies."

The toast provoked the customary table pounding and grunts of approval. Many others around the hall took their turns to offer up similar banalities until finally Lord Eugene came to his feet.

"To our most gracious host," he said with a respectful bow toward Elsea, "may her victory over Otto be as complete as her victory over his son." He shot a sideways glance at Charles as he drained his cup.

Charles caught the mockery in his eye. Though he knew he should ignore it, he could not resist the temptation to respond in kind. He got up quickly and raised his goblet. "To Lord Eugene," he began, "congratulations on my capture. May all your victories enjoy odds of a hundred to one."

By now the account of the lopsided chase through the Austrian countryside had become common knowledge, and the reference incited a hearty blast of laughter in the hall. Once again, Lord Eugene did not partake.

With the banquet now over, Elsea rose from her table to receive the obligatory expressions of gratitude from the guests. She made as little conversation as possible, and Charles detected her eagerness to conclude the unpleasant duty.

The hall was nearly empty when the guards came to lead Charles back to his cell. He wondered why Lord Eugene insisted on following them until they came through the door, and both guards suddenly grabbed his arms and slammed him against the wall.

Lord Eugene stepped up, and with their noses almost touching, hissed through clenched teeth, "Beware, Your *Highness*, I am not a man to be trifled with." On the last syllable, he drove his knee hard into Charles's groin, and he collapsed to the floor in excruciating pain.

Charles was still in a crumpled ball on the floor when he heard the door slam closed. Eventually, the searing pain began to subside, and he was able to gently crawl onto his cot and stretch out cautiously.

He began to rethink the wisdom of continuing his ruse. If Eugene treated him this way when he thought he was the prince, what would he do when he discovered he was only a knight? Maybe it was time to confess, he reasoned. After all, the prince should be safe by now, and he had gotten a hot meal at the expense of the Duchess of Austria out of it for good measure; what more could he expect?

Yet the stubborn streak in Charles would not let him give up so easily. He would confess, he told himself, soon enough. Until then, it might be prudent to tread a little more softly in the presence of Lord Eugene—if he could manage it.

CHAPTER FIVE

Conspirators

The men of Elsea's council exchanged sullen looks as they took their seats around the table. The portraits of five generations of Babenberg dukes looked down on the solemn gathering, but could offer no advice to the dejected nobles. The duchess was not present, nor was she expected. Her council had learned by now that certain matters were better discussed behind her back.

Lord Raglan looked around the table. "My Lords," he began, "I regret to inform you that the new Emperor has rejected our latest petition. He still refuses to honor his father's agreement and insists on the return of our ancestral lands."

"It would seem your diplomatic skills are waning," noted a smug Lord Eugene. "Perhaps it is time for a less subtle approach. In my experience, the clever application of the right amount of gold has never failed to change even the most stubborn of minds."

"Conrad is no man of simple tastes," pointed out Kirchenbetter. "It will take more than a few coins to change *his* mind. Our coffers are nearly exhausted. Where do you propose we find this gold?"

"Why, the duchess herself has unwittingly given us the answer," smiled Eugene. "We only need squeeze Otto like an apple to make cider, and buy Hohenstaufen favor with Wittelsbach gold!"

"Bribery always begets more bribery," warned Raglan. "In the end, the only thing that gold will buy us is Otto's wrath."

"He already is our enemy," replied Eugene.

"Some enemies can be reasoned with."

"Do you mean like the reasonable Duke Otto who is ravaging our frontier at will?"

Raglan had no reply.

"So," continued Lord Eugene, "diplomacy has failed and you are too noble for monetary *enticements*. You know that leaves us with but one alternative."

"Eldridge," frowned Raglan.

"Speaking of which," inserted Keinmeyer, "what response has he made to our latest query?"

Eugene pulled a folded sheet of paper from beneath his shirt. "I received this communication only today," he reported as he handed it to Raglan. "I think you will find he has addressed our concerns most satisfactorily."

Raglan passed the letter to Keinmeyer without looking at it. "I have yet to see *anything* satisfactory about that self-styled duke. He is a rebel we should have put down three years ago."

"We were in no better position to do that three years ago than we are now," pointed out Eugene. "What we need is a more practical strategy."

"You call trusting a rebel a strategy?" asked Raglan. "I knew Eldridge when he was an insignificant margrave, and he was a notorious liar even then. What makes you think he has changed?"

"Because now he is a duke," replied Lord Eugene matter-of-factly.

"Ha!" snorted Raglan.

"My Lords," intervened Baron Keinmeyer, "let us not waste time debating Eldridge's veracity. That he has his deficiencies, none can deny, but neither can we deny our need for a marriage.

The Babenberg reign will perish unless we find the wench a suitable husband."

"Keinmeyer is right," agreed Lord Eugene. "Our world is unraveling before our eyes." He grabbed the letter from Keinmeyer and held it up. "Here is a way to reunite with Styria short of war and at last give the duchess a measure of legitimacy. We will solve two complex problems with one simple marriage."

"And let us not forget the Holy Father," added Bishop Prochaska quickly. "A lawful marriage to a genuine house is all that stands between us and his blessing."

"Ah, yes," replied Lord Eugene with a roll of his eyes, "let us not forget the Holy Father."

Raglan rapped the floor sharply with his staff. "I tell you I do not trust the man!"

"Since when did we have to trust a man to take advantage of him?" asked Eugene with a dramatic shrug. "We need a marriage. It would be utter folly to turn away the only man from here to the English Channel willing to wed the monster."

"Lord Raglan," tried Kirchenbetter in a calmer tone, "what Lord Eugene is trying to say is that regardless of your reservations, which we all share, we have no other options. If you have a... uh... more *appealing* solution, please show us."

All eyes turned on Raglan.

"Perhaps Otto can help us," he suggested.

"Otto?" sneered Lord Eugene. "Are you suggesting we hold the prince captive until his father delivers us a ransom of a lonely noble bachelor?"

"He would have to be very lonely indeed," smirked Kirchenbetter.

"Do not speak so crudely," admonished Raglan. He shifted himself in his seat and continued. "What if we return the prince safely and without preconditions as an overture to restoring the good favor we once had with Bavaria?"

"But Otto tried to help us once before," noted Kirchenbetter.

"That was four years ago," retorted Raglan, "and this time we have his son to bargain with. A grateful Duke Otto might be willing to assist us. He is held in high esteem by some of the oldest houses in Germany. A good word from him on our behalf may be all we need to achieve our purpose."

The doubtful barons looked across the table to Lord Eugene.

"Lord Raglan," began the equally dubious Eugene, "even if we allow ourselves to imagine the duke will somehow have forgotten Her Lady's past indiscretions, a fanciful conjecture to say the least, what you are proposing would mean using the prince as a form of tribute; one might even call it a *bribe*. That would require overruling the duchess. You know perfectly well she intends to use Prince John to humiliate Otto. She will not be happy."

"She is not happy about many things," conceded Raglan. "But in this she will have no choice. We will inform her of her duty in the morning."

"And what about Eldridge?" asked Keinmeyer. "What response should we make to his offer?"

Again, all eyes turned to Raglan.

"It is my hope we will find our solace in Bavaria," he admitted. "However, it would be foolish to burn any bridges just yet. Lord Eugene, you may write a favorable reply to Eldridge. Encourage him, but be certain to make no promises. We will meet with the duchess tomorrow regarding our new plans for Prince John. However," he paused to look them all in the eyes, "we must be careful to say nothing to her about Eldridge, and especially matrimony, just yet."

"Indeed," returned Keinmeyer, "her reaction will be as unpleasant to endure as it will be unseemly to behold, and the longer we can postpone it the better."

Lord Eugene leaned back in his chair and looked around at his fellow nobles. "My Lords," he smiled, "our long nightmare may at last be over. Whether he is Styrian or Bavarian, by this time next month we could finally have a groom for the Babenberg beast!"

He and the barons enjoyed an overly embellished laugh.

CHAPTER SIX

Strange Stirring

Charles paced his tiny quarters with a new appreciation for the fate of a penned animal. The sound of his door unlocking caused his heart to leap.

"Prince John," said the guard who appeared inside, "Lord Raglan wishes to see you."

Overjoyed for any excuse to escape the monotony of his cell, Charles did not even ask the purpose of the summons. He happily followed two guards to the second floor, and across a now empty great hall, until they came to the door that Elsea had disappeared through the first time he saw her. As they approached the threshold, however, they heard the shouting of an argument from behind the door. The guards stopped abruptly and exchanged fearful looks.

Judging from their reaction, Charles gathered they were not expecting this and yet were not surprised either. He returned their expressions of embarrassment with his own look of complete indifference all the while straining his ears to their utmost eavesdropping ability. Though the thick door muffled the words, he recognized the voices of Raglan, Eugene, and the duchess. He understood enough to discern Elsea was upset about something.

The obscure debate continued a few minutes more until suddenly the room went quiet. The first guard took a deep breath, stepped up to the door, and rapped his knuckles three times. The door flew open, and there stood a red-faced Lord Eugene.

"What took you so long?" he snapped. But before the startled guard could answer, he added in a softer tone, "Please come in, Prince John."

Charles stepped inside what he assumed was some kind of private dining room. In addition to the elegant tapestries covering the walls, he noted the large paintings of all the great figures of the House of Babenberg. He recognized a young Duke Leopold and his son, Frederick, but did not see one of Elsea. Three tall windows opened at one side, and the fresh air and sunlight of a warm spring day filled the room.

Charles glanced from face to face, subtly searching for clues to their verbal battle. Keinmeyer, Kirchenbetter, and the bishop sat around a long oaken table. The barons reposed like men well sated after an enjoyable meal. Prochaska seemed unsettled, yet relieved, as if a painful thorn had just been pulled from his hand. Lord Raglan, leaning against the sill of a window, looked like a father who has had to reprimand an unruly child, but feels guilty for being too excessive. Lord Eugene's face was more difficult to decipher. Apparently, he had mastered the art of concealing his true emotions. Yet the way the corners of his mouth turned upward ever so slightly beneath his moustache betrayed his sense of triumph. One look at Elsea answered the most pressing question: whatever the argument had been about, she had lost.

Charles studied her with a new interest. She stood alone near the only other door like a scolded servant waiting for permission to leave. Her arms were folded tightly across her chest, and though she held her head proudly, her defiant expression could not mask her obvious humiliation. For some reason which he could not understand, the thought that these men were responsible for her disgrace made him angry. He looked back again at her council and despised them all.

"Please be seated, Your Highness," said Lord Raglan. "We have something to discuss with you."

Lord Eugene offered him a seat. Charles sat in the one next to it.

"Prince John," said Raglan, "we will avoid useless pleasantries and come right to the reason we have called you." He took a step closer and leaned on his staff. "We know that Duke Otto has been permitting these border raids because he hopes to provoke us into a war we cannot win."

Charles made a motion to protest, but Raglan cut him off. "We have not brought you here to dispute that fact. What we wish to know is do you believe your father would be amenable to a proposal to resolve our conflict and avoid this war?"

"Lord Raglan," said Charles with a shrug of his shoulders, "whether or not the duke can be swayed from his current policy would of course depend on what it is you are proposing."

Raglan returned to his place at the window, each deliberate step accompanied by the sound of his staff tapping on the wooden floor. Charles saw Elsea tense in anticipation of his answer.

"First, we will waive all rights we have to a ransom for your person and return you to your father as soon as circumstances permit. Secondly, as a show of our good faith, we will pay a tribute to the duke of a thousand florins in gold. All we ask in return is a meeting with His Grace at a location of his choosing. I think you will agree, Prince John, that we are in earnest and that this is an honorable offer."

Charles tried to present a calm front as he soaked in the ramifications of what he had just heard. Until now, he had no idea how he was ever going to make it back to Bavaria alive. The last thing he expected was being sent home like some kind of peace offering.

As important as this development was, however, Charles was not giving it his full attention. He had noticed the scowl on Elsea's face as Raglan listed their terms. "So that's what it is," he said to himself, "they are forcing her to bargain with Otto." He recalled her boasting before a crowded hall that she would make Otto beg forgiveness from his knees. The prideful Elsea intended to shame the duke, but they now insisted she honor him.

"I cannot speak for Duke Otto," said Charles at last. "Nevertheless, it is my opinion that he will find your proposal worthy of consideration, assuming, of course, that the duchess is in agreement." He paused to look Elsea in the eyes. "Are you also in favor of this offer, Your Grace?"

Elsea had not spoken a word since his arrival. It was obvious to him they meant her to be quiet and acquiesce to the proceedings. He leaned back and enjoyed a twin feeling of contentment for having irritated the council while showing her a proper respect.

Kirchenbetter and Keinmeyer gave each other a look of consternation. Lord Eugene clasped his hands behind his back and walked stiff-legged to the window near Raglan. Charles watched Elsea closely and thought he detected a hint of gratitude glide across her countenance. They wanted her to be silent and submissive, but he had rescued her. He was confident she understood his intention, and it took a determined effort on his part not to smile.

A long silence followed as everyone waited to hear her reply.

"Prince John," she began in a restrained voice, "I depend on my council for advice in matters of state, and I have learned to trust their judgment. They have persuaded me that their approach is better for Austria. I therefore endorse this proposal to Duke

Otto. It is our hope that you will be so kind as to express these things in writing to your father so that we might dispatch a courier this very day." She ended her speech and glanced over at Raglan and Eugene who stood shoulder to shoulder at the window. She made a face that said, "Was that good enough?"

"A letter to the duke is a small thing to ask, Your Grace," replied Charles who pretended not to notice the look she gave them. "I only have need of pen and paper."

Bishop Prochaska took the letter from Charles and handed it to Raglan. The count, with Lord Eugene looking on, read it carefully, then passed it to the barons.

"Prince John," said Raglan, "you are to be commended. Your service this day may have enabled us to avoid a costly and utterly unnecessary war. I believe I knew your father well enough to tell you that he would be proud."

"I have only done my duty, Lord Raglan," cautioned Charles. "I cannot predict Duke Otto's response."

A clearly annoyed Elsea spun to leave the room; but before she went through the door, she looked back at Charles and shot him a curious look. He had no idea what it meant. Yet even more difficult for him to understand was the strange stirring he felt as he watched her go.

CHAPTER SEVEN

Mother and Daughter

Elsea relaxed in her favorite chair in a room lined on three sides with bookshelves. The shelves reached to the ceiling and were crowded with leather scrolls, paper rolls, and hardbound volumes of every description. Over many years, and at great expense, her grandfather had gathered hundreds of copies of the literary works of antiquity from all over Europe and the Near East. Duke Leopold often spent hours in this very room teaching himself from the classics of ancient Greece and Rome. By the time he died, he had amassed one of the best libraries in all Germany.

Elsea's father, however, thought little of such learning. What could a stack of worm-eaten papers teach him he did not already know? He never ventured into the room much less open any of its dusty volumes. Elsea was still a child when one day she found the abandoned library. Something about the old tomes and parchments fascinated her and she pestered her father to teach her to read them. To placate her, he employed a tutor who showed Elsea the secret to deciphering the mysterious markings that filled the yellowed pages. The task quickly became an obsession and she was soon reading complex works and asking penetrating questions that even her tutor could not answer. Yet most of all, she discovered the unexpected joy of escaping the stark realities of her life by immersing herself in the history and philosophy of long-forgotten people. When she became duchess, she enlarged the room to include her personal residence so as to be even closer to her beloved books.

Sitting across from Elsea, in her usual chair near the dormant fireplace, was Dorianne, her lady-in-waiting. Dorianne was small, yet carried herself with an effortless confidence. She was plain looking, yet pleasant to look at. She kept her shoulder length black hair braided simply in the back making her look older than her sixteen years.

Dorianne was repairing a worn-out shirt while Elsea read from a musty manuscript laid out across her lap. Only the sounds of needle and thread working in and out of the old cloth, and the occasional rustling of old paper when Elsea turned a page disturbed the intimate quiet of their privacy.

"What happened at the council meeting today, My Lady?" asked Dorianne.

"As usual," replied Elsea, casually turning a page, "they treated me like a fool. Only this time they found it amusing to do so front of Prince John."

"What did they want?"

"In their collective wisdom, they believe I should return the prince and beg Otto's pardon for his trouble."

"Perhaps that's a good thing, My Lady," suggested Dorianne, still focusing on her work. "The prince is an honorable man and deserves to be sent home."

"Honorable!" blurted Elsea. "We caught him in the very act of stealing. Where is the honor in that?"

Dorianne tilted her head in thought. "I think God allows *princes* to steal," she decided. "They're lords, after all."

"Lords would steal with or without God's permission, Dori."

"But Prince John seems different."

"What is so different about him?"

"He doesn't like Lord Eugene," noted Dorianne.

"Well, who does?"

"That may be true, My Lady, but I believe the prince insulted him at your dinner because he knows he's not a man of honor."

"Or maybe he insulted him because he is half-witted, because only a fool would go out of his way to make an enemy of Lord Eugene."

"No, no, very honorable," insisted Dorianne.

Elsea rolled her eyes. "And what other admirable traits have your astounding powers of observation detected?"

"He's a kind man," answered Dorianne confidently.

"Now he is kind," laughed Elsea.

"He has tried to be polite to you," reasoned Dorianne.

"Why should he be polite to me? He is the son of a man I loathe."

"I don't see what that has to do with it, My Lady."

"Dori, you are a marvel indeed. You have gained all this insight into his very soul without speaking a single word to him. You sound like one of the Gypsy women in those smoky tents at the fairs. Do you read palms as well? Perhaps you can tell me my fortune." She finished with a burst of forced laughter.

"Laugh if you like, My Lady, but the prince is kind, he's honorable, and I like him." Dorianne nodded her head emphatically at each of her points, but did not look up from her needlework.

"Well, I think he is up to something," replied a no longer smiling Elsea. "And I am not fooled by his courtly charm. If he hopes to endear himself to me by his gracious tone he will be disappointed. It is plain to see he is working at some ploy."

"What ploy is that, My Lady?"

"I am not sure," admitted Elsea, "but I feel he is mocking me somehow. You should have seen how he pretended to care about my opinion in front of the council today. It was perfectly obvious to him I am against their ridiculous scheme. I saw the look on his face: he enjoyed watching my humiliation."

"I think you make things more difficult than they need be, My Lady. An honorable man *should* care about your opinion. You are a duchess."

"You are too innocent," sighed Elsea. "You still believe the world is full of good people."

"Not so, My Lady. Living with you has taught me there are many bad men in the world, but I don't believe the prince is one of them."

"Well, I have learned never to trust first impressions," confessed Elsea. "All men want you to believe they are made of gold, but scratch the surface, and you will discover the lump of clay beneath. Believe me, Dori, we shall soon find out that your honorable Prince John is not what he appears."

"That may be, My Lady, but until then I will think him kind."

Elsea said nothing more for a long time. She kept making trips to the stacks, but could not seem to find anything of interest. Returning one last time with another volume, she sat down with a sigh. "Dori," she said at last, "I would rather not eat alone tonight. What do you think of having some guests for dinner?"

"Do you mean the council?" frowned Dorianne.

"No, thank you," answered Elsea. "I have had enough of them for one day. I mean, well, *one* guest. I think we should invite your upright prince to dinner. Now that we are to make love to his father, the council insists I show him a few royal courtesies. Though I see nothing good coming from it, I believe I could tolerate a meal with the man."

After Dorianne left to inform the cook and servants, Elsea broke open the book in her lap giving the appearance that she cared for what she saw written in it.

CHAPTER EIGHT

Trial by Water

When Prince John and his men first entered the swamp, the water was only a few inches deep, and their horses glided along easily between the trees and the overhanging branches. The thick strands of moss that hung from the branches would occasionally tangle about their heads, but except for the insatiable mosquitoes, the men had no complaints. They smeared themselves with mud in hopes of discouraging the voracious insects, and everyone expected their passage through the watery forest would be a brief one.

When they eventually came to a break in the trees, they slapped each other on the back in celebration. Their elation was short-lived, however, for they discovered they were not out of the swamp, but at the edge of a large body of water. The stench that rose up with the gathering mist told them this was no freshwater lake. A quick investigation revealed that the water was shallow enough to traverse on horseback. William recommended they press on, and the men plunged into the slime covered pool.

Navigating by the moon's faint glow, they had been pushing forward in single file when the man riding point suddenly disappeared from view in a great swirling slosh of water. Horse and rider quickly resurfaced, and a furious struggle began to rescue them from the deep hole.

Several more immersions later, the horses began to balk and

refuse to move forward. William ordered everyone to dismount and lead his animal by hand. Each man held the reins of his horse while wading cautiously ahead through the chest-deep water hoping to avoid the next hole. William gave his reins to another man and led the horse of the young prince who insisted on remaining mounted.

It was past midnight when the man in front announced excitedly that he had reached firmer ground. The rest of the column scrambled up from the mire to discover they had now entered a marshy area with tall reeds and muddy footing. They were not out yet, but the drier ground encouraged them. They remounted their horses and continued with new hope.

Their despair soon returned. The mud, which was shallow at first, got deeper, and the horses began to bog down. It took the combined efforts of the weary men, pushing and pulling, to break them loose from the suction effect of the dreadful morass. There were long stretches where they could only move forward step by agonizing step. Reduced to a crawl, they still saw no discernable difference in the terrain ahead.

"William," protested Prince John, "these conditions are odious to me. How much longer must I endure this reek in my nostrils?"

"There's no way to be sure, My Lord," panted William. "We may be yards from the end, or leagues. You must be patient and not dwell on your discomfort."

The impatience of the prince soon became contagious. Tempers flared and the men cursed the mud and the mosquitoes. The swamp, like some evil sentient being, seemed determined to trap and kill them. A feeling of hopelessness began to permeate their thoughts like the way the odor of the marsh seeped into their skin. Both man and beast had reached their limit of endurance.

When the setting of the moon robbed them of what little light they had, William called a halt. "We need to rest."

"Rest!" blurted John. "How do you expect us to rest in here?"

"We'll have to sleep on horseback," explained William. "There's no helping it."

William had the men search their food bags. To their immense disappointment, they could produce only a single crust of bread which, when split six ways, provided barely a mouthful. They washed down this morsel of a meal with last of their fresh water.

"We shall find more rations tomorrow," promised William.

"That thought does little to alleviate the pain in my stomach now," moaned the prince.

The men arose from their restless sleep at the approach of sunrise. By the gray light of dawn they saw a line of trees a short distance ahead. After they readjusted their saddles, and cinched up their loosened belts, the little column began its grueling march anew. Leaving the marshy reeds behind, they entered a swampy forest like at the beginning.

"I do wish you would lead us out of this cursed hole," grumbled John. "I have never experienced a more horrid night in all my life. I am beginning to doubt your skills as a navigator."

William pointed ahead to a low ridge they could see through the trees. "There are no swamps in the hills," he smiled. "We should reach dry ground soon, My Lord."

On they went. The rising sun helped raise their spirits, and the hungry men gave up complaining. As they plodded steadily forward, the hills grew larger. Nevertheless, when midday came and went, William had to confess to the prince that his estimate of the distance to the edge had been too optimistic. Their morale sagging again, they began to dread another night of misery in the stench and mud.

By now, they no longer looked like the finely attired knights of the prince's elite guard. They had long ago discarded helmets and armor, and their tattered clothes hung from their bodies in shreds. The swamp mud stained their skin, and the wispy weeds of the marsh intertwined their hair. The further they progressed, the more things clung to them: mosses and vines, wet grasses and leeches, and the never relenting clouds of mosquitoes. It seemed the swamp was slowly absorbing them until nothing remained of their humanity, and they wondered if this was how it killed its victims.

The sun was an hour from passing below the horizon when they at last broke out into dry country. All of them, including the prince, threw themselves down on their faces and kissed the grassy ground, praising God from the depths of their souls.

CHAPTER NINE

Private Dining

Charles and Elsea sat at opposite ends of the table in the room where he had earlier written the letter to the duke. To Elsea's left was Dorianne. Except for the sentries standing guard by the doors, and a few servant girls fluttering about the room with the items for the meal, they were alone. The invitation to the private dinner surprised him, and he wondered if it had something to do with his gracious gesture towards her that morning. Maybe this was her way of thanking him? He studied her face for clues to her thoughts, but could find none.

Apart from the obligatory greetings in which her attitude was minimally polite, Elsea had not spoken. After the servants placed the main dishes, they began to eat in silence. Unused to such somber meals, Charles debated within himself whether he should blurt something out to get a conversation going. He wished his training for knighthood had included a lesson or two on table etiquette.

At last, Elsea looked up from her dish. "Prince John, have you met Dorianne, my lady-in-waiting?"

Elsea's sudden question caught him in the middle of chewing a stringy piece of pork. He recalled hearing once that speaking around a mouthful of food was poor manners, and instinctively knew not to spit out his cud as he might have done before a campfire on campaign. The only option left him was to dramatically accelerate his chewing while holding up a finger to indicate he had heard her question and would answer in due time. He looked ridiculous, and he knew it.

He swallowed hurriedly, and said, "I saw the young lady at that first dinner, Your Grace, but I did not know her name until now."

"Dorianne," he said facing her, "that is a beautiful name. I like the way it sounds."

"Thank you, Prince John," replied Dorianne, "you are very kind." She glanced at Elsea and lifted her eyebrows slightly.

"How long have you served Her Highness?" he asked, hoping to make the most of the meager beginnings of a dialogue.

"Her parents were servants of my father," cut in Elsea. "But they both died the same week of a plague. I used to have a whole hive of attendants buzzing about me. They fretted and fussed over me so, but I dared not trust a single one. A passing comment in my bedchamber at night would be common knowledge among the stable boys by breakfast; so I got rid of them all. Dorianne is the only personal servant I need."

"Her Grace found me hiding beneath a stairwell," continued Dorianne as soon as Elsea finished. "I was crying because my parents were dead, and I was afraid I would be sent away. I was born in this castle and had never been outside its walls. My Lady heard me crying, and she told me to be quiet and that she would take care of me. And she has taken very good care of me, Prince John. Now I have clothes, and food, and a wonderful room."

Charles looked down the table at Elsea and tried to reconcile this account of her generosity with the rumors of her cruelty.

"Dorianne, you are boring the prince." scolded Elsea.

"On the contrary," replied Charles, "I find this story most compelling. I had no idea you were so..."

"Benevolent, compassionate?" she interrupted. "I am none

of those things. I needed a servant I could trust, and Dorianne needed a new master. I am very practical, nothing more."

Charles held up his cup and gave it a slight tilt toward Elsea. "Well, here is to more *practicality* in the world," he said with a smile.

She frowned and looked down at her food. The silence returned.

"I have heard that you are an excellent rider, Your Grace," ventured Charles hopefully.

"My father insisted my instruction include all things equestrian," she answered with thinly veiled boredom. "He was a man who got what he wanted."

He took this ambiguous response as a promising start. "It is too bad that we have met under these circumstances. I would have enjoyed riding with you. I share your love of horses."

"You are mistaken, Prince John. I did not say that I love horses, only that I ride well because my father saw to it that I did. Furthermore, I am not in the habit of riding with anyone but myself and certainly not with Bavarian Princes."

Though rebuffed again, Charles was not yet defeated. Seeing the painting of a young Frederick on the wall behind her gave him an idea. "Is that your father?" he tried.

"Yes," she answered without looking up. "The artist was more than generous, and his impression of him is more fanciful than factual." She turned toward a vacant place on the wall. "My brother's portrait would have hung there—if he had lived."

"Ah, right next to your grandfather, Duke Leopold. I have heard he was Austria's greatest duke."

At this, Elsea spun her head around. "And I suppose by that you mean to say that I am the worst. I can see you imagine yourself a clever man, Prince John, so it may disappoint you to know that you are not the first to point out my deficiency in that regard. Hardly a week goes by that someone does not remind me of Leopold the *Glorious*. Leopold was so great, and Leopold was so wise! By which they imply I am neither great nor wise. I have grown weary of it, and I will thank you for not spoiling further what is already a dreary dinner with any more allusions to my inadequacies!" On this last word she pounded the table so hard it made her plate jump.

He was still trying to fathom how she had inferred a criticism from his innocent comment when a servant girl approached the table to refill Elsea's drink. She tipped the pitcher too quickly, however, and the contents came gushing out all at once toppling the cup and sending a frothy wave washing over the table edge onto Elsea's lap.

"Look what you've done, you clumsy fool!" shouted Elsea.

"Forgive me, My Lady," cried the panic-stricken girl attempting to wipe up the mess.

"Oh, give me that," barked Elsea as she grabbed the cloth from her. "Go and see if there is something in the kitchen you can ruin."

She started to mop up the spill, but suddenly stood up and threw the cloth onto the table with a wet slap.

"What is the use in pretending?" she said. "I do not enjoy making small talk, Prince John. I never understood the point of it. I will have the guards return you to your cell and spare the both of us further drudgery. Come, Dorianne, we shall retire."

She turned toward the door, but Charles felt he must say something before she left. "I hope you are not leaving because of me," he grinned. "I know my table manners are not what they should be, but I do not recall ever chasing anyone away."

Halfway to the door, Elsea stopped and faced him. "What is in this for you?"

His polite smile melted. "What do you mean?"

"Why are you playing this game?" she pressed.

"What game?"

"Why are you pretending to befriend me? Let me tell you plainly that there is nothing about you that interests me. I can think of no reason why I should not hate you. In fact, I do hate you. I hate everything that Otto holds dear. What agreement did Raglan and Eugene make with you anyway?"

Charles felt himself grow warm and knew he was close to losing his temper. Experience had taught him that in circumstances like this he should keep his mouth closed. As usual, he ignored his experience. "It is I who should be asking you what *your* game is!" he fired back as he came to his feet.

Elsea's eyes opened wide, but Charles hurried on, "My game, as you call it, has been very simple: treat a lady as a lady until proven otherwise. If there is something I should be ashamed of in that I am sure I do not know what it is. Perhaps you will be so kind as to enlighten me. As for agreements, I again plead ignorance. I have made no agreements with anyone save the one in which you were an eyewitness to in this very room. If you recall, you assured me you supported it. So, once more I am at a loss to know my crime. The only thing you have said which I can find any truth in is that you hate me. That, I believe, is indisputable."

He intended to say more, but the red glow of her face told him he had already said too much. She clenched her fists at her side and took a step back into the room. He prepared himself for what he knew was coming. However, to his surprise her face began to soften, and the green light slowly returned to her eyes.

She spun on her heel and grabbed Dorianne by the hand. "Good evening, Prince John," she snapped on her way out the door.

All that evening, Charles rehearsed in his mind the bizarre dinner. He deeply regretted losing his temper, but his emotions confused him. In the morning, when she looked so alone and vulnerable, he felt compelled to help her. Yet tonight she had made him angry, and he took pleasure in offending her. "One minute she's as helpless as a lamb and the next she's as fierce as a lion," he said to himself.

He could not decide which one intrigued him more.

CHAPTER TEN

Spring Walk

Charles awoke from his second nap with a groaning yawn. He was unsure of the time, but his growling stomach suggested his lunch should be on its way. Just then, he heard the sound of jangling keys and his door clanged open. However, instead of a servant holding out another bowl of lukewarm gruel, an empty-handed guard entered followed immediately by Lord Raglan.

"Good day, Prince John," he said. "I hope you had a pleasant night."

Charles stood and stretched himself. "Better than a night in the rain," he conceded.

The old count motioned for the guard to leave. "I want to thank you for the letter you wrote the other day," he said in a low voice after he was gone. "It is my hope that this will be but the first step in the reconciliation of our two houses. There was a time when the Babenbergs looked to your family for protection." He waited for a reply, but Charles was too busy fighting off another yawn.

"It may be a week or more before we are able to send you home," continued Raglan. "I see no reason why you should not enjoy a little fresh air each day until then."

The unexpected practical turn in the conversation revived Charles like cold splash of water. "I should welcome any relief from this boredom," he gushed.

"The prince needs to stretch his legs," explained Raglan to the sentry waiting outside. "You will escort him to the battlement walkway and permit him to enjoy the sunlight."

"Yes, My Lord."

"You are a man of honor," Raglan noted to Charles. "I trust a single escort will be sufficient?"

"I shall be as docile as a newborn calf," answered Charles with a bow.

Raglan left the cell, but not before adding, "I hope to speak again of our mutual concerns, Prince John."

The guard led Charles through the castle to a hallway he had not seen before. Arriving at the foot of a narrow stone staircase, they began a long ascent of a spiraled stairway. The steps twisted on and on until at last they reached a small landing at the top with a low wooden door. His guard pushed it open, and Charles was nearly blinded by the sunlight that flooded the stairwell. They stepped out onto the battlements high atop the wall. A parapet walkway, wide enough for a carriage and paved with tightly laid stone, completely encircled the castle. Charles paused to soak in the sunshine and enjoy the warm spring breeze that blew across his face.

From this vantage point he could look out on the countryside for miles in every direction. Close by were the outer walls of the fortress and the courtyard he had passed through the day he arrived. Sprawled out along the swift running Danube, still swelling from the melting snow of the Alps, was the bustling town of Vienna. Beyond, lush forests and fertile farmland stretched off to the horizons broken only by scattered barns and herds of sheep and cattle grazing peacefully. It was a stunning view, and Charles was impressed.

He had been there only a few moments when he heard the sound of women talking. From around a corner of the walkway suddenly appeared the duchess with Dorianne at her side.

Elsea stopped short. "What is *he* doing here?"

"Lord Raglan ordered that the prisoner be allowed some fresh air, Your Grace," stammered the guard.

"Why was I not informed?"

"I don't know, Your Grace," answered the guard with bowed head.

"Your Highness," said Charles, coming to his rescue, "if my presence here is an inconvenience, I will gladly return to my humble quarters."

"Far be it from me to go against the wishes of Lord Raglan," she answered with a wave of her hand. "You may fling yourself from this wall for all I care." She took Dorianne by the arm, and they continued on their walk as before.

Charles watched them stroll down the parapet. Just before they disappeared around another traverse in the wall, he caught a glimpse of Elsea turning to look back at him. She was out of view in an instant, however, and he wondered if he only imagined it.

"Your duchess has a most singular approach to conversation," he said to his sole companion. "Is she often like this?"

His escort did not reply at first and continued looking out over the wall. "If His Highness is a gentleman, he'll not expect an answer."

Charles received the rebuke with a nod of his head. Settling for something less controversial, he asked him to describe what he was seeing. There followed a long oration as his guard-turned-guide eagerly pointed out a string of hamlets, hills, bridges, and forests. It seemed to Charles that every patch of trees and cluster of buildings had a name and its own peculiar story. He did his best to pretend a respectful interest, but forgot every detail within seconds. His escort was still droning on when he heard again the approach of the women who by now had come full circle along the wall.

"You're still here?" asked Elsea as they came around the corner.

Charles was not convinced the astonishment in her voice was genuine. He gave the guard next to him a slap on the back. "This remarkable fellow has been giving me a most extraordinary account of your splendid country, Your Grace. Why, Tacitus of ancient Rome could not be more informative." The long look she gave him confused him, but he assumed she was not amused.

"If it is a history lesson you wish, Prince John, allow me to fill the gaps of your knowledge. There is no one in this castle who knows the story of my people better."

Her suddenly pleasant tone caught him by surprise. He quickly recovered, however. "You would do me a great honor."

Elsea motioned him alongside, and they began a leisurely walk together with Dorianne and the guard following a few strides behind.

Mindful of their combative dinner the previous night, Charles hoped to take advantage of what was certain to be a harmless topic. "This is a wonderful view," he declared with confidence.

"I imagine the impression is stronger the first time," she replied casually, "but I no longer notice it. I come here for the solitude. Since a child, I have rarely missed an afternoon in good weather."

They stopped by an embrasure at a part of the wall that gave the best view of the town a short distance away. "There is our magnificent Vienna," she sighed, "the town my grandfather built. From Paris to Kiev, and Hamburg to Constantinople, more wealth passes through here in a single month than most German cities in a year. I suppose it is what makes us such an attractive prize and why my enemies will not leave me alone."

He noted her melancholy tone. "You are in a difficult position, Your Grace, and I do not envy you."

For the first time since they began their walk, she turned to face him. The sunlight caught her eyes, and they burst into a blaze of emerald. He did not know eyes could be so green.

"You know not the half of it," she said as she looked away and broke his trance. "I do not know what is more vexing: the conspiracies of my enemies or the conniving of my own council."

"They are perhaps too overbearing," he admitted. "But surely they are concerned for your welfare."

"Ha!" she blurted, "you are more naive than Dorianne. I do not doubt they have many concerns, but I can assure you my welfare is not among them."

Her latent fiery spirit seemed poised to break out. Charles hoped to apply a little balm. "Perhaps it only seems that way," he thought might work.

It did not.

"Prince John," she huffed, "permit me to enlighten you with a few of the realities of my *concerned* council. I will begin with the barons 'K' and 'K.' Excuse me, but I often forget which is which. Their aspirations have never gone beyond a pantry brimming with food, a cellar of inexhaustible drink, and an endless parade of pretty servant girls to amuse them. Their sole fear in life is that I might deprive them of even a single moment's pleasure. Then there is the pious bishop. He hopes someday to be a cardinal, but it seems I am an obstacle to his red hat. Rome, they tell me, does not approve of a woman ruling the House of Babenberg. Yet Prochaska is a saint compared to that devil Eugene. A more unscrupulous man you will not meet this side of Hell. Why my father placed such trust in him I will never know."

"What about Lord Raglan?" he asked when she stopped to catch her breath. "He appears to be a reasonable man."

At the name of Raglan, she relaxed some. "I am told my grandfather thought highly of him," she said after they resumed their walking. "There was a time I felt I could trust him as well, but even he has changed since the Emperor died."

"Is your life all dreariness, Your Grace?" He flung an arm toward the sky. "Is there no sunshine at all?"

They walked in silence a moment as she thought over his simple question. "At least they no longer pester me with that marriage nonsense," she sighed at last.

"What marriage nonsense?"

She gave him a puzzled look. "Are you the only man east of the Rhine who does not know of my curse and my foolish father's quest?"

"Is it so famous a story?"

"Infamous is a better word," she replied. "After my brother died, my father was determined to preserve the Babenberg dynasty by any means. He insisted I marry a German nobleman and produce a male heir. Though I was barely fourteen, he wasted no time. He searched the length and breadth of the Holy Roman Empire for a year. He sent emissaries to every House in Germany, great or small, but could not find me a husband."

"I am sorry to hear that," he said in his best sympathetic tone. "It must have been most discouraging for you."

"Discouraging!" she laughed, throwing back her head. "It is plain how little you know me, Prince John. For one whole year I had not a peaceful night's sleep so great was my fear of his finding success!"

Charles looked down at the pavement stones and tried to let this shocking revelation sink in. "You mean," he said looking up again, "you do not want to be married?"

"I can think of no worse a fate. No torture ever devised by the Inquisition could compare with being bound to any man!"

Charles opened his mouth to speak, but no words came.

"What is marriage but a more clever form of serfdom?" she asked. "I am suffocating in men who want nothing more than to abuse me. My council I inherited, but why, I ask you, would I voluntarily inflict even more misery upon myself? Like most men, you no doubt think my beliefs unreasonable. Ask yourself, therefore, do you know of any woman made happier by marriage? My father had no affection for my mother that I could discern. Why, look at your own mother. Your uncles compelled her to marry for their own political ends. You will not say she is happy, will you? Otto got all the power, pomp and prestige. What did she get, but a few frilly things and a comfortable room in which to await the sweet relief of death? I do not see what is so holy about matrimony, Prince John, and you may be sure the day you hear of my wedding announcement will be the day you hear of my mysterious disappearance!" She punctuated the last word with a stamp of her foot.

Charles was speechless. He had never heard such thoughts as these. He was certain her thesis was wrong, but try as he might he could not find where. His father left his mother when Charles was too young to remember, and she never spoke of him. Was *she* ever happy? he wondered. Would she have been better off having never met him, whoever he was? Shaking himself free from his perplexity, he pronounced feebly, "This is a perspective I am unfamiliar with, Your Grace."

"I can see this *perspective* distresses you," she said with a hint of sympathy. "Let us change the subject. Why not entertain me with some of your doubtlessly enchanting plans for Bavaria when you are duke."

"When I am duke?" he asked with unfeigned surprise.

"Yes. Your father is nearly as old as my grandfather was when he died. You could be duke by this time next year. So tell me, will you raise taxes for another glorious crusade to at long last rescue Jerusalem from the godless infidels? Or maybe you will build a new city and name it after yourself; we have such an awful dearth of cities named after pompous men, you know. Perhaps you will free your precious serfs, and benevolent Bavaria will lead us all to a new era of enlightenment. Why, I am sure your head is bursting with ideas."

Though completely devoid of any ideas, Charles's head was indeed bursting as he strained to keep it all straight: was he Charles pretending to be John, or John pretending to be Charles? Her puzzled face brought him around. "I do not really have any plans," he answered in his noblest tone. "I try not to dwell on those things."

She stopped and spun to face him. "Try not to dwell on those things," she repeated. "I have never heard anything more absurd."

"There is nothing absurd about it," he returned with an air of false confidence. "It is man's responsibility to be concerned with the present and leave the future to Almighty God."

"What does God have to do with it?"

"Everything: it is man's duty to serve God."

"How can you say that? You are a prince. You will soon be a duke and rule Bavaria. Everyone knows you cannot rule men and serve God!"

"And I say the man who does not serve God," he replied, standing a little taller, "does not deserve to rule men!"

They stood face to face, deadlocked. Suddenly, Elsea burst out in genuine laughter. "What an intriguing man you are: a philosopher-prince with the morals of a peasant! I am sure the courtiers at home hang on your every word."

Charles was not sure how to answer and so kept his mouth

closed. They resumed their walk, but did not speak again until they reached the door that led to Elsea's tower.

"Dorianne believes you are trying to be kind," she said, nodding in Dorianne's direction. "I imagine you have a great deal of experience being kind to women."

"Your Grace," he said, looking her in the eyes, "you will never meet a man with less."

She held his look a brief moment. "Enjoy the sunshine, Prince John." She and Dorianne vanished through the doorway.

CHAPTER ELEVEN

Honorable Advisor

Elsea slammed the door behind her and stomped her way across the room.

Dorianne leapt up from her chair. "Is there something wrong, My Lady?"

"Wrong?" answered Elsea. "What could be wrong? I enjoy being set upon by a pack of blithering fools. What better way to spend an afternoon? It was a pleasure to miss my dinner. Who needs food when basking in the glow of so much collective brilliance? So, no, nothing is wrong." She collapsed in her chair with her arms and feet splayed out at all angles.

"Shall I tell the cook to prepare your meal?" asked Dorianne quietly.

Elsea remained slumped in her chair, staring blankly at her outstretched feet. Dorianne returned to her needlework.

Eventually, Elsea got up and began to pace between the book covered walls. "You should have been there, Dori. I have not seen them so agitated since the day I told Otto to go hang himself. It was so frustrating. I swear if just one more person had said, '*We must seize this opportunity,*' I would have pulled my hair out by the roots!"

"What opportunity, My Lady?"

Elsea made a few more revolutions around her chair before stopping to face Dorianne. "They want me to marry Eldridge, the self-styled Duke of Styria! We should have crushed his rebellion three years ago; instead, I must wed him for his impudence!"

Dorianne laid her work in her lap. "I thought he was already married."

"It seems his poor wife recently met with a tragic accident. They say she fell from a horse and died. Ha! She probably threw herself off at full gallop just to end her misery. It is what I would have done."

"Oh, My Lady, you mustn't talk that way! It's a very great sin to destroy one's self. Only God has that right."

"But I suppose my nobles have the right to force me to marry?"

"You know I don't understand these things," confessed Dorianne with her calm returning. "But they are devoted to you and perhaps it's for the best."

"The only thing they are devoted to is their own comfort!" snapped Elsea. "They are so consumed with saving their precious fortunes they will sacrifice anything—especially me."

"You shouldn't let them upset you so, My Lady."

"Who says I am upset?"

When Dorianne did not answer her rhetorical question, she let out a moan and returned to her chair to resume her moping.

"Is Lord Raglan in favor of this marriage?" asked Dorianne after a long silence.

"Not yet," answered Elsea. "It is obvious this is Lord Eugene's doing. He has convinced the barons that Eldridge is their only solution, and they are boiling over with urgency. Fortunately, Raglan is not so enthusiastic. He said my decision could wait."

"Lord Raglan is a wise man."

"Shrewd is more like it," returned Elsea. "I think he has a plan of his own, but what it is, I have not a clue. I could extract no hints from him."

"So, what will you do?"

"That is my problem, Dori; I have no idea what I should do. My grandfather had many men in his day he could lean on for advice. I have no one. I need an advocate. I need someone who understands these things: someone I can trust."

"You need someone like the prince," suggested Dorianne.

Elsea's jaw hung slack a few seconds. "Dori, have you been listening at all? I said I need someone I can *trust*. Next to Eugene, Otto's son is the last man I would turn to for advice."

"The prince is an honorable man," insisted Dorianne. "Men of honor can always be trusted."

"Honestly, Dori, where do you get these childish notions? You do not even know the man. There is something different about him, I will grant you, something strange even. Why, did you hear him talking on the battlements the other day? He claims he is not concerned with the future. Have you ever heard anything more preposterous than a prince who does not care what he will do with a crown?"

"Maybe that's why you *can* trust him. He's not overly ambitious."

"His ambitions have nothing do with it. He is the son of my enemy! Have you forgotten that?"

"He doesn't act like an enemy," noted Dorianne calmly.

"And so thought Caesar of Brutus just before he slipped the knife between his ribs," returned Elsea.

"I don't know who Brutus is, My Lady, but I don't think the prince is like him."

"Oh, Dori, the things you don't know could fill a library." She went to a bookshelf and pulled down a yellowed tome at random. Back in her chair, she sat staring at the same page for the next half-hour.

"I suppose he would not even *want* to help me," she sighed eventually. "I have not gone out of my way to encourage him."

"No, you haven't been very encouraging," agreed Dorianne. "But you are a duchess, and he shouldn't expect to be encouraged."

"Do you really think the man I have been keeping locked up in a stone box will be able to help me?"

"I don't know if he can help you, My Lady. I only say that you can trust him to be honest." Dorianne looked up from her work and added, "And I think you know that too."

Elsea went back to her book, and they were quiet again for a long while.

"I will be disappointed, Dori," she predicted quietly.

"Maybe so," admitted Dorianne, "but at least you will have tried."

"Yes, at least I will have tried." She laid her book aside and stood to stretch herself. "Go wake that lazy cook, Dori. I'm famished!"

CHAPTER TWELVE

Enthralling Vision

The guards ushered Charles across the great hall to the now familiar room with the paintings and tapestries. The door was open this time, and they motioned for him to enter alone. Having no idea why Elsea wanted to see him, he stepped inside a pace, but stopped when he saw her standing near one of the windows in the middle of reading a paper she held in her hand. Not certain if she had noticed his entrance, he considered making a sound to alert her. He decided that would be impolite, however, and so opted to wait respectfully for her to finish.

The morning sunlight silhouetted her profile allowing him a unique opportunity to study her face while she read. As before, she kept her hair pulled back tightly and wore none of the paints or powders common for women of her position. From her forehead, along her nose, to her full lips, he discovered something he had not noticed before. "She must have been very beautiful before the pox," he concluded.

Nevertheless, imagining her beauty in the past did not stop him from admiring it in the present. Each time his eyes repeated their original survey he found new details, and he wondered how he could have missed her faintly strong chin and delicate ears. He knew his gawking was rude, yet he could not tear himself away. "Just one more second," he kept promising himself, but the more he dwelt on those feminine lines the more spellbound he became.

Suddenly, Elsea looked up and their eyes met. He turned aside quickly, hoping she had not noticed his staring.

She had.

"You have seen something unpleasant, Prince John," she noted without emotion.

"I do not know what you mean, Your Grace," he answered truthfully.

"Come now," she frowned, "insincerity does not become you."

He opened his mouth, but she interrupted his protest. "Your views on my blighted visage can wait till another day," she said. "I have a more pressing matter to discuss with you at present." She let out a pronounced sigh and tried to soften her look. "I know I have been critical of you, Prince John, perhaps unnecessarily so. Yet, you have impressed me as a candid person with a sound mind." She held out the paper. "My council gave me this correspondence yesterday. I wish you to read it and give me an appraisal of its merit, if you are able."

Profoundly grateful she had changed the subject, Charles politely took the letter. Written by Lord Rottermund, Duke Eldridge's notorious advisor, it turned out to be a windy marriage proposal: high with flattery, but low on detail.

He dropped his hands to his side when he finished. "The last I knew, old Eldridge already had a wife."

"She has conveniently died," she informed him.

"But, I thought you did not want to marry."

"Who said I want to marry? I told you about my father's illness. Now the contagion has spread to my council. This is their idea."

"I see," he said, not sure of what else to say.

The anxious look she gave him confused him even more.

"Your Grace," he asked with a shrug of his shoulders, "what is it that you want?"

She let out an exaggerated moan and snatched the letter from his hand before turning away and pacing to the other end of the room. When she came back, she stopped a few feet before him and looked him in the eyes. "I want your advice," she said quietly. "I have no one else I can trust."

So astounded was Charles by her simple request that he had to catch himself from staggering backwards. "Your Highness," he stammered after regaining his balance, "I am flattered you would place any value on my judgement, but I tell you in all honesty I do not know enough of your predicament to be of any service to you."

She hesitated a moment. "You are right," she agreed. "Please be seated and I will complete your education."

They sat down at the table, and she launched into a rapid summary of the events that had brought her thus far. "A century ago, Emperor Frederick Barbarossa raised Austria from a mark to a duchy and bequeathed it to my family as an inheritable fief. The terms of this agreement were written down in a document called the *Privilegium Minus*.

"For four generations our duchy passed peacefully from father to son within my family. Peacefully, that is, until my brother died. His untimely death meant we no longer had a male heir. According to the original deed, the duchy would revert back to the Hohenstaufen family. However, there was a little known clause in the *Privilegium* which stated the fief could also be passed on through the female line. Although my father's enemies disputed the interpretation of this clause, Emperor Frederick II promised he would honor it. So when my father was killed in Hungary four years ago my council declared me the rightful duchess of Austria, and under the protection of Frederick we enjoyed a few years respite. But Frederick died last Christmas, and his son Conrad has refused to recognize me as the legal heir. Now I have enemies springing up from behind every tree hoping to take advantage of my ... *predicament*, as you call it. My council believes that if I were to marry into some properly noble family it would restore my legitimacy and solidify my family's claim to our duchy."

She finished and leaned back in her chair. "Well?"

All the while Elsea was listing the litany of her woes, Charles could not help but consider the magnitude of the risk she was taking by confiding in him. How desperate her situation must be that she would turn to the son of her enemy for advice. Though she sat with her head held high, and presented her points like a disinterested tutor giving a well-rehearsed lesson, he could sense her unspoken helplessness. Just like the day when she asked him to write that letter, something stirred within him, and he was determined to help her even at cost of his life.

He bowed his head a long moment as he called upon every scrap of his mental acuity. Like a chess player, he analyzed her problem, trying to see all possible moves and their repercussions.

"First of all," he began after composing himself, "I advise great caution in any dealings with Eldridge. I would not trust that man to tell me the weather unless I could first look out a window."

"How do you know this?"

"A few years ago, Eldridge came to Bavaria and spent several days in the castle trying to convince Otto to assist him in his impending revolt against your father. One night, I caught him abusing one of the servant girls. He offered me a fistful of gold for my silence, but I refused. I reported it to the duke, and within the hour he was driven from the castle with the sound of Otto's rage ringing in his ears."

"Another item to add to the long list of reasons to despise him," she observed. "But my council knows his true character well enough. How then do you explain their sudden infatuation with him?"

"They fear losing the lands they have held for generations, and they see no other option," he answered matter-of-factly. "Put yourself in their place and see the problem through their eyes."

"The last thing I want to do is to put myself in their place!"

"Your Highness," said a calmer Charles, "if you would be a duchess then you must think like one. You must know the motives of all you deal with, whether friend or foe."

"Motives!" she snapped. "Nothing could be easier to discern: they want to keep their wealth at my expense."

"You see, this is what I mean. From their perspective this marriage would help you as well."

"Prince John, are you trying to advise me or mock me?"

He raised his hands, palms facing her. "Have you considered what you would get from this marriage?"

"Yes: a pig for a husband!"

"You will reunite with Styria," he said, ignoring her outburst. "You will gain an ally, and perhaps restore your family's legitimate claim and keep your ancestral home."

Elsea rose and stood back from the table. "So this is your grand wisdom? I should marry Eldridge and make everyone but myself happy? I do not wish to insult you, Prince John, but you are no better than my council."

"I have not yet finished, Your Grace," he replied quietly. "I only wanted you to see that their view is not without merit. As I see it, however, their plan depends on too many factors beyond their control." He stood up and began to count on his fingers. "First, the Styrian nobles must be willing to support Eldridge in a war, perhaps even with the Emperor himself, for control of

Austria. Second, he must be able to give you a son. It is a matter of speculation as to which of these two are the most implausible. What will more likely happen is that on the first moonless night he will slit your throat while you sleep, and have you, and any who support you, thrown into the Danube. Eldridge is not a man inclined to share power."

Elsea took a deep breath and let it out slowly. "You have shown me the hazards of their plan, Prince John, and for that I thank you, but you have given me no hope." She took a step closer, glanced at the open door and whispered, "What shall I do?"

Charles did not know she could speak so softly. He let himself stare into her green eyes a few seconds longer than necessary before whispering back, "Your Grace, there is only one man who might be able to help you."

"Who is this man?" she pleaded.

"Duke Otto," he said.

"Otto?"

"Yes. Bavaria is more than strong enough to stand up to your enemies. You must seek his aid."

"We already sent that letter," she said, throwing her hands up.

"You need more than cordial relations, Your Grace. You need an ally."

"Well, how am I to acquire this ally?"

Charles braced himself before answering. "Beseech Otto's forgiveness and swear to him your fealty," he said quickly.

"Now I know you are mocking me!" she shouted. Pacing again, she struck her palm with a fist. "Ask forgiveness of that man! Kneel in homage before him like a slave and lick his boots… never!"

"You must not let your pride keep you from doing what is best for you, Your Highness."

"And I suppose you think humiliation is for my *best*?"

"Humility is a virtue," replied Charles. "The duke tried to help you when you first became duchess. If you had become his vassal then, you would not be in this difficulty now."

"And so these are the choices you lay before me: be chained to Eldridge, or enslaved to Otto. I scarce can decide which one is more repulsive."

"You must change your opinion of Duke Otto, My Lady. He is your enemy only because your father made him one; but you may yet win him to your cause."

"I see you are indeed your father's son," she sneered. "You are here to finish what he began. How proud he would be." She grabbed her hair in both hands. "I knew this was a bad idea," she screamed. "I could have gotten better guidance from a milk maid!"

"Your Grace," he answered after the echo of her scream died away, "it pains me to see your distress. Please believe I have only your welfare in view. Otto is an honorable man and can be trusted. I believe even Raglan thinks the same."

"How do you know what Raglan thinks?"

"He hinted as much the day he permitted me to walk the battlements. If you will allow yourself a moment to think it through, you will agree that Bavaria is your best hope."

Elsea's mouth hung open a second. "You talked to Raglan the day we met on the battlements?"

"Yes, I have said so, it is no secret."

"Ah, things are becoming clearer," she declared, "and I have been such a fool not to see it! Raglan knows perfectly well I walk those walls at the same time every day. I can just see the two of you in some darkened corner thinking up your clever plot to sneak yourself into my confidence."

Though Elsea was nearly beside herself, Charles could see her anger was not born of hatred, but of desperation, and thus his compassion for her only grew. He came around to her side of the table. "My Lady," he said softly, "there is no plot to deceive you. I have given you the best counsel I know. I am sorry I could not do better, but why can you not see that I am in earnest?"

The sincerity in his voice chased the scowl from her face, and they studied each other without speaking.

"This is not the advice I expected," she admitted quietly. "Your proposal is a difficult one, Prince John, and I will need time to think on it."

She signaled for the guards, and they returned Charles to his cell.

CHAPTER THIRTEEN

Apology

At Raglan's urging, Elsea reluctantly agreed to dine with her nobles again. The lords crowding the great hall buzzed with excitement. It was rare for their reclusive duchess to call them to dinner two nights in the same month, but twice in the same week was unheard of. Elsea's council sat around the head table talking quietly while they awaited the arrival of the final two dinner guests.

"I see the duchess is late as usual," noted Lord Eugene, "but what could be keeping the prince?"

"He will arrive shortly," Raglan assured him. "I ordered he be given a bath and a clean change of clothes." Looking carefully around at his tablemates, he added in a lower voice, "We would do well to have a care for his comfort."

"I understand he and the duchess have been seeing quite a bit of each other," noted Lord Eugene with a sly smile. "Is this your doing as well, My Lord?"

The barons exchanged snickering glances.

"A better relationship between the prince and Her Grace can only work to our advantage," replied Raglan.

"The question is," observed Eugene with a wink at the barons, "whether more time with the duchess can make *anything* better."

He and the barons burst out in laughter.

A sudden murmur of surprise swept across the room as Charles strode into the hall with only a single escort at his side and a smile on his face. Clean and freshly shaven, he now wore a shirt of white linen with the red shield of Babenberg embroidered across his chest. To those who did not know better, he looked like a renowned knight of Austria. Lord Raglan rose and directed him toward an empty chair at the end of the table.

"Am I to believe you have become a Babenberg knight, Prince John?" smiled Prochaska.

"My former garments were in much need of repair," explained Charles. "I am sure Duke Otto would understand."

His new wardrobe sparked more polite comments, and everyone did his best to humor him. Even Lord Eugene made an effort at civility, albeit a half-hearted one.

The sentry near the throne announced Elsea, and the knights and nobles gathered for the meal stood and dutifully applauded as she entered and took her seat. Bishop Prochaska asked the blessing, and the meal began.

Charles looked up often at Elsea while they ate. He was curious to know if she had considered his advice from the morning, but she would not return his glances. She kept quiet and seemed content to permit Raglan and the others the burden of conversation.

"Have you noticed the fruits of Lord Raglan's labor, Your Grace?" asked Lord Eugene as he forked another piece of meat onto his plate. "Why, I believe the prince could pass as one of your knights."

"I am sure Prince John finds the irony most amusing," she remarked without looking up.

"We hope your stay here has not been too unpleasant, Prince John," tried Prochaska.

"I have slept on softer beds, Your Excellency," admitted Charles.

The bishop turned to Raglan. "Can we not remedy that, My

Lord? After all, we wish to send Prince John home with a favorable impression of our Austrian hospitality."

"I shall see to it personally," nodded Raglan.

Baron Kirchenbetter finished a long drink from his goblet. "Bed or no bed, I imagine the prince is understandably anxious to return to Bavaria," he said. "Though Her Lady's table has no equal in all Germany," he paused to let out a loud belch, "a prisoner's life must be very dull indeed."

"You mistake my sentiments, Lord Kirchenbetter," inserted Charles. "I am quite content with my circumstances for the present." He looked down the table and studied Elsea's face to see if she understood his meaning, but her blank expression did not change.

"I am afraid you will need to be content with your circumstances for a few more days," noted Raglan. "We are still awaiting the duke's response to your letter."

"Lord Raglan," said Keinmeyer, "if His Highness is to be here a few days longer, may I suggest he attend the upcoming tournament? I think it would be a pleasant break from the tedium of this castle."

"Tournament?" asked Charles.

"Her Grace believes a tournament would be a splendid way to celebrate the arrival of spring," explained Raglan.

Charles looked again to Elsea. "It sounds exciting."

"It is Lord Raglan's idea," she replied flatly. "He is convinced my subjects would appreciate a day of frivolity. My father believed tournaments were an unnecessary extravagance, and it has been many years since we had one. I defer to Lord Raglan's opinion in these trifles."

"Well, I for one am looking forward to the joust," continued Baron Keinmeyer. "I believe this time we shall have a new champion."

"Hear, hear!" proclaimed Baron Kirchenbetter. "It is about time Lord Eugene's man was unseated."

Lord Eugene sat back and stroked his short beard. "Perhaps the two of you wish to place a small wager on the outcome."

The barons gave each other a quick look and then blurted, "Agreed!"

"Let each of us place twenty-five florins in a bag," proposed Keinmeyer. "The purse will go to the one whose man makes it the farthest in the tournament."

"Ah, fifty gold pieces to the winner," declared Lord Eugene as he rubbed his hands together. "I will never make so much money with so little effort."

Bishop Prochaska waved a half-eaten chicken leg at the three of them. "My Lords, you discard your money like the clean bones of this bird." He tossed the leg over his shoulder to illustrate his point. "That is money the Parish of Vienna could use to build new village churches and provide priests for our flock. You must learn to think of the eternal, and not," he finished with a wag of a greasy finger, "the temporal."

Lord Eugene wasted no time in replying. "You are quite right my good Bishop: if only we worked at expanding the kingdom of heaven with as much zeal as you put into expanding your girth, the Gospel would be known from here to Cathay!"

He and the barons enjoyed another round of laughter.

The frowning Prochaska reached for another chicken leg.

Lord Eugene broke the silence that followed by rising to offer a toast. "To Austria and Bavaria," he said holding up his cup, "may our new friendship with Prince John lead to happier and more peaceful days ahead."

This provoked the appropriate grunts of approval. Charles watched Eugene's face as he returned to his seat. He was certain he did not mean a word of it.

The meal was at last over. Elsea rose from the table, received the requisite words of thanks from her guests, and headed off to her rooms. One by one, the lords departed until the hall was empty and only Charles remained. He was sitting at the table wondering why the guards had not come for him, when Elsea reentered the room. He started to stand, but she motioned for him to stay seated.

She sat down directly across from him, placing her hands on the table only inches from his. The heat radiating from her fingers made his heart beat faster.

The hall was empty but for the two of them, nevertheless she began in a voice not much above a whisper. "I wish to apologize for my obstinate attitude this morning, Prince John. I have thought the matter over, and I now see the wisdom in your counsel."

"You have no need to apologize, Your Grace. I should not have presumed to know what is best for you."

"I did not think you presumptuous," she replied. "On the contrary, your view on the matter has given me a perspective I had not considered."

Charles sensed she wanted to say more and waited for her to continue.

"Prince John," she said, looking down at her hands, "if this, uh, *reconciliation* you spoke of is to be successful, how do you recommend I proceed?"

He gave some thought to her question before answering. "Begin with a letter," he suggested. "Let Duke Otto know you regret your former behavior and make clear to him that you wish to restore the broken friendship between your families."

"Would he even receive a letter from me?" she asked. "Would not a letter from you be better?"

"No," he answered quickly.

"You seem so sure. Certainly your word would have great sway with the duke. After all, he is your father."

Charles folded his arms across his chest. "He will not be swayed by any letter from me."

"But you had no objections when we asked you to write that letter the other day."

"That was different," was all he would say.

"I do not understand."

"I cannot explain my reasons, Your Grace. I can only urge you to write to him yourself and to do so without delay."

She pulled her hands back and looked at him a moment. "You give this advice in good faith?"

"I believe it is your best course, Your Grace, but only you can decide what is right for you."

She stood up from the table and paused with her hands resting on the back of the chair. "I will not pretend it will be easy for me to write such a letter, Prince John, but if this succeeds you will have done me a great service that I shall not soon forget."

She headed for the door, but stopped at the threshold. "Will Lord Raglan be sending you to the battlements tomorrow?" she asked.

"I believe so, Your Grace."

Charles was not sure if he saw her smile faintly on her way out, but he wanted to believe he did.

CHAPTER FOURTEEN

Dilemma

Charles sat back against the cool stone of his cell wall and sighed within himself. William and the prince must surely have made it back to Bavaria by now, and so his little game had more than achieved its purpose. The only reason to continue with this deception was purely for his own amusement: he enjoyed watching the most important nobles of Austria fret over the cleanliness of his clothing and the softness of his bed.

Yes, he enjoyed making fools of them all—all of them, that is, but Elsea. *Her* feelings had suddenly become important to him, and thus his dilemma. Would she have sought the private counsel of a simple Bavarian knight this morning? Would she have apologized to Charles, the peasant's son after dinner tonight? He knew the answer to those questions, and it did not cheer him.

Once, as a young page, he befriended a girl his age that also lived in the castle. She was the daughter of a prestigious knight, and he was the son of an unknown father. They were both too young to understand why that should matter. He and the girl played together whenever they had no lessons to practice or chores to do. It was always the same game: he was the chivalrous knight and she was the fair maiden in need of his protection. In their childish way they believed they were in love, and they promised each other they would always be together.

Their idyllic world ended the day her father sent her away

to a convent to complete her education. She would learn to be a lady of the court. They both cried bitterly when she had to leave, and he missed her terribly at first. However, his long hours of training with William and a growing friendship with the young Prince John helped him not to think about her, and soon he all but forgot her.

Many years went by until the day she unexpectedly returned. Charles was astonished at the change. She went away a cute little girl, but came back a glorious angel. The way she turned her head, the way she laughed, the way she veiled her face captivated him completely. Even the way she moved seemed more like floating than walking. For two days, he peeked around corners watching her, aching for an opportunity for them to be alone again as they were when they were children. Though she gave no indications, he was certain she was just as eager for their reunion.

One day, they met each other accidentally in one of the castle passageways. Charles stopped and smiled, but she and the woman escorting her seemed impatient to pass.

"I've been waiting for a chance for us to meet again," he grinned.

She took a step back. "Do I know you?" she frowned.

"Jennifer, it's me, Charles, don't you remember?"

She looked at him a little more intently, until finally a forced smile came to her lips. "Of course," she said flatly, "you are Charles. How have you been?"

"Very well," he gushed. "I'm so glad you're back." He glanced at the woman beside her before adding, "Perhaps we can meet later at our..."

She stumbled back from him as if he had just asked her to eat a worm.

"What's the matter?" he stammered.

"I am the daughter of Sir Teulon," she answered with her chin held high. "I shall be married to a baron next month. You are a… a…" she looked him over from head to toe, "a dirty, frumpy, foolish peasant boy. Do not be so absurd!" She gave a jerk to her shoulders as she and her companion pushed their way by him and disappeared down the hall.

Charles was devastated. He had never before considered how others perceived him. Later that day he found a mirror and studied himself intently. Looking back at him was a tall and gangly boy just turned seventeen. His thick brown hair, not yet tamed by a comb, was wild looking. He wore a baggy tunic covered in greasy stains from doubling as his napkin. His belt, a gift from William, and which up to that moment he had been proud of, looked too big for him. His hands and face were the same shade of grimy.

He acquired a low opinion of his own attractiveness that day. He had not yet learned that most of the ills he saw reflected in that mirror could be cured by an hour in a bath and a visit to a laundress. That day indelibly impressed upon him the belief he would never be more than an ugly boy with an undesirable pedigree.

His close proximity to Otto's court allowed him to further his education when it came to the female sex. Over the next few years, he had opportunity to see many young women come and go, all remarkably like Jennifer. They were always beautiful, and always adept at flirting with the sons of the nobles. Invariably, Charles found his original attraction to their physical beauty dampened by their personal shallowness. They cared only for fine clothes and finer gifts. They noticed only handsome men of means, the wealthier the better, and Charles soon despaired of ever attracting their attention.

As he grew older, he engrossed himself in his duties to the duke and prince. Meeting the requirements for becoming a knight was demanding work, and it left him little time to dwell on his desire for female companionship. Until a few days ago, he thought himself finally immune to those feelings.

Meeting Elsea had changed that. He had never known such a woman. She had depth to her soul and strength of character mingled with a sweet vulnerability that touched something deep inside him he could not identify. He was not sure what had happened to him that morning. He closed his eyes and could still see her standing before that window. Did she know the effect she had on him? Was it possible she was not aware of the power of her own beauty?

He knew he had to make a decision. As was his habit, he tried to be honest with himself. That he enjoyed her company, he could not deny, but he was tortured by the thought that his only appeal to her was as Prince John. The minute she learned the truth would be the last minute he would ever see her again, and he was not ready for that minute just yet. Besides, they would soon hear from Otto and his deception would be known to all. What harm could come from drawing out his masquerade a day or two longer?

So bolstered in his course by these flimsy justifications, he turned over on his cot and tried to sleep. Instead, the warmth of her hands, the color of her eyes, and the sound of her soft voice kept flooding his mind. The more he thought of her, the more difficult sleep became. He was in agony. But he was not complaining.

CHAPTER FIFTEEN

Forgery

Duke Otto sat brooding in his chair near the window, unable to enjoy the glowing red sky left behind by the setting sun. His wife rushed into the room and startled him out of his gloom.

"Otto, Otto," she blurted between gasps for air. "There's a messenger!"

The duke jumped up. "What messenger?"

"He entered the walls," she panted, "a few minutes ago... Lord Savoyen is bringing him here."

"Calm yourself, Agnes. *Who* is here?"

"A rider," she replied catching her breath, "from Elsea!"

"Elsea!" exclaimed her husband. "This may be the news we have been waiting for."

Otto headed for the door, but met a smiling Savoyen coming through holding out a rolled up piece of paper. "It is from Prince John, My Lord!"

The duke took the letter and immediately turned away to read it.

"What does it say?" asked Agnes, peeking over his shoulder.

"All is well," sighed a relieved Otto. "Our John will soon be home."

"Please," she pleaded, "at least let me read it!"

He laid a hand on his distraught wife's shoulder. "He has little to say of interest to you, my dear, but you may read it if you wish." He handed her the letter and turned to Savoyen. "There is something odd here, Savoy. They caught my son plundering their estates and could have demanded every coin in my treasury. Instead, they are willing to return him with a tribute and ask only for a meeting. What can this mean?"

"It means the security of the Austrian pretender and her lackeys is more precarious than we even dared imagine," answered Savoyen. "It is clear they are desperate to gain your favor."

Agnes tapped her husband on the elbow. "This is not John's writing," she declared.

"What!" exclaimed the two men.

"This is not John's writing," she repeated. "I am sure of it."

Otto snatched the letter from her hand and rushed to the window. Frustrated with the rapidly fading twilight, he ordered her to bring him a lantern. She took a burning stick from the fireplace and lit a candle instead. With Agnes holding the candle, and her husband the letter, the three of them huddled together and studied the mysterious correspondence anew.

"I believe she is right," admitted Otto, "but who would have written such a letter?"

"Charles," said Savoyen confidently. "I recognize his letters."

"Why would Charles write to us in the name of the prince?"

Savoyen had no answer.

"Our John is dead!" gushed Agnes. "And Charles has had a hand in it!"

"Agnes," groaned her husband, "you know Charles better than that. Please try to think rationally, my dear."

"But he has written you a letter and called himself John. How do you explain that?"

Husband and wife both turned to Savoyen.

"Since there is no denying Charles has written this letter," noted the duke's counselor, "we can only conclude it is part of some ploy to gain the prince his freedom."

"Are you saying they knowingly sent a forgery?"

"That is unlikely," answered Savoyen. "Charles must have found a way to convince them it was authentic. You know how clever he can be. We can furthermore deduce that John must be alive as well. Otherwise, their offer to return him would be utterly pointless."

"Well, what shall we do?" asked an anxious Agnes.

"That, at least, is not a difficult question, My Lady. We reply with all haste and agree to meet them as they suggest. Assuming they are in earnest, and there is no reason to believe they are not, we will have them all back by this time next week."

"Where is the courier now?" asked Otto.

"He is waiting in the antechamber, My Lord. His orders are to return to Vienna with your response."

"Bring him here," ordered the duke.

As soon as Savoyen left the room, Agnes grabbed Otto by the arm. "Do you really believe all that?"

"Savoy is right, my dear. They must have our John, and their promise to return him must be sincere. Bluffing about it would get them nothing but my wrath. I cannot speak for that woman, but Raglan would know this."

Savoyen returned with the messenger.

"I am concerned for my son's health," said Otto as soon as he crossed the threshold. "Is the prince well?"

"He is quite well, Your Grace," answered the courier without hesitation. "I saw him at dinner in the great hall with Her Grace but four nights ago."

Otto looked over at his wife who looked up at the ceiling and crossed herself.

"And what do you know of the contents of this letter?" asked Savoyen.

"I know that My Lord Raglan is most hopeful of arranging a meeting with His Grace."

Savoyen gave Otto a smiling nod.

"Lord Savoyen will prepare a letter for your return to Vienna," said Otto. "You may inform Lord Raglan that we accept his offer. We will meet his delegation in Hogisfeld seven days from today. Once Prince John is safely in Bavaria, we may proceed with certain limited discussions. I promise nothing more."

"Yes, Your Grace."

"You see, my dear," said Otto after they were gone, "there is no need for concern. Our son will be home within a week."

"Thank heaven!" she exclaimed. "I am going to the chapel to offer more prayers." She hurried from the room as quickly as she had entered, taking the candle with her.

Savoyen found Otto sitting before his fire when he returned. He pulled up a chair beside him. "This is a joyous day, My Lord: not only will both your sons soon be returning, but it appears you have at long last forced Elsea's hand. She will undoubtedly use John to seek your aid, and thus our position with Austria has never been stronger."

"I see the hand of Raglan in this," noted Otto. "God knows he is the only thing standing between that witch and whatever latest devilry has struck her fancy."

"Raglan is a good man," agreed Savoyen, "but the news I hear out of Austria these days is that he has become too feeble. Lord Eugene is the one to watch now. The man has more spies than the Pope has priests. They say he has riders stationed strategically all over the Empire so that a nobleman cannot sneeze at sunrise without Eugene hearing about it by sundown."

"What do I care about conniving nobles?" complained Otto. "The world will never be rid of them. I care only for the return of my sons. And once Charles is back, I intend to keep my promise to his mother."

An awkward moment of silence followed Otto's declaration. Savoyen moved his chair a little closer. "My Lord," he began quietly, "there is something I wish to speak to you of regarding that matter."

"Well, speak on then," replied Otto.

"You must reconsider your promise to tell him the truth," he said flatly.

"Will you never have an end with your scheming?" asked the now exasperated Otto. "Can you not see how it only wearies me now?"

"My Lord, I would be an indolent counselor indeed if I did not remind you how close we are to our long sought for ends," continued a determined Savoyen. "Conrad has fallen out of favor, and the electors are murmuring for a new king. Your name is on the lips of many of the princes, and the throne of all Germans is at last within our reach; now is not the time to jeopardize the support of your wife's brothers."

"Yes! I have heard it all before," replied Otto, "and I tell you this time I will not be dissuaded." He sat back and folded his arms across his chest.

Savoyen took a long breath and tried again. "If you will not be dissuaded for your own sake, My Lord, then at least consider the welfare of Charles."

"What do you mean?"

"If you care for the boy at all, you will not claim him as your son."

"Enough with these murky words, Savoy; speak plainly or hold your tongue."

"You know Agnes's brothers only helped save your father because they hoped one day to have a duke for a nephew," Savoyen reminded him. "As your firstborn, Charles would have a legal claim to that title."

"Ha!" snorted Otto. "Charles does not want to be duke."

"It matters not what Charles wants, My Lord. As long as he is alive, he will be a threat to their aspirations. No doubt you will protect him, and let us hope for many years to come, but what do you think will happen after you are dead? You know Hechten and Lichten as well as I do: they will seek his life the moment you are in the ground. They will not tolerate a rival to their John."

"I told you I do not wish to hear these things, Savoy."

"These are indeed difficult words, My Lord, and I take no pleasure in speaking them, but they are the truth nonetheless. Your blessing will become his curse; your name will become his death warrant. He will spend his days doubting whom he can trust, his nights fearing to close his eyes, and every meal wondering which bowl of soup will have the poison."

Otto slumped back in his chair. "My heart breaks for the boy," he moaned "He has everything my poor John lacks, but a name."

"The boy does indeed have a rare gift," conceded Savoyen.

"Oh, why did I not marry her, Savoy? Hang the throne and all it stands for! I was Count Palatine of the Rhine Sea. Charles would have inherited my title and lands. Dana and I could have had many such children. We could have loved each other and grown old together in peace." He reached up and pulled the circlet from his head. "What has this wretched coronet ever given me except misery?"

"My Lord," smiled Savoyen, "you need not despair. Much good still awaits the boy. He will be John's trusted advisor and enjoy the esteem that comes with it. He will live out his days in comfort and want for nothing. Why, someday, we can even find him a worthy bride to keep him company. By not telling him the truth you will give him the best chance for a long and happy life. This is not something to sorrow over."

The duke leaned his head back and went quiet for a long while. "You might be right, my old friend," he said at last. "Why should I inflict upon him the very life that has brought me nothing but anguish?" He sat up with a new gleam in his eye. "I will spend what time I have left providing something better for him. I think I will begin with that worthy bride you mentioned." He clapped his hands together. "And I know just the woman!"

CHAPTER SIXTEEN

Storm Without

With nothing in his cell besides a pitcher of water and the wooden bucket that served as his toilet, Charles was left to study the cracks and crevices in the walls for his entertainment. Breakfast and lunch had come and gone and still Raglan had not sent for him. He began to despair.

The sound of footsteps in the hall filled him with new hope, and he sat up instantly on his bed. His door opened, and his now familiar guard entered. "My Lord," he said with a slight bow, "Her Grace wishes to speak with you."

Charles sprang to his feet. "The duchess herself has called for me," he thought. He followed his escort calmly enough through the castle, but when they reached the familiar stairway, he sprinted up the steps and to the fresh air of the battlements. Waiting for him, with Dorianne at her side, was Elsea. He tried his best to look unmoved, but was unable to keep himself from smiling.

After they exchanged a few properly formal pleasantries, they began another stroll along the parapet. Though Charles thought it curious, he was pleased to see that Dorianne and the guard had remained behind. The spectacular view was the same, but the clouded sky hid the sun, and a steady breeze out of the north foretold a coming storm.

"Thank you for rescuing me from the boredom of my cell, Your Grace," he said politely.

"You are welcome," she replied politely.

They eventually reached a far corner around a traverse. Here, Elsea stopped, leaned over the wall through an embrasure, and pointed off into the distance. "Do you see that small house near the three trees on this side of the stream?"

He followed her arm until he located the little thatched-roof home a mile or so away that matched her description. "Yes, I see it."

"I was born there," she said without emotion.

Charles looked again, this time with genuine interest. "I assumed you were born in this castle."

"My father was on one of his endless campaigns in Hungary," she explained, still looking over the wall. "Though my mother was well advanced with child, she insisted on visiting him. She was on her way home when she was overcome with the pangs of my birth. They rushed to get her back to Vienna, but that hut was as close as they got. A few years ago, the lord who works that land wanted to tear it down to make room more for crops. I put a stop to it the moment I heard of it. He grows rye right up to the doorstep now, and no one even lives there. I've never visited it, but it reminds me of my mother somehow, and it comforts me to know it is still there." She paused, then added, "I am sure you find that quite strange."

"There is nothing strange about cherishing the memory of one's mother, Your Grace."

She stepped back from the wall and they continued their walk. "Unlike you, Prince John, I did not have a pleasant childhood, and there are few things from it I care to remember, much less cherish."

"My childhood was not as pleasant as Her Grace seems to believe."

"Well, according to the stories I have heard, Otto dotes on you on like a mother hen. They say you are the most pampered man in Bavaria."

Charles did not like the new twist in the conversation. "I would hardly call my life a pampered one," he replied a little stiffly.

"It is not a bad thing to have a father who cares for you," she said in a softer tone. "My father refused me nothing, but neither did I ever hear a kind word from him. I envy you in a way."

Her soft answer caused him to relax again. "Duke Otto is indeed generous," he admitted, "but I have struggles to face like anyone else in this world."

On they walked, oblivious to the rising wind and the thickening clouds.

"This world, as you call it, is full of things I do not understand," she said.

"Like what?"

"Look at us for example," she answered. "We are both the same age. We both speak the same language. We were both born into noble families. I am a duchess, and you will soon be a duke. However, you have a mother and father who care for you, while both my parents died before their time. I am beset on all sides by greedy men with nothing in common save their wish to steal from me my birthright, while you will have the duke's coronet handed to you on a down-filled pillow. Men honor you, but they revile me. How can two people be so similar and yet be so different?"

"There is no denying that there is much wrong in the world," he agreed. "But we cannot let that discourage us. We must look beyond it to the day when God will undo those wrongs and make all things right."

"There you go talking about God again," she said, stopping to face him. "You mention Him more than most priests I know."

"I sometimes think I do not mention Him enough," he smiled. "God is the one who gives our lives purpose."

"Purpose?" she repeated, not returning his smile. "I see no *purpose* to this life. In fact, I see no proof that God is even there. I gave up on that fairy tale long ago."

"We cannot see the wind either," he retorted, pointing over the wall to a cluster of trees swaying in the breeze. "But we can see its effects."

"Hmmm… the effects of God we can see," she replied, as if thinking aloud. "I would be grateful to hear an example, for I see none."

Charles tried to recall the hundreds of sermons he had heard at Mass. Though he rarely missed a Sunday, most of what he knew of God came from his mother. It was her simple grasp of the truths of scripture and her deep faith in her savior that had a bigger impact on him than all the priests he ever knew. Aware that Elsea was still waiting for an answer, he suddenly recalled something his mother often told him. "What about love?" he asked.

"What about it?"

"Love is a gift from God," he answered. "He proved His own love toward us when He sent His only Son to die in our place." He amazed himself with his quick thinking and struggled to hide the touch of pride he felt.

"What you call love," she shot back quickly, "I call a myth. Men have made women believe in love so they will marry them and bear their children and grow sick from working to clothe and feed them and not complain when their husbands find younger women to please them."

He was annoyed by how quickly she had dismissed his brilliant point, but she hurried on before he could think of a reply.

"I have a whole shelf of romantic poems, Prince John. Not surprisingly, they are all written by men." She clasped her hands over her heart and threw her head back. "Oh, love is so deep, and love is so consuming, and love is so undying, and love is so, so... so what? Whatever it is, there has been precious little of it directed my way!"

Charles sensed she was getting the better of him in the argument, and it irked him that he could think of nothing profound to refute her. "Maybe that has something to do with the way you treat people," he blurted.

"How do I treat people?"

"You treat them meanly!"

"Ah, so now I am mean—how loving of you to point that out."

"I did not say you are mean," he corrected her. "But why do you go out of your way to offend everyone?"

"If I offend everyone, it is because I am not afraid to tell them the truth, and if the truth is offensive, what is that to me? I will not make myself a liar for fear of bruising someone's ridiculously tender feelings."

"And yet you wonder why you are without friends. Can you not see how hard you make things for yourself?"

"So you believe a softer approach would be better. What a sparkling gem of advice you have given me: Elsea the wet nurse! I must say, Prince John, it does carry a certain ring of authority. I will make the change immediately, and I am sure it will solve all my problems."

A howling wind was coming over the wall, and they now had to shout to be heard.

"If you do not wish to be serious, so be it," said Charles. "I am only trying to help you see that you might be the cause of your own unhappiness."

"Now you sound like the ever-virtuous Lord Raglan," she frowned. "It is easy for him to be the epitome of tact and diplomacy; he is a man. I, in case you have not noticed, am not. Maybe if I was a man I could play make-believe like the two of you. My father taught me I must demand respect. I think that would be obvious, especially to you."

"You cannot demand respect," proclaimed Charles, now reduced to platitudes, "it must be earned."

"Yes, I recall hearing that when I was a child just like the stories of goblins living under my bed. I have since learned that men will never respect a woman they do not fear."

"It is better to be loved than feared!" he insisted nobly.

"What charming poetry," she shouted, "but I do not live in a poet's world, and I tell you for the last time I do not see this love you so admire."

"Of course not. You drive people from you like a dog drives sheep!"

"Sheep is the last word I would use to describe the beasts that stalk me. No one cares for my welfare!"

"What do you expect with the way you act? Who could love you? Even the way you dress frightens people. Just look at your hair…"

He meant to say more, but her sudden reaction stopped him in mid-sentence.

The fury drained from her face, and she reached a hand up to her head. "What's wrong with my hair?" she asked weakly.

In an instant, Charles went from hot anger to cold remorse.

She continued to stand before him touching her hair, waiting for his answer. "Well, nothing," he fumbled out finally. "It is just that... uh... it is not as becoming as it could be... that is, of course, if you chose to wear it that way." He studied her face to see if his feeble explanation had done any good.

The wind now roared along the parapet, and the sky had turned black as night.

"We must go," she said abruptly before she brushed past him and headed back the way they came.

Charles stood there for several seconds until he realized she was leaving without him. He trotted off after her.

"Your Grace!" he shouted above the wind.

She walked faster.

He picked up his pace so that he was only a few feet behind her and tried again. "Please wait, My Lady."

She stopped, but did not turn around.

"Your Grace," he said to her back, "it is a great fault of mine to speak without thinking, and I have often regretted my hasty speech. Please pay my words no heed. I did not mean to disparage you." He wanted to say something that sounded better, but those were the only words that came out.

She began to run.

Leaving him behind, Elsea reached Dorianne just as the first scattered drops of rain started to fall. Without breaking stride, she took her by the arm as they went through the door.

A flash of lightening sizzled across the sky. The boom of thunder that immediately followed shook the stones and broke open the clouds. In seconds, Charles was drenched through to the skin.

CHAPTER SEVENTEEN

Storm Within

That afternoon a storm beat against the walls of Elsea's castle. The relentless wind brought down a sideways rain, and a cold dampness permeated the stone halls. Elsea weathered the tempest in her quarters with Dorianne. Like the wailing wind outside, she circled restively through her rooms mumbling to herself.

On one of her many revolutions, she stopped and looked down at Dorianne. "Why should I care?" she frowned, but before the confused Dorianne could open her mouth, she resumed her uneasy journey.

Exhausted from having worn a path through her rooms, she finally flopped down in her chair with a groan and went still. Dorianne was placing more logs on the fire.

"Dori," asked Elsea at last, "what happened to our mirrors?"

"Would you like me to get you one, My Lady?"

"It's not that important," yawned Elsea. "I was only wondering."

Dorianne dropped the piece of wood into the flames and left the room. Shortly after becoming duchess, Elsea had ordered all mirrors removed from the castle. The servants, however, had only hidden them. Dorianne went to a closet that had several and returned with a small hand-held one.

Elsea seemed surprised when Dorianne held it out to her,

but after another unconvincing yawn she took it by the handle and turned it down in her lap.

Dorianne sat down and began cutting out material for a new shirt. Elsea sat staring ahead at a shelf full of books as if looking at something and yet clearly looking at nothing. At last, she stirred herself and lifted the mirror to her face. She turned her head and twisted the glass at all angles looking at her reflection. "What does he know anyway?" she mumbled.

"What was that, My Lady?"

"Nothing," replied Elsea. She stood up and went back to her previous travels, only this time she did so while studying herself with the mirror as she walked. Once more, she dropped into her chair. "Dori," she announced, "I have decided to change the way I wear my hair."

Dorianne answered her with a wide-eyed stare.

"I am bored," explained Elsea with a shrug, "and there is nothing better to do."

Dorianne went to her room and returned a moment later with a comb in one hand and a brush in the other. She pointed toward a short stool. "Sit here."

Elsea obeyed without a word, and Dorianne went to work. It was a new experience for them. Elsea had always worn her hair in the same fashion and never allowed Dorianne to touch it or offer any helpful suggestions. The first task was to undo the current creation. Elsea kept her long hair twisted so tightly it looked like a coil of coarse rope piled atop her head. Dorianne had to remove the various pins and strings that held it in place. After setting her hair free from its bondage, she began the long process of combing it out. This was as difficult for Dorianne as it was painful for Elsea.

"Ouch!" cried Elsea at each snag and snarl. "Are you trying to rip it out?"

"It can't be helped, My Lady," continued Dorianne undaunted. "Please sit still."

She finally managed to comb out her hair to its full length and paused long enough for Elsea to bring the mirror up and appraise the progress. Her hair hung down to the middle of her back, and the combing had a teasing effect that gave it an artificial body. Elsea was unrecognizable.

"It is longer than I thought," she observed. "What now?"

Dorianne circled her, grabbing sections of hair and weighing them in her hands. "It needs to be cut," she pronounced like a doctor prescribing a cure, "and washed."

"Do you think so?" Elsea asked meekly.

"Yes," answered the confident Dorianne. "I'll sharpen the scissors and call for the water."

An hour later, Elsea knelt over the rarely used basin in her room that served as her bathtub. Dorianne poured hot water over her head and worked the bar soap into her hair. After rinsing out the lather, she ordered Elsea back to the stool.

Doing her best to keep an even line, Dorianne used the scissors to cut away the hopelessly frayed last few inches. At their feet fell the wet clippings. Picking up the comb, she parted Elsea's hair down the middle and combed it out straight on all sides. She took two large strands near each temple and braided them around to the back like a small wreath. After a few more strokes with her brush, and some final touches with her comb and scissors, Dorianne stepped back, her face beaming.

"What do you think?" asked Elsea.

"See for yourself!" gushed Dorianne.

Elsea lifted the mirror and studied herself intently. She touched her hair tenderly as if afraid to ruin it. "It is the way my mother used to wear her hair," she whispered.

"Yes, My Lady," replied a smiling Dorianne. "You look just like her."

Holding the mirror before her, Elsea got up and walked slowly through her rooms. She came back to Dorianne and wrapped her arms around her, but said nothing.

They returned to their familiar places as if nothing had happened, and Elsea opened another yellowed volume in her lap. She had been reading from the same page a long while when she looked up from her book. "I do not feel like eating alone tonight," she said casually. "Please tell the cook that the council will dine with us."

"Yes, My Lady," replied Dorianne as she set aside her needle and thread and rose to leave.

"Oh, I almost forgot," added Elsea, but stopped to stifle a mysteriously sudden yawn. "I suppose we should inform Lord Raglan that he may invite the prince if he wishes."

Dorianne gave her a prolonged look. "Yes, My Lady."

CHAPTER EIGHTEEN

Divine Witness

With heads bowed against the driving rain, William and his bedraggled band rode their horses toward a group of thatched-roof huts they had seen from a distant hillock. Their concern about causing alarm proved unwarranted, as they had seen no living thing save a few barking dogs and the huddled cattle lowing mournfully behind split-rail fencing. The freshly plowed fields gave evidence of recent human activity, but the smoke curling up from the chimneys told them the local residents preferred staying dry.

They eventually reached the center of the twenty or so dwellings clustered around the intersection of two roads. They had hoped to meet some compassionate serfs who could offer them a meal, but it now looked as if they might have to go knocking door to door like beggars.

William turned in his saddle and looked around. "My Lord," he said, pointing with an arm dripping with water, "look at that large stone structure farther up the hill. Whoever lives in that home is no peasant. We'd do well to begin there."

They stopped their horses before a gate in a tall fieldstone wall that surrounded the main building. A sentry, taking shelter in a raised hut on the wall, paced back and forth stomping feet and rubbing arms in a losing battle against the damp cold. His preoccupation with his discomfort kept him from noticing the approach of the strangers. He snapped to alert at the sound of snorting horses.

"Who goes there?" he yelled.

As previously agreed, William did the talking. "Good afternoon, my friend," he shouted back with a smile. "We wish to see the lord of this fine manor."

The man leaned out an opening of his little box and peered down at them through the rain. "What do you want?" he shouted.

"I've told you, my friend, we wish to see your lord."

After giving them a longer look, the man jumped down from his perch and ran up a stone path toward the main house. He returned a few moments later, followed by an older broad-shouldered man with a long sword dangling from his side. The old man clambered into the hut and looked down upon the armed, though disheveled, riders.

"As God is my witness," he bellowed, "we must be at war!"

"I assure you, Sir," returned William. "I'm not aware that we are at war."

The man studied William again even more closely. "As God is my witness," he roared, "you are returned from a crusade and bring news of the Holy Land!" Before William could correct him, the man shouted for the gate to be opened. "You must get out of this blasted rain!" he hollered down to them.

The old man met them in the courtyard as they came through the gate. He grabbed the reins of William's horse, and led them up the path, barking orders at every step. Servants were soon scampering about like ants disturbed from their colony. While grooms took their horses to the stable, a smooth-faced squire led the men into the house. In the center of the main room was a circular fieldstone fire pit, and the chilled men huddled around it as close as the blazing flames would permit.

From another part of the house came the booming voice of the old man. "Theresa, Theresa, come see who is here!"

He came through the door with a short gray-headed woman who boldly approached the men now sitting on the floor before the fire. "What's all this talk of wars and crusades?" she growled.

William came to his feet and gave a polite bow. "Upon my word, My Lady, we are not crusaders, and we are not at war."

"Well, who are you then?" asked the old man.

"My name is William, My Lord, and these are my companions. We've been on a long and difficult journey and are in need of food. When we saw your manor through the storm, we had hoped we might purchase some provisions here."

"I do not sell food," replied the man. "But when it comes to hospitality my home has no equal in all of Frioul. Isn't that right, Theresa?"

His wife's scowl melted somewhat. "We must first do something about their clothing," she grumbled. "The stench alone would kill a rat." She ordered them to remove their stained and tattered rain-soaked garments and for her servants to burn them. "They are not fit for rags!" The servants brought in a wicker basket brimming with tunics, shirts, and breeches, and dumped them out onto the floor. No two colors or sizes were the same, but the grateful men rummaged through the pile and pulled on the ill-fitting garments without complaint. Just as they were putting the finishing touches to their new wardrobes, another bevy of servants entered and handed each man a steaming bowl of venison stew. So quickly did they reach the bottom of that first bowl that Theresa decided to bring in the whole pot. She circled the fire ladling out fresh helpings until each man confessed his inability to eat another spoonful.

William handed his empty bowl to the old man. "You've been most generous, Sir," he sighed contentedly, "but we've not been properly introduced. To whom do we owe our most sincere gratitude?"

The big man rose from his chair. "This is Theresa, my good wife of more than thirty summers. And I am Sir Vincent, a knight of Lord Hesse, who is vassal to Lord Carra, who is vassal to Lord Coehorn, who is vassal to Lord Harrant, who is vassal to Lord Hiller, who is vassal to the Margrave of Frioul: Lindenau the Weak!"

"He is not Lindenau the *weak*," opined Theresa with a roll of her eyes.

"As God is my witness, he is weak!" retorted her husband. "How else can you explain our lamentable state of affairs? The Empire is in crisis. Glory and honor hang all about us like ripe fruit for the picking. Bold men are performing daring deeds, forging their names upon the rocks of time with their bare hands. Yet what does the great Lindenau do? He complains that my quota of goat's cheese is too small. Goat's cheese I say! Pay no mind that a kingdom awaits a valiant man; I must beseech my poor goats to give more milk!"

Theresa looked over at William and shook her head. "He thinks anyone who doesn't go to war twice a year is weak."

"And what's wrong with war?" asked Vincent. "It's the sinew and lifeblood of all great kingdoms. It is man's destiny!"

"Please, Vincent, our guests are too weary to hear of the destiny of man today."

"Quite right, my good woman," he admitted reluctantly as he took his seat again near the fire.

"You look a little old to be a knight," observed Prince John.

"I may be old now, young man," replied Vincent, "but I was once the greatest knight in all Frioul, as God is my witness!" He paused and added in a meeker tone, "That was before my, uh, *temporary* retirement to this humble estate."

"You're the lord of this excellent manor then?" asked William.

"The one and only Lord of Tengen at your service, Sir," he answered with a bow. Vincent looked more closely at William. "You have the bearing of a great knight as well, Sir. Pray tell, what brings you to Frioul?"

"We are returning from a mission for Duke Otto," answered William simply.

"Duke Otto!" bellowed Vincent. "As God is my witness, there is a man who knows what he's about." He stood up, drew his sword, and began marching back and forth thrusting and slashing at unseen foes. "Duke Otto understands the times," he announced between parries. "From what I hear, he is but a handbreadth away from being King of all Germans. No goat's cheese for a man like Otto, you may be sure. *He* knows what both edges of a sword were made for!"

"Please, Vincent," said Theresa sweetly, "put that thing away before you hurt someone."

Vincent dutifully returned his sword to its scabbard and sat down. Suddenly, he looked over again at William. "Duke Otto, you say? Then you must be Bavarians. What sort of mission would bring you so far south with so few provisions?"

"We were ambushed by the shameless Austrians!" blurted Prince John.

William gave him a quick look that kept him from saying more.

"My companion is correct," inserted William calmly. "Several days ago we were attacked by a company of Austrian knights. In our effort to escape them, we were forced to take this route home."

"Ah, so the vixen of Vienna has made another enemy has she?"

"It would seem so," replied William.

"There is no disputing she is Frederick the Quarrelsome's daughter," said Vincent. "She hasn't a friend from Hungary to Holland, but her enemies are as plentiful as mice in a granary. As God is my witness, the Babenbergs will not long be masters of Austria."

Theresa pulled her shawl tighter around her shoulders. "I don't see why she's so detested. How is she any different from half the princes in Germany? They slight and offend each other as if it were their religion."

Vincent leaned in toward William. "You must forgive my dear wife," he said, tapping his head with a finger. "She doesn't understand these things like you and I."

"I think I understand perfectly well, my dear husband: she has something that other men want. And I say curse those men who start wars because they can't be satisfied with what God has already given them. If they ruined only themselves it might be pity enough, but to destroy so many innocent lives and cause so much misery to satisfy their lusts makes it a sin."

"Peace is always preferable to war, My Lady," agreed William.

"Ah well," replied Theresa, "you men might find this topic stimulating, but debating war and peace always makes my head ache. Come Vincent, it's already dark. We must see that these men have comfortable bedding for the night."

William came to his feet. "We're indebted to you for all your help, but we've imposed upon you enough. We're dry and well fed and the rain seems to have slackened, we must be on our way."

Theresa ignored his polite, though half-hearted, refusal and ordered her servants to spread out blankets and animal hides on the floor before the fire. "We rise with the sun," she warned them. "I shall see that you have a proper breakfast before you leave."

"You are most gracious, My Lady," said William. "When we reach home, I'll inform the duke of the kindness you have shown us here."

"Thank you, William," answered Theresa.

After seeing that the servants had restocked the fire, she and Vincent left the room.

William stretched himself out on the thick wool blankets. "Well, My Lord, we've only a few more days of riding over good roads through safe lands and we'll be home."

"Thank God," yawned John from beneath an animal hide.

CHAPTER NINETEEN

Unleashed Beauty

A bewildered council discussed in hushed tones the possible reasons the duchess could have for calling them to dine at her private table so late in the day. It was not like her to spend time with her wearisome lords of her own volition. No one was more surprised than Charles. He sat quietly in the same seat he had used the night he dined alone with Elsea and Dorianne. After their argument that afternoon, the last thing he expected was a dinner invitation.

The sentry announcing the duchess's arrival caused all conversations to cease, and the six men stood dutifully as Elsea glided into the room with her freshly cut hair bouncing as she walked. She reached her place at the head of the table and glanced around at them with a smile in her eyes. Dorianne's simple hairstyle had transformed her, and her guests were speechless.

An obviously proud Lord Raglan was the first to break the peculiar silence. "My compliments to you, Your Grace," he said. "When I saw you come through the door, I thought I was seeing a vision of your dear mother."

A blush came over Elsea's face that only increased her attractiveness.

She took her seat, and it soon became clear that not only had she changed her appearance, but she was in a rare good mood and had a pleasant word for everyone. Everyone, that is, but

Charles. She would listen with raptured gaze to Lord Raglan's numberless stories of the days of yore, and laugh at the Barons' inane jokes, but for Charles she had not so much as a glance.

It was plain to him that she was genuinely enjoying herself, and he became envious of the consideration she was giving the others while ignoring him. All night he kept trying to catch her eye like a dog begging at the table, but she would not throw him a scrap. Even worse was having to listen to everyone have a turn at remarking on her newly unleashed beauty.

Typical was Bishop Prochaska. "My Lady, I must say that your hair tonight is most becoming."

"Thank you, Your Excellency," she replied with another blush, "but it was all Dorianne's idea. She insisted it would look better this way. I try to humor her when I can."

Charles had lost track of how many tales Lord Raglan had regaled them with when the servants began collecting the dishes. He handed over a plate still piled high with food.

"Prince John," said Baron Keinmeyer, "you have hardly touched your dinner. Are you feeling unwell?"

"I do not have much of an appetite this evening," explained Charles. "I think it has something to do with the weather."

"Or maybe you are homesick for something," reasoned Kirchenbetter.

"Or maybe it is not some *thing* as much as it is some *one*, eh?" added Eugene with a wink and a nod toward Charles.

Elsea was reaching for her chalice when Lord Eugene made his vulgar suggestion. She froze with her hand above the rim, but did not look up.

"I admit I miss the company of my good friend William," replied Charles.

Elsea picked up the cup and brought it to her lips.

"Prince John," began Raglan as he eased himself back from

the table, "our long awaited tournament will be held tomorrow. Is it still your wish to attend?"

"It would be an honor, Lord Raglan," he answered quickly.

Raglan looked from Charles to Elsea and back to Charles. "As a distinguished guest, you will of course sit on the dais with Her Grace. You have no objections to that, do you?"

Charles looked down the table at Elsea who would still not look up. "None at all," he said.

With the table now clear, Elsea motioned to her servants that the evening meal was over. Her guests rose to offer their thanks for the honor. This was only customary, of course, but tonight's compliments possessed true enthusiasm and were actually believable. For once, Elsea had been a charming host. It had been a pleasant evening, and the lords of her council left the room with full stomachs and merry hearts. The sound of their laughter echoed across the great hall as they headed back to their quarters.

Elsea and Charles were the last two standing in the room. They faced each other from opposite ends of the table.

"Well," she said, with her arms folded across her chest, "you have not yet graced me with *your* verdict."

With considerable effort, Charles resisted the impulse to confess he never saw a more beautiful woman in all his life. "You look remarkable, My Lady," is what he settled for.

"You must get some sleep, Prince John," she replied as she turned to leave. "It will be a long day tomorrow, and they will call for you early."

Once again, Charles rolled over on his cot berating himself for what he had said on the battlements that afternoon. Why could he not learn to keep his mouth closed? Among the torrent of conflicting emotions washing over him, he now discovered a new one: jealousy. He could not decide what galled him more: the interest those hypocrites suddenly discovered in her, or the way she clearly enjoyed it.

When at last he did manage to fall into a shallow sleep, he lapsed into a nightmare. He saw her sitting on her throne looking as beautiful as he knew her to be. Gathered around her were the members of her council. On bended knees, they placed boxes of jewels and bags of coins at her feet and pleaded for her hand in marriage. Laughing and flirting, she complained that it was such a hard decision; she wished she could marry them all. Charles was there too, standing at the far side of the room. He kept calling her name, but she would not look his way and only laughed the more at the attention of her suitors. He awoke with a start, his brow beaded in sweat and his heart racing.

CHAPTER TWENTY

Secret Mark

Harried stable hands scurried about the courtyard completing last minute tasks for the long-awaited tournament. Elsea's grandfather had hosted many of the popular gatherings featuring martial exhibition as entertainment. Leopold's lavish events often lasted days and drew hundreds of knights from all over Austria. However, much like the infrequent tournaments of Elsea's miserly father, today's modest endeavor would be over by sundown.

Raglan greeted Charles in front of the stables and gave him a spirited chestnut mare to ride. Urging his horse forward, he moved up alongside Elsea who sat astride a white Arabian stallion. Slowly, order emerged from the chaos, and the cavalcade of nobles and knights was ready at last. At a command from Lord Eugene, the duchess's escort swung onto their horses. The gates opened, and accompanied by the blaring of trumpets, Elsea and Charles led the colorful procession on their stately walk to the field.

Outside the castle, a large crowd anticipated the appearance of the duchess, and a loud cheer went up when she finally emerged from behind the walls and crossed the drawbridge. Elsea waved to the enthusiastic peasants and townspeople as she led her entourage down the road. The people stood back to allow the resplendent knights and lords to file past two by two and then fell in behind, becoming part of the parade. Last night's storm had cleared. As the sun climbed higher, the wind changed to out of the south and the temperatures began to rise. The day promised to be one of the warmest yet in an already unseasonably mild spring.

The tournament concept originated as a way for the highly trained and expensively equipped knights to maintain their battle efficiency during the exasperating interludes of protracted peace. Among the many events were archery shoots and horse jumps, along with team and individual battles on horseback. Though they used training weapons for the more dangerous events, injuries, sometimes fatal, were not uncommon. This was especially true in the mock battle which featured high-speed charges.

It was customary to declare a holiday when holding a tournament. For the overworked serf this meant a day without labor. It also meant a day of feasting. Part of each noble's obligation to the duchess was to provide his share of food and drink which varied according to his stature. The excited serfs knew that today they would not be going home hungry.

As they approached the field, scores of tents came into view standing opposite a brightly festooned platform that served as the viewing stand for Elsea and her highest ranked nobles. Over the tents fluttered the knights' brilliantly colored banners; each distinctive design representing their individual houses. Farther down were the booths erected around already burning fires. The smell of roasting pork, beef, venison, and every kind of fowl wafted along in the morning breeze. A long row of tables stood end-to-end, ready to receive the bounty of the prolific cooks.

The nobles left their horses and took their places on the platform. After Bishop Prochaska gave the invocation, Lord Raglan came to the front and faced the assembled knights who hoped to win a small share of glory that day. They stood with their hats removed and heads bowed while Raglan reminded them of their oaths of fealty and the sacred honor of their duchess which they were sworn to protect. Several thousand eager spectators lined an area marked off by stakes and ropes.

When Raglan finished, Elsea stepped forward and the knights respectfully knelt down before her in the still damp grass. She held up a long white kerchief over her head and let the wind blow it back and forth before releasing it. When it fluttered to the ground, the crowd burst into cheers. The tournament had begun.

The first competition was the archery shoot. This event was open to anyone regardless of rank, and young men from all over Austria came to vie for the title of best archer. The competitors stood to the left of the platform facing whitewashed circular boards placed at a distance of twenty paces. The only mark on each board was a small black circle in the center. The object was to hit the black circle. Anyone who missed, even by the tiniest margin, was eliminated. After each round, the targets were moved farther away and the number of archers who missed increased until only one remained.

Being declared the best archer carried great honor. The winner received a small leather bag containing several gold coins from the duchess's own hand. The victor that day was a curly-headed blond of no more than seventeen who trembled so badly when he reached out for the bag that he dropped it. Only Elsea's quick reflexes kept it from hitting the ground and adding to his embarrassment.

Charles sat to Elsea's right and slightly behind. Although the occasional feat of daring on the field would get his attention, he spent most of his time watching her. She laughed and cheered and carried on like a child at her first public outing. It was clear her enthusiasm was sincere, and he enjoyed seeing her so unguarded.

Though archery shoots, horse jumps, races, and javelin throws fascinated the onlookers, the highlight of any tournament was always the display of the knights in combat. The last and greatest of these demonstrations was the mock battle. Two teams of knights entertained the crowd with three hours of breathtaking charges and collisions. One by one the combatants were unhorsed until only two remained.

To the right, in a livery of bright red, was one of Baron Kirchenbetter's knights. Facing him was Lord Eugene's champion in deep blue. The blue knight had never before been defeated and was the crowd favorite. At their respective ends of the field, squires feverishly prepared their lords for the final charge.

Eugene leaned over to Kirchenbetter. "I shall soon take possession of that gold, My Lord."

"We shall see," laughed the nervous baron.

After readjusting armor, and pulling on helmets, the two knights climbed into their saddles and dipped their lances in salute to the duchess. The spectators pressed closely against the ropes, and a hush fell over the field. At a nod from Elsea, the two men spurred their horses into a gallop. A loud roar rose up from the throng as they closed rapidly with lances leveled. In the flickering of an eye, the blue knight's lance shattered into a hundred splinters, and the red knight toppled end over end to the ground. The cheering mass knocked down the ropes and swarmed the field to congratulate their hero. A crestfallen Kirchenbetter handed Eugene a jangling leather bag.

When the final contests were completed, and the last of the victors had approached the podium for their rewards, it was time to begin the feast. On cue from Lord Raglan, the people began to line up at the tables. Most of the excited serfs had never seen so much meat in one place. For some, today would be their first *legal* taste of venison. The food and drink would be served until it ran out. Back in the time of Duke Leopold that may have taken two days. Today, Elsea's subjects would be content if the meats, breads, and cheeses lasted long enough to stuff down their third helping.

Elsea dined with her council at a separate table before the dais. After they finished eating, Raglan, Eugene, and the barons excused themselves and drifted off to visit with some of the heroes of the day. As soon as they were out of sight, Elsea looked furtively in all directions and whispered to Charles, "Follow me."

They snaked their way through the crowd of jubilant peasants thronging around noisy enclaves of jugglers, acrobats, dancing bears, singing minstrels, and fast-talking merchants hawking everything from eastern spices to fine pottery and colorful cloth, to where Lord Eugene kept the horses. Except for the two guards, who had strict orders never to let the prince out of their sight, they had left the field unnoticed. Just as they reached the horses, however, Lord Eugene came running up to them.

"What are you doing?" he panted.

"The prince's legs are cramped," reported Elsea. "We shall take a short ride."

Lord Eugene's eyes widened. "Alone?"

She nodded toward the guards. "These men will be with us."

"Does Lord Raglan know about this?"

"Of course," she answered without hesitation.

"Well, at least tell me how long you will be gone," he demanded.

"We shall be but a few minutes," she promised as she mounted her horse.

Charles followed her example, but before he turned to catch up to her already trotting animal, he could not resist a parting shot. "Be not concerned, my good man, I shall see that the duchess is well cared for."

"Why are you still standing here?" growled Eugene at the guards. "Get on your horses and follow them, you fools."

Elsea had slowed down to allow Charles to catch up, but as soon as he was alongside, she lashed her horse. "Now we shall see who can ride!" she laughed. She was instantly several lengths in front before Charles knew he was in a race.

They splashed across a trickling stream and galloped down a long meadow toward a wooded area ablaze in the bright green of its fresh leaves. Elsea rode her animal hard and it was difficult for Charles to keep his mare from losing more ground. They stood in their stirrups with knees bent, leaning against the bouncing necks of their horses. Elsea would look back over her shoulder and goad him with things like, "Come on, old Raglan is faster than that!"

Each time she turned around her smile was brighter, her windswept hair more striking, and the excitement in her voice more captivating. Charles did not know where she was taking him, and he did not care. If she led him off a cliff at full gallop, he would plunge to his death the happiest man on earth.

They were swiftly coming up on the woods. Charles saw a gap in the trees and expected her to angle in that direction. Instead, she headed straight for a snake-rail fence that was over five feet high.

Only a few strides from the fence, she turned once more to taunt him, "Follow if you can!" Suddenly, her horse left the ground and in one graceful motion, she soared up and over the top rail, landed on the other side, and rode off through the trees without breaking stride.

Charles had no idea if his horse could even jump, but he was willing to risk a broken limb or two to keep Elsea in sight. He felt the mare gather herself below him, and in one powerful leap they were in the air. Time stopped briefly as he and the horse floated silently above the ground; only the wind rushing past his ears told him he was moving. They cleared the fence and landed perfectly. From behind, he heard dull thuds and loud groans. He looked back and saw two horses trotting away with empty saddles.

They broke out from under the trees into an even larger field. Elsea slowed her sweating stallion to a canter and guided him toward a jumble of moss covered stones. She stopped when she reached them, and Charles reined in his mare beside her. Both animals were panting and covered in a frothy white film.

"We should walk them for a few minutes," he advised.

They got down and led the fatigued horses in circles around the stones. Charles discovered that what he thought was only a random pile of rocks was actually the remains of an ancient building. The intact foundation outlined what had once been its many rooms, and one end still reached up several feet above the ground. There was something peculiar about the old dwelling, and he stopped to study its crumbling walls.

"What is it?" asked Elsea.

"I am not sure why," he answered, "but I have this feeling I have been here before."

"How odd it is that you should say that," she said, "because this is what I wanted to show you."

They tethered their horses, and he followed her to the other end of the strangely familiar building.

"I have not been here since the day my ever-ambitious father tried to impress *your* father with that lavish tournament. Do you remember?"

The expression on his face told her he had no clue what she was talking about.

She pointed to a cluster of trees on the other side of the field. "You sat right over there next to my brother and me," she reminded him. "You were quite shy and scarcely spoke a word all day. You never left your father's side the whole time. As usual, my father's diplomacy was as fruitless as it was tactless, and that was the last time we ever saw each other."

"Uh… yes… I remember now," stuttered Charles. "I was but a child then, of course."

"My poor brother had to remain on the dais all day," she went on, "but I snuck away when things got too boring and found these ruins. There was a peculiar boy already playing here by himself. He was pretending to be some sort of king, and he invited me to join him. I never had any friends who asked me to play like that before. Naturally, it was all very childlike: we were the monarchs of a great kingdom and this was our castle." She led him along the trace of a central hallway as if giving a tour. "This was the room for our servants, and that room over there was for our meals on cold days because it was closest to the fireplace. This big room was our great hall where we would entertain important visitors from all over the Empire. Over here is where we put our thrones side by side. We took a sacred vow to rule our kingdom with justice and compassion. These last two rooms were our own. We imagined ourselves as husband and wife coming here after a busy day among our subjects and privately discussing the cares of our realm."

Charles listened intently, not daring to interrupt her.

"The boy told me of a great Viking warlord he once read about in a book. The legendary king tattooed his name onto his wife's arm. He asked if I wanted a tattoo like the great Viking queen. He said all we needed was a sharp point and some charred wood from a fire. He had a small knife, but I was afraid, so he let me mark him first. She rolled up the sleeve of her right arm. "Can you see it?" she asked. "It hurt too much to do our whole names, so we made only a small mark."

He leaned in, and halfway between her elbow and shoulder, he saw a small faded-black 'X'.

"The hours flew by like minutes until finally my mother sent some servants to find me, and I had to go. But the boy promised he would return someday, and we pledged never to forget our secret marks."

She opened her mouth to say more, but stopped.

"My Lady," he asked quietly, "what do you wish to tell me?"

She took a deep breath, as if bracing herself. "I regret the harsh things I said yesterday. No doubt you think me colder and more unfeeling than ever. I told you this story because I want you to know I was not always this way. For a while I even imagined that boy and I were in love, and I prayed God every day to bring him back." She paused before adding quietly, "He never did, of course. And so that is all I have ever really known of love, Prince John: a childish mark on my arm to remind me of a childish dream."

Her sad tone caused his heart to race, and he struggled to hide the effect she was having on him. "I believe love is more than a dream, My Lady," was all he dared say, "and I hope someday you will find it so."

They both went silent.

"We should go," she said at last. "Lord Eugene will surely sound the tocsin if we are not back soon."

The rubble of one of the walls separated them from the horses. Charles got to them first and waited for her. She tried to leap over the stones in one bound, but caught her foot and fell toward him. He reached out instinctively and grabbed both her hands in his. They ended up with Elsea standing on his toes looking up at him.

He stared into her face. The scars were easier to see in the light of day, but he looked beyond them. The same cruel sun that highlighted her blemishes made her lips pinker and her green eyes dazzle more brightly. A gentle breeze blew a few strands of her hair back and forth across her face partly hiding, partly revealing her features. "Are you unharmed, My Lady?" he asked softly.

"Yes," she replied, before retaking possession of her hands.

They rode their horses at a leisurely walk retracing the same ground they had raced over earlier. Elsea had not spoken since she nearly fell, and Charles chastised himself for holding her hands so long. They were approaching the woods where they had jumped the fence, when Elsea's entire escort came thundering through the trees and rode up to encircle them.

"What is the meaning of this?" demanded a startled Elsea.

"Lord Eugene is concerned for your safety, Your Grace," explained the captain. "He sent us to find you and bring you back."

"I will return when I please!" she exclaimed.

"Yes, Your Grace," said the captain, but gave no indication of leaving.

She stared at him a moment more and said in a calmer tone, "If you must be here, then at least keep to the rear."

"Yes, Your Grace."

Elsea and Charles continued on their way, and her escort fell in behind.

"Why must they always treat me like a child?" she sighed.

The setting sun dispersed what remained of the lingering crowd, and Elsea and her nobles began the short ride back to the castle. As soon as the door of his cell closed behind him, Charles stood up on his cot and rolled up his right shirtsleeve. By the fading light coming through the window high above, he frantically searched his shoulder until he found the small 'X.'

CHAPTER TWENTY-ONE

Bold Impulse

A yawning Charles sat up on his cot, rubbing his bleary eyes. He had spent a sleepless night reliving a long buried memory. Before Elsea's father had his falling out with Otto, he had invited the duke and young prince to Vienna and hosted a tournament in their honor. Royal protocol required Prince John to remain at his father's side, but Charles, a page to William at the time, had no such obligations. During a prolonged lull in the festivities, he slipped away to go exploring. He met what he thought was a peasant's daughter near some old ruins he had discovered. What were the chances that cute and clever girl would be Elsea?

The sound of voices interrupted his contemplations. The door swung open and a smiling Lord Raglan stepped inside.

"I have good news, Prince John," he beamed. "We have at last received a letter from your father."

Charles did his best to hide his sudden apprehension, but was confused by Raglan's obvious excitement.

"You will soon be going home," continued Raglan. "We leave the day after tomorrow for Hogisfeld."

"Duke Otto has agreed to your terms?" asked a stunned Charles.

"You seem surprised," observed Raglan. "Did you have any doubts?"

"Uh, of course not," lied Charles. Indeed, he had more than doubts. William and the prince should have made it home several days ago. What possible reason could Otto have to still meet with them?

"Prince John, I know the conditions here are not what you are accustomed to," Raglan paused to take a step closer, "but I hope they have not been overly oppressive."

"I have no complaints."

"Her Grace, at times, can be somewhat abrasive," admitted Raglan in a lower tone, "but I believe she has made an effort to show she can be amiable as well. I trust you will give your father a favorable report."

"Lord Raglan, you may be certain that I will speak of the duchess in the most flattering terms possible," replied Charles, grateful for the opportunity to speak truthfully. "I regret our time together has been so short."

"I am pleased to hear that," smiled a relieved Raglan. "I will not conceal from you my hope that Austria will once again find a friend in your father." He pointed toward the door. "Come, I have prepared more suitable lodgings. It is a shame I did not think of it sooner."

Charles followed Raglan and the guard to the same floor as Elsea's great hall. They brought him to a windowless closet previously used for storing the weapons and armor of the castle guard. Raglan had the room emptied and swept, replacing the shields, swords, pikes, and breastplates with a few pieces of simple furniture. Charles was pleased to see the room was larger than his former cell, and the air was much drier. The bed had a proper mattress and even a pillow and blanket. There was a small table, a simple chair, two oil lamps, and an inkstand complete with pen and paper.

"It is the best we could do for now," said Raglan. "I hope it meets your approval."

"I shall repose like a king," answered a thankful Charles.

Raglan moved to the door. "Lunch will be sent around shortly," he said. "Afterward, may I suggest some exercise on the battlements?" He glanced around behind him and added with a faint smile, "I believe the duchess will be there. Your arrival has had a most unexpected effect upon Her Grace, and I cannot recall ever seeing her so content. Perhaps it is because the two of you have so much in common." Without waiting for a reply, he left and closed the door.

As Raglan predicted, Elsea was there to meet him on the familiar stones. By now, Dorianne and the guard knew their part. Without a word from Elsea, they waited behind, and the duchess and would-be prince began their promenade.

They walked for several minutes in an awkward silence until Elsea at last said, "I hear Lord Raglan has provided you your own personal suite."

"I must be the envy of every lord in the castle," he laughed.

"I suppose he also told you that we received a letter from your father."

"He says I am to leave for Hogisfeld the day after tomorrow."

She turned to look out onto the fields growing greener by the day. "I imagine you are impatient for your freedom."

"On the contrary, Your Highness, my time here has been more enjoyable than you know, and I am not so eager to depart as you believe."

"But certainly there are people at home you are looking forward to seeing."

"My mother is no doubt anxious for me," he conceded. "And it will be good to see my friend William again."

"What about your father?"

"Yes... the duke as well."

"Is there no one else?"

"No."

"What, no beautiful princess your father wants you to marry?"

"I assure you, My Lady, there is no one my father wants me to marry."

"You are fortunate, Prince John. You have control over the important issues of life. Around here, they cannot wait to marry me off. Lord Eugene and the barons are still convinced Eldridge is the only hope for the Babenberg legacy. You see, I told you my life would be easier if I were a man."

"I am glad you are not," he smiled.

They arrived at the spot where they had argued the day of the storm. At this bend in the wall, Dorianne and the guard could not see them.

"I wrote to your father," she said.

"What did you say?"

"I did as you advised: I apologized for my former behavior and asked if there was any way I could make atonement."

"I know it was difficult, My Lady, but you have acted wisely. The duke is the kind of man who will be impressed by your gesture."

"I am not so sure, Prince John. Words on paper can often be misunderstood."

"Then I will be your advocate," he promised, looking her in the eyes.

The instant her eyes met his she turned her head away. An uncomfortable silence followed as they watched a flock of birds spiraling down in a long circle before landing in a freshly plowed field.

"I hope I did not bore you yesterday," she said, still watching the birds.

"What do you mean?"

"I mean with all that childish drivel about Viking kings and queens. It was rude of me to prattle on like that."

"You were never rude," he replied, "and yesterday was one of the most exciting days of my life."

She stepped back from the wall. "That is difficult to believe."

"I do not see why. The weather was beautiful, the games were thrilling," he looked her in the eyes again, "and I had a gracious host."

This time she returned his look for a long moment. "Why have you been so kind to me?" she asked. "I have done nothing to deserve it."

A small voice in his head told him not to do what he was thinking, but, as was his habit, he ignored it. He reached out and gently took her by the hand. "My Lady," he said quietly, "I can no longer hide my feelings for you."

Charles felt her hand tense in his.

"I am unskilled in coquetry, Prince John."

"Yet one more thing that I admire," he replied. He reached up with his other hand to touch her face. His bold impulse caught her by surprise, however, and she drew her head back with a start. He immediately let go of her hand and took a step back.

Elsea cleared her throat and looked out over the wall again. "We have had an exceptionally mild spring this year," she observed after a long pause.

"That always bodes well for the fall crops, My Lady."

"Lord Raglan says it hasn't been this warm in April since he was a boy."

"The peasants say a warm spring means a hot summer," he noted confidently.

"Well, I prefer a hot summer to a cold winter," she declared with equal confidence.

Having exhausted their collective knowledge of weather folklore, they fell silent.

Elsea ended their misery. "You must excuse me, Prince John. We are holding court today, and Lord Raglan tells me he has enough cases to last well into the afternoon. He insists that I attend these things."

"Certainly, Your Grace," returned Charles with a courtly bow. "As usual, Lord Raglan is correct, and I must not keep you from your more important duties."

They made their way back to Dorianne and the guard without speaking. Elsea took Dorianne by the arm. "There are pressing matters I must attend to, Prince John. Feel free, however, to enjoy the sun a while longer."

"Thank you, Your Grace," he replied with feigned indifference. "It is a welcome relief to stretch my legs."

"Lord Raglan tells me you will be leaving us in another day or two," she added casually. "Unless you have an objection, I suggest you dine with us tonight. It may be your last chance for a good Austrian meal."

Charles offered no objection.

CHAPTER TWENTY-TWO

Intuition

Elsea sat on her throne in the great hall. Sitting at a nearby table, with stacks of yellowed parchments spread out before him, was Lord Raglan. A line of nobles, each one eager for the duchess to adjudicate for him in some complaint, stretched out the door and onto the landing beyond. Though Raglan possessed enough authority to have presided over the tedious duty alone, he insisted on maintaining feudal tradition and expected Elsea to be present.

Most cases involved disputes between her nobles and usually centered on unfulfilled vassal obligations. Austrian society was a pyramid shaped hierarchy with the duchess at the top. In theory, all land belonged to Elsea, and all her important nobles were also her vassals by virtue of the piece of land called a fief which they had been given. A large fief could be subdivided permitting the lord to acquire his own vassals. This subinfeudation could be repeated many times, thereby creating multiple levels of vassals all the way down to a single knight living on a small manor.

Vassals were expected to provide their lord with certain days of labor, a percentage of the harvest, and even gifts on holidays. In the event their lord was threatened by war, they were responsible to rally to his cause with a predetermined number of well-armed knights and footmen. In return, the vassal received the protection of his lord and the use of his fief. It was on this land that the vassal was able to support himself and his family. The bond of commitment between a vassal and his lord was the bed-rock of feudal civilization. Enforcing the oaths and punishing those who broke them were vital to preserving order.

It was late in the afternoon when the last of the justice-seeking nobles had left the hall, and Elsea was finally able to return to her quarters. With dinner yet a couple of hours away, she and Dorianne sat in their familiar seats passing the time in their familiar way.

"I have decided you were right, Dori."

"Right about what, My Lady?"

"About the prince: he is not at all what I thought."

"I told you so."

"He said that he enjoyed his day at the tournament."

"I'm glad to hear it."

"Did I tell you how Lord Eugene sent the whole palace guard after us?"

"I believe you did, My Lady."

"What did he think—that Prince John might try to kidnap me? Really Dori, they do not know him like I do."

"Do you know him, My Lady?"

"Well, I think I know him better than any of *them*," proclaimed Elsea. "He is different, and I have never met a man who..."

"Yes, My Lady?"

Elsea stood and used her hand mirror to look at herself. "Dori, do I have any other clothes?"

"You have many shirts and tunics, My Lady."

"Not those," she sighed. "I mean... well, you know, *nicer* clothes."

Dorianne's eyes widened. "Do you mean a dress?"

"You need not say it like *that*, Dori. We will meet Duke Otto in a few days and it is vital I make a good impression. So, do I have any?"

"No, My Lady, you don't."

Elsea returned to her seat with a frown.

"But I think I know where I could find one," offered Dorianne.

Elsea's face lit up. "You do?"

"Lord Hagen's wife is very close to you in size. I'm sure I could get one from her."

"No, thank you," replied Elsea, slouching back in her chair. "Wearing someone else's castoffs is not what I had in mind."

"But I can alter it and make it better."

"I suppose it would take a long time?" guessed Elsea.

"I'll go right now. You can try it on, and I'll have it ready by dinner."

"I should like that very much, Dori."

The dutiful Dorianne left immediately on her mission. However, on her way to Lady Hagen's quarters, she took a detour and stopped by the recently converted storage closet. Boldly stepping up to the sentry on duty, she announced in an authoritative tone worthy of Raglan himself, "I am here on behalf of her lady the duchess; show me in to the prince."

CHAPTER TWENTY-THREE

Witness Moon

Elsea came to the table wearing a long green dress trimmed in white at the collar and cuffs. Around her waist was a braided chain of fine silver and on her head was a pearl-lined golden circlet. Charles glanced at Dorianne who answered his look of astonishment with a brief lifting of her eyebrows. "I see you have changed your attire, Your Grace," he said. "Is there a special occasion?"

"I intend to accompany Lord Raglan to Hogisfeld," she replied simply. "I asked Dorianne to find me something more appropriate for meeting a duke."

"You chose well," he smiled at Dorianne.

They sat down, and the meal began. Charles did his best to engage Elsea in conversation, but she seemed distracted and seldom gave him more than one-word answers. Several times he caught her staring at him, but the instant their eyes met she would look away. He was certain his rash behavior that after-noon was behind her sudden aloofness.

With so little dialogue between them time passed slowly, and Charles felt relieved when the uneasy dinner was finally over. He sat back to wait politely for the guard to return him to his new quarters. He was surprised therefore when Elsea suggested a walk on the battlements.

"At night?"

"I hope you do not believe I am afraid of the dark, Prince John. I think you will find our Austrian nights can be just as enjoyable as our Austrian days. Is that not so, Dori?"

"Yes, My Lady."

The cool evening air was indeed a pleasant relief from the stuffy castle interior. A cloudless sky allowed an unspoiled view of the full moon rising slowly behind the town. Its nearness to the horizon appeared to multiply its size making it look close enough to touch. Leaving Dorianne and the guard at their now usual place, Charles and Elsea walked alone in the moonlight. They stopped when they came to their familiar corner and leaned against the stones of the wall still warm from the day's sun. Standing close to each other, they stared out at the innumerable pinpricks of light flickering throughout the town below.

Elsea seemed content to remain silent, but Charles could no longer bear the tension. "You are very quiet tonight, My Lady."

"I suppose I am," she admitted.

"Have I done something to upset you?"

"I would not be standing here if you had."

"Then what is it?"

She turned to face him, but said nothing for a long moment. "Why did you say those things to me today?" she asked quietly at last.

"Do you wish I had not?"

Again, she hesitated. "I only wish I could believe they were true."

The soft tone of her voice combined with the way the moonlight fell upon her face was too much for him. He stepped closer and took her hands in his. "I told you I can no longer hide my feelings for you, My Lady, but I do not know how to give them voice. I think of you when I am awake, and I dream of you when I am asleep. You have wounded me somehow, yet it only hurts when we are apart."

"Do not mock me," she pleaded.

"If I mock you, then I mock myself, for there is nothing I would not do to prove the depth of my feelings."

"How can you talk this way? Do you not see how wretched I am?"

Charles brought a hand up and lightly ran his fingers along her face. "I see only your beauty, My Lady."

She closed her eyes at his touch. "Scars have no beauty."

"I have never touched anything softer," he assured her. He traced her eyebrows with a fingertip. "Has anyone ever told you how becoming your eyes are in the sunlight?"

"No," she answered with eyes still closed.

He touched her lips. "Has anyone ever told you how inviting your mouth is when you smile?"

"I have never heard such words," she whispered.

"My heart is full of nothing else, My Lady."

He placed a hand on either side of her face, and softly kissed her mouth. She slid her arms around him, and they embraced each other with only God and the moon to witness their bliss.

"I told you I know nothing of love," she said, now stepping back to look him in the eye. "I know only that something has happened to me—something that I fear to lose. And yet I fear it will destroy me."

"Elsea, you have a power over me greater than you can understand. You are bound in my heart, and I could not destroy you without destroying myself."

"Is this love then?" she sighed.

"I do not know," he admitted, "but I want to find out."

"You know nothing about me," she warned him.

"Then teach me," he smiled, taking her by the hands. "Tell me everything: tell me every thought you have ever had, every deed you have ever done. I want to spend this night hearing nothing else."

"There is little of importance to tell," she smiled back. "My life has been a dreary one, and I expect you will soon be bored and have to beg for mercy."

"Then I will risk the boredom and trust in your mercy," he laughed.

Elsea intertwined her fingers in his and they began a slow walk along the darkened parapet. "I never wanted to be duchess." she began. "I would have died with my brother if it had not been for my mother's constant care. No one else would go near me, not even my own father. He warned her to stay away, but she refused to leave my side." She paused before adding quietly, "She died the day they buried my brother."

"She must have loved you dearly," noted Charles.

"I think about her often," she said. "I can hardly recall my father's face, but when I close my eyes at night I can still see her bending over me, and I hear her sweet voice promising me all will be well. I have never told anyone how much I miss her."

On they went through the night. Charles was always careful to deflect questions about himself, insisting he only wanted to hear about her. And so, from her joyless childhood to her combative council, Elsea poured out all her heart. They soon lost track of how many times they had passed Dorianne and the lonely guard. Sometimes they went by laughing like children. Other times they passed silently as ghosts. But mostly they drifted by arm in arm talking in hushed tones, oblivious to all else around them.

The moon was now well above them and the dew had begun to fall. The guard flung his arms back and forth around himself trying to keep warm. Charles noticed Dorianne was shivering and pointed her out to Elsea. The brave lady-in-waiting stubbornly insisted she was fine, but was betrayed by her chattering teeth.

"You should have said something," scolded Elsea as she wrapped her arms around her. Turning to Charles, she added, "I have enjoyed our brief walk, Prince John, but I think I should take Dorianne inside now." She was almost to the door when she stopped and turned around. "I am sure Lord Raglan provides you with adequate rations, but breakfast is not the sort of meal one should eat alone. May I call you to my table in the morning?"

Charles did not need to answer.

CHAPTER TWENTY-FOUR

Heart Triumphant

The last few hours with Elsea would not leave his mind. Whatever Charles had thought might come of all his deceptions he had not foreseen this. Tonight he had held her, and she had held him. For good or ill, tonight his life had changed forever.

He wandered from corner to corner of his lonely room seeking refuge from the anguish in his soul. Like two great armies met on a contested field, his heart and mind battled for the mastery of his will. His heart begged him to pursue her love. His mind mocked him for a fool. If they truly loved each other, said his heart, then his father's name should not matter. She is a duchess, laughed his mind; she could never love a nameless peasant.

Desperate for relief, he tried escaping into fantasy. He let himself dream of holding her close and basking in her words of love. He let himself dream of riding with her playfully through sunny glens every day and forever. His mind shattered his idyllic reveries with its heartless logic.

Just when he thought he could no longer bear the torment, a third voice spoke up. He had lied to her, said his conscience, and he should tell her the truth. Charles found the argument of this unwelcome intruder even more difficult to refute, but he tried nonetheless.

It was true he had lied, he admitted, but he had never *intended* to deceive her. Alas, his conscience was not soothed. What about the doubts she expressed and the way he had encouraged her to trust him? How could he look her in the eyes and tell her he was a liar after all that? His conscience cared not for this trifle either. It would not be content until it had ruined what was the most wonderful night of his young life. He had lied, it persisted, and he should tell her the truth.

He collapsed onto his bed, his mind a whirl of confusion, and no closer to an answer. Exhausted, his thoughts began to wander. He recalled Dorianne's surprising visit that afternoon and a sudden idea struck him. No one knew Elsea better than Dorianne; why not ask her for advice?

This hasty inspiration gave him his first glimmer of hope. The more he dwelt on it, the better it sounded, and he sat up on his cot filled with a new optimism. Perhaps Dorianne could give him a feminine perspective he had not considered, he reasoned. She might even urge him to keep his secret for now. After all, he would be going home the day after tomorrow. Why, maybe *she* could tell Elsea the truth. Would it not sound better coming from her?

Charles let out a sigh of relief. He would say nothing until he could meet with Dorianne in private. He had, of course, no idea how he would arrange that, but he need not dwell on that small detail for now.

"I'll ask Dorianne tomorrow," he whispered to himself as he laid his head on the pillow.

His triumphant heart rejoiced over its vanquished foes.

CHAPTER TWENTY-FIVE

Royal Return

Unable to bear the suspense of waiting, Duke Otto was determined to reach Hogisfeld in advance of Elsea. The stone walls echoed with the noisy drone of excited Bavarians cinching up saddles, tying down packs, and strapping on armor. Servants and footmen whirled throughout the courtyard loading carts and harnessing horses, and every corner seemed ruled by a barely restrained chaos. Since they could not be certain how long they would be gone, the methodical Savoyen insisted on bringing everything they might need on a protracted stay from the castle. Within the vehicles were enough tents, furniture, and food to establish a small village upon their arrival in Hogisfeld.

Savoyen went up to a stout man busily going over a list of items scribbled on a long scroll of paper. "Is everything in place, Louis?"

"Yes, My Lord," answered the harried man. "You may leave when you please."

Savoyen crossed the courtyard and informed the duke.

"Finally," grumbled Otto. Placing a foot in his stirrup, he was about to swing himself onto his horse when the sentry above the gate yelled down that a lone rider was galloping toward the castle. Horse and rider soon came thundering over the drawbridge, through the gatehouse, and into the crowded courtyard. The young man spun his horse in a tight circle. "I have a message for the duke," he shouted over Otto's head. "I have a message for the duke!"

"Be careful you do not step on him!" Savoyen shouted back.

The mortified courier jumped off his horse and knelt at the feet of Otto.

"I beg your pardon, My Lord."

"Never mind that," said the duke. "Give me your message, and be quick about it."

The man looked up with a smile. "Prince John is returning, My Lord!"

"Of course he is returning," snapped Savoyen. "We are on our way to Hogisfeld for that very purpose."

"No, My Lord," beamed the young man, "Prince John is coming now. He's less than a mile from the castle."

This pronouncement produced an outburst of cheers from the tightly packed courtyard. Knights and servants slapped each other on the back as if celebrating a great achievement.

Savoyen looked up to the battlements. "You there," he yelled, "can you see anyone on the main road?"

"I see six men coming this way, My Lord."

The duke and Savoyen bolted for the gate. They passed under the portcullis and beyond the wall and looked down the road. There were indeed six riders approaching the castle, but their nondescript clothing made it difficult to identify them.

"I recognize William," said Savoyen at last, "and John is beside him!"

"Praise God!" exclaimed Otto.

When they reached the bridge, Otto ran up and clutched John by the leg. "It is good to see you, my son!" he exclaimed. "Are you well?"

"I am weary, but well, Father."

The duke looked over the faces of the other riders as he

escorted John through the gate. "Where is Charles?" he asked anxiously.

Another spontaneous cheer erupted when they entered the courtyard, and William had to answer over the sound of the merriment. "I regret to say he's not with us, My Lord.

"You mean they did not release him with you?" asked Savoyen.

"We weren't released," explained William. "We were ambushed the first day, and we had to split up to avoid capture."

"But what about the letter?" asked Otto.

"What letter?"

"The one from Charles," said Savoyen.

A smile exploded across William's face. "You've heard from Charles! He is well then?"

"Charles disguised himself as me so I could escape," exclaimed John as he slid down from his horse. "I owe him my life, Father."

Savoyen looked around at the crowd pressing in on them and leaned in closer to the duke. "My Lord," he said in his ear, "I suggest we go inside and discuss this mystery in private."

Duke Otto gave his old friend a nod. "Yes, let us retire to the hall."

The four men made their way through the sea of excited knights and nobles vying with each other to offer their congratulations. When Otto reached the top of the flight of steps leading to the main entrance, he turned to face the cheering men.

"There will be a great feast tonight in honor of my son's safe return," he shouted.

This produced an even more robust display of gaiety and backslapping. Otto and Savoyen slipped away from the celebration and led William and the prince into the castle. Rushing to meet them as they crossed Otto's hall was Agnes. She flung herself at John, nearly knocking him off his feet.

"My son, my son!" she gushed between alternating hugs and kisses. "Thank God you are alive!"

"Please Mother," returned the blushing prince. "I am quite alright; there is no need to fuss over me so."

"But you are supposed to be in Hogisfeld, my darling," she answered with another hug. "And what has happened to your clothes?"

News of the prince's return spread quickly through the castle, and a small crowd of curious well-wishers was now gathering in the hall. Savoyen took John by the elbow and pulled him and his clinging mother toward a door leading to one of the duke's private rooms.

"Come, Prince John," he said, "we are all eager to hear of your Austrian exploits."

Once behind the door, everyone listened intently as William recounted the morning the Austrians took them by surprise. He described their daylong flight and near capture, placing special emphasis on Charles's clever plan and noble sacrifice. Agnes covered her ears with her hands as he and John took turns describing their ordeal in the swamp. William concluded with a favorable account of Sir Vincent, Lord of Tengen and the dreary, though uneventful, final leg of their journey.

William looked over to Lord Savoyen when he finished. "That is our story, My Lord. But tell us, what news have you of Charles?"

"Until a few moments ago, we were expecting Charles to return with you and Prince John," explained Savoyen. "But now, all things have become clear."

"Clear?" exclaimed Otto. "I am more confused than ever!"

"There is nothing confusing about it," replied Savoyen. "You heard yourself how Charles disguised himself as the prince. As implausible as it may seem, it is obvious they think he is indeed

Prince John. What is more, I believe they still do. How else can we explain the second letter from the duchess herself?"

"But how could he have fooled them this long?"

"That too is no great mystery, My Lord. The young men are close in age, their features are not too dissimilar, and none of them have seen the prince since he was a boy many years ago. As clever as Charles is, it would not have been difficult to convince them he was John."

"It won't be long before they hear the real Prince John has returned," inserted William. "When that happens, Charles's life won't be worth a dried fish."

"William is correct," agreed Savoyen. "There can be no telling what that woman will do when she discovers she has been holding an imposter this whole time."

"You must do something, Father," blurted John.

"But what can you do if he is still in Vienna?" asked Agnes.

"If they are yet unaware of the deception," mused Savoyen aloud, "they should be preparing to leave for our meeting as planned."

"Then let us waste no more time," declared Otto. "I promised the men a feast, but it will have to wait; tell them we ride for Hogisfeld in one hour."

"As a precaution," suggested Savoyen, "we should send a letter ahead to the duchess. We must warn her to do the boy no harm."

"Make it so," ordered Otto.

"Sir William," he said after Savoyen left, "your conduct in ensuring the safe return of my son has once again confirmed my trust in you."

"You are most kind, My Lord," answered William, "but it was Charles who risked his life to make our escape possible. I hope My Lord will remember that."

"I will not forget it," promised Otto. "Of that, you may be certain."

Out in the courtyard, a group of boisterous knights gathered around the men just returned with the prince. The four celebrities regaled their auditors with the account of their arduous journey. No one noticed the man in a dark hooded cloak listening discreetly at the edge of the crowd. Neither did anyone notice him slithering his way across the yard to one of the stables and reemerging a few minutes later on a coal-black horse. Passing casually through the open gates, he cantered down the road and was soon out of sight.

CHAPTER TWENTY-SIX

Condemned

Charles paced the floor of his windowless room, uncertain of the time. He had been awake for several hours waiting for the guard to take him to breakfast with Elsea. He of course looked forward to seeing her, but was even more anxious to speak with Dorianne. Still without a clue as to how he would arrange that, he nevertheless sat down at his modest table and again rehearsed his explanation. Suddenly, his door opened, and a guard came into the room. Right behind him was Dorianne.

"Prince John," she said with a polite bow, "Her Grace has been called away to an unexpected meeting. She sends her regrets for not being able to share breakfast with you this morning."

An astonished Charles came to his feet unsteadily. All morning he had been picturing a dozen ways he might find a quick moment to confide in Dorianne. Her walking through his door and standing before him was not one of them. He felt it was a good omen.

"Dorianne," he said. "I wish to speak of a matter that is of concern to the duchess."

She waited patiently for him to continue, but he glanced at the guard standing by the door.

"Thank you," she said to him, "you may wait for me outside."

When the door closed, she turned and gave him a faint smile.

"I have something difficult to tell you," he said, "something about me."

She stood a few feet from him on the other side of the table. "Yes, My Lord," she replied quietly.

Charles gripped the back of the chair before him with both hands. "Do you believe I love your lady?"

"Yes," she answered with confidence.

"Do you believe that I would never cause her harm?"

"Yes," she answered with even more assurance.

He paused to take what he feared would be his last breath. "I am not Prince John," he blurted. "My name is Charles…"

The words had scarcely left his lips when Dorianne sucked in her breath loudly and brought both hands to her face. She stepped back from him so quickly that she struck her head against the wall behind. All Charles could see through her fingers were her terror-filled eyes.

He had hoped she would understand his plight. He had hoped she might have some sympathetic words of wisdom to help unravel the knot in his stomach. Instead, a sudden wave of panic surged through him that washed away all traces of that castle made of sand. If this was Dorianne's reaction, he could not bear to imagine Elsea's.

Desperate to explain himself, he poured out his story. He told her why he had to pretend he was the prince in the first place. He confessed that he did not have the courage to tell Elsea the truth once he knew he was falling in love with her. He promised he never intended this to happen, and he begged her to believe him. Like a vile criminal before a stern judge, he beseeched the teenaged Dorianne for mercy; with one word she could pardon or condemn him. He ended his heartrending revelation with the words, "Dorianne, what should I do?"

She wasted no time in contemplation. "You must tell her," she pronounced through the fingers of her hands.

He was condemned.

She brought her hands down. "You must tell her before she hears it from someone else."

Charles was taken aback by the simple warning. Until this very moment, it had not occurred to him how dreadful it would be for Elsea to learn the truth secondhand.

"Yes, you are right, of course," he agreed reluctantly. "I will tell her as soon as I can. Do you think she will call for me today?"

The horror in Dorianne's eyes had faded, and she was again the unflappable lady-in-waiting. "She will send for you at dinner tonight," she answered calmly. "You must find a way to tell her then."

"I will try," was all he could promise.

She went out the door and left him standing by the table.

He never felt so alone.

CHAPTER TWENTY-SEVEN

God Knows

Charles stared down the table at Elsea and speculated on the cause behind her obvious despondency. He wondered if perhaps Dorianne had not already alerted her to his treachery and glanced over at her with raised eyebrows. She replied with a slight shrug of her shoulders and a shake of her head. On they labored through the gloomy meal in total silence.

The servants were dutifully clearing away the dishes when Elsea suddenly pushed back from the table and ordered everyone, including Dorianne, to leave the room. She came down to Charles's end of the table, and he could plainly see the apprehension in her face.

"Prince John," she began, "I had hoped to breakfast with you this morning, but my council insisted I endure another exhibition of their incomparable wisdom."

"I am sure it was important," he said.

"Unfortunately, it was." She looked down at her hands before continuing. "We received another letter from Eldridge. It seems he is losing patience with us and is threatening to revoke his offer unless we act soon. Lord Eugene and the barons are quite anxious and even more zealous for me to say yes."

"Yes to what?"

"Marriage, of course."

"What did you say?" he asked, surprised by his sudden jealousy.

"I informed them of my reluctance in most unmistakable terms," she assured him. "But you should know by now that what *I* want is irrelevant. Lord Raglan is all that stands between me and that brute, but even he will relent eventually, and I will have to do what they want in the end." Looking him in the eyes she added anxiously, "Or find something better on my own."

"Something better?"

She continued to hold his eyes with hers, but did not answer.

"Elsea," he whispered. "What is it?"

"Do you care for me?" she asked.

"You know I do."

"I mean *really* care for me."

"I have never cared more for anyone in my life," he declared with unfeigned sincerity.

"Enough to marry me?"

Charles did his best to steady himself. "You hardly know me, Elsea."

"I know I would rather marry you than Eldridge," she answered quickly. "I have been thinking it through all day. You are a prince of the House of Wittelsbach, and I am the last of the ruling line of Babenbergs. Our marriage would ally our two houses and solve all my problems. My council would have to agree."

"That is true," he admitted, but his voice lacked conviction.

"Well?"

"Well… it is only that I am not free to marry whomever I please."

"Are you saying your father would prevent it? Does he detest me so much that he would refuse an alliance with me? Would not an heir on the Austrian throne be worth overlooking our differences?"

He knew she was right. Otto would never let his personal grievances prevent him from taking advantage of so easy a coup. Easy, that is, if he was really Prince John. His mind reeled as Dorianne's admonition again echoed through his head. Since his confession that morning he had agonized over how he could tell Elsea the truth. Her unexpected proposal had made that task more difficult than he could begin to fathom, and yet tell her he must.

He took a deep breath and opened his mouth, but after one look into those imploring eyes, his resolve vanished completely. He turned away a moment to gather himself, but when he stared back into her expectant face, his feckless courage deserted him once more. How gladly he would have traded this moment to leap into a den of lions bare-handed. Yet in this one thing he was powerless to act. God forgive him, but he had not the strength to break her heart.

He pulled her to himself and held her tightly. "Elsea, my darling," he whispered in her ear, "God knows I cannot live without you. No matter what may happen, you must never doubt that."

She returned his embrace, and they held each other without speaking until she forced herself to pull away. "We leave for Hogisfeld in the morning," she said. "We must not tell anyone of our plan until we are able to speak directly to your father. I am certain you will be able to persuade him. After all," she smiled, "you have done so well persuading me. I will look for you in the morning, my love."

He watched her leave the room. The joy he saw in her face only added to the anguish in his heart.

CHAPTER TWENTY-EIGHT

Without Compassion

Excited nobles of every rank crowded Elsea's hall. The duchess was leaving for Hogisfeld and the unprecedented meeting with Duke Otto. Every man understood the significance of this day, and the room buzzed with their anticipation. Near the windows overlooking a busy courtyard, Raglan and the rest of the council stood talking in low voices while they waited on Elsea.

"I still say we should send a reply before we leave," declared Baron Kirchenbetter. "It is too important a matter to delay."

"Let Eldridge simmer in his own juice a while longer," replied Raglan. "You seem to expect things not going well in Hogisfeld."

"It is only that I believe in setting the hook when the fish is biting so hard," returned Kirchenbetter.

Keinmeyer agreed. "After all, Lord Raglan, you cannot really believe we will get anything better from Otto, do you?"

"My Lords, we are about to enter into the most important negotiations since the death of the Emperor. We must not go into this meeting with half a heart and one eye on the door."

"I stand with the Count," interjected Bishop Prochaska. "We should approach this interview in earnest. We may find that God will answer our prayers for peace in Hogisfeld, not in Styria."

"Yes, we will all be thankful when God answers our prayers," smirked Lord Eugene.

"Your prayers are appreciated, Your Excellency," said Raglan.

"Nevertheless, we need to do our part as well. We must choose our words with care, as the slightest indiscretion could dash our hopes. Once we have released the prince, I intend to suggest reopening the old trade routes. It will be an appropriate first step, and I need not tell you how profitable that could be for all of us."

"Profit," exclaimed Kirchenbetter, "now there is a subject one need not pretend an interest in!"

"Your concern is misplaced," noted Eugene. "The five of us understand our responsibility well enough. It is Her Highness that is the weak link in the chain of your aspirations. How many trade routes do you think the duke will reopen after she entertains him with one of her little tantrums?"

"You are too critical of her," returned Raglan. "She has changed since Prince John arrived, and I believe she can be trusted to do her duty."

"Prince or no prince, she has never shown us she can be trusted to do her duty," countered an unconvinced Eugene. "It would be foolish to believe she will act any differently now. It is imperative that you remind her of the consequences her behavior will have on the prospects for our success."

"Very well," sighed Raglan. "I will find a moment to speak with her if that will ease your mind."

"Speaking of her nastiness," said Kirchenbetter, "what is keeping her? I could have had a proper breakfast if I had known she was going to be this late."

"I intend to eat in the saddle," laughed Eugene. "A crust of bread and a wedge of cheese is all the breakfast I will need today."

"Yes, we all know you are a true Spartan, Lord Eugene. But some of us require a little more than peasant fodder to sustain us."

Lord Eugene slapped him on the shoulder. "I am afraid you would not enjoy campaigning with me, My Lord."

"There are few men who would," agreed Kirchenbetter.

At that moment, a sentry announced Elsea into the hall, and all eyes turned her way. She wore her hair up in a simple braid, and looked resplendent in the soft yellow riding tunic Dorianne had made for her. A spontaneous cheer went up from the nobles gathered to escort her to Hogisfeld.

Elsea approached Raglan. "Is everything in order?"

"Yes, Your Grace."

"Where is Prince John?"

"We were only awaiting your arrival to send for him," explained Raglan.

"Then let us proceed at once," she smiled. "I am eager to reach Hogisfeld. If we do not dawdle along the way, we will make the river before the town by sundown."

Lord Eugene gave Raglan a nudge with his elbow.

Raglan looked around himself. "Your Highness," he said in a low tone, "I hope you are aware of the significance of this occasion."

"Certainly I am aware," she replied, her smile fading. "Why do you even ask?"

"What Lord Raglan is trying to say," added Lord Eugene, "is that it would be unwise to jeopardize our plans with, shall we say, any *unseemly* displays."

Elsea looked at each of her council members in turn. "Is this what you were talking about before I came in?"

"Your Highness," replied Lord Keinmeyer, "it is only fitting that we overlook nothing as we prepare. I am sure you understand."

"What I understand," she said through clenched teeth, "is that once again you have gone out of your way to insult me."

"No one is insulting you," insisted Raglan. "We only wish to advise you that any unnecessary harshness could undermine our expectations."

"And just what are your *expectations*?" she asked.

Before Raglan could answer, a servant stepped up to Lord Eugene and whispered in his ear. "I beg to be excused, Your Grace," apologized Eugene, "a matter has arisen that requires my immediate attention."

After Eugene left the circle, Lord Raglan continued, "Our hope is that we might begin with a modest proposal for renewed trade."

"A modest trade proposal!" she laughed. "Is that the best you can do? You think yourself a clever diplomat, Lord Raglan. I will have you know that I have ensured the security of my reign without help from any of you."

"How is that?" asked Raglan.

She lifted her chin and threw back her shoulders. "Prince John and I are to be married! So you see, Lord Raglan, I intend to get more than trade agreements at Hogisfeld."

Elsea's astounding revelation rippled outward from her council to every noble in the hall. Within seconds, a noisy celebration broke out. Bishop Prochaska gushed with praise and the dumbstruck barons begrudgingly stammered out congratulations.

Lord Raglan studied her face carefully. "Is this true?" he asked over the sound of the jubilation.

"It is true," she replied coldly. "You may ask the prince himself if you do not believe me."

A smile slowly spread across Raglan's face. "Your Highness," he beamed, "you are to be commended. This will be one of the happiest days in my life."

Well-wishing nobles soon pressed in around Elsea. It was as if she had just promised every man in the room a fabulous wealth. Everyone was eager to show his approval, and their enthusiasm was overwhelming. She blushed at the adulation and returned their smiles with her own.

Just then a voice shouted above the merriment swirling around Elsea. Lord Eugene threaded his way through the press waving a paper above his head.

Your Highness," he bellowed. "Your Highness!"

The consternation on his face and the edge to his voice made it clear he had ominous news. A more compassionate man would have asked to see the duchess in private. Lord Eugene was not burdened by that sentiment. He reached Elsea and stood before her holding out the paper. Though the boisterous nobles had now gone silent, Lord Eugene felt it necessary to proclaim at the top of his voice, "Your Highness, the prince is an imposter!"

When the laughter turned to groans and the celebration to sorrow, no one saw Dorianne slip from the hall and run out through the doors.

CHAPTER TWENTY-NINE

Confession

Once more, Charles read the letter it had taken him all night to write. It was only a single page, but contained his entire confession. After last night's dinner he sat in his self-pity a long time, rebuking himself for his weakness. He was supposed to tell her the truth and destroy her hopes. Instead, he had built those false hopes even higher. He intended to tell her they could never be together, but ended by letting her believe they would never be apart.

He drifted aimlessly around the room, tortured by his hopelessness, always coming back to the need to tell her. Noticing the small inkstand for the first time, an idea occurred to him: he would write what he had not the heart to say. Yes, it was a cowardly substitute, but perhaps it was better this way. She would read the letter and hate him, and it would at last be over.

As he folded the paper on the table, he heard the sound of footsteps running down the hall. His door flew open, and Dorianne rushed in.

"The duchess knows!" she exclaimed.

He jumped up from his chair. "But how could she?"

"Lord Eugene has announced it to everyone!"

"Eugene," he moaned, striking his forehead with the heel of his hand, "why did it have to be him?"

"My poor, poor Lady!" cried Dorianne. "Why didn't you tell her?"

Through the open door, Charles saw four guards marching quickly down the corridor. He grabbed the paper from the table and stuffed it into Dorianne's hand. "You must see that she gets this," he said.

Before she could answer, the guards burst into the room.

"You there," barked one of them, "your presence is required in the hall." They bound his hands behind his back and pushed him from the room.

Word of what happened spread quickly, and it seemed to Charles that all of Vienna was trying to squeeze into the hall to witness his downfall. He felt hundreds of eyes boring into him as the guards hurried him through the murmuring crowd. They led him up to the foot of the dais where someone gave the back of his legs a painful kick, and he dropped to his knees.

Lord Raglan stood to the left of the dais and Lord Eugene to the right. Elsea sat sideways on her throne with her legs draped over the armrest refusing to look at him.

Lord Eugene stepped forward grasping a crumpled paper in his fist. "You are not Prince John," he boomed, "true or false?"

Charles looked up at Elsea. He saw how pretty she looked in her new yellow tunic and could only imagine the happiness she must have felt when she pulled it on that morning.

"True or false," repeated Lord Eugene.

"True," answered Charles.

A loud groan swept across the hall.

"Your name is Charles," bellowed Eugene, "son of a mere peasant, true or false?"

"True," said Charles with his eyes still on Elsea.

"You have willfully deceived Her Grace with your despicable lies, true or false?"

Charles hesitated.

"Answer the question!" demanded Lord Eugene.

"True."

A piercing wail rent the air as Elsea sprang from the throne. Grabbing a sword from the side of the sentry nearest her, she ran at Charles. She stopped short and stood over him holding the heavy blade above her head, poised to slay him on that very spot.

He knelt before her without flinching. At last able to look her in the eyes, he wished desperately for some power of word craft, some poetic gift that would endue him with the words to ease her pain. Alas, all he could do was whisper the only thing that came to his mind, "I am sorry."

She dropped the sword which clanged loudly on the floor and stumbled back as if struck by a hammer. "How dare you!" she screamed. "Every word out of your mouth has been a lie!" She turned her back on him and covered her ears as if afraid he might utter some new folly.

He did not.

"Take this liar away!" she shouted to no one in particular. "Get him out of my sight. Send him to the dungeon. Let him rot in the darkness!"

The guards jerked him to his feet and dragged him through the now jeering crowd toward the doors.

"I hate him," she shrieked, "I wish he was dead!" She spun around to hurl more of her rage upon him, but found they had already hauled him from the room. Sprinting after them, she burst out onto the landing just as he disappeared around a turn of the stairwell below her.

She gathered herself for one more blast. "I hate you!" she screamed with all her might. "I wish you were dead!"

The stone walls amplified the dreadful curse and pierced his heart like a dagger. He realized they were the last words he would ever hear her say.

CHAPTER THIRTY

Bottom of the World

The guards hauled Charles deep into the bowels of the castle. With each step of the decent, the air grew damper, and a rancid stench from something recently dead filled his nostrils. At the bottom of a narrow stairwell, they dragged him along a passage so confining they had to lower their heads and rub shoulders on the walls. A small lamp hung from the ceiling, its sputtering flame losing the battle with the musty gloom. They stopped at last before an iron grated door that opened into a stone box not quite large enough for a man to stretch out in full length. They pushed him in with his hands still tied behind his back and slammed the creaking door closed. The dark silence that fell down upon him pressed him to the floor.

Charles reeled as if struck by lightning. A few moments ago, he had been wondering how to get Elsea his letter, still clinging to the desperate hope she might yet forgive him. In one blinding flash, his world had collapsed around him, and he now lay at the bottom of its ruins. No previous sorrow he had ever known had prepared him for this. His natural optimism had deserted him and left behind in its place a hungry despair that sought to consume his will to live. He remembered Dorianne's words just before they came to drag him before the duchess. "My poor Elsea," he whispered into the blackness around him, "my poor, poor Elsea."

Lord Eugene was quick to meet the duchess as she reentered the hall. "What do you wish done with the prisoner, Your Grace?"

"I want him out of my sight," she barked, still catching her breath. "I never want to see him again! Do you understand? *Never!*"

Lord Eugene rubbed his bearded chin a brief moment. "Let the order be given, and I will send him bound to Duke Eldridge. I have information that this unworthy cretin has offended His Grace in the past. He would undoubtedly receive the imposter as proof of your friendship."

Elsea had already turned to leave, and she stopped with her back to him. "See to it," she snapped, before walking on.

Lord Eugene gave an embellished bow to her back before spinning on his heel and heading for the exit.

A short time later, he was in the barracks handpicking the men, the horses, and even the wagon they would use to transport Charles. Though the journey would be a long one, he insisted they leave without delay. While the horses were hitched, and some provisions were hastily stuffed into a bag, Lord Eugene met with a hooded man in a corner of the courtyard. "You will meet them before the bridge at Fairfield," said Eugene. "You know what to do."

"Think no more on the matter, My Lord," replied the hooded man. "The deed is as good as done."

CHAPTER THIRTY-ONE

Whirlwind

Far above the cell where Charles now lay in a heap on the floor, in the room where he had last held Elsea, a tempest raged. Servants and nobles fled before a feminine whirlwind, leaving behind only the inanimate objects to weather her storm.

Lurching back and forth unpredictably, she overturned tables and hurled chairs. She pulled down the paintings of her noble kin and smashed their gilded frames to kindling. The shards from exploding plates flew in all directions. Imported lanterns of fine glass and candlesticks of polished silver sailed through the air like missiles. To the growing wreckage around her she added shattered vases and crushed flowers. The feather stuffing of ripped-open pillows floated down like a soft snow. The bravest knight dared not enter that maelstrom of destruction. Even Dorianne could only peek through the doorway, fearful of risking the power of her lady's vortex.

With nothing left to destroy, she now staggered from corner to corner able only to hurl the fragments and make the rubble fly. Gradually, her winds subsided, and she sank to her knees on a tapestry that lay at her feet in a twisted mound. Covering her face with a torn cushion, she sobbed into its soft folds.

Dorianne was at her side instantly. Kneeling beside her, she placed an arm around her heaving shoulders. "I am here now, My Lady."

Elsea leaned into her. "Why, Dori?" she whispered.

Dorianne had no reply but to tighten her gentle embrace.

CHAPTER THIRTY-TWO

Heading South

Charles was still slumped over in his dark dejection when the guards came to hustle him back down the cramped passage and up the narrow stairs. He stumbled along mindlessly until they thrust him through one last door and into the blinding light of day. Were they hauling him to his execution? Would this be his last glimpse of the sun in its sky? Pulling him across the courtyard to the barracks building, they turned him over to a captain who ordered him thrown into the back of a well-used wagon. It was only then that he realized he was leaving the castle.

A few minutes later, the wagon carrying Charles and three guards lumbered toward the gate. Before they passed under the portcullis, he caught sight of Lord Eugene a short distance away leaning casually against the wall.

"Goodbye, My *Lord*," said Eugene with a wry smile. "Give my regards to His Grace."

It seemed to Charles that Lord Eugene was unusually cheerful.

They crossed the drawbridge, and Charles broke himself free of his despondency long enough to look up at the battlement walls looming high above him. He strained his eyes to find the corner where he had confessed his heart to Elsea in the moonlight. He wondered if she was there now, gratefully watching him trundle down the road and out of her life. Not until the castle had disappeared from view did he tear himself away to look about.

He was sitting in the back of a rickety wagon with his hands still bound behind him. Across from him sat a guard old enough to be his grandfather. In the front were two others. Holding the reins was a heavyset man with a red and puffy face. On the seat next to him was a man so thin and frail he barely filled out his clothes. Charles thought it odd that men like these were taking him back to Bavaria. Perhaps this was what Lord Eugene found so amusing.

The two old mares labored to pull the wagon along the road through the open farmland. The guards in front were engaged in a low conversation, but no one spoke to Charles. He looked up at the sky and saw that a storm was moving in from the north. The morning sun would soon be behind clouds. At this pace, it would take them nearly two days to reach the Bavarian border. He did not look forward to two days of being cramped, bound, and jostled around like an animal on the way to market.

They eventually came to a crossroads, and Charles was surprised when they turned south. He prodded the guard sitting across from him with his foot and nodded to the west. "Bavaria is that way."

"Bavaria!" grunted his traveling companion. "The poor boy thinks we're going to Bavaria."

The guards in front burst out in a derisive laughter.

"It'll be a long time before you see Bavaria again," said the one with the reins, "if old Eldridge has anything to say about it."

His comrades enjoyed another round of merriment.

Though this was startling news for Charles, it at least explained Lord Eugene's smirking farewell. He sighed within himself, "What else can go wrong?"

Hour after hour, they rumbled along their bumpy way. Despite the jarring ride, the guard across from him had managed to fall asleep sitting up, his head rocking and swaying with the motion of the wagon.

The sleeping guard gave Charles an idea. Sunset was only a few hours away. Though his hands were tied, his feet were not. Darkness, and the inattention of his overseers, might provide him an opportunity to escape. He decided he would bide his time until sundown. At the first wooded area they passed through, he would jump up and throw himself over the side. If his plan worked, he would be several strides into the trees, before his lethargic fellow travelers could react. Despite his depressed state of mind, he was optimistic about winning a foot race with three old men in the dark.

Having come up with his plan, Charles settled down to wait. To convince them of his indifference, he pretended to be asleep like his aged companion. Real sleep was the last thing he was capable of however, as his mind swam with thoughts of what might have been.

CHAPTER THIRTY-THREE

Second Thoughts

Although it took much coaxing, Dorianne was at last able to get Elsea to her feet. She shuffled her way back to her rooms where she slouched in her chair staring blankly at the bookshelves, ignoring Dorianne's every attempt to comfort her. Several hours later, the patient lady-in-waiting was still maintaining her vigil when Elsea suddenly stood and headed for the stairwell. Dorianne was right behind.

She followed her all the way to the battlements, and they walked the familiar parapet until they reached the corner where she had often talked with Charles. Though the clouds of a coming storm obscured the sun, the wind was strangely still. Elsea paused here a while, looking out over the town and farmland far below.

"So," she said at last, "his name is Charles."

"Yes, My Lady," answered Dorianne quietly.

"I am not surprised," said Elsea. "The name John never suited him."

"No, My Lady."

Elsea lightly ran her hand over the stones of the wall. "I want to talk to him."

"Now?" asked Dorianne.

"Yes," she replied, "have him brought here."

"As you wish, My Lady."

Dorianne ran to find the nearest guard and returned a few minutes later to wait with her mistress. They had been waiting much longer than necessary, when a sentry came running up to them.

"Your Highness," he panted, "the man you've asked for isn't in the castle."

"What do you mean he isn't in the castle?"

"He's not here, Your Highness. He's been moved."

"By whose orders?"

"They say Lord Eugene gave the order, Your Highness."

"Where has he been taken?"

"I don't know, Your Highness."

Elsea threw her hands in the air. "Well, what did Lord Eugene tell you?"

"We can't find him either, Your Highness."

"Has anyone thought to ask Lord Raglan, or has he too vanished like a fog?"

"Yes, Your Highness. I mean no, Your Highness. I'll find him immediately, Your Highness." The guard bowed low and scurried off on his new mission.

When Elsea and Dorianne finally went below, they found Lord Raglan waiting for them in the main room off the great hall. The servants had already cleared away the debris from Elsea's rampage. The table and chairs were back in place, but devoid of the colorful tapestries and majestic paintings, the once regal room now looked barren and dreary.

"Lord Raglan," said Elsea before she had scarcely stepped through the door, "where is the prisoner?"

"He should be in the dungeon where you sent him," shrugged Raglan.

"I am told that Lord Eugene has given orders for him to be moved, but no one seems to know where," she replied.

"Then Lord Eugene is the one we need to speak with."

As if on cue, Lord Eugene glided into the room. "I understand you wished to see me, Your Grace."

"What have you done with the prisoner?" she barked.

"Have you forgotten?" he asked calmly. "You ordered him sent to Duke Eldridge."

Raglan turned to Elsea. "Is this true?"

"I do recall Lord Eugene making mention of something like that," she admitted reluctantly. "But I did not expect him to act so swiftly."

"What possible reason could there be for sending him to Eldridge?" asked a perplexed Raglan.

"I have information the imposter is an old enemy of His Grace," explained Eugene. "Who knows, but he may have deceived him in a similar fashion; it is apparent to me now that he is an accomplished liar. By this time tomorrow half the Empire will be laughing at our expense. Sending this charlatan to Styria rids us of someone who has made fools of us and demonstrates our good faith to Duke Eldridge. What concern is it of ours if he receives a just reward for his crimes?"

"Are you implying his life is in danger?" blurted Elsea.

Lord Eugene paused to rub his chin. "I cannot say for certain."

"We do not know what value this man may have had to Duke Otto," grunted Raglan. "You should have consulted me first. You have acted rashly, Lord Eugene, and I do not share your opinion that any good will come of this."

"I do not care about any of that," interrupted Elsea. "I want him returned."

"Is that still possible?" asked Raglan.

"A swift rider should be able to catch them before they reach the border," conjectured Eugene coolly. "If that is what you wish, Your Grace."

"It is what I wish!" she snapped.

"Very well. I shall see to it. But it will take several hours to reach them, and perhaps longer to bring them back."

"Even more reason to act without delay," she shot back. "Send me word the instant you have any news."

Lord Eugene bowed properly and left the room.

Raglan watched him leave and then turned to Elsea. "My Lady," he began in a low voice, "this matter with the man who called himself Prince John…"

"His name is Charles."

"Yes, Charles," he continued, "this unfortunate development has affected all of us. I hope you do not in any way hold yourself responsible. The man was a clever deceiver. I am ashamed to admit he fooled me as well. You must not blame yourself."

"Of course I do not blame myself. You are right—he was a cunning fraud. Even Lord Eugene was taken in by him."

Raglan took a step closer. "My Lady, I hope you will not let this regrettable affair affect you *personally*."

"Lord Raglan, I assure you that whatever effect you feel this man had on me is purely of your own imagination. I merely think it prudent that he answer a few more questions before we dispense with him. That is all."

"I see," answered Raglan. He looked as if he wanted to say more, but then thought better of it.

After he left, Elsea and Dorianne returned to her rooms to pass the time while they waited for word from Lord Eugene. Refusing to retire to bed, Elsea soon fell asleep in her chair. Dorianne covered her with a blanket.

CHAPTER THIRTY-FOUR

Ambush

Charles rubbed his back against the wall of the wagon trying to scratch a pesky itch. His movement awoke the guard across from him.

"These ropes are too tight," he complained.

"I'm sure they are," yawned the man.

"Well, could you please adjust them? I am starting to lose the feeling in my hands."

"Look here, boy," he replied with a wagging finger, "our orders are to deliver you to Duke Eldridge. No one said anything about making sure you got there in a good mood with both hands. Now sit still and be quiet." Fluffing up the provisions bag he was using as a pillow, he leaned back to resume his nap.

Charles had not really expected to have his ropes loosened. He knew he would be able to wriggle himself free once he was safely away. But he was relieved to see that his keeper was still more concerned with catching up on his sleep than keeping an eye on his charge. The sun had just set and the cloudy sky made the dusk even darker. Up ahead, he could see the hazy outline of what looked like trees along the road they were traveling. He would need the cover of woods to escape. As they got closer, however, he noted that the forest was small and there were open fields on all sides. He would have to wait a little longer.

An hour later, darkness was fully upon them. The wind had

picked up and the smell of rain was in the air. His fellow travelers complained bitterly among themselves that their orders were to ride straight through the night. They were experienced enough to know they had been given an ignoble assignment.

"I don't see why we can't pull off the road once we hit Fairfield," said the thin man. "Who'd know?"

"Maybe you don't care who'd know," replied the red-faced man with the reins. "But I can tell you if Lord Eugene hears of it, it'll cost me my head. The way that man has eyes behind every bush, it wouldn't surprise me if we were being watched this very minute."

"Why don't we just slit his throat and be done with it?" suggested the one in back. "We can say he tried to escape."

"Oh, there's a clever one for you," noted red-face. "Why didn't you mention that to his lordship when you had the chance? Maybe you could've saved us all a long trip."

"Well, I'm not looking forward to riding through the rain all night with nothing to warm my belly. Can't we at least stop in Fairfield for a hot meal?" He shook the food bag at them. "There's no sense in gagging on stale bread and moldy cheese all the way to Styria, is there?"

"We'll see," was all the man with the reins would offer.

Though Charles was thankful that red-face had overruled the proposal to slit his throat, he was now more determined than ever to get away. He certainly did not want to find out how a night in the pouring rain might affect their cheerful dispositions.

At long last, he sensed they had entered a thickly forested area. There were trees along both sides of the road now, and he smelled the distinctive aroma of rotting leaves. He told himself this might be the best chance he would get and began to rehearse mentally each step of his plan. His first move would be to jump up and out of the wagon in one quick motion; several hard running strides would put him into the forest. From that point, he would use the woods and the cover of darkness to elude his pursuers. What he would do beyond that, or how he would find his way back to Bavaria, a fugitive, on foot and without friends or money, he had not considered. He would think of that later.

They were rounding a bend in the road when Charles was sure he heard the unmistakable sound of a horse snorting. He looked up at his escorts, but they seemed oblivious to the noise. The one in back rested with his chin on his chest and the ones in front continued to stare ahead at the road, their heads swaying in rhythm to the rocking of the wagon. Nevertheless, he was certain he had heard something, and he sat up with all his senses on alert.

Suddenly, a hissing sound rushed past his head followed by several thuds and a loud groan. The guard across from him slumped over on his side. The feathers of several short arrows of the kind fired from a crossbow protruded from his chest. For a brief second, Charles thought that this was some kind of a rescue effort. He quickly dismissed that notion when he felt the hair on his neck rise as another bolt whistled by his ear.

"They are trying to kill us all!" he thought.

The men in front were now aware of what was happening. The one with the reins lashed the horses unmercifully to break them into a gallop, and for a moment it appeared as if they would ride out of danger. Their brief respite evaporated when a cluster of mounted men erupted from the trees on either side of the road and began chasing after them. Charles could hear more crossbow bolts whizzing by.

"It's an ambush!" the thin man screamed hysterically. "We need to…" Before he could finish he was hit by several arrows at once. He swooned to his left and toppled onto the road. The red-faced man did not look back nor let up on his frantic lashing.

The bulky wagon, pulled by the old mares, was no match for the men galloping after them, and Charles saw they would soon be ridden down. He decided not to wait to find out their intentions. Rolling over onto his back, he brought his knees up to his chest. Quickly working his bound hands down and around his feet, he was able to get his hands in front of him. He rolled over onto his stomach and peeked over the back wall, keeping a low profile so as not to invite any more arrows his way.

There was no more time for contemplation. Placing his hands on the sideboard, Charles jumped clear. He hit the ground hard and tumbled several times end over end. He came to a dizzy stop, but the sound of pounding hooves brought him around. He sprang to his feet and ran for his life into the trees.

"There he goes," someone yelled, "after him!"

"It's me they want," he now realized.

The cover of the darkened forest gave him a feeling of protection. It would be difficult for the men on horseback to chase him down now. He was immensely disappointed, therefore, when after going only a short distance he broke out into an open field. He considered plunging back into the narrow strip of woods, but could hear several voices coming from that direction.

Turning to his left, he ran along the tree line as fast as his legs could propel him. He intended on heading into the woods again to double back on them, but before he could, he discovered that the trees had completely ended. He was now running through a freshly plowed field parallel with the road. From his left, came the sound of the horses chasing down the wagon, but it was the hoof beats behind him that alarmed him the most.

Through the darkness up ahead he thought he saw another forest. He ran toward it with all the speed he could muster. Though his legs were aching and his lungs burning, he knew he must not let up. He looked over his shoulder, and saw three riders chasing him. The rider in front was right behind.

In desperation, Charles tried something he had once learned from William. When the lead rider was only a few strides away, he suddenly threw himself into a ball at the front legs of his horse. Horses by instinct avoid stepping on living things, but his unexpected move did not give it time to react. Charles's body struck the horse just below the knees causing it to trip and stumble. The momentum of the animal caused it to somersault over Charles without landing on him. The surprised rider flew head first to the ground like a spear.

Charles got back on his feet, sprinted over the rider's body, and made the woods just ahead of the second rider. After only a few strides, he came to the edge of a small brook. It was not a forest after all, but only a scattering of trees lining each side of the stream. Without pausing, he turned to his right, running along the bank and away from the road.

The second rider shouted into the night that their quarry had changed direction. Charles heard whooping replies coming from what seemed like everywhere. Hoping the stream might slow them down, he turned left and plunged across the knee-high water. The opposite bank was slippery, and he had a moment of panic as he struggled to pull himself onto dry land. The noise of horses splashing through the water added to his anxiety. He scrambled out into a grassy field gasping for air. The ground began to rise beneath him, and the uphill running was rapidly draining what little stamina he had left. He did not know how much longer his endurance would last.

Just then, he heard a sound that sent a wave of hope surging through him: several dogs were barking up ahead in the darkness. He knew he must be near a village or a town of some kind.

Perhaps he could find help there. Summoning all his remaining strength, he pulled hard in the direction of the barking dogs.

When he finally reached the crest, he saw a few twinkling lights of a small village below him. The downhill running made it easier on his aching legs and his courage began to revive. The dogs were barking louder and the village was getting closer. One more minute and he would be safe.

Suddenly, another rider appeared from out of nowhere. He held a long club in his hand, and as he came up on Charles he swung it fiercely. There was a loud crack like the breaking of a tree branch, and Charles knew no more.

Two riders sat atop their horses looking down on the body stretched out in the grass. From the direction of the village, a group of people led by a man with a torch and barking dogs was heading toward them.

"Finish him," said the first rider.

"He *is* finished," returned the one with the club. "I cracked his skull like a walnut. Finish him yourself if you don't think so, you've got a bow."

The first rider lifted the crossbow at his side and let fly a bolt that hit the motionless body with a soft thud.

The barking dogs were almost to them now.

"Let's go," said the one with the club. "We've done what we came for."

They cantered into the darkness just as the villagers arrived. Far from being a mob of vigilantes, they turned out to be a large man, his two teenaged children and the family dogs.

"What do you think they were doing, Father?" asked the boy.

"You can be sure it was nothing good," the man answered confidently.

The two dogs sniffed around in the grass, noses to the ground and tails wagging.

"I think they found something," said the girl.

Her father held up his torch above the excited dogs. The dancing light revealed the body of a man lying face down on the ground. Blood oozed from his head, soaking into his white shirt. The man knelt down and placed a hand on his shoulder.

"Who is he?" gushed his daughter.

"I don't know," declared her father, "but whoever he is, he's dead."

CHAPTER THIRTY-FIVE

Premonition

The loud crash of thunder that echoed through the castle halls awoke Elsea with a frightening cry. Dorianne was at her side instantly.

"Something has happened to him!" exclaimed Elsea.

"To whom?"

"To Charles," she answered, as she scrambled from her chair.

"You were only dreaming, My Lady," Dorianne tried to assure her.

Dorianne's calm tone only made Elsea more frantic. "Something has happened to him," she repeated, "something awful."

"But you can't know that."

"I do know it!" insisted Elsea. "Send for Lord Eugene. I want to speak with him."

"My Lady," hesitated Dorianne, "it's very late; are you sure?"

"Yes! Have him meet me in my dining room."

Lord Eugene came through the door with one hand over his mouth and in the middle of a long yawn.

Elsea wasted no time with pleasantries. "Lord Eugene, what have you heard from the riders you sent out?"

"I have not heard anything yet," he answered with a shrug of his shoulders. "I did not expect to hear anything till morning."

"And just what *did* you expect to hear in the morning?"

"Your Grace, I do not know what you mean."

"Something has happened to him," she declared.

"Something has happened!" he repeated with an alarm in his voice that possessed everything but sincerity. "How do you know?"

"Never mind how I know!" She looked over at Dorianne, and then took a deep breath to calm herself. "What time in the morning do you expect them to return?"

The concern on Lord Eugene's face melted as quickly as it had appeared. "Late morning," he speculated, "perhaps closer to midday."

"So long?" she asked. "I thought you said they would be back in a few hours."

"I said it would take that long just to reach them, Your Grace, assuming there were no problems." He pointed to one of the darkened windows. "This storm will undoubtedly make it more difficult."

"Very well," she sighed, "inform me immediately upon their return."

"Of course, Your Grace, I had every intention of doing so."

He turned to leave.

"Lord Eugene," she said, stopping him before he reached the door, "if anything should happen to him, I want you to know I will hold you responsible."

Lord Eugene took a step back into the room. "Your Grace, I am not sure what makes you think I have acted improperly in this unfortunate matter. May I point out that you are the one who wished him dead, and you are the one who gave the order to send him to Eldridge? I was following your orders when I sent him, just as I am following your orders now by having him recalled. Throughout this whole affair, I have only done my duty.

What I do not understand is why you allow this man to trouble you so. He has lied to you. He has mocked you most cruelly. What is he to you that you should care whether he lives or dies?"

"What he is to me is none of your concern!" she snapped. "I expect you to see to his safe return. That is all you need to know."

"As you wish, Your Grace," he replied with an exaggerated serenity that bordered on contempt. "It is, as I have said, my duty to carry out your orders."

She held him with a cold stare a moment. "I have nothing further to discuss with you."

Lord Eugene gave an appropriate bow and left the two women alone.

"He has done something, Dori. I just know it."

"I fear you are right, My Lady. I've never trusted that man."

CHAPTER THIRTY-SIX

Angel of Mercy

The thunder was now coming right behind the flashes of lightning, and the gusting wind threatened to extinguish the man's torch. Unperturbed, the girl knelt down in the grass alongside her father and placed a hand on the stranger's back. "How do you know he's dead?" she asked between booms.

"Christa, I know a dead man when I see one," he replied.

"He's seen hundreds in the war," gushed her brother. "Isn't that right, Father?"

"But he's still warm," pressed his daughter. "Aren't dead men supposed to be cold?"

"He'll be cold soon enough, my dear."

"Yeah, he'll be cold soon enough," repeated the boy.

"Oh be quiet, Andre," rebuked his sister.

Christa grabbed the man with both hands. "Help me turn him over," she said.

Andre looked at his father, but neither one moved.

Grasping him by his shirt, she tried to roll him over. "Help me, Father," she grunted through clenched teeth.

Her obedient father placed a strong hand below the man and with little effort rolled him onto his back. All three of them gasped at once.

"Look at his shirt!" exclaimed Andre. "He's a Babenberg for sure. Do you think he has any gold, Father?"

"I don't care if he has a wagon full, my son, I wouldn't touch a farthing of it. Come children; we must get away from here."

Another flash of lightning was followed instantly by a crack of thunder, and scattered drops of rain began to fall. The fearless Christa bent over the stranger with her ear close to his face.

"What are you doing?" gasped her father. "The storm is upon us; we must leave at once!" He reached out for her, but she suddenly lifted her head.

"He's alive!"

"What!"

"I can hear him breathing!"

Christa moved aside and motioned for her father listen for himself. He hesitated a second, then leaned over as his daughter had done.

"He's breathing," he agreed, "just barely. But there's nothing we can do for him, Christa. We've got to get away from here."

"Father, you see for yourself he is alive. We can't just leave him."

"Knowing he's alive only makes it worse," warned her father. "This man can only mean trouble."

"But look at his face," she pleaded. "He's a good man."

"Whether he is a saint or a sinner has nothing to do with it. Someone wanted him dead, and they might be back any minute to finish the deed."

"Don't you remember Father Harmon's homily last Sunday? It's our Christian duty to help him!"

"Christa, the Good Samaritan didn't have to worry about someone riding out of the dark and murdering his family. Look at him more closely—good men don't end up in a field at night with their hands bound and covered in blood."

A violent blast of wind blew out the torch, and with the sudden darkness that engulfed them came a cold rain. The gusting wind made it difficult to be heard, and even the dogs were now whining in the dark.

Christa stood and looked up at her father. "Very well," she yelled above the wind. "I'll drag him to the village by myself!" She reached down and took hold of the man's shirt collar. After several seconds of grunting and slipping in the wet grass, she had moved him a few inches.

"Oh, get out of the way," groaned her father.

He dropped down on one knee, pulled the injured man into a sitting position, and slung him across his broad shoulders.

"Thank you, Father," said Christa. "It's the right thing to do. I just know it."

"That's what you always say," he grumbled as they started back.

Andre ran ahead and burst through the door of their home. "Mother, look what we found!"

His mother met them as they came in out of the pounding rain. When her rain-soaked husband stepped through the door, she let out a scream. "For goodness sake, Antonie, what has happened?"

"Now don't get excited, Kara," he answered, attempting to sound composed while standing with a bleeding stranger draped over his shoulders. "It's only another bird with a broken wing your daughter insists we bring home. Where should I put him?"

Kara pointed toward a bed near the fireplace. "Lay him down on Andre's bed for now."

Antonie laid the man down, and Kara got out a knife to cut away the ropes from his wrists.

"Father," cried Andre, "he's got an arrow in him!"

The feathers from a short arrow protruded through the clothing on the back of his right arm. The shirt sleeve was soaked with blood, and he was still bleeding from the wound at the back of his head.

"What's happened to the poor boy?" wondered Kara aloud.

"Boy!" exclaimed Antonie. "Someone has tried to kill him, and that's men's work. Now I'm certain we shouldn't have brought him here."

"Would you have left him out in the storm to die?"

"He's going to die anyway," predicted Antonie. "It would've been safer for us if he had died out there."

Kara tore some of the bloody shirt away to reveal about six inches of a feathered arrow sticking out from his arm. The arrow had penetrated clean through, and the rest of the shaft with the bloody arrowhead stuck out the other side.

"Well, I don't think this is enough to kill him," she declared with modest confidence. "I guess we should try to pull it out."

"Now hold on there, woman," warned Antonie. "I agreed to bring him in out of the rain, that's all. There's no reason for you to start playing midwife. You don't even know what you're doing, do you?"

"I think I know we can't leave that arrow in there. Why are you so anxious?"

"I'm not anxious!" he declared, puffing out his chest. "It's my duty to protect this family, and I don't think dragging half-dead criminals in out of the rain is a good idea. I expect a young girl like Christa not to understand that, but a grown woman like you should know better."

Kara was wiping blood away from the arrow wound and did not look up. "I keep telling you, she's not a young girl anymore. She's older than I was when I married you, or have you forgotten? And what makes you think he's a criminal? Maybe someone tried to rob him."

"Rob him? Do you think thieves tie you up before they shoot you full of arrows?"

"Why can't they?"

Antonie looked up at the ceiling. "You women just don't understand these things."

"Perhaps not," she agreed, "but I wouldn't be so quick to judge him just yet."

She tried to bind the arm wound with the small rag she was using, but blood was dripping onto the floor. "Christa," she called out without turning, "bring me another cloth."

There was no answer.

Kara and her husband turned around to scan the room. Andre was sitting on a stool near the table. The dogs were lying on the hearthstones contentedly soaking up the heat of the fire. Christa was not there.

"Where did she go?" asked Kara.

"She went out," said Andre.

"What for?" asked his stunned father.

"She left right after you laid him on my bed," replied Andre with a shrug of his shoulders. "I thought you saw her leave."

Husband and wife looked at each other and shook their heads.

After Kara checked the other room in the house, Antonie opened the door and went out into the rain. He returned shortly to report that he had searched the barn, the nearby field, and the road in both directions. He could not find her anywhere.

"Where could she have gone?" asked Kara.

Her husband paced the room with his hands clasped behind his back. "Who knows?" he moaned. "This is just like her to disappear without a word. First, I end up with a criminal in my home, and now my daughter vanishes into the night. Oh, Lord, what have I done to deserve this?"

At that moment, a dripping wet Christa came through the

door followed by a short woman whose wet gray hair was matted down both sides of her face.

Antonie's face went ashen. "What's *she* doing here?"

"Father," his daughter smiled at him, "you know perfectly well why she's here."

"What will you do next?" demanded her exasperated father. "Will you get Father Harmon to sound the tocsin so the whole village will know?"

"Know what?" asked Christa.

"Know what?" repeated Antonie. "Know that we're sheltering a brigand, a cutthroat, a... a... a fugitive from justice, that's what!"

Christa laid a hand on his arm. "Father," she said sweetly, "I told you he's a good man. We must help him if we can."

"We *are* helping him," he said, looking over at the old woman, "but I prefer we did it alone."

The old woman's name was Sarah. Her face was thin, almost gaunt, but her many layered dress with overlaying frock made her look heavyset. Hanging from her shoulder was the brown leather bag that never left her side. She lived alone and survived on the food, clothing, and other gifts the villagers brought her in return for healing their sick and injured. Whether broken bones, lacerations, fevers, or convulsions, nothing seemed beyond her ability. None of them understood her methods, and local gossip held that her healing power lay in witchcraft. Nevertheless, whenever their health was in jeopardy, she was the first one they called. If she was a witch, they trusted she was the good kind.

Ignoring the distraught Antonie, Sarah pointed at the injured man. "Is that him?"

"Yes," answered Christa, "is there anything you can do?"

"My dear girl," she replied as she brushed her way past Antonie, "I won't know until I've seen him."

CHAPTER THIRTY-SEVEN

Evil Tidings

Elsea's interview with Lord Eugene had anything but a settling effect, and for the rest of the night she and Dorianne were in constant motion. Elsea had left explicit instructions with the sergeant on duty at the gate to notify her the moment any news of Charles arrived. She nevertheless insisted on going there every hour to see for herself. They even went to the battlements once, though the darkness and wind driven rain made it impossible to see anything.

As dawn neared, she dragged the sleepy Dorianne up to the wall once more to look down the barely visible road. The rain had stopped, and the wind was gone. The sky grew slowly brighter in the east, revealing scattered patches of fog still clinging to the ground, and the birds had begun their morning songs. The idyllic scene was a sublime precursor to another beautiful spring day.

They searched the road for any sign of movement, but saw nothing. Disappointed, Elsea sighed and turned to leave, but stopped when Dorianne laid a hand on her shoulder.

"My Lady," she said pointing at a small speck in the distance, "what's that?"

The two of them strained their eyes peering down the road a few more seconds until Elsea exclaimed, "It's a man on horseback!" She bolted toward the door that led below with Dorianne close behind.

Elsea flew down the stairs and sprinted along the hallways as if the castle was on fire. Running wildly around a corner, she collided with a sentry coming quickly the other way. The force of their collision knocked the young man down.

"Your Highness," said the mortified man as he jumped back to his feet, "please forgive me, I thought you were in your rooms. The sergeant sent me to get you."

"What did he say?" she panted.

"He says to tell you that the person you were expecting has returned."

Elsea raced on to the gatehouse. Waiting for her there was the sergeant of the guard standing next to one of the four men Lord Eugene had sent to retrieve Charles.

"Did you find him?" she blurted.

"Yes, Your Grace," replied the sodden and weary man, "we found them near a small village before the town of Fairfield."

"Well?"

"One of our men was on the road and the other two were in the wagon."

"What about the prisoner?"

"It was a difficult search in the dark during the storm," explained the dejected man, "but we finally found him in a field a short distance from the road."

"So where is he?"

"We left him there, Your Grace."

"But Lord Eugene sent you to bring him back."

"The others are bringing him, Your Grace, later this morning."

"I do not understand!" exclaimed the exasperated Elsea. "Why did you not bring him back now as you were told?"

"Your Grace," he answered, looking down at his feet, "they're all dead, including the prisoner."

Elsea's shoulders slumped and she took an unsteady step to the side. Dorianne reached up discreetly and took her by the arm. At Dorianne's touch, Elsea stood a little taller. "How did this happen?" she asked flatly.

"We're not sure, Your Grace. It seems they were attacked by a group of bandits."

"Has Lord Eugene been informed?"

"No, Your Grace."

"See to it," she ordered. "And inform Lord Raglan as well."

"At once, Your Grace."

Elsea leaned on Dorianne all the way back to her quarters. The same halls and stairs she had flown down only moments before they now traversed in a struggling silence. Once back in her rooms, she did not argue when Dorianne suggested she try to get some sleep. Still wearing the same yellow tunic from yesterday morning, she collapsed onto her bed and stared up at the ceiling. Dorianne positioned her pillows and tried to make her comfortable, then quietly left the room being careful to leave the door open should Elsea call for her. She lay down on her own bed, whispered a prayer for her lady, and was asleep instantly.

CHAPTER THIRTY-EIGHT

Strange Medicine

Sarah had scarcely sat down on a stool next to the wounded man before complaining she needed more light. Kara and Christa searched the house for every candlestick they owned, while Antonie scrambled to add more logs to the fire.

Christa lit the last candle and set it on the small table next to the bed. "Is there anything else I can do?" she asked.

The old woman was busy removing various oddities from her oversized leather bag. She plunged her arm in to the elbow and pulled out a roll of soft deerskin. "Lay this out on the table," she said. "Then get me some water."

Christa untied the cord binding the pouch and unrolled it across the table revealing a strange assortment of shiny tools. There were short knives, peculiar needles, thin sharp nails, an intricate pair of scissors, and a tiny version of the kind of tongs a blacksmith might use. No two of the bizarre implements were the same, but all had identical white handles.

"These are beautiful," said Christa. "Where did you get them?"

Sarah pulled the cork stoppers from two small glass bottles. "I got them in Alexandria," she replied, waving the vials under her nose, "a city in Egypt. The handles are made from the tusks of an elephant."

"Have you been to Egypt?" gushed Christa.

"A few times," answered the old woman matter-of-factly.

"Ha!" snorted Antonie. "I suppose you stop by there on your way to the moon."

Sarah laid a hand on Christa's arm. "I need that water."

While Christa went for the water, Sarah began her inspection. She gave the bloody arrow wound barely a glance before ordering Antonie to roll the injured man onto his side. Holding a candle in one hand, she probed the head wound with the fingers of the other.

She made a few grunts, stopped, and held up the candle. "Hold this," she said to no one in particular.

Kara took the candle, and Sarah now continued her examination with both hands. For the next few minutes, she poked, pushed, squeezed, and grunted. Blood flowed from the wound, soaking the bedding and turning her hands red. "Where is that water?"

"Here," said Christa as she retrieved the small iron pot that was hanging over the fire.

She set it on the table, and Sarah quickly washed her hands turning the water a light pink. After drying her hands with a cloth from her bag, she took up the small scissors and clipped away at the bloody hair until a jagged gash about three inches in length emerged. Using the miniature tongs, she carefully picked out the clumps of hair from the bleeding wound then shaved the stubble left behind with one of the ivory-handled knives. The blood now flowed even more quickly.

"You're making it worse!" exclaimed a flabbergasted Antonie.

"I was mending torn skin before you learned to feed yourself, young man," replied Sarah without looking up.

"Ha!" was all Antonie could say.

She at last put the blade down and washed her blood stained hands once more in the iron pot. She handed Christa an unusual needle bent like a fishhook and a short length of a thick thread from a spool. "Thread this, girl."

While Christa performed her new task, Sarah sprinkled a small amount of green and yellow powders from each of the two vials directly into the bloody gash.

Taking the needle from Christa, she suddenly plunged it through both sides of the wound, drawing out the thread as if she were only repairing a torn garment. Kara let out a soft groan just before she dropped the candle and collapsed onto a nearby chair.

"I need more light," grumbled the old woman.

No one moved.

"I can't see what I'm doing," she said with more urgency.

Christa picked up and relit the candle. "Is that better?"

Sarah grunted in the affirmative and went back to work. In a few minutes, the wound was stitched closed, and the blood flow stopped.

"I didn't know you could do that," said Christa.

"Your skin is no different than the animal hides you sew together," replied Sarah.

"Don't let this old woman impress you too much, my daughter," smirked Antonie. "I once saw a man sew a whole arm back on. Now he was a *real* physician."

Turning her attention to the bloody arrow, Sarah ordered the now recovered Kara to lift the wounded arm to allow her access to both sides. Using one of her blades, she cut the barbed iron arrowhead from its wooden shaft. After smearing another mixture of powders onto the cleanly cut end, she grabbed the arrow by the feathers and pulled it from the arm. The entry and exit slits closed instantly, and the bleeding was reduced to a trickle. She ended by wrapping his head and arm with long strips of cloth from her near bottomless bag.

"Pay attention to how I do this, girl," she said.

When the last bandage was in place, she directed Antonie to lift the injured man while Kara and Christa propped him up into a sitting position with blankets and animal hides.

The old woman washed and dried her hands one final time. "You'll need to keep him like this and not let any weight rest on the back of his head," she warned. She meticulously repacked her bag, but left behind a pile of the cloth strips.

"Will he live?" asked Christa in almost a whisper.

"His head wound is quite serious," Sarah pronounced without emotion. "It's why he's still asleep."

"But will he live?" pressed Christa.

"We'll know in a day or two," she shrugged. "If he awakes by then, he might live."

"And if he doesn't?"

"If he doesn't wake within the next few days," answered Sarah, "then I don't expect he ever will. You should prepare yourself for that."

She slung the strap of her bag over her shoulder and stood to leave. "Till then, you must change the bandages twice a day as I showed you. It's all we can do for now."

"I'll come again," she promised on her way out the door. She looked back at Antonie and added, "At midnight, on my broom."

CHAPTER THIRTY-NINE

The Fourth Man

It was early afternoon when Dorianne entered the room to wake her mistress. To her surprise, Elsea was sitting up on the edge of the bed, head hung down, and her long hair concealing her face.

"What is it?" she asked from behind the curtain of her hair.

"Lord Raglan and the council have called for you, My Lady," Dorianne answered quietly.

"Why?"

"I overheard them talking about a message from Duke Otto."

"Otto! What does *he* want?"

"I don't know, My Lady. Do you wish me to tell them you are not able to come?"

"You know I cannot do that," she said, forcing herself to stand. "Come, Dori; let us see what new tune my puppet masters have for me today."

Waiting for them in her dining room was a strangely subdued council. A doleful Father Prochaska sat across the table from the not so jovial barons as Lord Raglan pensively paced the floor with head bowed. Only Lord Eugene, leaning leisurely against a wall with his arms folded across his chest, seemed unaffected by the somber mood.

"Why have you called me?" asked Elsea.

Raglan stopped his pacing to study her. "Have you heard what has happened?"

She returned his penetrating gaze with a blank face. "They tell me he is dead."

Raglan nodded. "But that is not why I called for you." He held out a sheet of paper toward her. "We have just received a disturbing letter from Duke Otto."

"What have I done now?" she sighed.

"It seems this man Charles does have, rather *did* have…" he looked at Lord Eugene as he corrected himself, "some value to Otto after all, and he has warned us to guarantee his safety. It is a great shame we did not know this sooner."

"Yes, it is a great shame," she agreed half-heartedly. "So what should we do?"

"That is what we are discussing, Your Highness."

Elsea looked over at the man leaning against the wall. "What does *he* say we should do?"

"Your Grace," began Eugene, not bothering to unfold his arms, "there is little we *can* do, except, of course, inform the duke of this most unfortunate incident."

She paused a moment as if considering his suggestion, then turned again to Raglan. "And what exactly do we know of this *unfortunate incident?*"

"Apparently, they were attacked by some kind of highwaymen," explained Raglan. "I expect to learn more once the patrol returns with the remains. However, Lord Eugene is correct: there is little for us to do now beyond returning the body to Otto along with a complete explanation and our sincerest regrets."

"Is that it?" asked Elsea. "Here's what's left of him—sorry he's dead. You know Otto better than any of us; do you think he will believe such nonsense?"

"What else is there to believe?" interrupted Lord Eugene.

"What if Duke Otto believes we killed him out of spite?"

"Your Highness," groaned Baron Kirchenbetter, "our situation is grave enough. Let us not compound our woes with wild and groundless speculations. It is plain to anyone the poor man has fallen victim to a band of thieves and cutthroats. Regrettably, this sort of thing happens all too often these days. The duke will understand this. He knows a deed as hideous as you suggest is beneath us."

"Is that so?" she wondered aloud with her eyes once more on Lord Eugene.

Lord Eugene unfolded his arms. "My Lady, I deduce from your tone that you believe I have played a role in the scoundrel's demise. As I told you last night, after you ordered me to recall the miscreant, I did all in my power to ensure his safe return. I was as astounded as you when I heard the dreadful news this morning. This letter from the duke is equally unexpected. The man was but a common knight without a drop of noble blood. Who could know that one so contemptible would mean so much to a man like Otto? If you will permit me to say so, Your Grace, I believe your familiarity with this man has affected your judgment."

Elsea's face reddened and she took a step closer to Lord Eugene. Just then, a soldier rushed into the room.

"My Lord Count," he said bowing to Raglan, "the men you have been expecting are returned!"

"Have you seen them?" asked Raglan.

"They've brought back a wagon," he answered while crossing himself, "with our people, My Lord."

"Inform the men I will be down shortly to question the patrol."

"Yes, My Lord."

Raglan was the first to break the uncomfortable silence that followed the messenger's departure. "It is necessary that I verify the reports, but we have much yet to discuss in view of our new circumstances. We will meet here again in half an hour's time."

He headed for the door. Elsea was right behind him.

"My Lady," he said in a low voice, "this will not be a pleasant task. It may be better for you to remain here."

"You need not concern yourself with my feelings," she said. "I intend to see for myself, and I will not be dissuaded."

"As you wish," replied Raglan.

A group of soldiers were huddled together at the far side of the courtyard. At the sight of Lord Raglan and the duchess coming toward them, they moved back to reveal the rickety wagon. Raglan stepped up to it without breaking stride. Elsea, however, stopped short and closed her eyes.

Raglan peered over the side a brief moment and then spun to face the soldiers. "There are only three bodies here," he declared.

"What do you mean?" asked Elsea.

"The man called Charles is not in the wagon, My Lady," replied Raglan,

Elsea rushed forward and seized him by the arm. There, stretched out like logwood, were the three soldiers that had escorted Charles the night before. Exposure to the hot sun had already begun to bloat their bodies. A cloud of flies buzzed around them and crawled on their blankly staring eyes and bloody wounds.

"I was told you were bringing back four bodies," said Raglan to the sergeant who had led the patrol.

"I assure you, My Lord, there *were* four."

"Well, where is the fourth man?"

"This one and this one were already in the wagon when we found them," replied the sergeant pointing at the dead men, "and that one was in the road. It took us a while, but we found the prisoner in a nearby field. After I sent the courier to inform Lord Eugene, we went to get the wagon. We put the one from the road in back and rode over to get the fourth man: the one in the field. But when we got there, he was gone. I swear that's how it happened, My Lord."

"But the messenger you sent back told us they were all dead," noted Raglan.

"Yes, My Lord."

"But if the fourth man was dead, then where is he?"

"I can't explain it, My Lord."

"Perhaps you were mistaken, and he was still alive."

"But, My Lord," protested the sergeant, "his neck was broken!"

"And do you not think it odd that a man with a broken neck gets up and leaves when your back is turned?"

The flustered sergeant had no answer.

"Enough of this!" snapped Raglan. "Send for the captain of the guard at once."

"Yes, My Lord," replied the sergeant before scurrying off.

"We should return to the others, My Lady," advised Raglan. "There is nothing more to be learned here."

He started to step away from the wagon, but Elsea still held his arm and would not let go. "Lord Raglan," she asked quietly, "do you really think he may be alive?"

"It is a possibility, My Lady, but *only* a possibility. You must not to allow this confusion to raise your hopes. Of one thing I am certain: whoever attacked this wagon was very good at killing."

Elsea released his arm and they returned to the great hall where they met the captain, still breathing hard from having run all the way.

"My Lord Count," he panted, "I was told you called for me."

"Follow me," ordered Raglan.

Bishop Prochaska stood when Raglan and the duchess came back into the room. "My Lord, while you were gone, we were discussing how we should handle the return of the ill-fated man's body."

"Your requiem may be premature, Your Excellency," said Raglan bluntly. He paused to sweep his glance over his auditors' puzzled faces. "They did not bring back the body of Charles."

"What!" exclaimed Kirchenbetter.

"It is possible," said Raglan after a quick look at Elsea, "that the man may not be dead."

Father Prochaska clapped his hands together. "Heaven be thanked," he gushed. "This is glorious news!"

"On what do you base this surprising revelation?" asked Lord Eugene.

"The sergeant is convinced he was dead when they found him," answered Raglan, "but when they returned a short time later to retrieve the body, he was gone."

"Then he was not dead," concluded an exultant Prochaska.

"My dear Bishop," said Lord Eugene, "let us not be carried away with wishful thinking. There may be other explanations you are overlooking."

"Such as?" said Raglan.

Lord Eugene placed his elbow in his left hand and stroked his short beard a moment. "For one, a roaming bear, or a pack of wolves for that matter, could have dragged his body off into the bushes. The beasts of the field have to eat too, you know."

"That is one," said Raglan. "Do you have another?"

"Someone could have taken his body," shrugged Eugene.

"And why would anyone do that?"

"My dear Count, you ask for 'why,' the best I am able to suggest is a 'what' or two."

"I see that," observed Raglan. "But it is the question *why* that concerns me the most. Why would someone attack three soldiers escorting a nameless prisoner in a worthless cart pulled by two broken down horses?"

"And *why* do you insist on making things so complicated?" countered Lord Eugene. "Experience has taught me the simplest answers are most often the correct ones."

"No doubt you have a simple answer for us," returned Raglan.

"It is quite plausible," began Eugene, "that in the dark, the bandits mistook them for men of wealth, maybe even merchants traveling to the town of Fairfield, and therefore easy victims. Naturally, our valiant soldiers defended themselves nobly against the rogues. Overwhelmed by the sheer brutality of the attack, however, their heroic stand ended tragically."

"An interesting conjecture," replied Raglan.

"If the man is still alive," noted Prochaska, "he may be gravely injured, and a proper search should be made for him without delay."

"Precisely," agreed Lord Raglan.

Turning to the man who had been waiting near the door, Raglan continued, "Captain, you will prepare a company of mounted men to depart within the hour. You will proceed to the area where the attack occurred. Cordon off the roads in all directions, and stop anyone who attempts to leave. At first light, you will begin a search of every field, stream, and clump of trees. You will look in every hut, house, and barn, and you will send back a rider every hour to report on your progress. Is that clear?"

"Yes, My Lord Count." He bowed once and left the room.

"My Lords," said Raglan after he was gone, "I need not tell

you the importance of finding this man. Whether he is alive or dead, we should know by tomorrow. If he is alive, our course is unchanged: we return him immediately and continue our negotiations with Otto."

"And if he is not?" asked Lord Eugene.

"If he is not alive," Raglan paused to glance at Elsea, "then we will have no choice left to us but Eldridge."

The count gave a nod to indicate the meeting was over, and each man took leave of the duchess and exited the room until only Raglan remained with the Elsea.

"My Lady," he said solemnly, "I feel I must repeat my earlier warning. It is quite likely that the sergeant is correct and that this man is already dead. You should therefore prepare yourself to face the possibility of dealing with Eldridge and all that entails."

"Lord Raglan," returned Elsea with a newfound confidence, "you have often accused me of always seeing things in their worst light. Now I think you are the one who refuses to accept good news when you hear it. Dorianne and I will join you in the morning to follow the progress of the search. I want to know the minute they find him."

CHAPTER FORTY

Renewed Hope

After they left Raglan, Elsea led Dorianne to the battlements. Having suddenly lost the lethargy she started the day with, she practically skipped her way up the steps. Unable to keep up with her rejuvenated lady, Dorianne fell behind. She caught up to her standing before the wall, looking out at the town below.

"Dori," asked Elsea as soon as she came alongside, "why do you believe in God?"

"I've never thought about why I believe, My Lady. Maybe it's because I know my Savior lives within me. He comforts me and cares for me. He is as real to me as the sun and the moon."

"But you can see the sun and moon. You can't see God. What makes you think he is even there?"

"It's true I can't see Him, My Lady. But I hear His voice when the priests read to me His holy words, and I know He hears my voice when I pray."

"Do you still pray, Dori?"

"Every day, My Lady."

Elsea stepped back from the wall. "Have you ever prayed for something important—something that meant the whole world to you?"

"When my parents died, I prayed to God for help."

"And did He?

"Yes, My Lady," Dorianne answered quietly. "He sent you to rescue me."

"And have you been rescued?"

"You know I have," scolded Dorianne.

"My precious, faithful Dori," smiled Elsea, "did it ever occur to you that God may have sent *you* to rescue *me*?"

"It pleases me that you think I've been a help to you, My Lady."

Elsea took Dorianne by the hand, and they began to walk toward the door that led below. "I did something today I have not done since I was a child," she said.

"What was that, My Lady?"

"I prayed."

"What did you pray for?"

"It was right before I looked into that wagon," explained Elsea. "I did not pray to any of the Saints, but I closed my eyes and begged God Himself. I prayed that he, Charles I mean, was still alive and that he would not be in that wagon. And it was true, Dori, it was true! I prayed that he would come back and…" she stopped herself.

"And what?"

"I must get ready for tomorrow," said Elsea.

"Tomorrow?"

"Yes, tomorrow is when Charles returns, and I must look my best."

"But remember what Lord Raglan said, My Lady. What if they don't find him? Or what if…"

"Dori!" exclaimed Elsea. "Have you not been listening? God has heard my prayer, and Charles is coming back tomorrow."

"Yes, My Lady," answered Dorianne after too long a pause.

CHAPTER FORTY-ONE

Irony

Lord Eugene's living space did not approach the multi-room splendor of men like Raglan or the barons. Even Prochaska had better quarters than the man charged with protecting the duchess. The room given to Eugene was only large enough to hold the most essential furniture. He did at least have a window, however, which allowed him to look down the road leading to the castle gate. On more than one occasion foreknowledge of an approaching visitor had worked to his advantage.

Eugene leaned back in his chair behind the table that was his desk and looked up at the cloaked man standing before him. "In other words, Geulf, you have failed me."

"No, My Lord," replied Geulf.

"No?" returned Eugene with a lifting of his eyebrows. "I gave you a dozen men and a simple task. Yet, somehow you were not able to overcome three decrepit guards and an unarmed man with bound hands. Worse than that, now you tell me he has disappeared and may still be alive. Please explain to me how that is not a failure."

"But, My Lord," protested Geulf, "he must be dead."

"And yet we have no body to prove it. You will understand my skepticism."

Geulf opened his mouth to reply, but Lord Eugene cut him off. "So, it was our man they found dead?"

"Yes, My Lord. We think he fell from his horse during the chase. We went looking for him when he failed to meet up with us."

"At least you had sense enough to retrieve the body," conceded Eugene. "And you believe those villagers dragged the imposter off somewhere?"

"It's the only explanation, My Lord."

"But why would they bring a dead man in out of the rain? Perhaps he was not as dead as you believe. What if he was able to move off on his own?"

"That's unlikely, My Lord. As I've told you, his wounds were mortal."

Lord Eugene stood up from the table and made his way to a large chest in the corner. "The road of life takes many strange turns, Geulf."

"How so, My Lord?"

"Consider how just two weeks ago I was struggling to convince the council to negotiate with Eldridge. Suddenly, this charlatan shows up and within a few days beguiles everyone, undoing all my painstaking progress." He lifted the lid of the chest and bent over to rummage through the cache of papers it contained. "Yet, between the rising and setting of a single sun, the man is disgraced, Raglan and the duchess are humiliated, and all now must look to me for help with Eldridge. In one day, my position has become stronger than ever." He stood up clutching a long leather scroll. "Do you not see the exquisite irony? The shrewdest man in Austria is saved by a Bavarian fool. If I were a religious man I would say I see the hand of God in this."

"Then My Lord is no longer concerned about the missing man?"

Eugene's scowl returned. "Of course I am concerned! This trickster could still threaten my designs for Eldridge. I underestimated his importance to the duchess. Who knows what new folly will cross her mind if she learns he is still alive." He came back to the table and unrolled the scroll which turned out to be a finely painted map. "Show me exactly where the ambush occurred."

Geulf studied the map a moment and pointed. "Here, My Lord."

"If he survived the attack, but was as seriously injured as you claim, then he would need to find refuge," speculated Eugene. "And here is where he would find it." His finger rested on a symbol indicating a small village along a stream near the town of Fairfield. "What is the name of this village?"

"I believe it is called Longwood, My Lord."

"Yes," agreed Eugene, "Duggen is lord there. The old man is almost as blind as he is deaf. He will give us no trouble. I want you to send two of your ablest men there immediately. Instruct them to pass themselves off as blacksmiths or wainwrights, traveling through looking for work."

"What should they do, My Lord?"

"The usual: blend in, ask questions. If the deceiver is cowering there, then someone will know. No secret is safe in a small village."

"But Raglan will have a whole company of men searching that area tomorrow," noted Geulf. "Certainly they'll find him first."

"Do you think I have not thought of that?" snapped Eugene. He sat down and leaned back in his chair again. "If he is hiding in some grassy glen or has crawled off to die among the shadows of a local forest, then Raglan will indeed find him. However, if someone within the village has given him shelter, his people might not be so fortunate. This is where a more subtle approach may work better."

"If he is in that village," said Geulf, "I believe we can find him."

"If he is in that village, I *expect* you to find him," returned Eugene. "Remember to be discreet. A badly wounded man will need help. People will talk, they always do. Follow the rumors and the gossip, and you will find our man. But do nothing rash. Dispatching him a second time will not be so easy. He must disappear without a trace this time, and we will have to deal with any witnesses who can report seeing him. I trust you will succeed if given another opportunity?"

"You may be sure of it, My Lord," promised Geulf.

"It is settled then," said Eugene. "You will personally supervise the placing of our people in Longwood. Keep me informed of your progress, but be certain you put nothing in writing." From his pocket, he produced a small leather bag that jingled as he set it on the table. "You will need this."

Geulf scooped up the bag, bowed low, and left the room.

CHAPTER FORTY-TWO

Thwarted Rescue

Charles opened his eyes and struggled a few seconds to focus them on the unfamiliar ceiling. He turned his head to look around and was startled by a young girl sitting at his side only inches away.

"Who are you?" he asked.

"My name is Christa," she smiled.

He sat up and swung his legs out to stand, but as soon as his feet hit the floor an excruciating pain from the back of his head overwhelmed him. His vision went blurry and he suddenly felt as if he were spinning in circles. So real was the illusion that he reached out for the girl to hold onto before he spun completely away. Beads of sweat began to form on his forehead and he feared he was about to vomit into her lap.

To his immense relief, he found that closing his eyes made the spinning stop. He heard the girl telling him to lay down, and he allowed her to guide him back onto the bedding being careful to keep his eyes tightly shut. He stayed motionless in that position for several minutes until at last he felt his nausea subside. Though his head still throbbed with pain, he was thankful he had not gotten sick in front of the girl.

From the table across the room, Christa's parents had witnessed his failed attempt to stand. Antonie sat frozen in his chair, but Kara rushed over to help her daughter. There was no need, however, as Christa ably returned him to his bed on her own.

Charles cautiously opened his eyes again, ready to close them at the first sign of any spinning. He discovered that as long as he kept still and did not turn his head to either side, the queasiness did not return. "Where am I?" he asked.

"You are in Longwood," answered Christa.

"How did I get here?"

"I think we're the ones who should be asking the questions," said Antonie, who had now moved to the foot of the bed so that Charles could see him. "Who are you, and what were you doing in that field the other night?"

Charles opened his mouth, but could think of no answer to give. "What field?"

"The field at the edge of our village," Christa quietly reminded him. "You were badly wounded when we found you."

He brought his hand up to touch his head, but a sharp burning pain shot through his right arm, and he let out a groan. "What has happened to me?"

"That's what we'd like to know," pressed Antonie. "You had an arrow in you, and your head was beaten in. Who wants to kill you? What crimes have you committed?"

Charles thought for a moment, but nothing came to his mind. "I do not know," he said, "I remember nothing of that night."

"Ha!" snorted Antonie. "Do you think we villagers are fools? Do you expect us to believe you can't remember nearly being killed?"

"Why shouldn't we believe him?" interjected Christa. "He's been asleep for two days, and his mind is still cloudy. He can't answer all these questions right now. I'm going to get Sarah; she'll know what to do."

"You're not going anywhere while the sun is up," warned her father. "We don't want the whole village wondering what the old woman…"

The sound of dogs barking outside interrupted him in mid-sentence. Andre burst through the door. "Father," he shouted excitedly, "Father, there are soldiers here!"

"Soldiers!" exclaimed Antonie. "What do they want?"

"I don't know," gushed Andre, "but little Franz says they're searching everywhere!"

The color drained from Antonie's face. "I told you," he said to no one in particular. "I tried to tell all of you, but no one would listen: they're looking for him!"

"Oh, Father you mustn't let them take him!" begged Christa.

"It's too late for that now," he replied, looking up at the ceiling to avoid her pleading eyes. "I warned you that no good would come of this. Who knows what sort of trouble this man has caused, or what the duchess will do to us when she finds out we've been sheltering him."

Kara went up to her husband and placed a hand on his shoulder. "They might not be here for him," she suggested. "You must go out and talk to them."

"My dear, soldiers don't ride into little villages to chat about the barley harvest. They're here for a reason. The old witch has betrayed us!"

"She would never do that, Father," insisted Christa.

"I'll go out and speak to them," he said gravely, "but no one is to leave this house while I'm out there. Do you hear me?" He spoke these last words giving Christa his fiercest look. Calling for Andre to follow, he opened the door and went out.

As Antonie exited the house his panic-stricken expression changed instantly to one of jovial warmness. A young man in the uniform of a sergeant in the palace guard waited at the head of a line of horsemen that had just stopped in front of his door.

"My Lord," he said to the sergeant, "good day to you. My name is Antonie and I am Lord Duggen's steward on his manor here. On behalf of My Lord, and of my family, I welcome you to our fair village of Longwood. How may I help you?"

The bleary-eyed sergeant, who had now been awake for the better part of two days, looked down on him. "I'm not a lord."

"Forgive me, captain," said Antonie, "but you have the bearing of a nobleman, and I was mistaken. May I at least offer you something to eat?"

Before the sergeant could answer, he turned to Andre. "My son, go and get the captain and these good men some bread."

Andre dashed into the house and returned quickly with a loaf of bread in one hand and a wedge of yellowed cheese in the other.

Antonie broke off some of the bread and cheese and handed it up to the sergeant. I apologize for having nothing better to offer you, My Lord. If only I had known you were coming I could have had a proper meal waiting for you, but no one ever tells me these things."

Andre took the rest of the bread and cheese and went down the line of knights. The grateful soldiers tore into the morsels like starving men.

"Are you here to protect us from those bandits?" asked Antonie.

"What bandits?" replied the sergeant around a mouth full of bread.

"Why, those wicked men that attacked Her Grace's soldiers the other night, of course. It was an awful affair, My Lord. They say there were dead men strewn everywhere! The village has been in an uproar ever since, and I have not had a peaceful sleep in two nights. Please tell me that you have caught them."

"We're not looking for bandits," answered the sergeant with a belch. "We're looking for one man—been at it all day."

"But My Lord, you've so many men," observed Antonie with a sweep of his arm toward other soldiers in a nearby field. "This person must be very dangerous!"

"I don't care about dangerous," declared the sergeant as he bit off another piece of bread. "I've dealt with worse."

"I should think so, My Lord. Certainly, such a despicable character will pose no difficulty for a man like you. But tell me, My Lord, what does this rogue look like? Perhaps I've seen him."

"He's young," mumbled the sergeant around the bread, "and he was wearing a Babenberg shirt. They say he goes by many names; one of them is Charles."

Antonie rubbed his chin and furrowed his brows. "Hmmm, I don't recall anyone by that name, My Lord. What sort of dreadful crime has he committed?"

The sergeant glanced around once and then leaned over. "All I can tell you is that the duchess wants him," he answered in a low tone.

"Ah, the duchess herself!" gushed Antonie. "Then you are on important business indeed, My Lord. It must be a great honor to serve Her Grace and to live in that castle. I have a cousin who once lived there for a whole month. Oh, what splendor! Oh, what magnificence! I truly envy you, My Lord. Please forgive me for keeping you, but what do you intend to do?"

"I'm to search the buildings of this village. How many people live here?"

"That's an excellent idea, My Lord! We have fifty-three families living in Longwood. I'm the steward and this is my home here. Over there is my barn where I store my grain, and in the winter, the few cattle and horses I have. You can see where the other homes start up ahead. Beyond those trees by the stream is our mill and oven. We're a simple folk and are not used to trouble of any kind. Most of our people are working in the fields. Do you wish me to have them gathered here for an interrogation?"

The sergeant looked around at the peasants moving about on their plots of land. "I don't think I'll need to see them just yet."

"A wise decision, My Lord, for you must continue the search without delay! Before you do, however, may I humbly make but one request?"

"What is it?"

Will you please have your men search my barn: both floors *and* cellar? My wife will worry me to death if she thinks there is some fugitive from Her Grace's justice hiding in there."

The sergeant turned to the men behind him and nodded towards the barn. Two soldiers left the line and rode over to it. They reemerged a few minutes later, shook their heads, and climbed back on their horses.

"Thank you, My Lord," said Antonie. "My wife will be so relieved." He clutched his hands together as if in prayer. "If you'll not think me too bold, My Lord, may I impose upon you for but one more favor?"

"Now what?"

A broad smile broke across Antonie's face. "Will My Lord please search my humble lodgings personally? My poor daughter is quite ill—burning up with fever. We've never had a man so important in our village before, and it would be a great honor for her to meet you. I am sure it would make her feel better." Antonie took a step towards the door as if he expected him to follow.

The sergeant looked over at the door of his house, and then back at Antonie. He readjusted himself in his saddle. "I don't think it'll be necessary to search this house," he said. "You're the steward, after all."

Antonie let his shoulders slump appropriately.

With that, the sergeant popped the last piece of cheese into his mouth, took a tug from his water skin, and signaled to the men behind him. The weary men resumed their sluggish ride toward the rest of the village. Antonie grinned widely at each soldier who cared to look his way as they rode by. As the column moved along, men would leave the line to investigate the various buildings they came upon. After they were far down the road, he and Andre returned to the house.

Closing the door behind him, Antonie crossed the room to his wife and daughter. Kara and Christa sat clutching each other near the bed where Charles lay.

"They're gone," he said calmly.

Christa ran to her father and hugged him. "I was so worried for you, Father," she cried. "You were right: it was dangerous to bring him here, but I just know we did the right thing. I hope you aren't angry at me anymore."

"Hush my girl," he said, as he patted her on the head. "Let's hear no more of it. Praise the Saints, there's been no harm done."

He casually walked to Christa's bed, slowly sat down, and fainted.

CHAPTER FORTY-THREE

Fruitless Vigil

As soon as Dorianne tied off the last thread, Elsea hurriedly pulled the new dress over her head. She studied herself with her mirror while Dorianne shook out the folds. "You have outdone yourself this time, Dori," she smiled.

"Thank you, My Lady," replied Dorianne without smiling back.

After breakfast, they joined Lord Raglan in the great hall to await what Elsea was certain to be the soon return of Charles. By midmorning, a stream of couriers began arriving at regular intervals to report on the progress of the mission. The first messengers had no details of significance. Raglan reminded an apprehensive Elsea that the search was just getting underway; he did not expect to hear anything important until at least noon. Midday had come and gone, however, and still the reports were negative. The heavy rain of the fateful night had washed away all clues, and no one had seen or heard anything of the missing man. If not for the wagon full of dead bodies, there would have been no evidence that anything exceptional had even happened.

As the day wore on, Dorianne suggested that Elsea retire to her quarters for some rest and a meal, but she refused. The more messengers returned with nothing to report, the more she insisted the next rider would have important news. In the end, Dorianne ordered a small plate of cold meats brought to the great hall. Elsea nibbled a few bites now and then, but otherwise left it untouched.

It was now well past sundown, and the promising sunlight that had come through the windows gave way to the dreary flickering of burning tapers.

"My Lady," said Raglan, "the hour grows late. Would you not be more comfortable in your rooms? I will continue the vigil on your behalf and promise to send a runner as soon as I hear anything."

Elsea had been quiet the last few hours, and she did indeed look weary. "Thank you, Lord Raglan," she said after stifling a yawn, "but I am really not tired, and I can wait here just as comfortably as in my rooms."

At that moment the sentry on duty at the door announced yet another courier.

Raglan stood to indulge himself in a long overdue stretch. "Well, what news do you have?" he groaned.

"My Lord Count," began the soldier, "my captain sends his regards and says that we've completed the search as you ordered. We've covered the entire countryside, including every building and dwelling of Longwood. He's not there. My captain wishes to know if you desire us to investigate a new area."

"You are certain you have searched the fields and woods as I directed?"

"Yes, My Lord. He's not there, and none of the peasants of the region have seen or heard of him."

Raglan looked over at Elsea who was now standing as well. "We have done all we can, My Lady," he concluded in a sympathetic tone. "I recommend that the company be recalled."

She did not answer.

"However, if you wish, I will order them to renew the search in the morning."

"Thank you, Lord Raglan," she said at last, "but that will not be necessary. I believe you are right, and we have done all we can. It is a shame, but these things sometimes happen, and we will just have to make the best of it. Come Dorianne, it is time for us to retire. I shall see you in the morning, Count."

She headed for the door, but Raglan stopped her. "My Lady," he said, "this does not prove he has come to harm."

"Your encouragement is quite unnecessary, Lord Raglan. My only concern in finding him was to avoid further difficulties with Duke Otto. It now seems that is no longer possible."

She glided from the room with her head held high, and the hem of her new dress making a rushing sound along the floor. She was followed by a yawning Dorianne holding a lone candlestick.

The instant Elsea reached the hallway she staggered to the side, and slumped against the wall. "He is gone, Dori," she moaned. "He is gone, and I will never see him again."

"I am sorry, My Lady," was all Dorianne could offer.

Elsea pushed off from the wall and ran the rest of the way back to her rooms. Once through the door, she began to tear at her beautiful dress. Dorianne watched quietly as what had taken her hours to make flew to pieces in seconds.

Now in her underclothes with Dorianne's creation in a tattered heap at her feet, she stumbled across the room and collapsed onto her bed. She pulled a pillow to her face and cried into it, "Even God has forsaken me!"

CHAPTER FORTY-FOUR

Locked Mind

Charles tried to keep still while Sarah rewrapped the bandage around his head. The pain had subsided some since he first awoke, and he could now sit up without becoming dizzy. It was well into the evening, and Andre and the dogs were fast asleep on Christa's bed in the corner. Christa and Kara stood ready to offer Sarah any assistance, but Antonie sat at the table, his face alternating between frowns and scowls.

The old woman returned to the stool near the bed. "Let us try again," she said. "What is your name?"

"You said my name is Charles."

"Stop trying to pretend you didn't know that," snarled Antonie.

"Please darling," smiled Kara, "let Sarah do the talking."

Antonie folded his arms across his chest and turned his back on them.

"Where are you from?" continued Sarah.

Charles again searched his mind for the answer. For hours now, he had been trying to remember things as simple as who he was and where he was from. He would close his eyes and struggle to recall mental images of his life, but each time his mind responded with only shifting clouds of an impenetrable fog. Occasionally, the haze would thin and he thought he could make out some shape in the gloom, but then a fresh bank of the thick mist would roll in and he was lost again.

"I cannot remember," he sighed. "What is wrong with me?"

"Tell me what you *can* remember," asked Sarah. "Do you have a mother and father?"

Charles closed his eyes again and thought for a moment. "Yes," he said with some excitement. "Yes, I can remember my mother." A wave of relief swept over him as he was able to recall this small fragment.

"What about your father?"

"Nothing," he said after a long pause.

"Close your eyes and think about your mother," urged Sarah. "How old are you in your memory?"

"I think I am about six or seven years old," he answered after a minute. He kept his eyes closed and concentrated on the memories of his childhood. His mother was young and beautiful. She was always busy fixing meals, repairing clothing, or feeding animals. She seemed a contented person and yet lonely somehow. He could not remember any other family.

"What about your shirt?" interrupted Christa, holding up the white shirt embroidered with the red shield. "It has the Babenberg insignia. Are you a Babenberg? Do you know the duchess?"

"I am sorry," he said, looking at the shirt Christa had washed and mended, "but it means nothing to me."

Sarah started putting things back into her bag. Only after she had returned every item to its proper place did she look up at Charles. "I've seen this before," she said, "but never in someone so young."

"Why can't I remember anything?"

"Ah, but you can," she answered. "You remember your mother now, and perhaps in time you'll remember more."

Charles's eyes widened. "Perhaps?"

She reached out and gently touched his head. "Your wound

is quite serious," she said. "It's a wonder you're even alive. You must be thankful for that."

"But, is there anything you can do?" He looked at the bag on her shoulder. "Is there no medicine?"

"There's no medicine for this, young man. If your memories return, they'll return on their own. Sometimes there's a key that unlocks the mind."

"What sort of key?"

"There's no way to know," she explained. "It could be a familiar sight or sound, or maybe even a food. It might be one of those, or none of those. I cannot tell."

"But I will remember?"

"I once heard of a man who never found his old memories."

"But what will I do if that happens?"

"You'll do what he did," she assured him, "you'll start again with new memories. You won't miss what you can't remember."

She stood to leave and turned to the mother and daughter. Though Kara was standing closest to her, Sarah addressed her comments to Christa. "Keep feeding him as much as he can hold down. He should be able to walk by the morning, but don't let him overly exert himself. I have done all I can, and his healing will be but a matter of time. You may remove his bandages in another day."

She opened the door and went out into the night.

As soon as the door had closed, Antonie was on his feet. "I always thought the ancient one had sniffed too many of her potions, but now I'm sure of it. Have you ever heard anything more outlandish?"

"Father," said Christa, "I think Sarah knows what she's talking about."

"How would you know what she knows? Whoever heard of someone losing his memory overnight?"

Antonie turned to Charles. "You may have fooled these women, but you haven't fooled me. We both know you're running from the duchess for Lord knows what reason."

"Antonie," said Kara softly, "there's no reason to be so rude."

"He has good reason to be suspicious," interjected Charles. "These things are just as unbelievable to me."

"What's unbelievable," observed Antonie, "is that you can't remember getting shot through with an arrow and beaten nearly to death! My goodness, man, the duchess sent half the palace guard to look for you. Do you expect us to believe she was concerned for your welfare?"

Charles let out a long sigh. "You and your family have taken a great risk in saving my life, and I am most grateful. I promise I will stop taking advantage of your kindness as soon as I can walk. If that old woman is right, I should be able to leave in the morning."

At this, both women at once insisted that he must not think of leaving until he was fully recovered. Besides, they argued, where would he go, and what would he do? By their combined urgings they were able to effect a truce. He would allow him to stay, agreed Antonie, but only until Sarah said he was ready to leave. At which time Antonie promised to take him to the town of Fairfield where he could find employment or transportation to somewhere else.

With that settled, everyone prepared for bed. Christa insisted on helping Charles get comfortable, and he politely allowed her to fuss over him and tuck in his blankets. By now, he had heard the story of the night they found him and how she convinced her skeptical father to bring him home. Her constant care had given him time to study her. Though she was younger than him, she had the beauty and poise of an older woman. Her attentions were flattering, but he tried not to encourage her. As she meticulously positioned his pillow she bent over him so closely he could smell her hair. The sweet fragrance reminded him of something he was certain he should remember. But what was it?

Antonie blew out the last candle before he and the two women disappeared into the other room. Charles turned his thoughts to Sarah's *key*. Did she really believe that, or was she as crazy as Antonie said? Several times during their interrogation they had mentioned Elsea. The way Antonie kept insisting he was in some sort of trouble with the duchess he thought it best not to reveal that there was indeed something familiar about her name. He whispered it now into the dark. If she was his enemy, then why did he enjoy the sound it made? He drifted off to sleep still thinking of that name, clinging to it like a shipwrecked sailor amid the crashing waves of the sea.

CHAPTER FORTY-FIVE

Betrothal

Dorianne slipped quietly into Elsea's bedchamber. Though the mid afternoon sun lit up the room, Elsea still lay in her bed facing the wall. Dorianne crept up and reached out a hand.

"What?" Elsea asked before she had touched her.

"I'm sorry, My Lady," apologized Dorianne, "but the council wishes to see you."

"Is that what that knock on the door was about?" she asked without turning.

"Yes, My Lady."

Elsea rolled over and sat up. She placed her feet on the floor, but remained sitting on the edge of her bed for many minutes without moving.

"Get my clothes," she said at last.

Dorianne brought out her old garments. Despite sleeping a night and half the day, Elsea still looked tired, and she struggled to pull on her clothes as if lifting heavy weights. Once dressed, she let Dorianne lead her down the stairs of her tower. Dorianne slowed her walk to let Elsea keep up. As they approached the door to her dining room they heard a loud argument in progress. Elsea stopped several feet from the threshold and listened a moment. It would not have been the first time she had interrupted her bickering lords. Normally, this is where she would have steeled herself and hardened her countenance, but the haggard expression on her face did not change, and she went through the door without taking so much as a deep breath.

Her entrance stilled the voices instantly. All five members of her council were there. With Dorianne behind her, Elsea came a couple strides into the room and stood with her hands at her side.

"Why have you called me?" she asked quietly.

No one seemed eager to answer. However, a bolder Lord Eugene stepped forward to break the uneasy silence. "Your Highness," he began in a somber tone, "we have a matter of vital urgency to discuss with you."

Elsea replied with a weary stare.

"Your Highness," he continued, "the day we have all been doing our best to avoid is here. Duke Otto is using that unforeseeable incident with the imposter as a pretext to move against us. He says that unless we return him unharmed within three days, he will declare war."

She brought her hand up to smother a sudden yawn.

"Do you not understand what I am saying?" asked an exasperated Eugene.

"You are saying that Otto intends to declare war," she answered clearly. "I thought Lord Raglan had written a letter explaining everything."

"I did, My Lady," confirmed Raglan, "but perhaps we should have personally gone to Hogisfeld instead. We might have been able to convince the duke of our innocence in this matter."

"I keep telling you," countered Eugene, "going to Hogisfeld would have changed nothing. Otto's affection for the man is a pure fabrication. He is only using this affair as an excuse to do what he has always intended."

"Your Grace," interjected Baron Kirchenbetter, "you must understand what this means."

It means," said Elsea, "we will be attacked by the Bavarians."

"Well, yes, Your Grace," conceded Keinmeyer, "but that is not what Baron Kirchenbetter is asking." He hesitated a moment before proceeding. "You will no doubt recall the many deliberations we had regarding this possibility and the contingency we agreed upon should this day ever come."

There was a long silence.

"You want me to marry Eldridge," she said without emotion.

"Yes," stammered Keinmeyer, "yes we do."

"Have you discussed this among yourselves?"

"Thoroughly, Your Grace."

"And are you all in agreement?"

"We all agree it is for your best," he gushed. "This marriage will gain us an ally against Bavaria and strengthen your claim to the duchy. You and Eldridge will co-rule Austria and Styria. Your firstborn son will inherit the lands of your combined duchies. It is what your father would have wanted. You will at last have brought peace and security to Austria!

"If you are all in agreement," she replied as soon as he finished, "then what were you arguing about before I came in?"

Keinmeyer's jubilancy melted to a frown. His companions all looked to Raglan sitting at the end of the table, head down and both hands resting on the top of his staff. Elsea turned her gaze upon him as well.

"And what does my esteemed advisor, the great Lord Raglan, Count of Hohenberg, have to say about these things? Do you agree with the dear baron? Will my betrothal to the devil save my coronet? Will sacrificing my body on the altar of matrimony usher in a new golden age for Austria? Will the bards celebrate my marriage to the swine of Styria in rapturous melodies to generations yet unborn?" Though her sarcastic tone was familiar, the lack of passion in her voice robbed her words of their usual cutting power.

Raglan came to his feet with noticeable assistance from his staff. "My Lady," he began with a reluctant resignation in his voice, "I need not remind you that I have never been in favor of this particular strategy." He paused to glance at Eugene now standing by the window. "I was optimistic that we might find an ally in Bavaria instead of an enemy. Alas, all hope of that is now gone. I assure you, regardless of his motives, Otto's wrath is genuine, and he will not rest until he has laid us waste. Time is crucial. Otto could be outside Vienna in less than a month. We can expect no help from the emperor, and there will be a terrible war which we have little prospect of winning without allies. We have a pledge of protection from duke Eldridge if you will betroth yourself to him. I have served you, your father, and your grandfather faithfully my whole life, but I must warn you: none of us in this room will stand with you if you refuse to marry Eldridge. Being a duchess carries with it difficult and sometimes even loathsome responsibilities. And this, My Lady, is one of them."

Raglan returned to his seat, and all eyes looked to Elsea.

"What do I have to do?" she asked blankly.

"You have only to sign this letter we have prepared," replied Eugene quickly. "By this you will promise yourself to Eldridge, and he will pledge to you his protection. The marriage will follow his arrival in Vienna."

He laid the letter on the table and indicated to Elsea where to sign. She went to the table, took the quill from his hand, and signed her name.

Lord Eugene brought the letter around to the others to sign. Lord Raglan was the last. When Eugene put the letter before him, he paused to look up at Elsea. "Are you sure?"

"I did not know you had given me a choice," she answered.

Raglan picked up the pen and signed it.

"Is that all?" she asked.

"Yes, Your Grace," answered an elated Baron Kirchenbetter, "our meeting is concluded. We will inform Eldridge of your desire to marry. This is a great day for the House of Babenberg!"

The overjoyed Barons started toward her to offer their congratulations.

Elsea left the room.

CHAPTER FORTY-SIX

Recovery

With faltering steps, and assistance from Christa, Charles was able to leave his bed the next morning. He walked haltingly through the two rooms of their home, stretching his sore muscles like a calf set free from its stall.

After Antonie and Andre left for the fields, Kara and Christa went to work cutting pieces from a mound of freshly risen dough. They formed the sticky dough into fist-sized shapes and placed them on a board at the table. Charles sat across from them busily scooping spoonfuls of reheated dried-pea porridge from a wooden bowl. While the two women prepared their bread, they told him about their life on the manor.

The village contained only one oven capable of baking bread. There was also only one mill for grinding grain into flour. As was customary in the feudal villages, their lord owned and operated both these important structures and charged a small fee for their use.

Mother and daughter normally made the half mile trek to the bakery together once a week. Not all the women baked their bread on the same day, but there could still be a wait of several hours. Kara had heard of manors where they could bake hundreds of loaves at a time. In Longwood, they all had to wait patiently in line to use the one small oven. The village women had been complaining for years, and recently Lord Duggen had relented and promised to build a bigger oven.

In addition to the small fee to grind their flour and bake their bread, they had to pay Lord Duggen their yearly tithes, usually in the form of food, and present the customary gifts on Christmas, Easter, and Lord Duggen's birthday. Three fourths of all arable land on the manor belonged to their lord. The rest of the land was divided up among the families of the village. It was from these small plots that they were able to scratch out their meager existence. However, before they could attend to their own land, they had to work three and sometimes four days a week in Lord Duggen's fields.

It was Antonie's job to oversee this work. Duggen entrusted him with supervising the serfs. Many years ago he had been a personal servant of Lord Duggen and impressed him with his ability to read, write, and understand figures. When the previous steward of Longwood died he gave the job to Antonie. It was an important promotion as well as a great honor.

Being the steward of Longwood meant that Antonie had several advantages over his fellow serfs. For one, his home was much larger, practically palatial by village standards. Like everyone else, he still had to give his ten percent to the church, but as steward, he was exempt from paying Lord Duggen's tithe. Duggen also gave him a twenty acre parcel of ground, an enormous amount for such a small manor. More land meant more potential wealth. Yet, twenty acres was a large piece of land for one man, and it was difficult for Antonie to find the time to work it and keep abreast of his other responsibilities. Most men his age had several sons able to help with such work. Although Kara had given birth to four sons, only Andre had survived beyond his first birthday.

It was late in the afternoon when Charles was awakened from his nap by Antonie and Andre coming in from the fields.

"Where are the women?" asked Antonie.

"I guess they are still at the bakery," yawned Charles.

"It's getting close to sundown," complained Antonie. "If only Duggen would spend a little of that money we give him and build us a proper oven, baking a few loaves wouldn't take all day."

Just then, the door opened and Kara came through followed by Christa holding a basket of freshly baked bread.

Kara gave her husband a quick kiss. "The last few loaves are still hot," she said. "Is anyone hungry?"

"I'm starving!" exclaimed Andre.

"Wash the dirt from your hands," ordered his mother. "Christa, bring out what's left of that cheese—and the butter too. I think we'll use it up on this hot bread."

The five of them took seats around the table. Christa gave Charles her nicer chair and took the wobbly stool instead.

"How did things go in the field today, my husband?" asked Kara.

"Andre and I finally got the last third planted in rye," answered Antonie as he tore a piece of bread from his loaf. "And not a day too soon."

"What are you planting in the other two-thirds?" asked Charles.

"One third in clover," replied Antonie, "and I'm leaving the other third fallow."

"So you are using a three-field system," noted Charles casually as he spread some butter on his bread.

Antonie held up a slice of cheese he had just cut and gave Charles a long stare. "How do you know about these things?

"I am not sure," answered Charles, "but I think I understand farming. Next year you will rotate the crops."

"Interesting," said Antonie. "You can remember nothing of your life as a soldier, but you understand farming."

Kara gave her daughter a glance. "Perhaps Christa and I learned something today that will help you remember more."

"What is it?" asked Charles and Antonie in unison.

"Today at the oven," she began, "everyone was talking about the big uproar in Vienna last week."

"What uproar?" interrupted Antonie.

"Well," resumed Kara, "it seems there was this man," she looked at Charles, "a Bavarian, who infuriated the duchess for some reason. Theodora's cousin Eliza has a sister-in-law who lives in Vienna. She told her that the duchess flew into a rage and cut the man's head off with an axe in front of all the nobles of Austria."

"What does that have to do with me?" asked Charles.

Kara paused before replying. "Eliza's cousin's sister-in-law said his name was Charles."

"Aha," exclaimed Antonie, "so you *are* running from the duchess; that would explain why she sent a small army to find you the other day. *And* you are from Bavaria—that explains your accent."

"But he can't be *that* Charles," broke in Christa, "Elsea cut his head off."

"And I suppose you don't think it strange that another mysterious man named Charles shows up out of nowhere half-murdered?"

"But he doesn't even know the duchess," she argued.

"Or so he tells us," countered her father. He stood up, locked his hands behind his back, and began to pace. "It's all making sense now. You are from Bavaria, and you were sent here to… to…" He stopped and looked up at the ceiling for a moment and then spun around pointing at Charles, "…to assassinate the duchess!"

"Oh, Father!" pleaded Christa.

"Yet despite your clever Babenberg disguise," continued Antonie undeterred, "your plot was discovered—by the duchess herself no less. Naturally, she gave the order for your immediate execution." He stopped and faced Charles. "Do you deny it, Sir?"

"If what you say is true," replied Charles after a brief reflection, "then how did I end up here?"

"Easily explained," decided Antonie. "The duchess was sending you to Fairfield to face your well-deserved justice. Knowing that you would soon reap the bitter fruits of your crime, you made a desperate attempt to escape, but were grievously wounded before you could get away."

"But Father," blurted Andre, "those soldiers had dozens of arrows in them. If his hands were tied, how could he shoot a bow?"

"Sweetheart," added Kara softly, "why would the duchess send a man to Fairfield for an execution? The town doesn't even have a respectable jail. I only told you that story because it might explain where he is from; we certainly can't believe all of it."

"Why are you trying to defend him?" shouted the incredulous Antonie. "I tell you this man is a Bavarian assassin!"

"Theodora's cousin didn't say anything about assassins," noted Christa. "Why do you have to use such a word, Father?"

"And if he was to be executed," added her mother, "why did they leave him still alive?"

"And if they thought he was dead, why did they come back to search for him?" asked Christa.

Antonie had no response to these insightful questions.

"Come, my husband," said Kara, "finish your bread and cheese. The sun is down, and the fire needs restocking. You have another long day tomorrow and it's time for us to prepare for bed. This mystery can wait until the morning. I for one will not lose a moment's sleep worrying about Bavarian assassins."

"Besides, Father," said Christa, "Charles isn't ready to answer all these questions. Give him some more time, and he'll soon remember everything."

"Ha!" was all her father had to say.

CHAPTER FORTY-SEVEN

Fatherly Advice

Dorianne followed the servant into Bishop Prochaska's quarters. "Thank you for seeing me, Your Excellency," she said meekly.

"Of course, Dorianne," smiled Prochaska, rising to greet her. "My responsibilities as bishop keep me busy, but never so much that I cannot find time for *you*."

He offered her a rough-cut wooden stool and returned to his own overstuffed armchair.

"Tell me, is the duchess well?"

"That is the reason I've come to talk to you, My Lord. I know that you and Her Grace sometimes disagree, but I believe you are loyal to her."

She hesitated.

"What is it, my child?"

"I'm troubled for My Lady," she confessed.

"What is wrong?"

"I fear for her health, My Lord. She won't speak and barely eats, and it's all I can do to get her to leave her bed in the morning. She hasn't touched a book or gone to the battlements in over a week. I've never seen her like this before."

"Hmmm…," replied Prochaska, "perhaps we should consult the physicians."

"I have, My Lord, two days ago. One blamed the bad air in her Lady's quarters. He gave me some strange powders and said

I should burn them in her rooms to cleanse the air. We nearly choked from the smell, and I threw them out the first day. I saw no change in My Lady because of them. The other doctor said she was suffering from an imbalance of the humors. He gave me some herbs to mix into her drink, but it only made her cry all night. It pained me so to watch her."

"Many disturbing things have occurred in recent days," noted the bishop. "Her Grace has been under much strain and may only need some rest to fully recover."

"That's what I thought too, My Lord, but now I think she rests too *much*. She sleeps and sleeps, but always looks weary. I fear she'd never leave her bed were it not for my coaxing."

"Then, my dear child, I am afraid there can be only one explanation left to us." He leaned forward and added in a hushed voice, "It is clear to this old priest that Her Ladyship has been stricken with an ailment all too common among women. Though I admit I cannot explain it fully, I have often observed that the female sex find the approach of matrimony to be disconcerting. Undoubtedly, her impending marriage to Duke Eldridge is causing her anxiety."

Dorianne paused a moment to reflect upon the bishop's theory. "It's true My Lady did not wish to marry Lord Eldridge," she thought out loud.

"It is, I suppose, perfectly understandable," asserted Prochaska. "Thankfully, I can assure you that this phenomenon is always temporary, and her health will return of its own accord with the passing of a bit more time."

"Do you truly think so?"

"Yes, my dear, we need only be patient. My advice is to continue watching her closely and be ready to provide help when she is ready to receive it. I will also say a special Mass for her in the morning."

"Oh, Your Excellency, that would mean so much to me!"

"Say no more, my child," he smiled, giving her a tender pat on the head. "Now, it is late, has Your Lady eaten?"

"I was going to bring her something after I left here."

"Excellent! I think you should prepare some of her favorite food and take it to her. In my experience, a good meal is always the best tonic for even the worst of moods."

"Thank you, Your Excellency," said Dorianne as she stood to leave. "You've been very helpful."

An hour later, Dorianne set a dish of food on the table near where Elsea sat sulking in her chair. It was not much: two pieces of buttered wheat bread and a cut of cold chicken. Elsea leaned over, nibbled at the bread and pushed the chicken around the plate with her finger. After a minute or two, she slouched back in her chair, just as despondent as before.

Dorianne threw herself at Elsea's feet. "My Lady," she pleaded, "please tell me what's wrong."

Elsea's blank expression did not change at first, but as the imploring Dorianne continued to kneel before her, she hung her head. "Oh, Dori," she cried softly, "why did he have to say those things? Why did he have to make me believe he loved me? Am I so wretched? Did he hate me that much? Eugene is right: he was never more than a liar, and I should despise him for it. But instead of hating him with all my might, I love him with all my heart, and I don't know how to stop!"

Dorianne reached up and grasped her hands. "He did love you, My Lady."

Elsea yanked her hands back. "Please, Dori," she sobbed, "more lies will bring me no comfort. He could never have loved me— no one can."

"But he *did* love you," insisted Dorianne. "He told me so."

Elsea's sobbing quieted some.

"He talked to you?"

"Yes, My Lady."

"How did you, I mean…" Elsea sat up a little straighter and wiped her eyes with the back of her hand, "…*when* did you talk to him?"

"The night I went to Lady Hagen to get you that dress," explained Dorianne, "I went to Charles's quarters first."

"How did you get past the guards?"

"I told them I was there on your behalf," answered Dorianne coolly.

"What! Has everyone become a liar now?"

"It was not a lie, My Lady. What concerns you, concerns me. I saw how he was affecting you, and it was my duty to see if his feelings were sincere. So I asked him if he truly cared for you or not."

"Dorianne, one does not go around asking those kinds of questions. I am sure he was quite insulted by your impertinence."

"He wasn't insulted, My Lady. He said he loved you."

Elsea grabbed her by both shoulders.

"Did he say that?"

"Yes, My Lady. I wouldn't have said so if he didn't."

The disbelieving duchess studied her young lady-in-waiting a moment before launching into an interrogation that would have made the most zealous Spanish Inquisitor look merciful by comparison. Like an accused heretic on the rack, she forced her to confess every nuance of their conversation. What words did he use? How did he say it? What facial expressions did he show? She made her repeat her answers again and again, stopping her every few words to ask more questions. The patient Dorianne did her best to recall every detail.

When Elsea at last finished her examination, she slumped back into her seat. "Of course he told you all that, Dori. He was lying to you just like he was lying to me. Even you were beguiled; you are just too innocent to see it."

"I know he wasn't lying, My Lady, because he also told me he wasn't the real prince."

Elsea shot up out of her chair. "When did this happen?" she cried.

"The morning you sent me to tell him you had to meet with the council," answered Dorianne. "He asked for my advice."

"Now he is asking for advice! Dori, is there no end to your revelations? What advice could he possibly want from *you*?"

"He told me his real name was Charles. He said he had to pretend he was the prince so the true Prince John could escape. He asked me what he should do."

"And what did you tell him?"

"I told him he should tell you the truth before you heard it from someone else."

"Ha! It seems he was not as good at taking advice as he was at telling lies."

"No, My Lady," answered Dorianne. She then reached into her dress pocket and pulled out a folded piece of paper. "But he told me to give you this."

"What is that?"

"It's the letter he wrote."

"A letter!" exclaimed Elsea. "Is this a dream I am having? First, you tell me he was confiding in you behind my back the whole time, and now you tell me you have been hiding a letter from me. I can no longer bear the suspense, Dori. How many more surprises do you have?"

Dorianne came to her feet. "I wasn't hiding it," she declared. "He gave it to me the day the guards took him away. You know

I can't read, My Lady. I was afraid it would only upset you more, so I kept it in my pocket." She held out the letter again.

"What makes you think I want it?" asked Elsea, taking a half step back. "Why should I subject myself to anymore of his fables?" She pointed toward the fireplace. "Burn it!"

"Burn it?"

"Oh, give it to me!" Elsea grabbed the letter from her hand, crumpled it into a ball, and strode to the fireplace. She brought back her arm ready to throw it into the flames, but hesitated. "What could he possibly have said that would make any difference now?"

"Perhaps the truth," answered Dorianne softly.

"Truth," sighed Elsea. "I don't know what that is anymore."

One of the logs settled deeper into the coals with a sizzling pop.

"I don't know what those words on that paper mean," admitted Dorianne, "but if he is dead like they say, then that letter is all you have left of him."

Elsea stared a long moment at the crumpled ball in her hand. "I am going for a walk," she said finally. When Dorianne made as if she would follow, Elsea added, "Alone."

CHAPTER FORTY-EIGHT

Dreams

The servants had long since gone to bed, and only the night sentries were on duty. Still clutching the letter in her fist, Elsea glided along the quiet hallways searching for a place that offered privacy. Many of the vacant rooms she passed could have sufficed, but she walked by them without stopping.

Her unwavering course brought her to the threshold of the chapel, yet she hesitated to enter. Unlike her pious grandfather, Elsea seldom visited the small sanctuary. Apart from the occasional Sunday Mass, and the holy days when her attendance was mandatory, she avoided reminders of her spiritual emptiness.

She passed through the arched doorway and made her way to the front. The little refuge of Christianity was unpretentious, with a dozen short benches divided evenly on both sides of a narrow aisle. The frail light of a few candles illumined the marble statue of the Lord Jesus welcoming her with outstretched arms. She lit a candle from the altar and brought it with her to the first pew. For a long moment, she sat with her head bowed. Then, after taking a deep breath, she unwrinkled the crumpled letter.

My Dearest Elsea,

I have rewritten this letter many times, searching vainly for the right words to tell you the truth I have been hiding. But there is no gentle way to confess I have deceived you.

At home they think me brave, yet I fear to look into your eyes and speak the shameful truth. I owe you more than the meager words on this paper, but I have not the courage to watch your heart break.

I am not Prince John. My name is Charles, a mere knight in the prince's guard. It was because of that duty I switched clothing with His Highness to save him from capture on that day that now seems a lifetime ago. It seemed such a simple plan, such a harmless deception. How could I know I would meet someone who would conquer my heart and turn me into the most wretched of men?

There is no defending what I have done. You are the daughter of a duke. I do not even know my father's name. It was wicked of me to pretend these things do not matter and let myself hope that you might love me anyway. Instead of winning your love, I have earned your loathing. It is no less than I deserve, and I must learn to bear it, but I pray you will not let my crime embitter you, or make you despair of ever finding the happiness life has yet to give you. You have an inner strength far greater than you realize. Use that strength now to overcome my treachery and do what is best for yourself and Austria.

You still need to make a good marriage. When I return to Bavaria I will beseech Duke Otto on your behalf. I will implore him to find you a husband who will cherish you the way I had hoped to do. Though the very thought grieves me, I know another man more worthy than me must give you a son.

You were right about the poets. Their lilting lines give us but half the truth. I have learned there is another side to love, and I fear it is more than my heart can endure. I know not how I will ever get over you, but you must get over me.

For your own sake, you must make yourself forget you ever knew me.

I write these dreadful words knowing that you will soon read them and see me for the fraud that I am. It does me no good now to dream dreams that will never be. It does me no good now to wish that I owned the world if only to gladly lay it at your feet. But oh, my dearest, dearest Elsea, how I wish things could have been different. How I wish you could have been mine!

I will never forget the music of your laugh and the warmth of your smile. I will never forget the tenderness in your touch when you first put your hand in mine. I will never forget the sweet fragrance of your hair on the gentle breeze. The afternoon sun will always remind me of the gleam it brought out in your eyes. And with each full moon I will remember the night we held each other beneath its soft glow. These memories will soon be all I have of you, but I will cherish them to my grave.

I have prepared myself to lose you, but you may be certain that wherever I am, or whatever might befall me, I will never stop loving you.

Goodbye my love,
Charles

Elsea slid from the pew to the polished stone of the chapel floor. With the letter pressed to her lips, she knelt at the feet of the Lord Jesus, and wept softly, "Oh, my sweet Charles."

CHAPTER FORTY-NINE

Return of Resolve

Elsea's council crowded around a map of Austria, anxiously debating the best place to assemble the army. Elsea observed their hand wringing from her seat at the head of the table.

"We should take position as far west as possible," prescribed Baron Kirchenbetter with a dramatic sweep of his arm. "We must keep Otto out of Austria until Eldridge is able to join us."

"A noble, but naive strategy," argued Lord Eugene. "The only thing that will accomplish is to give Otto a chance to destroy the army *before* Eldridge can join us."

"No doubt you have a better idea," chimed in Keinmeyer.

"It is not a question of better, but of *best*," opined Eugene. "I propose we move to meet Eldridge and form our forces a day's ride to the south."

"That will leave everything between here and the border wide open!" gasped a stunned Kirchenbetter. "Why, Vienna itself could fall!"

"Baron Kirchenbetter," replied a more composed Eugene, "we are all aware that much of the land along the western frontier belongs to you. The Bavarians will likely wreak some havoc as they move through, but it will be inconsequential in light of the greater purpose."

"Inconsequential for you," observed Kirchenbetter. "None of

your property will be at risk. But what about the city, are you willing to sacrifice it as well?"

"Vienna will not be in jeopardy," promised Eugene. "Once Otto learns our combined armies are bearing down on him from the south he will be forced to give us battle on ground of our own choosing—assuming he does not altogether flee before us."

"Do not underestimate the duke," warned Raglan. "He is a captain of the first order, and his resources are great. Even with Styria's help, we may be no match for him."

"What if we kept our armies separate?" speculated Keinmeyer. "We could attack him from two directions simultaneously. He would not expect that."

This comment launched them all into yet more military pontifications and emphatic gesturing at the map.

"There will be no combination with Eldridge," announced Elsea over the babble.

Her lords went silent, and all eyes turned her way.

"What did you say?" asked Lord Eugene.

Elsea shifted herself in her chair. "I will not marry him," she declared casually.

Baron Kirchenbetter rolled his eyes, and Father Prochaska dropped his face into his hands. Lord Eugene looked up at the ceiling and shook his head from side to side. But for the sound of the wind whistling past the open windows, the room was quiet.

Lord Eugene was the first to regain his composure. "Your Highness," he began calmly, "your marriage to Eldridge is no longer a matter for discussion. It was settled when you signed that letter. Duke Eldridge will be here within a fortnight. If Otto has not begun his invasion by then, there will be a wedding. You have agreed to this, and there is no turning back now."

"I will not marry him," she repeated matter-of-factly.

Lord Eugene pounded the table. "You will do as you are told!"

"Do you intend to force me?" she asked, pounding the table on the word, *force*. "Will you tie me to the altar like an animal for a pagan offering?"

"Your Highness," sighed Kirchenbetter, "this is not the time for one of your tantrums. Eldridge is coming here, *with* his army. You have betrothed yourself to him, and he is expecting a marriage."

"If Eldridge comes here still expecting a marriage," she replied coolly, "it will not be my fault."

"What do you mean by that?" asked Keinmeyer.

"I have broken the betrothal. I sent him a letter by my fastest courier. I told him I would rather marry a flea-ridden dog than to spend even five minutes alone with him. I told him the only sympathy I had for his poor wife is that it took her so long to find the courage to kill herself. I told him the flames of purgatory must be a welcome relief from a husband so loathsome."

"You cannot do that," shouted Lord Eugene. "You are not allowed!"

"Not allowed?" she shouted back. "I am the duchess! Or have you forgotten that?"

"You are the duchess only because we made you one! Or have *you* forgotten *that?*"

"I assure you," she said through clenched teeth, "I will never forget what you have done to me." She stood up from her chair and looked around the table. "What a wicked and ruthless band of advisors I have! You would never have treated my father or grandfather this way. Yet me you must abuse. You cannot enjoy your own life unless mine is miserable. You even conspired to kill the only man who ever cared for me. You could not begrudge me that one small haven of comfort. Do you remember the day you each knelt before me and swore to me your loyalty? Well, where is that loyalty? I demand it now. I demand you rally to me and help save my throne from the invader. I demand it, and every one of you knows it is my right!"

She stopped to catch her breath, but said no more.

Lord Eugene, fists clenched and eyes ablaze, turned to Raglan who till now had endured Elsea's tirade looking down at the floor beneath him. "Are you just going to sit there?" he bellowed.

Raglan continued to look down at the floor for a long moment, but at last rose slowly to face her. "Your Highness," he began in a tone as calm as Lord Eugene's was agitated, "once again I stand in awe of how little you understand the impact of your impetuous conduct. To break your betrothal to Eldridge is one thing, but you did not need to insult him. He is a notoriously proud man, and there will be no mitigating this latest recklessness. Not only have you brought dishonor upon us and antagonized the only source of help we had, but you have given him justification to take by force what he expected to receive by marriage. It was uncertain whether we could fight one invader on our own. By this rash act, you may have given us a second enemy and thereby written your own death warrant. Waging war in a just cause is honorable, but this is suicide, and I will not support it."

Elsea looked to the barons. "And what of you two?"

"As usual," answered Kirchenbetter, "the count is correct in his political and military assessment. It would be madness to wage war on two fronts. I cannot, with a clear conscience, ask my knights to ride to such fruitless deaths."

"Do not speak to me of your conscience!" she barked. "Has your conscience ever prevented you from enjoying the coddled life my family gave you? Will your conscience trouble you when you break your vows to me?" She took a step back and looked around at them once more. "Is there anyone in this room who will stand with his duchess?"

The sound of a chair pushing back from the table broke the long silence that followed her challenge. Bishop Prochaska came to his feet. "I will stand with you," he said meekly. "Though I possess none of the tools of war, I will not cease to beseech the Lord of Hosts on your behalf."

"Do not be a fool, Prochaska," chided Lord Eugene. "Your pieties may suffice for a Sunday morning, but now is the time to stand like a man."

"Why, Lord Eugene," replied Prochaska confidently, "that is exactly what I am doing. We swore those oaths in the name of the Almighty. I will not be party to unholy matrimony or ungodly treason."

"Then you will be dead within a month," said Eugene.

"If God wills it, then so be it," answered the priest. He looked around at the others. "Is there anyone else who will join me?"

Lowered heads was their only answer.

Elsea stepped to the bishop's side and turned to face her rebellious council. "Very well then," she said, "you leave me no choice but to banish you from my court. I expect all of you to leave this castle before the sun goes down."

"What will you do?" asked Raglan.

"I still have my castle guard and a few loyal knights," she answered. "I will send out a call for more. My grandfather believed this castle to be impregnable. I shall soon put that to the test. Eldridge and Otto may well squabble over my bones in the end, but they shall pay a dear price for the right."

She left with Prochaska at her side.

"She has finally gone mad," growled Lord Eugene.

"If she has gone mad, then we share some of the blame," admitted Raglan.

"Are you going to let her ruin everything just when we are so close to success?"

"It seems to me everything is already ruined," noted Raglan. "We are at war with Otto, and another war with Eldridge is on the horizon. Since the council is dissolved, the duchess and her problems are no longer my concern. I am going home to await the result of these wars. The rest of you should do the same. Ere long we will know the name of our new master. Let us hope he is benevolent."

"You accept defeat too easily," pressed Eugene. "If we act now, we can still proceed as planned."

"And how is that?"

"We put the wench under arrest, of course. We marry her off to Eldridge whether she likes it or not. If we have to, we'll marry her by proxy!"

Raglan rose to his full height and glared into Eugene's face. "I may have broken my vows," he growled, "but I will never raise my hand against her. And I will not tolerate such shameful conduct in any of you. Do you understand? I will not tolerate it! She has ordered us to leave, as misguided as that may be, it is her right. I will meet each of you in two hour's time at the gatehouse. Do not be late." He brought his staff down hard on the floor. "Now go!"

Raglan glowered at the three men as they snuck from the room one by one. Once alone, he called for the captain of Elsea's guard to meet him in his quarters. A few minutes later, the young man stood before him.

"Her Grace may be in grave danger this day," warned Raglan. "You will increase the guard in her tower tenfold. No one is to see her without an escort. Shortly, Lords Keinmeyer, Kirchenbetter, Eugene, and I will be leaving the castle. You will close the gates behind us and not open them again except by explicit order of the duchess. Is that clear?"

"Yes, Lord Raglan."

"And captain," continued Raglan, "after today, you will be the only man left in the castle capable of giving Her Lady advice on military matters. Do not fail her, or you will have me to answer to."

"I will do my duty, Lord Raglan."

CHAPTER FIFTY

The Key

It had been two weeks since they found Charles face down in that field. No one expressed more surprise at his rapid healing than Sarah, though she did not seem too concerned that his memory had not returned. Her only answer to Charles's persistent questioning was to shrug her shoulders and advise more patience. Antonie's paranoia increased with each passing day, and he fervently insisted that Charles remain out of sight. Kara gave him as many menial indoor tasks as she could find, but there was a limit to how much butter he could churn, or rickety furniture he could repair. As the tedious hours crept by, he felt more and more like a fish trapped in a tidal pool longing for the open waters of the sea.

Antonie and Andre were rethatching the leaky roof over the barn. Kara was crushing up a pile of dried beans on a cutting board and scraping it into a pot stewing over the fire. Charles sat at the table, drumming his fingers, watching Christa put the final touches to a new shirt.

"What's the matter?" she asked as she pulled on her needle.

He paused before answering. "I think it is time for me to leave."

"Leave?" replied the surprised Christa. "How can you leave when you still don't know who or what you are?"

"I remember how to walk," he answered, "and that is all I need."

"But where would you go, and how would you provide for yourself? You have no money, you know."

"Perhaps I will go to Vienna."

"Vienna!" she laughed. "That's where your troubles began. I don't think going back there would be safe."

"Well, maybe Bavaria then," he tried. "If I am Bavarian, I might be able to find someone who will recognize me."

"No," she decided, shaking her head, "you simply can't go wandering all over Bavaria hoping to bump into to someone who remembers you. Who knows what sort of people you might meet? Not everyone in this world will be as kind as my family."

"But Christa," he sighed, "I cannot stay here."

"Why not? You have everything you need here: food, shelter, a doctor." She looked him in the eyes and added, "And people who care about you."

He pretended not to notice the look she gave him and turned his head away.

Christa put down her needlework and held up the light brown shirt. "It's all done," she pronounced. "Time to try it on."

He glanced down at the baggy shirt he was wearing. "What is wrong with this?"

"Don't be silly," she scolded. "That's one of father's old shirts. It's much too big on you." She proudly held up the results of her painstaking labor. "This is a proper shirt."

Charles could see further resistance was pointless, and he lifted his arms to let her help him pull off the old garment. With his arms bare, he got a better look at his arrow wound. He was pleased to see both holes had completely closed and looked healthy.

Christa interrupted his self-examination. "What's that mark on your arm?"

"What mark?"

"The one below your wound," she answered, pointing at it. "I notice it each time I change your bandage, and I've been meaning to ask you about it."

He followed her finger and found the black 'X.'

"It looks like some kind of tattoo," she noted, "but it's much too small."

The instant he saw the strange mark he knew that it meant something. He closed his eyes and once more peered into that stubborn fog. This time he saw a shape rise up: a young girl. "It is from my childhood," he said confidently. "A girl I once knew gave me this." The longer Charles focused on the girl in his memory, the more details he recalled. "I think I gave her the same mark."

"What a strange thing for children to do," declared Christa.

Charles continued to stare at the oddly familiar mark. He knew there was something more. He closed his eyes again and saw himself on a horse galloping across a sunny field. Looking deeper into the mist, he began to see someone else on horseback in front of him. Was he chasing this person? Suddenly, the other rider stopped and turned around. Charles was startled when he recognized the face. It was Elsea the day she took him to the ruins. A blaze of sunlight flooded his mind and drove the vapor of his forgetfulness away. He knew who he was. What was more—he remembered what he had done. He slumped back in his chair and hung his head.

"What is it?" cried Christa.

He took the new shirt from her hand and pulled it over his head. He knew she was waiting for an explanation, but he would not look up.

Just then, an ashen faced Antonie burst through the door.

"What has happened?" asked Kara.

"I just had a disturbing talk with Kellen the miller," he reported.

Kara came over, wiping her hands on a cloth. "What did he say?"

Antonie gave Christa and Charles a long look. "Kellen told me he met a couple of strange men yesterday."

"What was strange about them?" asked Christa.

"They claimed to be coopers coming from another town looking for work," explained Antonie.

"That doesn't sound so strange," said Christa.

"Well, Kellen just happened to need a couple of barrels repaired," continued Antonie. "He offered to pay to them good money to have them fixed, but they refused."

"Maybe they didn't have time just then," suggested Kara.

"Maybe so, but according to Kellen, they had plenty of time to ask a lot of questions."

Peculiar men asking questions got the attention of Charles, and he stood up from his chair. "What kind of questions?"

"They wanted to know all about that night we found you," answered Antonie. "They asked him if he had seen a strange man in a white shirt."

Christa gasped. "What did Kellen tell them?"

"Nothing," said Antonie. "He didn't know what they were talking about. But that's not all—Kellen said his nephew saw the same two men in Fairfield just this morning. Only there, they said they were *blacksmiths* looking for work."

"What could it mean?" wondered Kara. "Are they working for the duchess?"

"No," said Charles. "They are working for Lord Eugene."

"How do you know this?" demanded Antonie.

Christa interrupted his answer. "He remembers something," she said quietly.

Charles did not contradict her.

"Come man," blurted Antonie, "don't be so mysterious."

"I am indeed from Bavaria," he explained, not sure how much he should tell them, "but I am no assassin. I serve Duke Otto and have lived in his castle since I was a boy. A few weeks ago, I was part of a raid across your border. We were ambushed, and I was taken prisoner," he looked at Antonie and added, "by Lord Eugene."

"Is that how you ended up in Vienna?" asked Christa.

"I was kept prisoner there until they decided to send me to Styria. We were attacked along the way, and I believe Lord Eugene was behind it."

Antonie grabbed his head with both hands. "Don't tell me you made an enemy of Lord Eugene!"

"I am afraid so," admitted Charles, "and if he believes I am still alive then your family is in danger."

"A fatted calf at Christmas has a longer life than that man's enemies," moaned Antonie.

"Then I must leave at once," said Charles. "I am well enough to travel, but I need a horse."

"Where will you go?" asked Kara.

"Bavaria."

"What about Eugene's spies?" asked Antonie. "They might be watching the roads."

"I will travel at night and stay clear of the roads during the day. You will be safe after I am gone. If anyone asks about me, you only need pretend to be as ignorant as Kellen."

Christa slipped from the circle and slumped down on Andre's bed in the corner.

"I have nothing to pay you with," said Charles to Antonie, "but I cannot make it without a horse. Can you help me?"

"Yes, Father," said Christa quietly from across the room, "you must help him." It was more of an order than a request.

"I've got only one horse up to the kind of riding you'll be doing," replied Antonie. "She may not be fast, but she's as strong as any ox."

Charles, Christa, Andre, and Kara stepped out into the moonless night and met Antonie coming from the barn leading his mare behind him. Antonie gave the animal a tender pat on the neck and handed the reins to Charles. Christa held up a cloth bag. "Mother and I put what we could in there," she said. "If you are careful, it should last you three days."

Charles took the bag from her, tied it to the saddle, and then turned to embrace them one by one. He wrapped his arms around Christa last. "I owe you my life," he whispered in her ear, "and I shall miss you most of all. I am sorry I am not what you hoped I would be."

"You were always what Father said you were," she said looking up at him, "a bird with a broken wing that needed mending." She stepped back from him and placed an arm around her mother's waist. "Remember us well," she said.

Charles climbed onto his horse. "Which way to Bavaria?" he asked.

Antonie pointed down the road "You ride north for a while," he explained, "and turn west at the third crossroads you come to. It's not the fastest route, but you'll avoid the big towns. If you ride all night, you'll hit the main road to Bavaria by sunrise."

Charles looked around one last time at his adopted family.

"Thank you and farewell my friends," he said with a large smile. "I shall not forget your kindness."

He gently nudged the horse into a canter and disappeared into the gathering night.

CHAPTER FIFTY-ONE

One Condition

As he traveled alone through the dark, Charles rehearsed over and over that fateful week. Though her last words still cut his heart afresh, he made himself remember how she had held him that night when his dreams were still as real as the feel of her beating heart. That was the moment he knew she loved him, and he clung to that memory throughout the lonely night.

His concern over spies and malevolent men lurking in the shadows proved unfounded. Antonie's route helped him avoid the larger towns, and he passed unnoticed through the occasional villages he encountered. Except for a few brief naps below the trees on the side of the road, he continued west without stopping.

Early the third day, he came upon a quaint Bavarian village bustling with people going about their morning routines. The familiar accents and the welcoming faces that smiled up at him brightened his spirits, and he at last felt he was home. As he trotted away from the friendly strangers, a few puffy clouds floated above him, and the warming rays of the morning sun cheered him even more.

Eventually, the road he was on began to rise to a point on a low ridge. He knew when he got to the top he would be able to see into the wide valley beyond. In his eagerness to get there, he put his horse into a gallop and quickly reached the summit. What he saw caused him to bring the mare to a skidding stop.

He expected to see the small village straddling the stream that ran through the vale. Instead, spread out before him was a city of tents. Above the makeshift town floated the colorful banners of a score of Bavarian houses. Lavishly dressed knights covered the camp like a swarm of locusts. Smoke curling up from a hundred campfires formed a low-lying cloud that hung like a canopy over the men, horses, carts, and wagons. He knew there could be only one explanation for such a gathering.

An unknown man on horseback looking down on the camp drew the attention of the pickets, and soon four riders were heading up the road. "Who are you?" the lead rider shouted.

Charles waited until they came to a stop in front of him. "My name is Sir Charles," he reported with a beaming smile. "I am a knight of the prince's guard."

The leader of the squad gave his homespun shirt and farm horse a long look. "A knight, eh? You look like you just left your plow."

"Looks can be deceiving," replied Charles, still trying to smile. "Is Duke Otto here?"

"Hold on there," said the leader. "I'm the one asking the questions. Who did you say you were?"

Charles took a deep breath. "As I have said, my name is Sir Charles, I am a knight of Bavaria, and I serve Prince John."

"The only knight I know named Charles was killed in Austria a month ago."

"Well, as you can see, I am not quite dead. Now, please escort me to the duke."

"Isn't he a cheeky one?" laughed the soldier to his comrades. "Do you think we just let any peasant that can steal a plow horse ride in and chat with His Grace pretty as you please?"

Charles was quickly losing patience with his skeptical inquis-itor and had to remind himself the man was only doing his duty. After all, his story did sound farfetched. It occurred to him that it was easier to convince the nobles of Austria he was Prince John, than his own people he was Charles. Finally, an idea struck him.

"Is Sir William here?" he asked.

At the name of William, the man's expression changed. "You know Sir William?"

"Of course I do—I serve with him in the prince's guard. If you send for him, he can vouch for my identity."

He gave Charles another long look and then nodded at one of the other men. The rider wheeled his horse and took off down the road.

A few minutes later, Charles saw William galloping up the hill, lashing his horse hard the whole way.

"Charles," William called out. "Charles, is that you?"

"In the flesh, old man," Charles called back.

The two men jumped down from their horses and embraced each other in the road.

"I can't believe it!" exclaimed William. "They told us you were dead."

"I probably should be," admitted Charles, rubbing the back of his head.

"Oh, the duke will be overjoyed! He was quite beside himself when we got the report you'd been killed."

"What's going on?" asked Charles, pointing to the valley.

"Haven't you heard?" replied William with a slap on his back. "We're going to war!"

"With whom?"

"With Austria, of course. We're going to root out that witch once and for all. Why, I wouldn't be surprised if the duke has her properly burned at the stake."

William smiled widely at his prediction, but the look on Charles's face was less than jovial. "What's wrong?"

"Nothing," said Charles, "but it is vital that I see Duke Otto at once."

Inside the duke's tent, Otto, Savoyen, and Prince John were at a table finishing a late breakfast. The entrance of the two men threw them into a tumult of jubilation mixed with astonishment. Charles shook hands all around and embraced everyone. The emotional response of the duke, however, caught him by surprise. Otto hugged him far longer than appropriate, and Charles was certain he saw tears in his eyes.

The duke called for more food and made Charles sit down with them. The excited men all talked at once and begged him to tell of his adventure. Between mouthfuls of cold duck and long drafts from his mug, Charles regaled them with the story of his capture and his stay in the castle leaving out all but the most unavoidable references to Elsea. As he described how his simple ruse had fooled the greatest nobles in Austria the men pounded the table and roared with laughter.

They were especially interested to hear how he had come back from the dead. Charles recounted the night of the ambush and the Austrian family that saved his life. He made sure to emphasize Lord Eugene's role in his near demise, but made no mention of the duchess.

"Eugene's head will be the first one I lift," promised Otto. "After, that is, I lay that she-devil in her grave."

Everyone but Charles grunted his approval.

"This will be my first war!" proclaimed Prince John. "Father has given me and William command of the advance guard. Why, we might win this war all on our own."

"How is that?" asked Charles.

"The Babenberg beast is a worse general than she is a duchess," answered the smiling prince. "Our scouts tell us she still has not even put an army in the field. The road to Vienna is wide open! You must come with us, Charles, after, of course, you pay your respects to your dearly departed mother."

"My son," whispered Otto with a shake of his head.

"What has happened to my mother?"

"I should have told you," apologized William, "but I forgot in all the excitement."

"What has happened?" repeated Charles.

Savoyen reached across the table and put a hand on his shoulder. "We are all very sorry, Charles. Her illness worsened suddenly a few days after you disappeared, and she died unexpectedly."

"I knew it!" moaned Charles. "She tried to pretend she was not so ill, but I knew it."

"If it is any comfort to you," offered Otto, "I am told she passed on without pain and surrounded by those who cared for her."

"I should not have left her," lamented Charles. "There was something important she was going to tell me. Did she leave anything for me: a note or message of some kind?"

Savoyen gave Otto a subtle glance before answering with a straight face, "None that we know of."

"But Father Bernard found her the most peaceful place right near the old church," added the duke quickly. "When this Austrian affair is over, I will take you there."

An uncomfortable silence followed.

"My Lord," said Charles, "I wish to speak with you regarding a matter of great importance to me." He glanced at John and William and added, "In private."

Otto turned to the prince. "We will be leaving shortly, my son. It would be prudent for you and William to make one last sweep through the camp and report back to me on the readiness of the army."

Once they were gone, the duke slid his chair a little closer.

"My Lord, you must call off this invasion," blurted Charles.

"Call it off!" exclaimed Otto. "We have been assembling for ten days. We are striking tents as we speak, and we will cross the border before sundown. It cannot be called off now."

"But Elsea is not your enemy."

"If she is not my enemy, then I know not what the word means."

"I tell you, My Lord, there is no cause for this war."

"I think ridding the world of that wretch is cause enough," declared Otto.

"But what has she done to deserve your wrath?" pleaded Charles.

"A long summer's day would not suffice to list all her indiscretions."

Charles opened his mouth but Otto hurried on, "Besides, this war is no longer about my wrath or the Babenbergs' hapless last heir."

He gave Savoyen a nod.

"We have learned that Eldridge is preparing his own invasion," interjected the duke's counselor. "It seems she has dishonored him in some way, and he intends to have his vengeance. We are going into Austria if for no other reason than to take it before *he* does. Vienna is too valuable a prize to stand idly by and let slip through our fingers."

"But Eldridge is not strong enough to take Austria," argued Charles.

"Young man," countered Savoyen with a wry smile. "Austria no longer exists."

"What nonsense is this?" asked the stunned Charles.

"The House of Babenberg has at long last fallen," explained the duke. "Elsea has not assembled her army because she does not have one. Her nobles have deserted her."

"How can they abandon their lady in her hour of greatest need?"

"Why are you so surprised?" asked Otto. "The monster has managed to alienate everyone from page to Pope. It was but a matter of time before even her own people forsook her."

"My Lord, I wish you would not speak so harshly of her in my presence. I know her, and she is no monster."

"You seem to have developed a sudden concern for this woman," observed Otto. "There is not a man from one end of the Empire to the other who has a kind word for her, yet you spend a fortnight in her dungeon and return to tell us we are all mistaken. What sort of witchcraft has she worked on you?"

"There was no witchcraft, My Lord. I have been in her castle and have seen her struggle. She is a victim of the very men who swore to protect her. She rules Austria no more than I rule Bavaria."

"Did you hear that, Savoy?" asked the incredulous Otto. "She is a victim. She has made enemies of every prince in Germany, but it is not her fault—she is a victim!"

"It is true she has made mistakes," allowed Charles. "She is perhaps too proud and too impetuous, but she will listen to reason. I beg you, My Lord, call off this invasion. She may very well be in this predicament because of me."

"I do not care if she renounces all sin and joins a convent," groaned Otto. "Her newly found virtues will not stop the Styrian army. But even if Eldridge was to disappear in a puff of smoke, there is still Hechen and Lichten to consider. My so-called brothers-in-law have been pressuring me for this war since the day she snubbed me and refused to become my vassal. They are like two hounds baying to be let loose from their leashes. They smell the blood on the trail. To refuse them now when the prey is nearly in their jaws would risk a civil war, and you have no right to ask that."

Alas, Charles had no reply.

"Come now," said the duke in a gentler tone. "Let us talk no more of that woman and her endless problems. Lord Savoyen and I are eager to give you more cheering news."

Charles lifted his head. "What news?"

"We have at last found a way to reward your faithful service to the prince."

"What way is that, My Lord?"

A smile exploded across Otto's face. "We have arranged a most excellent marriage for you!"

"A marriage?" stammered Charles.

"Yes," said Otto clapping his hands before him, "and a brilliant one at that."

"But, My Lord, I am not ready for marriage."

"You will be after you hear the details," replied Otto. "Is that not so, Savoy?"

"It is indeed a spectacular marriage," agreed an enthusiastic Savoyen. "You will be the envy of every man in Bavaria. Do you remember that cute little Marie?" He did not wait for an answer. "Well, she is all grown up. You recall her father, Baron Scheindlin, had no sons. He has consented to let you marry his daughter. What is more, upon his death you will inherit his title and all the land that goes with it. Soon you will not only be a baron, but a *wealthy* baron!"

"And Marie is no small catch," added Otto quickly. "She is a remarkably attractive woman now. She was quite in favor of the proposal and was most distraught when we heard you had been killed."

Both Otto and Savoyen grinned widely in anticipation of Charles's heartfelt gratefulness. "Well, do not tell her I am alive," said Charles. "I will not marry her!"

"What!" exclaimed the two old men.

Charles got up from his chair and stood with shoulders back. "I cannot think of my own happiness as long as Her Grace is in peril."

"Now I know she has bewitched you!" exclaimed Otto.

"I am under no spell," insisted Charles. "If she is in danger, then I must help her."

"What help can you give her? She has two armies bearing down on her, and her own people have deserted her. This is the talk of a madman! Next you will tell me you are going to scale the Alps and command the spring snow to stop melting."

"My mind has never been clearer, My Lord. All I ask is that you let me return to Vienna."

The duke let out an exaggerated groan and shot Savoyen a frowning look. After a brief pause to regain his composure, he motioned for Charles to return to his seat.

"Charles," he began calmly, "you have always been wiser than your years. Please try to think wisely now. You have come through a vexing ordeal: you have been imprisoned, starved, shot, beaten and left for dead. Until a few days ago you could not even remember your own name. You have spent three days and three nights in the saddle without proper food or sleep. And if these things were not enough, you just learned that your dear mother has passed before you could tell her goodbye. Any one of these things might have broken a lesser man, and you are not to be blamed if your emotions are stirred and your judgment is clouded. I ask you, therefore, to consider carefully what you are turning down—a beautiful wife, wealth, comfort—all the things that can make one happy. What will you gain by this foolish venture you propose, but an unmarked grave in a strange land for a woman undeserving of the least of your passing thoughts?"

Charles sat with his head down as he pondered the duke's counsel. "I never knew my father," he said at last, "but my mother was kind and beautiful. She made herself sick from fretting over me, but she taught me the meaning of love. I have often wondered what sort of man could have walked away from such a woman, and I used to despise him for it. But what if he had to make the same choice I now face today? What if he had to choose between his ambition and the woman he should have loved? I wonder if he ever regretted his decision. I am grateful you think me worthy of this honor, but there is someone in Austria dearer to me than any wealth or comfort. I must help her if I can or live the rest of my life in regret. I know you think this unwise, My Lord, but perhaps there is a time when being wise is the best thing, but not the right thing."

Otto slumped back in his chair.

Savoyen stepped between the two men. "Charles, you cannot help her without going to war against your own duke. Will you betray the very man who reared you from a child and gave you everything you have?"

"I will not need to, My Lord, if His Highness will grant me two requests."

"What are they?" asked a solemn Otto.

"You said that the threat of Eldridge and pressure from Hechen and Lichten were forcing this war upon you."

Otto nodded.

"What if I can both rid you of Eldridge and give you the victory your in-laws demand?"

"And how will you accomplish this extraordinary feat?"

"First, you must give me time to defeat Eldridge," said Charles.

"Time?"

"If you cannot prevent the invasion, at least slow it down."

"I told you—we are already breaking camp."

"Begin your invasion as planned," suggested Charles, "but proceed slowly. Make frequent camps along the way. Stop to pillage every hamlet you come across. Sweep the countryside of livestock. Use any excuse, but give me time. Once you cross the border, Hechen and Lichten cannot debate your tactics. You are the duke, and you may wage war as you please. What is it to them how long it takes you to get to Vienna?"

"Even if we proceed at the speed of a tortoise, what good will that do you? Eldridge will reach Vienna before the month is out. He cannot be allowed to take the city. What is your plan to stop him?"

"I have none," admitted Charles, "but I will think of one."

"Ah, you will think of one," repeated Otto. "And without an army, or even a plan for one, you will turn back Eldridge with a supple flick of the wrist. But when I reach Vienna my in-laws will expect a victory."

"You will have that victory without fighting a battle," vowed Charles, "if you will grant me my second request."

"And what must I do to achieve this bloodless victory?"

"Elsea will never be secure until she can find a suitable husband," Charles answered. "She must marry into a respectable noble family. You need a victory and Elsea needs a husband. Find her that husband, My Lord, and I will give you your victory."

"You ask a difficult thing, Charles: you are asking me to save her."

"Is destroying her so important that you will not consider another way? There is no dishonor in a marriage alliance. The princes of Germany make these arrangements all the time. It was the basis of your own marriage. How difficult will it be to find her some worthy noble or distant relative? Your march through Austria will be one long triumphal procession. When you reach Vienna, Elsea will meet you on bended knee. You may make any stipulations you wish, demand any concessions you please, only let her keep her throne and her dignity. Surely, Hechen and Lichten cannot object to that."

"She is too stubborn," warned Otto. "She refused my help once before."

"I will persuade her, My Lord," promised Charles.

The skeptical duke looked up at Savoyen. "Well, what do you think?"

Savoyen rubbed the back of his head. "Any plan that depends on defeating the Duke of Styria with a phantom army is to be counseled against, My Lord."

"I am talking about the alliance, Savoy."

"My Lord, our plan rests on a quick strike to take Vienna. If Eldridge gets there before we do, it will mean a long and bloody siege, and who knows how many other princes will decide to get involved? Why, the Emperor himself might move against us. This is too great a risk for a theoretical alliance."

"But what if Eldridge never gets to Vienna?" pressed Otto.

Savoyen shrugged his shoulders and let out a loud sigh. "Well, the boy's idea does have *some* merit," he conceded reluctantly. "A marriage alliance would be more advantageous politically. The Emperor would have no legal claim against it, and a peaceful resolution of our dispute with Austria would be well received in Rome. If Charles is indeed able to succeed with that woman where heretofore all other mortal men have failed, we would achieve all our goals without the loss of a single life and gain the blessing of the Pope for good measure."

Duke Otto sat back in his chair, slowly stroking his beard. The only sound came from the neighing horses and shouting men outside. "Lord Savoyen is correct," he admitted finally. "This is a great risk, Charles. If Eldridge takes Vienna, it will be the undoing of all our plans." Before Charles could offer up a protest, Otto continued, "If I do this, she must win this war on her own. She must prove she deserves to wear the crown you want me to save. Marriage or no marriage, I will not ally myself with a disgraced duchess."

Charles tried not to let his relief be too obvious. "I understand, My Lord."

"In that case," continued Otto, sitting up again, "I will do all you ask. I will slow the army down, and I will find a suitable match for the Austrian Duchess." He stopped before adding, "On one condition."

"Name it, My Lord."

"After this crisis has passed, and assuming the two of you live through it, there will be two weddings: Elsea will marry into my family, and you will marry Scheindlin's daughter."

Otto's unexpected proposal gave Charles pause, but what choice did he have? "What you offer is more than I deserve, My Lord, and I will do all that you ask."

"It is settled then," said Otto. "Though I feel in my bones you will come to harm on this reckless quest, we will argue no more." He called for the guard. "But you will have no reason to fear highway bandits this time. You are on a mission for the duke, and so you will have a duke's escort."

The guard entered the tent. "You called, My Lord?"

"You will take Sir Charles to the stables," ordered Otto. "Let him pick out any horse he wants. Then take him to the armory and make sure he is properly clothed and equipped. And send for Sir William."

"Yes, My Lord."

Otto gave Charles a long embrace. "You have grown into an honorable man, and I wish you Godspeed. Upon my soul, I have never known anyone more worthy of His protection."

"Thank you, My Lord," said Charles. Before turning to leave, he added, "I will meet you in Vienna."

William entered the tent to find the duke finishing the final lines of a letter. He sprinkled some sand upon the paper, rolled it, and handed it to William. "I am sending you on a mission to Vienna."

"A mission, My Lord?"

"I want you to handpick two dozen knights and escort Charles through Austria. When you arrive in Vienna, he will present this letter to the duchess. This is a secret undertaking, and I have placed Charles in charge. Do you understand?"

"Completely, My Lord," replied William with a bow.

Otto left the table and came around to him. "William," he said in a lower voice, "You know how rash Charles can be at times. I fear he may needlessly expose himself to danger. I am very fond of the boy…" He could not finish.

William straightened himself to his full height. "I will surround him with twenty-four of the best knights in Bavaria and protect him with my own life if need be," he promised.

Otto shook William's hand. "Thank you, Sir William, your confidence provides me much comfort."

William left, and only Savoyen and the duke remained in the tent.

"You are taking a great gamble," noted Savoyen.

"Yes," agreed Otto, "and you of all people should know why."

CHAPTER FIFTY-TWO

Love's Orphan

Elsea slouched in her chair staring at the many books and parchments crowding the shelves of her walls. The ancient tomes were the leavings of some of the greatest minds of the classical world. Many of the mildewed volumes were the only copies known to exist, and their value was beyond measure.

However, their worth in gold was not why Elsea treasured them so. The thoughts and ideas of men long dead provided her a doorway to escape the perpetual despair of the land of the living. Over the years she had read all of them. Some were her favorites, and she would return to them often, plunging herself into a world of distraction however temporary and artificial it might be. But today nothing would do.

Scanning the stacks again, her eyes came to rest on a small chest tucked into the corner of a bottom shelf. She got up and retrieved the dust covered box and returned to her chair. Because she knew what was inside that box, she hesitated to open it. After a long moment, she lifted the lid and placed her hand on the only book in her library she had never read.

The book was a pristine hardbound volume that seemed immune to the ravages of moth or mold. She placed it in her lap and cautiously opened the cover. The vellum pages were filled with a beautifully flowing Latin manuscript centered between skillfully illuminated margins. Leafing her way through the pages, she found twenty-seven different sections, each with its own unique title and miniature gold and silver laced drawing. She turned back to the first page which read: *"The Gospel According to Saint Matthew."*

For the next three days, Elsea read and reread this book. Hour after hour she would study it, stopping only occasionally to rush through a meal Dorianne had brought before getting back to her chair and the next chapter. Her daily promenades along the battlements were now replaced with visits to the chapel. Even then, she took the book with her, clutching it to her chest like a fragile vessel of the finest glass. Late into the night she bent over the book, reading by the lamps and candles Dorianne kept freshly burning. When she could no longer keep her eyes open, she would carefully return the book to its box as if laying a sleeping infant in its cradle before staggering off to bed.

Throughout the course of those few days, Elsea and Dorianne hardly spoke. Grateful that Elsea was at least reading again, Dorianne was careful not to interrupt her. By the morning of the fourth day however, her curiosity overcame her caution.

"My Lady," she began as she set Elsea's breakfast beside her, "I've noticed you've been reading that same book all week."

Elsea closed the book and stood up to stretch herself. "It is the Bible," she answered with the widest of smiles, "or at least the New Testament."

"The Bible!" exclaimed Dorianne as she crossed herself. "I'm sorry for disturbing you, My Lady."

"Do not be so silly," laughed Elsea. "I am the one who should be sorry for ignoring you, Dori. That was very rude of me."

"You are never rude to me, My Lady."

"Well then, I should not have been so secretive. But this book has captivated me like no other, and the hours have flown by so quickly that I do not even know what day it is."

"It is Thursday," answered Dorianne, then added quickly, "You seem to have read the book many times already, My Lady."

"Indeed I have, Dori. There are things I confess are too deep for me to comprehend, and yet there is even more so simple that a child could understand. I see something fresh with each reading, and I feel I cannot get enough."

Dorianne's only reply was a puzzled look.

Elsea returned to her chair and motioned for Dorianne to sit beside her. She pointed at the shelves lining the walls around them. "Those books gave me insight into things I had not known, or even thought about before. The ideas in them intrigued me, but deep down I was never sure if I could trust them. I cannot explain it, Dori, but this book is different. These words are different: they are not the opinions of men, but the very words of God Himself, and I feel in my soul these words have the power to change me."

"But the priests give us God's words each week, My Lady."

"I used to think so too, but now that I have read this book for myself I can see how much they leave out."

"But what is there to leave out, My Lady?"

A now animated Elsea repositioned herself in her chair. "For one thing, they teach us to obey God because we fear Him; that if we are good to Him, He will be good to us. They teach us to fear hell, but never to love heaven. This book says I should obey God because He loves me. Do you see how important that is, Dori? I never before realized the depth of our Savior's love. He never caused harm, or uttered a lie. He cared not for wealth or comfort. Everywhere He went the people thronged Him, but He turned none away. He healed them, fed them, raised their dead, gave sight to their blind, and taught them the words of life. He walked among them as God because He was God. And all He asked in return was for them to believe Him. But instead, they mocked and scorned Him. And when He stood before the judge the very people He came to save cried, 'Crucify Him!' Even His closest friends forsook Him. Still, after all that, He prayed God to forgive them. Jesus died not because He was wrong, but because we were wrong. Even now He offers us forgiveness if we will but ask for it. Forgiveness, Dori, that is what I need; that is what I have always needed."

"But the priests offer us His forgiveness, My Lady."

"Yes, I have knelt before them too, Dori, but their words of blessing gave me no comfort. I knew I was a hypocrite and always left with more guilt then when I came. I need the forgiveness only God can give. I have been such a wicked person for far too long. Raglan always told me I was the source of my own misery. Even Charles, who knew me so briefly, could see that. I have wasted my life on a resentment and bitterness that robbed me of ever knowing joy.

"But I see things so clearly now. I used to think I had lost God, but now I see He never lost me. He may not have given me a father who loved me, but He gave me a mother who did. My council may have despised me, but did I not give them good reason? I complained that I had no friends, and yet you have been the truest friend anyone could ever hope for. I blamed God for abandoning me like an orphan, with no one to love me, but the one person that could have made my life bearable is gone from me because I could not control my pride. If only I had said no to Eugene's wicked scheme! Thank God you kept that letter, Dori. I would have gone to my grave wondering if that whole week was only make-believe. But now I know he loved me. He loved me when I was unlovable, and he made me feel beautiful when all the world made me feel ugly. How can I blame him for lying to me when I would tell a thousand lies this very minute if I thought it could bring him back? It is a shame I understand all this only now."

"I'm glad you're not upset with him anymore, My Lady. I still believe he was an honorable man."

"Yes, Dori. He was as honorable as I was dishonorable."

The two women fell silent for a moment.

"I will not be leaving this castle alive," declared Elsea at last. "Lord Raglan was right: I have written my own death warrant."

"Is it wise to stay here?" asked Dorianne. "Can't we go someplace safer?"

"You mean run away," said Elsea. "I will not pretend I have not considered it. Yet where would I go, and who would help me? Outside of Prochaska there is no one in Austria willing to risk his own welfare to save me. Raglan wearied himself trying to get me to see my place in history. He would not let me forget that my family has ruled Austria for over a hundred years. Whether it is fair or not, he would say, I am a Babenberg and therefore responsible for my family's legacy. For the first time in my life I appreciate that duty, and I will not run from it. If I do not survive this war, I will at least die as a Babenberg should. I will bring no more shame upon my family."

At Dorianne's look of dejection, Elsea smiled brightly. "Come now, Dori," she laughed, "I fear I have been too morose. Let us think on happier things. Let us go below and see what delicacies the cook is no doubt hiding in his cupboards. While we eat, I will read you some of these precious words. I cannot remember ever feeling so hungry, and yet so glad to be alive."

CHAPTER FIFTY-THREE

Intrigue

Side by side, Charles and William led the trotting column of Bavarians as they clattered across the stone bridge. The sun had already set behind them, but Charles insisted they keep riding. "We will stop for a brief rest at midnight," he promised William, "but then we must press on."

William gave a long whistle. "Are we to gallop all the way to Vienna?"

"We do not have much time," explained Charles to his big friend. "I am sorry the duke got you involved. This was supposed to be my affair."

"Have no regrets my young protégé. I should be thanking you for saving me from having to hold the prince's hand in the advance guard. Besides, your *affair* sounds more intriguing."

"Dangerous is more like it," said Charles.

"Since when did delivering letters become dangerous?" William pulled a small leather pouch from around his neck and handed it to Charles who slung it over his shoulder without opening it.

"Aren't you even curious to see what it says?"

"I already know," answered Charles. "Duke Otto is proposing an alliance with Austria."

"An alliance you say? Hmmm, well, I never pretended to understand diplomacy mind you, and I may not be as shrewd as

Lord Savoyen, but if the duke wants an alliance, why is he going to war?"

"I did not say he *wants* an alliance," pointed out Charles. "I was able to convince him to *propose* one."

"And just how was my former squire, recently risen from the dead, able to do that?"

"It was difficult," admitted Charles, "but not as difficult as it will be convincing the duchess to accept it."

"No doubt persuading the duke has filled you with confidence to persuade the notorious duchess herself. Good luck to you in that regard, my friend."

"Let us say I have a certain insight with Her Grace."

"And if *Her Grace* succumbs to your charming powers of persuasion, there'll be no war?"

"At least not with Bavaria—she will still need to defeat Eldridge."

William gave another whistle. "Yet another duke! I tremble to ask what he has to do with our affair."

"The great hog has a mind to take Vienna for himself," answered Charles.

"Why Charles, you are a bottomless well of information. How do you know all these things?"

"The duke told me."

"The duke told you! What a remarkable career you have found for yourself these days: an ambassador to duchesses, and a confidant of dukes. Is there anything else I should know?"

"Nothing too important," replied Charles with a half-smile. "Except that it is up to us to stop Eldridge and save Vienna."

William spun himself around in his saddle and looked back at the other knights in the company. "That explains why the duke told me to take these men. You, me, and our faithful band, are to drive Eldridge into the Danube and restore peace to the world!" He gave his thigh a slap. "You see, I told you your affair was more intriguing."

"I wish it were that easy," sighed Charles. "I do not even have a plan of battle to present to the duchess."

"Ah yes, the very duchess with which you have a certain insight," noted William. "Well, if it's a battle plan you need, at least you're talking to the right person." He placed a fist under his chin pretending to be deep in thought.

Charles could not keep from smiling.

"I have it!" he exclaimed, pointing a finger to the sky. "We advise the beleaguered duchess to gather her army, sally forth, and give that fat old man a sound thrashing. You and I can relax back at her palace eating venison roasted in garlic and onions twice a day until it's all over. There you have it: a plan as simple as it is profound. Lord Savoyen would be sick with envy."

"I forgot how entertaining you can be," laughed Charles.

"It's good to hear you laugh again," returned William. "You've been much too serious since your return."

"I suppose I have had a lot on my mind," agreed Charles. "But if I may continue to be much too serious a moment longer, there is another secret I have for you: the duchess has no army—her nobles have deserted her."

"In what kind of a world do nobles desert their duchess?"

"Suffice it to say they are not as noble as one might suppose. We must find a way to help her without them, and I was hoping you had some ideas."

"How does one win a war without an army?" wondered William out loud. "That's a difficult riddle indeed. Maybe you should tell me more about this Elsea and her wretched nobles. Perhaps between the two of us we can arrive at a solution."

For the next hour, Charles confided all he knew to his friend.

"So," began William when he had finished, "I let you out of

my sight for a few weeks and you fell in love with the Duchess of Austria?"

"Guilty," confessed Charles.

"And now you must convince her to marry a stranger, find her an army, and win her a war."

"I think you have summed it up adequately."

"You've made quite a mess of things, young man."

"Did I not tell you so?"

"And after the dust settles, you'll marry little Marie?"

Charles looked down at his saddle. "That is what I told the duke."

"Splendid! I think marriage would suit you most agreeably," opined William. "As for me, well, I don't believe matrimony and I are quite compatible. I'm a man of war, not love. I can teach you the graceful poetry of the short sword, long sword, axe, mace, club, lance, longbow, crossbow, knife and dagger. But when it comes to marriage, I'd be all thumbs; women are just too confusing."

"Have you never considered it?"

"I confess the thought recently crossed my mind. While you were falling in love with this Austrian woman, the prince and I met a strange fellow on our way through Frioul. His wife treated him tolerably well, and he seemed happy enough. Perhaps when I'm too old for all these exploits I too shall retire to that little fief of mine and find a sweet woman to bring me my hot soup on cold nights."

"You might find you would enjoy it."

"Maybe so, but I'm not ready for the quiet home life just yet. I enjoy my freedom too much. Take this morning for example: the duke says to me, 'William, gather a handful of knights and follow Charles to the gates of hell.' Without a second thought, I say, 'At once, Your Highness.' I scoop up my armor, buckle on my sword, and clamber onto my horse. I didn't have to make any long goodbyes to a teary wife or clinging children. Look at me now; because I have no one at home to worry about, I am free to concentrate on things like rescuing this duchess of yours."

"The birds of the sky must envy you indeed," remarked Charles.

"Now let's look at you," continued William. "What good has all this love nonsense done for you? You're obsessed with a woman you can't marry, on your way to talk her into marrying another man she doesn't even know. No wonder I can hardly get a smile out of you."

"I understand the appeal of the carefree life," replied Charles. "What you cannot understand is my viewpoint. I have discovered the joy of living to please someone besides myself. It has changed me, and I feel more alive than ever."

"What you call *alive* sounds worse than death by plague. I've never seen you so gloomy. I only hope I don't come down with it. Now, tell me this, my friend: who was it that took you under his wing and raised you from a pup when Duke Otto brought you in from the cold and said, 'Make a knight of him'?"

"You did," said Charles.

"And who was it that taught you the truly important things in life, like how to sharpen a blade, shoe a horse, or start a fire in the rain?"

"You again."

"And in all those years did I ever give you reason to doubt the wisdom of my philosophical views?"

"Not that I recall," smiled Charles.

"Well, I know even less about love than I do about diplomacy, but allow me to offer some advice on that subject."

"Offer away."

"You don't want to get mixed up with this duchess, love or

no love. You see, you and I are common men. The blood flowing through our veins is untainted by any trace of nobility. We understand the peasants because we are one of them. Give us a full belly at night, a warm bed under a roof that doesn't leak too much, and we can't be happier. These dukes and duchesses aren't like us. They spend their days fretting over palace plots and unpaid taxes. They fill their night's wondering how to make war with this one, or make peace with that one. They live swimming in splendor and yet can never enjoy a minute of it."

"There is some truth in that," conceded Charles.

"Now, here's my advice," said William. "After we find a way to save this Elsea woman, you do exactly what the duke says: you forget all about her and marry that cute baron's daughter. I've seen her recently. She's as strong as an ox. She'll bear you many sons—a dozen at least! And did I mention that her father owns one of the most beautiful slices of Bavaria you'll ever see? In a little while, they'll be calling you lord, and your only worry will be deciding which part of your land you'll be hunting that day. Talk about happiness, my friend—that is the kind of life you were meant for."

"I do not know if it is the life I was meant for," countered Charles, "but it seems to be the one I must settle for."

CHAPTER FIFTY-FOUR

Reunion

Elsea and Prochaska listened patiently as the captain did his best to explain the magnitude of their martial plight. Gesturing often at the map on the table, he methodically listed their many inadequacies and detailed the preparations, meager as they were, for the anticipated siege. The bishop's eyes had long since glazed over, and he made little effort to hide his relief when the captain's lecture was interrupted by a light knock at the door.

"What is it?" asked Prochaska of the nervous sentry who stepped inside.

"Your Excellency, there are two couriers from Duke Otto at the gate."

"Duke Otto! What do they want?"

"They are asking to see the duchess, and they insist they have urgent news that cannot wait. They seem to be men of some importance."

"What is so important about them?" asked Elsea.

"They have an escort of twenty-four knights, Your Grace."

"What!" exclaimed the now alert bishop. "How can so many armed men ride right up to our very door without any forewarning?"

"This is what I've been trying to tell you," lamented the captain, "we're not even able to properly screen our own roads."

Elsea looked at Prochaska and raised her eyebrows.

"It is indeed a lot of men, My Lady, but I am curious to learn what sort of message requires two dozen Bavarians to deliver."

Elsea nodded, and Prochaska turned to the sentry. "Tell the sergeant of the guard he may permit the couriers to enter."

"And be sure they're unarmed," cautioned the captain.

The young man bowed quickly and left the room.

Elsea went to one of the windows overlooking the courtyard and leaned out to let the warm breeze blow lightly across her face. She had been there but a moment when the sentry knocked again and escorted Charles and William into the room.

Prochaska staggered backward. "You!"

"Good morning, Your Excellency," said Charles. "It is encouraging to see Her Grace still has at least one loyal lord."

At the sound of his voice, Elsea pulled her head in from the window, but did not turn around.

"We were told you had been killed," stammered the bishop.

Charles patted himself on the chest. "I am living proof that one should not give credence to every passing rumor. Allow me to introduce myself properly this time. I am Sir Charles of Bavaria and with me is…"

Before he could finish, Elsea spun around and dashed across the room. The smile on her face told Charles all he wanted to know. Regrettably, she regained her composure just before she reached him, and they stood at arm's length, conversing only with their eyes.

A speechless Bishop Prochaska exchanged looks with the dismayed captain.

At last, Elsea stepped back and ran her hand across her eyes. "Sir Charles," she began, "I believe that I, uh, speak for everyone here, when I say that…" She stopped to wipe her eyes again. "… that we are greatly relieved to see you are well. Is that not right, Your Excellency?"

"Our merciful God has once again answered our prayers!" proclaimed Prochaska.

William tapped Charles on the shoulder.

"Your Grace," stumbled Charles, "Permit me to present to you my good friend, Sir William, the best knight in all Bavaria."

"It's an honor, Your Grace," said William with a respectful bow. "Charles has told me much about you."

"Sir William, any friend of Sir Charles is welcome in my castle." She waved a hand toward the other men in the room. "This is Bishop Prochaska, and this is Elburn, the captain of my guard. They alone have stood by me, and I trust their counsel completely."

"A man of the cloth," observed William. "We must talk theology sometime, Your Excellency. I've many questions I'd be eager to hear your views on."

"I am always eager to guide a soul in the knowledge of the Most Holy, my son."

Elsea and Charles had gone quiet again. It was left to Prochaska to break their enchantment.

"Sir Charles," he began, "we were informed you have pressing news for us."

Charles tore his gaze from Elsea. "What did you say?"

"The good bishop is asking about the message you carry," said William.

"Yes, we have come from Duke Otto," replied Charles. "He has authorized me to present this..." He pulled the small leather pouch from around his neck, reached into the bag and clutched the rolled letter.

"Present what?" asked Elsea.

"It is an offer to end the war before it begins," answered Charles without emotion.

"Is this true?" exclaimed Prochaska.

"The only way this war can end is with my death," declared Elsea solemnly.

"There is another way," said Charles, still holding onto the letter.

William took a step forward. "We have a message from the duke explaining everything. Perhaps my friend is having difficulty finding it in so large a bag."

Elsea held out her hand, and Charles reluctantly gave her the letter.

She moved to the window, unrolled the paper, and read:

Otto Wittelsbach, Duke of Bavaria,
Unto Elsea Babenberg, currently, Duchess of Austria,

As you must know by now, my army will reach Vienna before month's end. For reasons too numerous to list, I intend to depose you and make the city mine. As you possess not the means to stop me, you know this is no empty boast. Sir Charles, however, has endeavored to persuade me that I have misunderstood you these many years and that you might yet be reasoned with. I will not conceal my skepticism of his appraisal of your character. Nevertheless, in view of his fervent pleadings on your behalf, and out of respect for his opinion, I am prepared to make you this offer.

Assuming you are able to defeat Eldridge and save Vienna, I propose a marriage alliance between our two houses. You will marry my sister's youngest son, Kendrick. He is a man of modest vices and should make an adequate husband. By accepting this marriage you will become my vassal. In return, I will end this war and promise you the protection of my house. I will support your claim to Austria against all who might threaten it. Charles is convinced you will see the wisdom in this.

I have reared Charles alongside Prince John since he was a small boy. I need not tell you how dear he is to me. With a view to his future happiness, I have arranged a marriage for him as well. He will soon marry the daughter of a wealthy baron. Despite the grievous suffering Charles has experienced at your hands, he stridently professes some sort of infatuation with you. Such indiscretion in a young man is understandable. I warn you, however, not take advantage of these misguided feelings to interfere with his bright prospects. If you possess any wisdom at all, you will agree that this is what is best for him.

  O. W.

She turned from the window. "Do you know what this says?"

"Duke Otto is offering an alliance," Charles answered flatly.

Prochaska clapped his hands together as if in prayer. "Praise be to God!"

Elsea continued looking at Charles. "Have you read the letter?"

"There was no need to, My Lady."

She tucked the paper into the cuff of her sleeve and folded her arms across her chest. "You may return to your duke and tell him I accept his offer and agree to all his conditions without reservation."

Charles tried to pretend he was pleased with her answer. "I will dispatch a courier, My Lady. I came here for more than to deliver a letter."

"There is something else?"

"Are you aware that Eldridge is marching on you?"

"We have been following his movements for over a week," she answered matter-of-factly. "The captain believes he will be in sight of the city within four days."

"What measures are you taking to stop him?"

"Stop him!" she laughed. "I shall be fortunate if I have enough men to defend these walls."

"Holding this castle will not save Vienna," he warned her.

"Unfortunately," admitted the captain, "we don't have the means to defend ourselves *and* the city."

"And so you hope to survive a long siege in this fortress?"

"What other choice do we have?" replied Elsea.

Charles tossed the empty pouch onto the table that now stood between them. "Your Highness, most of Germany knows you have lost the support of your nobles, and little sympathy now remains for your cause among the princes. If you cannot defend your own capital it will only help convince the remaining skeptics that you do not deserve to rule Austria. Otto is an honorable man, and his proposal for an alliance is trustworthy, but it is up to you to prove you are a legitimate duchess. If you cannot keep Eldridge from taking Vienna, Duke Otto will have no choice but to take your crown himself. You must defeat Eldridge before he reaches the city or lose your throne."

"Then I am undone," she said with a shrug of her shoulders. "I told you—I have nothing to fight with. My nobles have left me defenseless."

"What about the serfs?"

"Because my nobles rule most of the villages, they have not answered my call for footmen."

Charles turned to the captain. "Does Her Grace have *any* troops?"

"We've sent word to recall the garrisons along the frontier in Hungary," he answered, "but they'll get here too late. The only troops we can count on right now are the castle archers, footmen, and Her Lady's mounted guard. Together, I could assemble three hundred fifty men."

"Is that it?"

"Well, before you arrived I was suggesting to Her Highness that we look to Vienna for volunteers. I believe the city could provide us six or seven hundred men."

"Added to what we already have, that will give us nearly a thousand," noted Charles.

"But our scouts report Eldridge has at least seven times that many. You can't hope to defeat him with so small a force."

Charles stepped up to the table. "Show me where Eldridge is now."

"He was here two days ago," answered the captain, pointing to a spot on the map.

"Is this the road he is using?"

"Yes, My Lord."

"That means he will be passing by all these villages," noted Charles, tracing a finger along a red line representing the road. "Can they provide us any men?"

"We'd normally expect the nobles there to bring in a couple thousand serfs and freemen," explained the captain, "but as Her Highness has said—they've not answered our summons."

"Then we must send someone with more authority." Turning to Prochaska, Charles added, "Your Excellency, we need you to ride through this area and recruit more volunteers."

"What makes you think they will listen to me?" asked the stunned priest. "I am a minister of God, not a mercenary of war."

"The peasants need to be reminded that their duty to Her Lady is as sacred as their duty to God," said Charles. "You are the best one to do that."

"My son, I am afraid you think too highly of the peasants' spirituality. They may fear God in the next world, but they fear man more in this one. Without the backing of an army of knights they will have no reason to heed my call."

"Then you will have to give them a reason," interrupted Elsea. "Tell them I will grant freedom to every serf who joins me."

"My Lady," warned Prochaska, "you cannot free the serfs without the permission of their nobles."

"I'm not in the habit of disagreeing with the church," inserted William. "But these nobles forfeited their rights when they broke their oaths of fealty. The duchess may give their land, and all who are bound to it, to whomever she pleases."

"Thank you, Sir William," said Elsea. "You may add *land* to the promise of freedom, Bishop Prochaska. Take several scribes and a chest of paper. Keep an accurate accounting of each man that rallies to my cause. If we live through this, they will have land and the freedom to enjoy it. I give my word."

Charles gave Elsea a nod. "How many weapons do you have in your armory?" he asked the captain.

"We've enough to equip an army of ten thousand."

"Good. Fill as many wagons as needed and accompany His Excellency. Go through all the villages you can in two days. Arm each man as he joins you. Sir William and I will use whatever men we can spare to impede Eldridge and give you the time you need."

"My Lord," protested the captain, "even if we're able to convince the serfs as you hope, I can't support this strategy. Eldridge is not leading an army of peasants. He has *trained* soldiers, stout and well-armed, and at least two thousand knights."

"We will have our own knights," Charles assured him. "While you are gathering the serfs, Her Grace will go to Lord Raglan and convince him to join us."

"Raglan!" blurted Elsea with a half-hearted laugh. "Sir Charles, we are more than grateful for the all consideration you are giving to our plight, but if you were depending on the Count of Hohenberg riding in at the last hour to rescue us all, then you will be severely disappointed. I assure you; he will not lift a finger on my behalf."

"Circumstances have changed," noted Charles. "You have a promise of peace from Otto, and with Lord Raglan's help we can now defeat Eldridge. If you explain these things to him, he will come."

"I have never been able to explain *anything* to that man. Sending me will do more harm than good."

"You are still his duchess, My Lady. You must at least try."

"But it will take me a whole day just to get to his estates."

"A day there, and a day back, means you will be able to reach the assembly point in time."

Elsea leaned on the table and hung her head. "You do not understand," she said from behind the veil of her hair. "He hates me and will only rejoice to see my downfall."

"He does not hate you," said Charles quietly. "Make him understand that you *need* him, and he will come."

She lifted her head. "Is there no other way?"

"Without him we fail."

"Very well," she sighed.

"It is settled then," said Charles, looking around the room. "The duchess will ride for Lord Raglan's help. Bishop Prochaska and the captain will sweep through all the villages within a day's ride and gather the serfs. William and I will take the footmen, archers and whatever men the city can provide and hinder Eldridge's march north." He pointed to the map again. "What is the name of this village?"

"Longwood," answered the captain.

Charles gave the table a pound with his fist. "We will form the army at Longwood in three days!"

The courtyard was a blur of bedlam as everyone from cow maids to cooks scurried to and fro loading carts and hitching horses. No one was quite sure of the reason behind the sudden urgency, or why everything seemed cloaked in secrecy. Rumors circulated among the harried servants carrying arm loads of weapons and baskets of food that the castle was being abandoned and the duchess was fleeing for her life. Others were equally certain that a great battle was about to be fought, but where or against whom could not be determined. A consensus rapidly formed, however, that all the commotion had something to do with the two Bavarians who had come through the gate that morning. The large man and his companion carried themselves like great lords and even the captain and Bishop Prochaska deferred to their orders.

William put his knights to work scouring the area around the castle for every farming implement they could find. "Shovels and pickaxes will be our most valuable weapons," he predicted.

Charles had earlier sent Prochaska and the captain into the city to muster the hoped-for volunteers. He and the sergeant of the guard were now inspecting the footmen and archers as they stood in two long ranks.

"We will fight a defensive battle," explained Charles to the sergeant. "These archers alone are worth a thousand men. Be sure they bring every arrow they posses. Do not leave a single shaft behind."

"I shall see to it, My Lord."

The hundred twenty men of Elsea's guard stood by their horses waiting to escort her to Raglan's estate. They gave an appropriate cheer when she strode into the courtyard. Her braided hair hung down her back in a long ponytail. A white vest emblazoned with the red shield of Babenberg covered a shirt of finely meshed chainmail that reached down to her leather breeches. She wore a black belt with black riding boots, and from her left hip dangled a broadsword. Dorianne came behind her struggling to fill out a baggy knight's tunic.

Elsea scanned the crowded yard until she spotted Charles. Leaving Dorianne by the horses, she came over and stopped a proper distance from him as frantic soldiers and servants swirled around them on all sides.

"Is it really you," she smiled, "or am I only dreaming?"

"It must be a dream," he smiled back, "because I had lost all hope of ever seeing your smile again."

They had to step aside for an overloaded cart pushed by three grunting men.

"Oh, Charles, my heart is bursting with all the things I long to tell you," she confessed over the neighing of a nearby horse, "but this is not the place."

"We will find a place when this is over, My Lady."

"But you cannot stay in Austria, Charles. You have done all you can—you have given us a plan and a hope. It is more than I deserve. You and your friend must ride away and save yourselves while there is still time."

"I will leave Austria," he said, "when you are safe."

"I know why you are doing this," she frowned. "You think you must make amends for some harm you imagine you have caused me."

"I do indeed wish there was a way to undo the harm I have caused you," he admitted. "But I am not here to make amends. I am here because you are here, and there is no place else I want be."

She stepped closer to him. "You do not know how much I want to believe that," she whispered.

He reached out for her hand, but a loud commotion from the other side of the yard stopped him. Bishop Prochaska and the captain came through the gate at the head of a straggling column of volunteers from the city.

Prochaska rode over to Charles and Elsea and swept his arm over the men shuffling in behind. "These are all we could get to follow us," he lamented.

"There is barely a hundred men!" exclaimed an astonished Charles.

"The men of the city place too much value on their comfort, my son," explained Prochaska. "They could not be persuaded to share your confidence in our daring endeavor. Only these men here, from the poorest streets of the town, were willing to risk the venture."

Charles looked again at the gaggle of city men laboring to form the semblance of a straight line. "We will have to make do with what we have," he sighed. "Be sure to give them a weapon they can handle."

"But this gives you barely four hundred men," protested Elsea. "You were counting on a thousand!"

"William and I will have most of the best troops, including our Bavarians," he replied. "Besides, we need only to slow Eldridge down till the serfs and Raglan can join us at Longwood."

"But what if Raglan will not be persuaded?" she pressed. "Is it wise to place all our hopes on him?"

"Alas, My Lady, I have no other plan. For the sake of us all, you must convince him."

Elsea looked up at the bishop and then back at Charles. "Then I will find a way," she promised.

The two friends watched Prochaska and the captain lead the train of rumbling carts stuffed with weapons, food, and scribes through the gate. The bishop wore a robe of bright yellow, and on his head was his tall miter. He looked back at his charges and pointed the way with his crosier.

"Is he going to wage war or to meet the Pope?" chuckled William.

Behind the procession of wagons came Elsea and her guard. Just before she disappeared under the portcullis, she turned to look back at Charles and held his gaze until she was out of sight.

"She certainly is different," noted William. "I didn't think you were ever going to convince her pay old Raglan a visit, yet she agreed to marry a complete stranger without making a peep. I told you women are too confusing."

"She can be unpredictable," agreed Charles.

"And she has a quick mind for a woman," added William. "That idea to free the serfs was a clever one."

"You will not meet anyone more intelligent."

"Who was that cute little thing riding with her?"

"That was Dorianne," laughed Charles. "Be careful with her; she is not as frail as she looks, and she is fiercely loyal to the duchess."

After the last of Elsea's guard cleared the courtyard, Charles turned to the men he and William would lead out next. Between the archers, footmen, and volunteers from the city, they had about three hundred fifty men. Except for their two dozen Bavarians, they had no knights.

"The road is clear," said Charles. "We have the toughest task and delay will not make it any easier."

Just then, the men of Elsea's guard came thundering through the gate and back into the courtyard.

"What has happened?" shouted Charles to the sergeant leading them.

"Her Grace sent us back, My Lord."

"You mean you have left her alone?"

"She chose our lieutenant and a few others to stay with her, but she sent the rest of us back."

"This will not do!" protested Charles. "You cannot allow the duchess to go riding across Austria unprotected in the middle of a war. You will take your men and follow her immediately."

"My Lord," said the sergeant, "that's exactly what she told me you'd say, and she ordered me not to return. She said you'll need us more than she will."

"I told you she was a clever one," said William after a long whistle. "She knows we can't refuse another hundred knights."

"Perhaps too clever," mumbled Charles.

The final group of mixed cavalry and infantry poured out of the castle and headed down the road. Except for the high stone walls, manned by a score of old and infirm guards, the castle was defenseless.

CHAPTER FIFTY-FIVE

Lady Raglan

It had been dark for many hours when Elsea and her reduced escort finally reined in their horses at the foot of a small hill. High above them, outlined by the faint moonlight, was Raglan's castle. Elsea looked up at the stone fortress made more imposing in the darkness.

"I have not been here since I was a child," she said to Dorianne.

"Who goes there?" cried a voice from above.

"It is the duchess," her lieutenant yelled back. "Open the gate!"

The lieutenant's announcement caused a stir of activity above them. The wicket door to the main gate soon flung open, and a lone sentry ventured out with a lantern.

"Where's the duchess?" he asked.

"Here," said Elsea.

The sentry held up the lantern, and when the light from the glass box flickered across her face, he sucked his breath in loudly. "Your Grace!" He took several steps back while bowing at the same time. "We weren't informed of your coming."

"I can see that," said Elsea. "Now open the gate. I wish to speak with Lord Raglan."

Elsea slid from her horse as soon as they reached the courtyard. "We have come a long way," she said to the man with the lamp. "Please tend to our horses and see that my people are fed."

"At once, Your Grace."

She turned to her weary lady-in-waiting. "Pray for me, Dori. I have no idea what I am going to say to him."

"Tell him the truth," advised Dorianne. "He'll listen to the truth."

Elsea gave her a weak smile and left to follow another sentry to the main keep. At the entrance, he knocked loudly at intervals until a sleepy-eyed servant girl eventually opened the door. When she heard that the woman standing on the threshold was the duchess, she let out a scream and fled down a darkened hallway. The mortified sentry was left to lead Elsea inside and wait with her in the dark. A few moments later, an elderly woman came down the hall holding a candlestick with three burning tapers. She carried herself with a confident elegance that was familiar to Elsea.

"Lady Raglan," said Elsea, "forgive me for calling on you unannounced at so late an hour."

"Say no more, Your Grace," smiled the old woman. "I am sure it is important. You must be starving after your long journey. Come, let us find you something to eat."

"You are most gracious," returned Elsea.

Lady Raglan extended her hand. "Take my arm, My Lady. These halls are kept so dark at night that even I feel blind in my own home."

Elsea took hold of her elbow and let her lead her down the corridor. Coming around a corner, they entered a room ablaze with light from the many lamps and candles a young girl was frantically lighting. After so many hours of riding through the dark, the sudden brightness caused Elsea to shade her eyes. In the center of the floor was a long table encircled haphazardly by several chairs. Two larger armchairs, draped in animal hides, stood in one corner near a cold fireplace. Another servant came in carrying a platter of bread, a small dish of butter, and a pitcher of milk.

Lady Raglan pulled a chair away from the table. "Please sit here and eat while you wait for my husband, Your Grace," she said as she poured some milk into a cup.

"Thank you," said Elsea. "We have been riding all day, and I am indeed famished."

Elsea sat down and went to work on the food, while Lady Raglan took a seat across the table and pulled a linen bag up onto her lap. She began removing small pieces of differently colored cloth squares and sorting them by color into little piles on the table.

Lord Raglan walked through the door just as Elsea finished the last piece of bread. "Lord Raglan," she stammered as she came to her feet, "I regret disturbing you this late at night."

"Your Grace…" he began, but then stopped to stifle a yawn, "…you need not regret visiting any of your subjects, regardless of the hour." He sat down in one of the chairs in the corner, leaned back, and folded his arms. "Well?"

Elsea returned to her seat. She pushed away the empty cup and platter and clasped her hands in front of her before looking up. "I have good news," she said at last.

"Is that so?"

"Duke Otto has arranged a marriage alliance with me," she reported through a forced smile. "He has promised to call off the war if I accept."

"A marriage alliance you say?" He again paused to indulge in an even longer yawn before continuing. "As I recall, we had arranged a marriage alliance for you with Duke Eldridge. You turned it down, remember?"

"That would be difficult to forget," she said quietly. "But Lord

Raglan, you must admit that an alliance with Bavaria is far superior. I thought you would approve."

"It is no longer my place to approve or disapprove anything you do, Your Grace. I am curious, however, as to how you were able to accomplish this amazing union. The last I heard, Otto was on his way to Vienna with an army, not wedding gifts."

"That is the other part of my good news," she said with a genuine smile. "You remember that man, Charles, the one we thought was dead?" She gave him a chance to nod his head. "Well, he is alive and has returned from Bavaria."

"So the enterprising young man who turned our world upside down survived his ordeal after all. I am glad to hear it, but what does he have to do with Otto's sudden benevolence?"

"Charles was kind enough to intercede with the duke on my behalf," she answered. "I think he felt honor-bound to help me after the way he…" she looked down at the empty cup, "…misrepresented himself."

"Well then, you are getting married, and I suppose congratulations are called for, but you did not need to wake me in the middle of the night to tell me. You could have sent a letter and saved yourself the excursion."

"That is not the only reason I came," she said. "As you rightly predicted, Lord Raglan, I am at war with Eldridge." She paused to take a breath. "It is a war I cannot win without your help."

"But you have Duke Otto now," he noted. "He is all the help you need."

"Unfortunately, his offer has a condition." She hesitated, then added quickly, "I must defeat Eldridge to secure the alliance. We are assembling an army now."

"An army?"

Elsea hurriedly described Charles's plan.

When she finished, Raglan got up from his chair and walked

over to the fireplace, acting as if he was suddenly interested in a particular candle on the mantel. "Let me see if I understand you correctly," he began after turning to face her, "you plan to fight Eldridge with an army of peasants you do not yet have; you let this Charles and his Bavarians run off with the only real troops you *did* have; and you have left the city open for Otto's taking. In all my life I have never heard of greater folly."

"It is not folly," she insisted calmly. "I trust Charles. He believes we can win with your help."

"So once more you have cast yourself off the cliff, and you need me to pull you back before you fall."

"Our situation is not as bleak as you portray it, Lord Raglan. There is no reason for Otto to take Vienna. He has promised me a marriage alliance."

"Like the one you promised Eldridge?"

"That was different."

"Ah, that was different," he repeated. "You agreed to marry Eldridge until, that is, you decided it did not appeal to you. Now you say you have agreed to marry another man. You sent us away because our advice did not appeal to you. Now you have discovered that life on your own does not appeal to you either. You will forgive me if I do not see anything in this whole affair that is different."

Elsea could give no answer but a bowed head.

Raglan began to pace before the fireplace. "No, there is nothing different here. You are the same petulant child we gave the coronet to four years ago. You have neither grown up, nor grown wiser, and nothing has changed. The trouble may be different, but the cause is the same. You have always been your own worst enemy. You snub Popes, dishonor kings, break vows, and disrespect nobles like a child playing fox and geese. Being duchess has been little more than a game to you. What did it matter to you if duke 'so in so' was offended or you slighted lord 'such and such'? You could not be bothered to even remember their names much less consider the effects of your actions. It never occurred to you that there might be times when the welfare of others could be more important than your own. I tried to teach you these things. I confess my total failure. I do not know what made me think you could ever learn."

He stopped his pacing and came up behind his wife who still pretended to care about the colored cloth squares. "My wife and I have outlived our children," he went on. "I have more wealth than I know how to enjoy. I am no longer a young man and do not have many years left. Have you ever asked yourself why I bothered to support you as long as I did?"

Elsea shook her head, but did not look up.

"I saw something in you," he continued, "a spark of courage, a flicker of genius, and I wanted to help you. You were the first German duchess to rule in her own right. I did everything in my power to establish you, but you tossed it all away like a child bored with a broken toy."

He finished speaking, and only the sound of the sputtering candles disturbed the silence.

Elsea at last looked up. "You are right," she admitted. "I have been wicked, and irresponsible, and reckless. I know that now. I resented being duchess, and I resented you for trying to make me one. I could not understand why any of it mattered. But I am different now, Lord Raglan. You must believe me. I want to live up to my responsibility, but I need your help. I have no one else to turn to."

Raglan let out a low sigh and came around to her side of the table. He pulled back the chair next to her and sat down. "You poor child," he said quietly. "Life has not been kind to you. Your brother should have been duke and saved you from this misery. Your beautiful mother should have lived to help you. Your wretched father should have given you either his love or his discipline, but he cursed you doubly by giving you neither. The council and I were not always fair to you; I suppose we expected too much. These things were not your fault. Maybe this whole tragedy was unavoidable; perhaps it is even your destiny. It hurts my heart to see you end this way, and I wish there was something I could do, but it is too late." He went back to his chair in the corner and sat down.

"But it is not too late," she pressed. "Charles says we still have two days. He believes we can defeat Eldridge if you will bring your knights."

"How many knights does Eldridge have?"

"We think he may have as many as two thousand."

"Two thousand!" he exclaimed. "It would take me a fortnight to gather that many." He waved a hand towards her. "You do not need me; you need a sorcerer. What you want cannot be done."

Elsea came over to where he sat and dropped to her knees. "My Lord," she said softly, "Charles is somewhere right now trying to fight an entire army with but a handful of men. He loves me too much and is risking his life for me. For his sake, I cannot return empty-handed. Please, Lord Raglan, I beg you."

"There is nothing I can do," he said, staring ahead to avoid her pleading eyes. "I am sorry."

She knelt before him a little longer, but said no more.

At last, she came to her feet. "Thank you for the bread, Lady Raglan," she said politely. "You have been very kind, but I must leave now. We have a long ride back and there is little time to lose."

She moved toward the door, but turned before leaving. "I cannot blame you for not wanting to help me," she said, "and I do not hold it against you. If this tragedy is my destiny, then it is only what I deserve."

As soon as Elsea was gone, Lady Raglan left the table and sat in the chair next to her husband. She placed a hand on his arm and patted it tenderly. "My husband," she said sweetly, "how many times have I sat in this very chair and begged you not to leave me for one of your pointless wars or useless crusades?"

"More times than I can remember," he answered. "You made it difficult sometimes."

"It was not easy staying here all alone waiting for the day a complete stranger would burst in to tell me I was a widow. I never understood the politics behind all those wars anyway. I do not even know why everyone is against that unfortunate girl now. You told her this was her destiny. I do not believe in that kind of destiny, my husband. I believe God places us on a path, but He gives us opportunities to change our direction. Maybe she is trying to change her direction. Maybe your path is to help her. Maybe your whole life has been leading to this very moment." She patted his arm again. "One thing I do know, my husband: you will be impossible to live with if she fails because you refused her."

Elsea met Dorianne and her escort in the courtyard. "Prepare to leave," she said to the lieutenant. "I know the men are tired, but there is no point in staying here." She returned Dorianne's questioning look with a shake of her head.

She had one foot in the stirrup and was about to swing herself onto the saddle, when they heard a voice call out from across the darkened courtyard, "Your Grace!"

A servant holding a lamp came running up to them. "Your Grace," he panted when he reached her, "Lord Raglan wishes to speak with you."

CHAPTER FIFTY-SIX

Sunday Homily

Charles watched the swallows swerving and swooping above the tall grass snapping up insects in their frenzied race to beat the setting sun. Something about the busy birds reminded him of a lazy summer day from his boyhood, and he leaned on his sword letting his mind wander. It was the awful moaning that brought him around.

He stood up and looked about at the shattered remains of the little army he and William had led out of the castle two days earlier. Groaning men crawled on hands and knees through trampled-down grass past comrades now staring blankly up at the sky. Others limped up the hill, hands clasped over ghastly wounds, yet thankful for any excuse to flee the next wave of carnage. The survivors, sheltering behind a low wall of freshly turned dirt, looked anxiously down the hill to where the troops of Eldridge's army were forming for the final assault.

"We are not going to make it," he complained to William.

On their way south from Vienna, Charles and William had chosen this spot near the village of Longwood as the best place to fight the main battle. They left behind the city men and some of the castle footmen with orders to build an entrenchment and continued on with the rest to meet the Styrians.

They had hoped to slow their advance by erecting a series of obstacles across the main road at natural chokepoints. The ad-hoc band would only have to fight brief skirmishes before retreating up the road to the next favorable piece of geography. The moments of delay caused at each encounter would add up to the precious hours they needed for Elsea and Prochaska to arrive with the rest of the army.

To their dismay, however, the normally cautious and methodical Eldridge hurled his troops forward with little preparation and even less regard for their welfare. Although the valiant Austrians and Bavarians inflicted many casualties, roadblocks they had expected to hold for hours fell in minutes, and Eldridge drove them north far faster than anticipated. An hour ago, they had reached the yet unfinished wall and the weary city men still feverishly trying to complete it.

At this point, the road Eldridge was following made a sharp uphill turn to the west. On the north side, the land rose quickly to meet thick, brush-choked woods that stretched for miles. To the south, the sloping ground ended abruptly at the bank of a fast flowing tributary of the Danube. The impassable forest to their left and the bridgeless river to their right meant Charles and William could safely ignore their flanks and concentrate all their strength on the stretch of open ground in the middle. They expected to have a full day to prepare for their final stand. Eldridge's relentless advance brought him to the half-built barricade a day ahead of schedule.

The footmen of the Styrian advance guard were nearly finished arranging themselves in their neatly dressed ranks. Riding up the road behind them was a long column of knights. Still further behind trudged the rest of the infantry followed by a train of wagons stretching off to the horizon. The rays of the late afternoon sun shone down on the knights lighting up the splendid colors of their heraldry and glinting off the polished steel of their armor.

"He does have a nice looking army," conceded William.

"What are we going to do?" moaned Charles. "We cannot hold this ground and yet we cannot retreat. Elsea and Prochaska are expecting to find us here tomorrow. Our only hope was to combine everything we had. If we are forced off this ridge, Eldridge will be able to destroy the rest of the army as it comes up, one piece at a time."

"It was always a plan more bold than practical, my friend," replied a more resigned William. "We've done all we can with flesh and blood. What we need now is a miracle."

The lead rank of the Styrian footmen stepped forward, waiting only for the signal to begin the last charge.

William tilted his head. "What's that?"

"What's what?" asked Charles.

"It sounds like music," answered William.

Charles strained his ears until he could hear what he thought was singing coming from above and behind them. It was faint at first, but grew steadily stronger.

"It sounds like the choir at church," declared William.

The other men along the wall could now hear the strains of song, and they looked up the road, wondering at its source. Soon, from over the hill above them came the unmistakable words of a well-known hymn:

All creatures of our God and King
Lift up your voice and with us sing
Hallelujah! Hallelujah!

Just then, Bishop Prochaska crested the hill, crosier in hand, as if coming to Mass. Behind him, marching four abreast, were hundreds of pike carrying peasants. They sang as they came, and their song rent the air and echoed down the hill.

Charles ran to greet them. "Thank God you are here!" he shouted.

"Thank God indeed!" shouted back Prochaska.

Turning himself around atop his horse, he motioned to the marching men like a general on maneuvers. Instantly, as if on parade, the column split in two, and the men filed by to the right and left. The exhausted survivors broke into hoarse cheers for their rescuers who continued to sing from the tops of their lungs as they filled the gaps along the wall.

While they passed by, Charles learned from the bishop that he had brought nearly two thousand men with him. Word of the land and freedom the duchess was offering spread so rapidly that the biggest problem he and the captain had was making sure they noted each man's name and place of residence correctly. The overworked scribes wore out quill after quill recording the volunteers who poured in from all directions. Prochaska left the captain behind to finish the recruiting. He expected him to come in soon with perhaps a thousand or more peasant-soldiers.

Prochaska noticed the bodies scattered about in the grass. "What is going on here?"

As Charles quickly explained their situation, the bishop's face turned a darker shade of red. He jumped down from his horse and strode to the wall. Stepping through the ranks of the newly arrived peasants, he scrambled to the top and waved his bishop's staff to silence his choir.

"Who are you that dare spill blood on the Lord's Sabbath?" he bellowed down the hill. "Have you no priests among you? Is this an army of pagan infidels before me?"

A lone horseman in black trotted forward from among a

group of knights clustered behind the footmen. "Go back to your chapel you old fool," he shouted back. "This is men's work!"

"So it is you, Lord Eugene," thundered Prochaska. "You are the one who has encouraged these men to hazard their souls. I am not surprised—you child of the devil! Have you forgotten the day you placed your hand on the box containing the holy relics of the saints? You have broken your oath of fealty and betrayed your God as well as your duchess. Is it not enough that you have cast yourself into perdition? Do you serve Satan so faithfully that you wish to take these innocent men with you? How proud you have made the Father of Lies!

"Listen to me, my children," he continued in a gentler voice. "You are right to obey your lords, but they are wrong to risk your souls by causing violence on the Lord's Day. Are there not seven days in the week? Are not six days enough for fighting that you must kill on the day our Lord rose in glory from the grave to conquer death? My children, I have knelt at the feet of His Most Holy Father. I have kissed his hand with the very lips I now plead to you with. I tell you this day you are in jeopardy of God's judgment. Attack if you will, but my conscience is clear. I have done my duty: I have warned you of your folly before God and man!"

Lifting his hands to heaven, he broke into a new song. The peasants behind him picked it up and amplified it a thousand times.

That day of wrath, that dreadful day,
When heaven and earth shall pass away.
What power shall be the sinner's stay?
How shall he meet that dreadful day?

At the bottom of the hill, the men waiting to attack looked up in awe at the charismatic bishop. The setting sun sat just off his right shoulder silhouetting his flowing robes and tall miter as he punctuated each of his warnings with a mighty shake of his staff. When the chords of his full-throated choir flowed down the hill, they took several halting steps backward, crossing themselves, and murmuring against their lords.

Lord Eugene spun his horse around and trotted back to the large man who dwarfed the horse he rode. Duke Eldridge sat atop the suffering animal flanked by Lord Rottermund and his closest nobles.

"Your Grace," said Lord Eugene, "sound the horn once more and finish this business."

Eldridge kept his gaze up the hill as if enraptured by the peasants' song. "It has been a long day," he noted at last. "I think we shall rest now."

"My Lord, are you going to let a foolish priest and a herd of peasants deprive you of a great victory? Send your knights forward now, and you will smash them like a pot of clay and win this war before the sun sets."

The duke turned from admiring the impressive bishop. "You are the one who promised me the Austrians had no army."

"This rabble is no army, My Lord. Sweep them aside with a wave of your hand and the road to Vienna will be open."

"I see you are a passionate man," observed Eldridge as he removed his helmet to reveal his perspiring bald head. "I have found that passion serves well in love, but it often leads to disappointment in war. I will be master of Austria, of that you may be sure, but not tonight. The men have been fighting for nearly two days and are in need of rest. My victory can wait for the sun of a new day."

He turned to a rider at his side. "Have my tent prepared," he bellowed. "And get those cooks busy. War gives me the best kind of appetite!"

CHAPTER FIFTY-SEVEN

Council of War

As Prochaska had promised, the captain of the guard marched into camp shortly after dark bringing another seven hundred volunteers with him. Anticipating the battle in the morning, Charles and William organized the peasants into three divisions and put them to work in shifts. While one division labored to improve the barricade, another stood by with weapons in hand in case of a surprise attack. A third division rested in the main camp behind the crest of the hill awaiting their turn on the wall.

The two friends walked along the wall offering encouragement to the busy men and making suggestions where necessary. Although the digging was tedious, the men toiled into the night without complaint, and Charles was pleased to see how quickly the work was going.

Having established a smooth routine, William insisted Charles return to the camp to get some sleep. "The captain and I can supervise the peasants for a while," he assured him. "I'll wake you when it's your turn."

The exhausted Charles trudged up the hill without protest. The men not working on the wall clustered around a hundred campfires scattered behind the ridge. They roasted meat over their fires and talked excitedly about the battle to come. Off to one side, Bishop Prochaska had improvised a confessional out of horse blankets strung up in a tree, and many of the men waited patiently in line to see their only priest. Charles found a quiet spot near where the horses were tied and stripped off his armor. Using a saddle for a pillow, he sank down into the soft grass and fell asleep within minutes.

Near midnight, William woke him with alarming news. One of the pickets had ridden up with word that a large body of horsemen was coming down the road about two miles to the rear. Fearing that Eldridge had somehow gotten behind them, they hurriedly roused the castle archers and the men of Elsea's guard from their long-deferred sleep. As soon as Charles finished strapping on his armor, he led the drowsy men toward the danger while William formed up his Bavarians and the off-duty division to prepare for an attack.

Charles and his men jogged along the road by the light of the half moon and soon met other riders who reported the unknown force was right behind them and coming fast. He ordered the men to spread out across the road and for the archers to ready their bows. The nervous men waited quietly as the sound of hoof beats grew louder. Suddenly, out of the darkness, there materialized the head of a long column of splendidly equipped knights. Charles recognized the second rider in the moonlight.

"Your Grace!" he cried.

An unknown voice calling out from the shadows caused the lead rider to pull back hard on his reins. The whole cavalcade collapsed upon itself like an accordion and came to a confused and thundering halt.

"Who goes there?" yelled the rider.

"It is Sir Charles, Lord Raglan."

"Charles!" exclaimed Elsea. "Are we too late? We passed many wounded men heading home who told us the army was destroyed."

"We nearly *were* destroyed," replied Charles, stepping forward. "But Bishop Prochaska arrived without a moment to spare."

"Is Prochaska here too?" asked Raglan.

"Yes, My Lord. He and the captain brought in almost three thousand men willing to fight." Charles stepped up to Elsea and removed his helmet. "You would have been proud of the bishop, Your Grace. He turned back the Styrians with nothing but his staff."

"Are you talking about *my* Prochaska?"

"Why are all these men here?" interrupted Raglan.

"We did not expect you until tomorrow and thought you might be Styrians," explained Charles. "Your arrival will be a great encouragement to the men."

He directed Raglan to an open field near the edge of the camp.

"Your men can use this area to rest," he told him. "How many did you bring?"

Lord Raglan muffled a groan as he climbed down from his horse. "Not nearly as many as we need, I fear. Her Grace insisted there was no time to lose, and so we had less than a day to call in my knights. If you had given me a week, I could have brought a thousand men to this fight. Considering our need for haste, we did well to bring in a little over three hundred."

The number was far smaller than Charles had hoped for, and he did his best to hide his disappointment as he took the reins of Raglan's horse. "At least *you* are here, My Lord. Your wisdom alone will be worth a thousand knights."

"You certainly have no lack of confidence," replied Raglan with a half-hearted laugh. "Come, young man, I am eager to see this army you have created out of thin air."

Charles and William led Raglan and the duchess through the camp and down the hill to the wall. The peasants were naturally excited to see Raglan, but when they saw Elsea, they erupted into spontaneous waves of heartfelt cheers. Everyone was eager to get a glimpse of the woman who had made his freedom possible and the grateful serfs crowded around to thank her. Their morale was high, and they talked and joked among themselves like men who had already won a great victory.

Charles gave the new arrivals a brief account of all that happened the last two days. Standing atop the wall, he showed them the features of the battlefield by the pale light of the moon. He pointed out the heavy woods to the left and the river to the right and explained why they chose this spot to fight the main battle. Spread out far below them, flickering peacefully like stars in the night sky, were the campfires of the Styrian army.

Raglan nodded his head in approval of the barricade which was fast becoming a one-wall fortress. "Keep them digging, young man. The fate of us all rests in this dirt."

A short while later, Elsea, Raglan, Prochaska, Charles, William, and the captain of the guard gathered around a campfire sitting on makeshift chairs of blankets and saddles. Dorianne slept in the grass behind her mistress.

Charles and William were explaining to Raglan how they had organized the army. The old count leaned back on his saddle, arms folded across his chest, listening attentively.

"William has formed the peasants into three divisions," reported Charles. "Each division is about nine hundred men strong."

"It'll take two divisions to man the wall properly," noted William. "That'll leave one division as a reserve."

"We split up what was left of the castle footmen to serve among them as officers," added Charles. "The archers will operate independently from behind the wall. When they run out of arrows, they will take up swords and join the peasants. Our most important force will be the mounted knights. Counting the men you and Her Grace were able to bring in, we have over four hundred men on horseback. These are our best troops and must be held ready until the last possible moment."

After Charles finished, Raglan turned to Bishop Prochaska. "Do you expect any more serfs to come in before noon tomorrow?"

"I believe it is a miracle that so many came as they did, My Lord. It would be presumptuous to hope for more."

Raglan leaned forward and held his hands to the fire. "You could not have chosen more favorable ground," he allowed, "and your battle plan is sound." He looked around at them and added, "But for two things."

"What do you mean?" asked Charles.

"First of all, you cannot count on the peasants."

"You are too critical," interjected Prochaska. "You saw for yourself their enthusiasm."

"They are in good spirits while they swing their pickaxes in the moonlight," conceded Raglan, still warming his hands at the fire. "But when the sun rises tomorrow they will be fighting trained footmen swinging short swords, and it is a fight they cannot win with enthusiasm alone."

"But we have the archers," inserted Elsea, "and over four hundred knights of our own."

"And that is our second problem," said Raglan. "Eldridge will use his footmen to pry us off our wall and force us to fight in the open. Once that happens, it will become a battle of knights, and we are far too outnumbered."

"Are you saying there is no hope?" asked Prochaska.

"I am saying we must make it a different kind of battle," answered Raglan.

"What kind of battle?" asked Elsea.

"It might be possible to make this a battle of maneuver, My Lady, but I do not know the area well enough to decide if it could work."

"I have a map, My Lord," offered the captain. From a leather sack at his side, he produced the leather map he had brought with him from the castle and rolled it out on the trampled-down grass.

Everyone crept closer to get a better view. Raglan pulled a burning stick from the flames and used it as a candle. "Show me where we are."

"We are here, My Lord," answered the captain, "just south of this village on the road near the river."

"Is this map accurate?" asked Raglan.

"I believe so, My Lord."

"But it shows only one road." Raglan pointed at the map again. "Do you know the name of this village?"

"It's called Longwood."

"Did you bring in any men from that village?"

"Why, my good Count," beamed Prochaska, "half the men of Longwood joined us this very afternoon."

"Is it possible to find one of these villagers and bring him here?"

The captain stood up. "I'll see to it at once, My Lord," he said before disappearing into the darkness.

"What is so important about a road?" asked Elsea.

"I said we must fight a different kind of battle," answered Raglan. "I am proposing a tactic that your grandfather and I once used on a pompous Italian noble when we were not much older than you are, My Lady."

"What tactic is that?" asked Charles.

"Since we cannot hope to defeat Eldridge in a standup fight

with his knights, we must make Eldridge himself our target. Cut off the snake's head and the body will die."

"How can we do that?" wondered Elsea. "You said yourself we too outnumbered."

"Eldridge will lead the battle from behind where he feels safe," explained Raglan. "He will have only a small guard for protection there. We will not need many men if we attack him from the rear, and that is why we need a road. While he is attacking our peasants along their wall, we will send our knights around his flank and get behind him. Bring Eldridge down, and this war is over."

William gave a long whistle. "My Lord must have been very bold when he was younger."

"Probably too bold," smiled Raglan wryly, "but we won the battle."

Just then, the captain entered the circle of light. At his side was a large man dressed in homespun.

Charles jumped to his feet. "Antonie!"

A bewildered Antonie looked down at Bishop Prochaska and Lord Raglan crouching near the fire and back to the well-dressed knight standing before him. "Have I done something wrong, My Lord?"

"Antonie," said Charles, "it's me."

The big man's jaw hung open.

Charles went up and embraced him. "This is the man that saved my life," he said to William as he slapped Antonie on the back. "What a strange coincidence that we should meet again like this."

Elsea came to her feet, and the instant Antonie recognized her he dropped to one knee. "Your Grace!" he exclaimed with head bowed.

"Please stand," she said. "If it is true you saved the life of Sir Charles, then you are an honored guest at my fire."

Antonie stood, but kept his head bowed. "I had little to do with it, Your Grace. It is Christa, my daughter, who hardly left his side for a week while he was recovering from his wounds, who deserves the credit. Without her tender care, I don't believe Charles, I mean *Sir* Charles, would've lived."

"Christa," said Elsea as she looked over at Charles, "I regret to say I have never heard of her. Perhaps when all this is over I will have the opportunity to thank her personally. We are all grateful for whatever assistance she rendered Sir Charles."

Raglan saw the look they gave each other. "Antonie," he cut in, "we need to know if you are familiar with the area east of us."

"I've lived within ten leagues of this very spot my whole life," replied Antonie with confidence.

Raglan motioned for him to step closer to the map. "Can you tell us if this map is accurate?" He pointed to the place in question. "Are there any roads running through here?"

Antonie knelt in the grass over the map a moment. "I wouldn't call it a road, My Lord, but there's an old trail that runs through these woods here." He traced his finger along the map. "The sheep and goat herders used to use it as a shortcut to get to the pasture land by the river."

"How good of a trail is it?" asked Raglan.

"I'm not sure, My Lord. It hasn't been used in years."

"Could knights on horseback use it?"

"Anyone on horseback uses the main road over here," replied Antonie.

"But is it possible for horses to go through *this forest*?" pressed Raglan.

"The trail is very faint and overgrown in many places," answered Antonie, "but a good horse should be able to make it."

Raglan pointed to the map again. "How long would it take to ride from here to here?"

Antonie stood up, shaking his head. "It's difficult to say, My Lord. You'd have to ride north for about an hour, and then east for a couple more, just to get to where the trail begins. Once on the trail, it's several hours of difficult riding through the woods straight south."

"Could the trail be followed at night?' asked Raglan.

"At night!" blurted Antonie. "My Lord, no one dares use that trail at night."

"Why not?" asked Charles.

Antonie looked around at his audience. "Everyone knows that forest is haunted. That's why the peasants stopped using it. Only a fool would enter it after dark!"

"I am not concerned with the spirits," sighed Raglan. "Do you know the trail well enough to lead my men through?"

"My Lord asks a difficult thing. I've never used that trail at night. It's a long ride, and I'm not very good on horseback."

Elsea stepped closer and placed a hand on the big man's shoulder. "Antonie," she said softly, "it is very important to me that Lord Raglan be able to get his knights through that forest tonight."

At Elsea's request, Antonie snapped to attention as if a soldier on inspection and then dropped again to one knee. "I didn't know it was important to Her Grace," he said. "If Her Grace wishes it, I'll do my best to lead them through."

"Thank you, Antonie," said Elsea. "Your service this night shall not be forgotten."

Charles slapped him on the back again. "That's the spirit!" He turned to the captain and added, "This man has a long ride before him; please see that he gets a proper mount. I owe him a good horse anyway."

"Yes, My Lord."

Antonie rose and followed the captain.

"Lord Raglan," began Charles after they were gone, "if Antonie believes it will take six or seven hours, we must plan on eight or nine to allow for delays. You should leave within the hour if you are to reach the rear of Eldridge's army by midmorning."

"The knights must indeed leave soon," agreed Raglan, "but I will not be leading them: you and William will."

"But my place is here with the main army," replied an astonished Charles.

"You heard Antonie," returned Raglan. "It is a long trail over difficult ground. You will need to ride hard with no time to rest. I am too old for these things now and would only slow everyone down."

"This is where the most important fighting will happen," argued Charles. "I think William and I can better serve the duchess by staying here. Besides, we are Bavarians; surely your knights will be reluctant to follow us."

"You are incorrect on both points," answered Raglan. "Holding this hill is not the key to victory. Our hopes depend on making a surprise assault with every knight we have. The captain and I are fully capable of directing the battle here until you can get through. As for our Austrians following you Bavarians, you forget that we are allies now. My knights are some of the finest in all of Germany, and they will do their duty to win this battle. I told you I am too old to make this ride. Tell me, young man, who do we have better than you to lead this attack?"

"The count is right, my friend," admitted William.

Although William's unexpected surrender undercut the argument he was trying to make, Charles stubbornly refused to give in without at least one concession. "We cannot take all the knights," he insisted. "If this line collapses before William and I can get through, the duchess will need help to escape. You cannot deny the wisdom of that."

Raglan gave the request a brief thought. "Very well," he relented. "I will keep the palace guard here, and you will take the rest through the forest. Her Grace and I will hold this hill until you can deliver the crucial blow. Everything depends on bringing Eldridge himself down, and the sooner you leave the better."

"Sir Charles," said Elsea, "I would like to speak with you briefly before you go."

"I am afraid he has no time for that," interrupted Raglan. "He must prepare to depart. I will inform the men that he and William will be taking charge of the regiment. You should go with Bishop Prochaska, My Lady. It would help with morale if you visit some of the peasants at their campfires before retiring tonight."

Charles looked across the fire to Elsea. He suspected Raglan's motive for keeping them apart. She was now pledged to marry Otto's nephew, after all. Nevertheless, he knew it would be easy to ignore his wish, and he briefly considered it. "Lord Raglan is right," he conceded reluctantly. "We must organize the men for the long ride. Perhaps there will be a few minutes before I go when we might talk."

She held his gaze a moment before answering. "Yes, perhaps there will be a few minutes before you go." Turning to the bishop, she said, "Come Father, there are some peasants I need to thank."

CHAPTER FIFTY-EIGHT

Destiny

Charles finished tightening the belt of his saddle and stepped back from his horse. He knew Raglan, William, and the rest of the knights were waiting for him at the other side of the camp, but he was in no hurry. He threw a few more sticks onto the fire, and checked again the straps tying down his provisions, blanket, water-skin, armor, sword, and helmet. At last satisfied he was ready, he reached for the reins.

"Charles," called a soft voice from out of the dark.

He spun around and saw her standing like a vision at the edge of the light, half hidden, half revealed by the flickering glow. He dropped the reins as she rushed to embrace him.

He lifted her off her feet and spun her around. "How did you get away?"

"Raglan thinks I am still with the bishop encouraging the peasants," she laughed.

"He is keeping us apart," he said, returning her to earth. "I am sure he thinks it is for our own good."

"He has always been a clever man," she smiled. "But speaking of things for our own good, I understand you are to marry a baron's daughter."

"How did you know?"

"Duke Otto said so in that letter you gave me. He seemed

351

quite pleased with your prospects and warned me not to interfere with his wedding plans for you."

"He does not trust you yet," he frowned. "But that will change after he meets you."

"Hmmm… I am not so sure about that," she mused. "But it appears he trusts me enough to let me marry his nephew, Kendrick."

"Ah, so Kendrick is my rival," nodded Charles. "I know the man. He is not too unpleasant a fellow."

"Is he as tall as you?"

"Quite a bit shorter, I am afraid."

"Oh well," she sighed, "one cannot expect to have everything. And what is the name of this baron's daughter who awaits your return, no doubt with a heart all-a-flutter?"

"Marie."

"I suppose she is a stunning beauty."

"So they tell me."

"And let us not forget that other girl—what was her name— Christa? Why, you must have a veritable harem of women hidden away all over the Empire."

Charles looked into her eyes lit up by the soft light of the fire and saw how she was forcing herself to smile. "It is true," he said, "but my favorite is the Duchess of Austria, and I would trade them all for her."

The touch of sadness that crossed her face pierced his heart like a cold blade.

"Elsea," he said, with a hint of urgency, "we may only have a few minutes, but there is something I must show you before I go." He knelt down closer to the fire and rolled up his shirtsleeve. "Remember this?"

When Elsea saw the small 'X' on his shoulder, she put her hands to her mouth and dropped to her knees alongside him.

"Are you that boy?" she whispered through her fingers. "The one I prayed for everyday?"

"I am your Viking King," he smiled.

"Oh, Charles, you were the happiest memory from my childhood—the only hope I ever knew. What is to become of us?"

"We both know the answer: you will marry Kendrick, and I will marry Marie, and we will return to our old worlds as before."

"Yes—our old worlds as before," she repeated. "It seems I am indeed trapped, just as Lord Raglan said."

"What do you mean?"

"He said my life was destined for tragedy."

"God does not force tragedy upon us," he replied confidently. "We bring it upon ourselves by the choices we make. Just look at all the trouble I caused pretending to be the prince."

"No, Charles, I have thought about it, and I think Raglan might be right. From a child, my life has been moving to this very moment, and I cannot see any way I could have changed it. Even now there is no good choice for me: to lose tomorrow's battle means death, but to win it means to lose you again. Dorianne wants me to run away, but how can I? Many have already died trying to help me, and the serfs are counting on me for their freedom."

"That is what I mean. If you have no good choices it is only because of what I have done."

"You must stop thinking that way, Charles. If you had not pretended to be the prince I would never have met you. What you call trouble was the best thing that ever happened to me. When you left I missed you so terribly that I lost my will to live. If you only knew how desperately I begged God to bring you back. I love you more now than when I thought you were a prince, and whatever harm you believe you have done me I have forgiven you for a hundred times over. God has taken something that could have been terrible, and He has made it wonderful. He has changed something in my heart. I see the world so differently now, and He used you to do it."

Charles stood and pulled her up to him. "Then Raglan is wrong," he said. "Our meeting is not a tragedy, and something good has come from it."

They held each other a long moment in the warm light of the fire.

"After tonight," he whispered into her ear, "we can never do this again."

"Do what?" she whispered into his shoulder.

"Build up our hopes. If we win this war, you will marry Otto's nephew, and I will marry Scheindlin's daughter. We must stop pretending it can be otherwise or we will drive ourselves mad. Let us chose to be grateful for the little time we had together."

She took a half step back, but still held his hands. "So after tonight, I will pretend you are just another pretentious knight, and you will pretend I am just another pompous noble?"

"It has to be that way."

"And what about tomorrow?" she asked. "I suppose you think it will somehow please me if you throw your life away for the sake of my wretched throne."

"I will not throw my life away for the sake of any throne," he promised. "But I will gladly *give* it away for you."

"And Raglan calls *me* stubborn."

"It is one of my many faults," he admitted with a faint smile.

"Since we were children our lives were bound together in secret," she said, touching the mark on his shoulder, "and even now we can only love each other in secret. Perhaps this too is our destiny."

He brought her hands up to his mouth and kissed the back of her fingers. "Perhaps," he conceded, "but it is also our choice.

I will never meet another woman like you, Elsea. I will choose to live a life worthy of your secret love, for you will always be worthy of mine."

"Goodbye, my love," she smiled. "No matter what happens to us, you will always be my Viking King."

"And you will always be my Viking Queen."

He let her hands slip from his, and she glided back into the shadows like a fading dream.

Charles stood staring into the dark long after she was gone. He was still standing there when William came trotting up on his horse.

"Here you are," he said. "Everything is set. Raglan has made his speech and the bishop his prayer. We've the double blessing of church and state. All we need is for you to give the command, and we're off."

Charles looked down at his hands still warm from her touch. He let out a long breath and turned to face his friend. "Have you made a count of our knights?"

"Of course," replied William. "Counting you and me, we have twenty-two Bavarians. Including your friend Antonie, we have three hundred twelve Austrians."

"Good," said Charles, "I want you and our Bavarians to stay with the duchess."

"What!"

"I have this sense of dread that will not leave me," confessed Charles. "Something is going to happen to her, I just know it. I want you to protect her."

"Protect *her!*" exclaimed William. "She'll have three thousand men and an eight foot wall in front of her. You're riding off into a haunted forest with a few hundred knights we were at war with only four days ago. Besides, Raglan agreed to keep her palace guard here for that."

"I do not trust these Austrians," countered Charles. "Too many of them have betrayed her already."

"The duke gave me those knights to protect *you*, my friend, not the Duchess of Austria. If anything happens to you, I'll never be able to show my face in Bavaria."

"And if anything happens to her…"

"She is pledged to another man! Why do you even care?"

"You know why."

William threw his head back and let out a loud groan. "Now you see what I mean: this love nonsense only confuses things. You need to be concentrating on killing Eldridge, not thinking about some woman you can never have."

Charles stepped up to William's horse. "Can't you see? That is the very reason you must stay behind. I will not be able to concentrate on my duty unless I know she is safe."

"She will be in the biggest battle of her life tomorrow," argued William. "How safe do you think she'll be?"

"She will be safer if you are there, and that will be enough for me."

William slid off his horse and grabbed him by the shoulders. "So, you get to go off on the glory ride and leave me behind to play nursemaid to the Austrians. Is that how it's to be? Well, there's only so much a few Bavarians can do, you know. If you don't stick a skewer through old Eldridge by midmorning, none of us will live to see their wedding day."

"Do not worry," said Charles as he climbed into his saddle. "You take care of Her Grace, and leave the Styrian Swine to me."

CHAPTER FIFTY-NINE

Peasants

Elsea watched the morning sun come up behind the Styrian army as she pulled down the ear flaps of her helmet. A lone knight, holding a long staff from which fluttered the red and white banner of the house of Babenberg, stood silent guard beside her.

Raglan had insisted the army be in place and prepared for battle while it was still dark. Since the gray light of dawn, more than two thousand peasants and soldiers had been crouching anxiously behind their barricade which stretched a quarter mile from the river on the right to the brush-choked woods on the left. By taking dirt from the downhill side, they had created a dry moat in front which made the wall facing the Styrians over eight feet high, while the uphill side defended by the Austrians measured only five. The archers held their bows and the footmen their short swords. The serfs, however, wielded the simplest of all weapons: the eight-foot pike. Waiting in reserve behind the crest of the hill, were the rest of peasants and the hundred twenty Austrian and Bavarian knights.

Raglan, Prochaska, and William cantered on horseback along the wall on one final inspection. As they rode by, the peasants shook their pikes and cheered. Raglan's noble bearing impressed them, and the big Bavarian amused them. The bishop, in all his ecclesiastical glory, made them proud. Although Lord Raglan led the trio, they shouted the loudest for Prochaska bringing up the rear. When they reached the river, Raglan turned and led them up the hill to where Elsea waited on her horse. They came to a stop on either side of the duchess.

"What brave men they are, Your Highness!" beamed Prochaska. "They will serve you well today."

Elsea gave him a quick smile and turned to Raglan. "Do you think they will hold?"

"They will be brave," predicted Raglan, "as long as we keep Eldridge on the other side of that wall. It is the most we can expect of them. Every hour they do so gives Charles more time to get into position. We rise or fall on his attack." Looking over at William, he added, "All the more reason why you should have gone with him."

"As I've already explained," replied William calmly, "Charles believes we Bavarians will be of more service here."

"Perhaps you Bavarians are accustomed to acting on your own impulses," scolded Raglan. "We Austrians have found that obedience is the superior virtue. Battles are rarely won by men following their whims."

"Charles isn't following a whim," insisted William. "He believes three hundred of your knights will be sufficient for the task you've set for him. I know Charles, and he'll not fail us."

"You still should not have let him talk you into it," complained Elsea. "You are his friend, and you should have stayed with him."

"He can be very persuasive, My Lady," he answered with a shrug. "But I sent the able captain along in my place." He looked back at Dorianne sitting on her horse a few paces behind Elsea and smiled.

She returned his smile with a frown before looking away.

From their vantage point on the hill, they watched their enemy move into position with a methodical precision. The Styrian footmen formed up in three distinct lines. The men in front carried tall rectangular shields and short double-edged swords. The archers readied their bows in the second line, and men with scaling ladders and hundreds of dirt-filled baskets came last. Duke Eldridge positioned himself in the middle of the hindmost formation of his knights resting in the rear.

"They don't seem to be in any hurry," observed Elsea.

"They believe they have no reason to be," replied Raglan. "All the better for us."

"Old Eldridge fights the way he moves," quipped William, "painfully slow."

"But once he commits to a fight he is like a dog with a bone," returned Raglan. "He will not let go."

Styrian commanders barked out commands as the men closed files and dressed ranks. Finally, the three lines came to attention, and an eerie hush fell over the field.

Raglan turned to Elsea. "The dog is ready, My Lady."

From below, a long and loud horn blast shattered the peaceful silence. The nearly five thousand footmen stepped off on a deliberate march up the hill tramping shoulder to shoulder through the dewy grass. When they reached bow range, the mass of soldiers came to an immediate halt. The front line knelt down, and holding their shields before them, formed their own artificial wall. The archers stepped up to the shield line and began releasing flight after flight of arrows into and over the barricade. The peasants instinctively ducked their heads, and though some arrows struck a few careless men, most sailed harmlessly over them.

Raglan ordered Elsea's archers to refrain from returning fire. "You will have better targets soon enough," he promised. "All they are doing is providing us more arrows to send back."

Suddenly, the men in the third line gave a mighty shout and

charged through the archers and the shield wall. Under the cover of the storm of hissing arrows, they rushed up the hill with the ladders and baskets. Jumping down into the moat, they leaned their ladders against the barricade and began emptying the baskets of dirt at the base of the wall. The horn sounded again, and the first line dropped their shields and sprinted for the ladders yelling at the tops of their lungs. In a matter of seconds, hundreds of Styrians were swarming the wall.

At a signal from Raglan, the archers ran forward and began shooting over the heads of the peasants. Their targets were only paces away and impossible to miss, and the bowmen fired as fast as they could nock an arrow. Some of their victims crumpled forward onto the pikes of the peasants, while others collapsed on the wall hindering their comrades who continued to climb up from behind.

All the Styrians wore helmets, and most had a vest of thick leather protecting their upper body. The peasants wore nothing but the farming clothes they came in. From the wall above them, their assailants slashed and hacked at them with their short swords, severing necks and cleaving heads. The farmer-soldiers stabbed their enemies in the face as they crawled up the ladders, or jabbed with their pikes at their unprotected legs and groins. Raglan and William rode up and down the line shouting commands and giving encouragement.

Though many men on both sides fell under the blows, the attackers had not yet crossed the wall. The screaming, shouting, hacking, and bleeding went on without pause until at last two horn blasts echoed above the din. Eldridge's men scrambled out of the moat and made an orderly retreat down the hill dragging their ladders and empty baskets behind them. They filtered through the archers and picked up their shields. A loud and spontaneous cheer went up from the serfs who had withstood the attack. When the cheering subsided, all was quiet save for the groaning of the wounded.

William turned to Raglan. "That's one."

The two men went to the wall and peered over. Raglan took note of where they had emptied the baskets. At evenly spaced intervals near the center, three piles of dirt already reached half way up the wall.

"They are building ramps," he said. "They want to get their horses across."

Bishop Prochaska came down the hill to assist the wounded and offer prayers for the dying. Dozens of bodies lay on the ground at the places where the fighting had been the deadliest. Many wounded streamed to the rear, some collapsing after only a short distance from loss of blood. The fortunate ones were able to make it to the camp where the peasants in reserve did what they could to bind their ghastly wounds, but could offer no remedy for their pain. Their blood-soaked garments and muffled moans had an unsettling effect on the men waiting their turn to go the wall.

Raglan and William worked quickly to clear the wall of bodies and prepare the men for the next assault. The serfs dragged their friends to the rear and threw their enemies over the wall. After making a quick count of the survivors, Raglan sent Prochaska to bring three hundred more peasants down the hill to replace their losses. The three men made one more pass along the wall to bolster spirits and returned to Elsea watching from her place above them.

"They did well," reported Raglan, "but it was not as serious as it seemed. Eldridge was only testing us. He now knows the strength of our defenses and how we intend to fight. The next blow won't be so light." He looked up at the sun and added, "I hope Charles is getting close."

After Eldridge's men reorganized their depleted ranks, and refilled their baskets, they arranged themselves as before. The horn blew again and the second attack came forward in a rush. Using the ladders, they clambered once more to the top of the wall. Following them were the men with the baskets who worked feverishly on improving the ramps. The battle reached a deadlier level of intensity, and the combat everywhere was bitter.

The fighting had already lasted longer than the first attack, and the Styrians were now coming over the wall and jumping into the midst of the beleaguered peasants. Raglan sent Prochaska up the hill to bring down the rest of his serfs while Elsea's archers kept up a relentless fire into the mass of men climbing across the barricade. The sound of the battle reached a crescendo as the roar of the combatants mixed with the metallic clanging of swords and spears. Men dropped where they stood or stumbled to the rear holding bloody arms or heads. Raglan and William slid from their horses and personally led the newly arrived peasants to the points most in danger of collapse. Through sheer force of will, they kept the men fighting and holding the line.

Just when it seemed they could not last another minute, two horns blew, and the attackers receded as before. The gasping peasants responded with a feeble cheer.

"That's two," panted William.

He and Raglan leaned over the wall. In many places on the floor of the dry moat bodies were piled several feet high. Raglan pointed at the dirt ramps, which now reached the top of the wall and were wide enough for horses to ride two abreast.

"They won't need ladders anymore," he warned.

William noted the bodies strewn before the wall and gave a long whistle. "At least we made them pay for it."

Elsea surprised both men when she slipped in between them. "Is it over?" she asked.

"I am afraid not, My Lady," answered Raglan. "Eldridge has only begun to flex his arm, and we have no more peasants in reserve. I will bring the knights down and have them ready."

"You must be careful, Your Highness," advised William. "We're within bow range here. It'll be safer for you farther up the hill."

"I know quite well why Charles sent you back, Sir William, but you must put it out of your mind. These men defending this wall are more important than my safety."

"Well," inserted Raglan, "unless Charles acts soon, none of us will be safe."

Raglan and William had just finished getting their knights in place, when they heard the horn again. The Styrians gave another bloodthirsty cheer and started up the hill. They brought no archers or ladders this time. As Raglan expected, the attackers converged on the dirt ramps. In three places, they came across the wall like water spilling over a dam. They slashed, stabbed, and clubbed at the defenders from the top of the barricade while others jumped down and fought fiercely to rupture the line. The peasants battled back with equal fury, and at first, the line held.

A continual stream of new men coming over the top plunged into the throng below them, and the opposing forces hacked away at each other at close quarters. Killing at such range required no skill. So tightly packed were the men in some places that the dead, wedged between friend and foe, were unable to fall to the ground.

Despite the fortitude of the peasants, the leadership of Raglan and William, and the steady volleys of arrows from the archers, the overwhelmed peasants began to yield foot by foot, and the line was in danger of breaking. It was then that Raglan ordered the knights into the battle. William led his Bavarians on foot at the breach on the right, while Raglan took half of the Austrians and attacked the left. Elsea gathered the remainder and led them against the center. She wielded her broadsword in both hands, and charged into the Styrians with a fierce shout.

Grasping his great sword, William waded into the mass of men pouring over the wall. To his left and right he hewed and sliced with a savage energy. Like a boat passing through a stormy sea, he moved steadily forward, leaving broken bones, cracked skulls, and severed limbs in his wake. His faithful band of Bavarians followed him against the raging tide, and as the intensity of their counter blows grew, the resolve of their opponents diminished. William and his Bavarians at last forced the attackers in their area back over the wall.

Raglan's counterattack had also pushed the Styrians back, but Elsea struggled to move forward in the center. Raglan and William now turned on this pocket of resistance from either side. Together, the three of them closed the last fissure in the line. The horn sounded at last, and the remaining attackers fled down the hill, staggering and stumbling as they went. The exhausted peasants collapsed to the ground made slippery with blood.

There was no cheering this time.

A layer of bodies, two and three deep, littered the area near the three ramps. Bloody men limped or dragged themselves away, and from everywhere came the wretched moans of the wounded unable to move. Raglan met Elsea and William near the middle of the wall. They did their best to avoid stepping on the dead and dying all around them.

"We are very vulnerable right now," warned a panting Raglan. "We must regroup while we have time."

Bishop Prochaska joined them. The hem of his robe and the cuffs of his sleeves were drenched in blood. "How much more of this must they endure?" he pleaded.

"I don't know," said Raglan without looking him in the eyes.

"I'm sorry," said Elsea. "They have done so much, but the battle is not yet won."

Prochaska's eyes widened when he saw Elsea's face. "My Lady, you are injured!" Elsea wiped a hand across the part of her face not covered by her helmet. She brought it down covered in blood. It was not hers. "I am alright," she assured him. "Come; let us tend to the wounded as best we can."

William gathered a group of peasants to once more clear the wall of the dead and wounded. However, even the strongest men now struggled to move the heavy bodies, and the grisly task went slowly. Archers who had run out of arrows scavenged among the dead pulling still useful shafts from their lifeless victims. Meanwhile, Raglan reformed the line and counted survivors. He placed the knights, now numbering less than a hundred, back in reserve.

Elsea joined Raglan to watch their enemy prepare for yet another attack. This time, however, the footmen did not form ranks. Instead, fifteen hundred colorfully equipped knights came slowly up the hill on their horses. Moving in three long parallel lines, they passed through the depleted ranks of the worn-out footmen and went into position. Eldridge stayed at the rear with his last five hundred knights.

While the Styrians readied themselves, William walked along the top of the wall from one end to the other. He joked with the peasants about how they would at last be able to kill some noblemen. The nervous men looked up at the big man whose chest and arms were red with blood. "Don't let those fancy clothes fool you," he laughed. "They've got flesh and bones underneath just like you and me. Jab them where they don't have any armor and they'll bleed out like gutted pigs."

When he finished his tour, he jumped down from the wall and returned to where Elsea, Raglan and Prochaska now waited on horseback in front of the remaining knights. Once out of sight of the peasants, William's carefree demeanor changed. He pulled himself atop his horse and gave Raglan a somber look.

"They won't survive this assault," he told him. "I can see it in their faces. They've gone beyond fear and are on the verge of panic."

"Is it as bad as that?" asked Prochaska.

"They've held off twice their numbers for over four hours," replied William. "It's more than we had a right to expect. They're fought out and can do no more. Before those knights make it halfway up the hill, your peasants will fly from this wall like dead leaves in a wind."

"Why is he using his knights now?" asked Elsea.

"He's been waiting to see what we had in reserve," explained Raglan. "That last attack showed him we are down to only a handful of knights. They'll use those ramps to come over the wall, and without the peasants, we can't stop him."

"But we must hold," insisted Elsea. "Charles has not yet attacked."

"What could be keeping him?" wondered Prochaska. "It is approaching noon. I thought you said he would be here by now."

"Maybe the journey required more time than we anticipated, or perhaps the Styrians discovered our maneuver," suggested Raglan. "Whatever has caused his delay is not important now. If William is correct about the peasants, we have only a few minutes to make a decision."

"What decision?" asked Elsea.

"My Lady," said Raglan after a pause, "we have done all we can here. We have made a valiant stand, but we must now consider your welfare and plan our escape."

"Escape!"

"Yes. We can head for my estates in the north and gather more knights—you'll be safer there."

"How can you talk about being safe?" she replied. "Charles is counting on us to hold this hill. He may be about to break out of that forest even as we speak. What will become of him if he attacks a whole army by himself?"

"Charles knows how to take care of himself," William tried to assure her.

"You are not one to talk," she retorted. "You should have stayed with him in the first place. A fine friend you are!" She pointed to the peasants still cowering behind the wall. "What about these men? Are we just going to ride away and leave them to their fate?"

"Eldridge's goal is Vienna," replied Raglan. "The peasants will be safe once they discard their weapons and disband."

Elsea walked her horse forward a few paces. "And what about them?" she asked, pointing at one of the rows of haphazardly strewn bodies. "These men died for me today. Am I to be remembered as the duchess who encouraged hundreds to die, but fled for her life at the first sight of blood?"

"What do you propose?" asked Raglan.

"We must stay and fight," she said.

"Fight with what, My Lady?" asked William. "Once they begin their attack, there'll be no stopping them."

"Then we don't wait for them to attack," she replied coolly. "We attack first."

The only answer the three men gave her was the shock on their faces.

"I say we attack with our knights," continued Elsea undeterred. "We charge their forward line and do as much damage as we can before retreating. They will not be expecting it. At worst, it will give us more time. Who knows, but even a quarter hour might be all that Charles needs."

"But we've barely a hundred knights," noted Raglan. "Look down that hill; there must be five hundred men in the first line alone."

"Lord Raglan," said Elsea in lower voice, "I know I have often grieved you with my childish behavior. Please believe I am not being childish now. You know what condition Otto placed on his offer of alliance. If we flee from this battle, is there any hope of stopping Eldridge from taking Vienna?"

"None, My Lady," answered Raglan.

"If we lose the support of Otto," she continued, "is there any hope of retaining my coronet?"

"None, My Lady," he repeated.

"So, I will lose everything by running, but might gain everything by fighting." She nudged her horse a little closer. "You knew my grandfather better than anyone. Tell me, Lord Raglan, what would Duke Leopold have done?"

Raglan looked up at the sun, then over at Prochaska and William, and finally back to Elsea. "He would have fought to his last ounce of strength," he answered, "and prayed for Charles to arrive."

William pulled his blood-stained sword from its sheath. "You wait here, Your Highness," he said. "We'll make this charge for you."

Elsea looked Raglan in the eyes but did not speak.

"No, Sir William," said Raglan breaking her gaze, "it is Her Grace's place to lead us."

Elsea looked up at the knights waiting behind Raglan. "I believe this attack is our best hope for victory," she said confidently. "We must gain more time for Sir Charles and our Austrian knights. I will force no man against his will, and I will make this ride by myself if need be." She looked up and down the line once more before adding, "Any man who does not wish to follow me may leave now."

None stirred.

The last of the knights filed through the small opening in the wall the peasants dug out. They formed up in two equal lines in front of the barricade. Nothing stood between them and the Styrian knights but the trampled-down grass and the scattered dead. William and the Bavarians were in the front with Elsea.

Lord Raglan had ordered Bishop Prochaska and Dorianne to remain with the peasants. "If Eldridge breaks through," he warned them, "you must lead them away as best you can."

Raglan walked his horse back and forth before the knights. "We will strike the center of their first line," he shouted. "Stay close together and keep moving forward. When I give the signal, we will circle to the left and fight our way back to this wall and reform. We must disrupt them as much as we can. Every minute we delay their attack increases our chances of victory."

Coming up alongside Elsea, Raglan leaned in close. "No matter what happens in the next hour," he said, "you have made this old man proud." He drew his sword and held it above his head. Elsea and the knights behind her did the same. Twirling his sword above him, he bellowed, "Honor! Courage! Austria!!" The men gave a cheer and started down the hill at a gallop with the banner of the house of Babenberg fluttering proudly at the front.

CHAPTER SIXTY

Last Ride

For the third time since they entered the forest, Charles and the captain had to stop to allow the rest of the column to catch up. Antonie had not exaggerated when he said the trail would be difficult. There were many twists and turns, and in some places the path was so slender the knights had to pass through single file. At one point during the night the column stretched out almost two miles. In the daylight, on an open road, this would not have posed a problem. In the dark confines of the confusing forest, however, Charles could not risk riding on and letting half his men get lost.

He glanced up through the trees at the sun while they waited for word from the captain. "We should have been there by now," he complained to Antonie. "How much farther do you think it is?"

"With or *without* stopping?" asked Antonie.

"Without," sighed Charles.

"I think we are at least an hour from the edge."

"This is our last stop," grumbled Charles. "Once the rear catches up, we will push on as fast as we can. Thirty men on time will be better than three hundred too late."

The captain at last rode up to them. "The column has closed up, My Lord, but we are still stretched out on this trail. It took me almost half an hour to reach you from the back of the line."

"There is nothing we can do about it now," said Charles. "Antonie believes we are getting close to the end. Perhaps the going will improve, and we can make better time." He gave his horse a gentle nudge, and the long line of knights crept forward again.

More than an hour later, the serpentine formation continued to wend its way through the forest. Charles suspected the tail of the column had fallen behind again, but was determined to press on regardless. The unexpected delay in reaching the battlefield was beginning to wear on him, and he struggled against a growing sense of foreboding that they would be too late. Adding to his annoyance, the trail in some places grew so faint as to disappear. Antonie twice had to dismount and snoop around like a dog on a scent until picking up the trail again. These delays, combined with several days of little sleep, only increased his anxiety.

He looked over his shoulder at the big man riding behind him. "Really, Antonie, this road of yours is atrocious. We could have crossed the Alps and been halfway to Rome by now."

"I told all of you it wasn't a road," Antonie shot back. "It wasn't my idea to bring a whole army through a dark forest on an old goat path."

Charles turned around and resumed his sulking. He was looking up at the sun, trying to guess the time, when suddenly the captain riding in front pulled back on his reins and raised a hand.

"What is it?" asked Charles as he came alongside.

The captain pointed ahead. "Look!"

Charles followed his arm and saw more sunlight coming through the trees up ahead.

Antonie joined them. "We're at the end."

"Thank God," declared Charles, "and not a moment too soon."

The three men put their horses into a canter and quickly

arrived at a place where the trees thinned out and they could see a sundrenched field before them.

"Bring the rest of the men forward," Charles said to the captain, "but assemble them here under the cover of these trees. Antonie and I will scout the area."

He and Antonie slipped from their horses and jogged ahead to see where the end of the trail had brought them. They had only gone a short distance into the sunny field when Charles suddenly dropped to the ground pulling Antonie by the arm with him. Peeking discreetly over the tall grass waving in the breeze, the two men looked upon at the entire Styrian army spread out before them.

"You're a genius, Antonie!" whispered Charles. "You've brought us out right on top of Eldridge, and he has no clue we are here. We could not possibly have hoped for better. I take back every word I said back there."

"I can't believe it actually worked," replied a wide-eyed Antonie.

From their secret perch, the two men made a quick appraisal of the battlefield. The barricade was still intact and seemed well manned by the peasants. Charles pointed to the cluster of mounted knights behind the wall. "There is the duchess next to the red and white banner."

"Look at all those bodies in front of the wall," said Antonie.

"They've certainly been hard pressed," replied Charles, "but the important thing is we made it in time. Raglan and Elsea are still holding the hill, and we have gotten completely behind old Eldridge. Look at him," he said, pointing to the large man whose back was to them. "If I had one good archer with me we could take him down from here."

"What about all those knights around him?" asked Antonie.

"We will make a plan as soon as the rest of the column catches up," answered Charles. "You stay here and keep an eye on them. I am going back to get your Austrian brothers organized."

Charles crawled through the tall grass on hands and knees. Once safely back inside the shadows, he jumped up and ran to where he left the captain. The arriving knights had grown to several dozen.

"Where are the rest?" asked Charles.

"They're coming, My Lord. I'm afraid they got too spread out again. It'll take at least half an hour for everyone to close up."

Charles was busy untying his armor from his horse. "Do the best you can," he said, "but be sure to keep them in these woods. Antonie has put us dead center behind Eldridge, and I want to stay hidden." He pulled his armor over his head and was tying together the straps when Antonie came running up to them.

"Something is happening," he panted.

"What is it?" asked Charles.

"Come and see."

Arriving at the field, the two men crawled along until they could see the battlefield again.

"Look," said Antonie, "the Styrians are moving their knights forward. What could it mean?"

"It means we have less time than I thought," answered Charles. "Eldridge would not commit his knights unless he believed the battle was nearly won. I've got to hurry those Austrians up."

He crept back to the trees and ran up to the captain. "How much longer?"

"I'm not sure, My Lord. We've a hundred twenty now, and eight or ten are arriving every minute."

Charles rubbed his eyes with the heels of his hands. "We can't wait twenty more minutes. Eldridge is getting ready…"

An out of breath Antonie ran up and grabbed him by the arm.

"Now what?" blurted Charles.

The big man did not speak, but motioned for Charles to follow him. The two men ran back to the field.

"Look," said Antonie when they reached their spy nest.

They watched as the tiny group of Austrian and Bavarian knights finished crossing the wall and formed up in two lines on the hill facing fifteen hundred Styrians.

"What is Raglan doing?" asked a bewildered Charles. "He was supposed to hold the hill until we could make our attack."

"I'm no general," admitted Antonie, "but that doesn't look a wise battle tactic to me."

"There is nothing wise about it," agreed Charles. "The safest place to defend…" He lost his train of thought when he saw Elsea and her knights draw their swords and start their charge down the hill. Charles jumped up. "Elsea!"

Antonie reached up and pulled him down by his belt. "Be quiet," he whispered loudly. "You'll give us away."

Charles leapt up and sprinted into the forest.

"How many men do we have?" he shouted to the captain as he scrambled onto his horse.

"We're up to a hundred eighty, My Lord."

"Good, I am taking them now. Stay here until the rest are up and then lead them into the battle. Attack wherever you think you can do the most good."

"But in fifteen more minutes the whole regiment will be ready," protested the captain.

"I don't have fifteen more seconds," Charles shouted over his shoulder. "The duchess is in danger!" With that word, he put his horse into a cantor with a hundred eighty of Raglan's best knights behind him.

The astonished nobles around Duke Eldridge all talked at once as they tried to find explanation for what they saw happening up the hill.

Over the sound of their babbling, Lord Eugene spoke out, "It is as I told you, My Lord: the woman is mad! What further proof do you need?"

"Indeed," replied Eldridge, "only the insane would think to keep us from breeching that wall with such a disheveled gaggle of knights."

"Perhaps she is preparing to surrender," offered Rottermund.

"That is unlikely," doubted Eugene. "Surrender would be the prudent thing to do, but she knows not the meaning of the word."

"Whether she possesses more wisdom than Solomon or is a raving lunatic makes little difference now," noted a gleeful Eldridge. "This battle is over, and I will be master of Austria before the noon meal!"

A sudden groan swept through the nobles. "Look, My Lord!" someone yelled.

Eldridge and his flabbergasted lords watched as Elsea and her slender band began their desperate charge.

"The audacity!" exclaimed Eldridge. "Does she think so little of my knights? She insults me and every man of Styria." He turned to his right. "Lord Eugene, I have had enough of this woman's insolence. Bring me her head on one of her peasant's pikes, and I will double the size of your fief."

Eugene drew out his sword from its scabbard. "Nothing would please me more, My Lord," he smiled. He spurred his horse and started forward.

With William to her right and Raglan to her left, Elsea stood up in her stirrups, pointed her sword forward, and led the charge at full gallop. The suddenness of their attack caught the knights of the first line off guard. Before they realized what was happening, the fearless flock of Austrians and Bavarians burst upon them. The violence of the impact tore a small hole in the line, as fifty Styrian knights went down at once. It was here that Raglan had intended to begin the long circle back to friendly lines. The unexpected ease of their small victory, however, combined with the sudden rush of their emotions, propelled them forward down the hill toward the second line without breaking stride.

These knights, having learned from the fate of their comrades in front of them, were better prepared. Drawing their swords, they gave a cheer and charged up the hill. The two forces met in a brutal collision that sent men and horses tumbling in all directions. Having lost their forward momentum, Elsea's knights now fought from a standstill. The wings of the second line began to bend in on them, forcing the outnumbered attackers onto the defensive.

"Keep together," shouted Raglan. "Keep together!"

Recovering from their initial shock, the first line of Styrians now turned around to attack the Austrians from behind. The unscathed third line, sensing an easy victory over the duchess herself, started forward as well. Lord Eugene, eager to claim his reward, was at their head. In a matter of minutes, Elsea and her valiant knights were trapped and fighting for their lives.

Charles and his knights spilled out of the forest in a confused jumble. Gripped by panic for Elsea's safety, he had not thought through what he would do next. He halted them near where Antonie still waited.

"Go back to the captain," ordered Charles. "Tell him to

bring the rest of the regiment out as soon as they are ready. I want him to support my attack." He thought it best not to let Antonie know he was still figuring that part out.

By the time Charles turned around again, Elsea was completely encircled. From his vantage point the knights around her looked like a small island ravaged by stormy waves on all sides. The first idea that crossed his mind was to ride to her rescue. Yet, between him and the duchess stood the five hundred knights of Eldridge's last reserve as well as a few thousand idle footmen. Even the topography, which he had used to his advantage previously, now worked against him. The river to his left and the forest to his right meant there was no way around them. Charles thought quickly and gave orders for the knights to divide into three troops.

He pulled his helmet on and pointed to Duke Eldridge. "That is the man we came to kill," he shouted. "Her Highness will not be safe as long as he continues to live." He drew his sword and held it above his head. Rearing his horse up on its hind legs, he yelled, "God bless the man who brings him down!" He brought his horse under control. "For our Duchess and for Austria!"

The Austrians gave a loud cheer and took off at the gallop.

Eldridge and his nobles enjoyed themselves immensely watching Elsea's demise.

"Lord Eugene had better hurry if he wants his trophy," laughed Rottermund. "There won't be much of her left soon."

"I believe you are right," agreed a chuckling Eldridge. "Too bad we can't get them word to save her for last."

The sound of a throaty cheer, and the rumble of hoof beats from behind, cut short their laughter. The duke and his lords spun around just in time to see the Austrian knights galloping down on them from out of nowhere.

Eldridge instantly spurred his horse hard in the opposite direction and bolted up the hill toward the wall. He looked back at the stunned men he left behind. "Stop them you fools!" he yelled.

Charles and the Austrians struck the astonished Styrians like a thunderbolt. Slashing and thrusting with their swords, they tore a wide gash in the line and emptied scores of Styrian saddles. Most had not time to even draw a weapon. Ignoring the startled survivors, Charles and his men chased Eldridge up the hill and through the resting footmen. The weary men rose up and cheered their duke thinking he was riding forward to the battle. Their celebration ended abruptly when they realized the knights behind him were not Styrians. They scattered like a flock of birds as the Austrians galloped over them, striking them down at will. Nevertheless, the delay caused by overcoming the near defenseless footmen allowed Eldridge to reach the safety of the knights closing in on Elsea but a few strides in front of Charles. The duke turned his horse about and cried, "Save me!"

The Austrians slammed into the rear line of knights, and their charge came to a halt. Charles exhorted his men to get Eldridge, but the Styrians resisted them bitterly. The knights who originally protected Eldridge regained their composure and now attacked from the rear. Soon, Charles found himself in the same predicament as Elsea: surrounded and outnumbered.

The two beleaguered bands were near enough to hear each other's shouts, but could not get any closer. Charles heard Raglan urging them to keep together, but saw that the Styrians had already managed to split Elsea's dwindling force in two. Elsea and her knights each fought two or three attackers at the same time. William and his Bavarians tried desperately to fight their way back to Raglan and the duchess, but the Styrians assailed them from every side. It was a fight they could not hope to win.

Seeing Elsea's plight fueled Charles with even more determination. Shouting above the deafening roar of the battle, he ordered the troops to either side to defend his flanks and rear. He would take his center group and fight his way to Eldridge. With their horses rubbing shoulders, he and his men wedged their way forward, step by step, hacking and slashing with a renewed ferocity. Eldridge continued to back his horse up the hill to keep a solid line of knights between him and the infuriated Charles.

From atop their horses in front of the wall, Prochaska and Dorianne watched the battle unfold. They had cheered when Elsea broke through the first line, but were horrified when she became surrounded. Charles unexpectedly erupting from the woods gave them a new hope that was soon dashed when he failed to catch the fleeing Eldridge. But now their greatest concern was for Elsea. Assailed from every direction, it was clear she could not hold out much longer.

"Oh, My Lord," pleaded Dorianne, "you must do something. Her Highness is in great danger!"

"I know, my child, I know," answered the anxious priest, yet he sat frozen in his saddle.

"Please, My Lord!" shouted Dorianne.

The young girl's urgent entreaty shattered the paralysis of the bishop. He looked behind him at the apprehensive peasants peering back at him from over the barricade. Wheeling his horse around, he trotted up to the wall. "Your Lady is in peril!" he roared. "She needs your help!"

The frightened look on their faces did not change.

He spurred his horse and galloped down the length of the

wall repeating his warning. When he returned to Dorianne in the center, he stopped and shook his crosier at them. "Who is on the Lord's side?" he yelled.

A few scattered voices offered up a frail, "We are."

Prochaska stood up in his saddle. "Will you stand idly by and watch your Lady die?" He roared louder, "Who is on the Lord's side?"

This time a few hundred responded.

The bishop removed his miter and placed it over his crosier. Holding it high above his head, he bellowed, "My children, your heavenly Father looks down on you. His glorious kingdom awaits His faithful servants, and we fear not death like the heathen!" Waving his bishop's staff before them, he gave one more mighty blast, "Who is on the Lord's side?"

Instantly, fifteen hundred peasants shouted back at the tops of their voices, "WE ARE!"

Prochaska put his hat back on and spun his horse around. Looking back at the peasants, he pointed his crosier down the hill. "God save our duchess!" he thundered and spurred his horse into a gallop.

The suddenly rejuvenated peasants grasped their pikes and spilled over the wall like angry hornets disturbed from their nest.

Elsea's knights now fought in three isolated pockets. Ignoring Raglan's band to his right and William's Bavarians to his left, Lord Eugene picked his way through the press of horses and inched toward Elsea in the center. When he finally made it to her small circle, only a handful of exhausted knights was left to defend her, and only one mounted soldier, already fighting three other knights at once, tried to resist him.

Eugene wasted no time with clever thrusts or parries. In one violent blow, he shattered his sword on the brave man's helmet, and he toppled to the ground. Casting his broken blade aside, Eugene reached down and grabbed his mace. Grasping the wooden handle, he held the heavy club with the spiked iron ball at the end over his head and closed in on Elsea. Locked in combat with two other knights, she was unaware of his approach.

Eugene came up behind her and swung the club fiercely. "Die you ugly wench!" he shouted as the deadly ball struck her between the shoulder blades.

Elsea cried out and collapsed onto the neck of her horse, her sword slipping from her hand.

Eugene urged his horse closer for a finishing blow. At that moment, the yell of the onrushing peasants overcame the roar of the combatants. The Styrians battling Elsea and Charles did not see the wave of enraged serfs coming on at a dead run until it was too late. Being closest to the wall, Eldridge and the cluster of knights around him were the first they encountered. The farmer-soldiers employed no subtle combat techniques. Groups of four and five simply rushed the tightly packed men on horseback, pulled them to the ground, and stabbed them to death with their pikes. Working from the fringe of the melee, Elsea's archers used up their remaining arrows, making every shot count. Surrounded and alone, Eldridge threw himself off his horse and begged for his life.

With their duke down and most of the leaders killed or wounded in Charles's first charge, there was no one left to give orders. The remaining Styrian knights now began to think only of their own survival. In groups of two and three at first, and then in dozens, they turned to flee from the furious peasants.

Already fatigued from having endured the worst of the battle, and demoralized by the surprise attack of Charles, the Styrian footmen looked on with alarm at the unexpected charge of the peasants. Suddenly, the captain and the rest of the Austrian knights burst forth from the trees at a full gallop. The startled footmen fled before the deadly wave wondering how many more Austrians were waiting to fall upon them without warning. What little resolve to stand and fight they still possessed evaporated when they saw their own gallant knights hurtling by in a jumbled stampede to the rear. Their contagious panic swept over the footmen like a strong wind, and throwing down their weapons, they joined the flood of refugees.

Lord Eugene shouted himself hoarse trying to get the Styrians around him to stay and fight. The ferocity of the peasants, the deadly arrows of the archers, and the fresh knights arriving from the forest were too much for them, however, and they too abandoned him. The exasperated Eugene cursed loudly, and hurled his mace at a group of peasants now running at him. He wheeled his horse and joined the shattered remains of the routed army streaming away to the south.

The knights who had been opposing Charles suddenly vanished before him and fled for their lives. He pressed forward through the wave of peasants chasing after them and came upon Eldridge encircled by a cluster of laughing serfs who poked and jabbed at him with their pikes. The disgraced duke cowered in the grass and pleaded with them to spare him. Charles slid from his horse and approached Eldridge with sword in hand. The peasants recognized him and took a respectful step backward.

The terrified duke looked up at the blood-spattered knight. "Mercy, My Lord," he whimpered, "have mercy!"

Charles brought his sword up over his head and paused as he considered slaying the man who was the cause of so much misery. "It is for Her Grace to decide your fate," he said as he brought his sword down, "but there will be no tears shed at your execution." He pulled himself back on his horse. "Keep him here," he said to the peasants. "If he attempts to escape, butcher him like a fatted calf."

Charles walked his horse through the debris of battle in the direction of the last place he saw Elsea. Discarded helmets, splintered shields, and abandoned weapons of every description littered the field. He had to guide his horse around the dead and wounded men strewn across the hillside. Knights and peasants moved up and down the slope, comingling in their search for fallen comrades. Still others took advantage of the opportunity to strip the dead Styrians of their rich apparel. The deafening and frenzied roar of combat gave way to an eerie silence, broken only by the groans of the wounded and men calling out for missing friends.

At last, Charles saw the familiar profile of his friend William as he stood with Raglan and Prochaska near a strangely somber cluster of men. He rode up to them and jumped down from his horse. "Where is the duchess?"

The look on William's face startled him, as did the sound of a woman crying.

"My Lady, My Lady," wept Dorianne.

Upon seeing Charles, Raglan and Prochaska stepped aside to allow him to enter the small circle. Kneeling on the ground, her shoulders heaving from her sobbing, was Dorianne. In her arms lay Elsea.

Charles threw his helmet aside and dropped to his knees beside her. "Elsea," he said.

At the sound of his voice, she opened her eyes. "Charles," she said faintly, "is that you?"

"I am here," he said, taking her in his arms.

"Is it over?" she asked, between struggling breaths.

"You have won a great victory, My Lady, and Duke Eldridge is your prisoner."

She relaxed slightly, as if relieved, then suddenly grabbed his arm. "Are you harmed?"

"No," he answered, fighting back his tears. "I am well."

"Thank God," she gasped.

As Charles looked down into her green eyes, his tears began to splash on her cheek.

Elsea reached up and gently touched his face. "Hush, my love," she said weakly. She brought her hand down, closed her eyes, and went limp in his arms.

"My Lady!" screamed Dorianne.

CHAPTER SIXTY-ONE

Supplicant

Bishop Prochaska laid a hand on Dorianne's heaving shoulder. "There now, my child," he said tenderly. "You must get the better of your grief."

Charles looked up imploringly at Raglan.

"We have sent to Fairfield for a physician," Raglan assured him.

"Fairfield is too far," replied Charles. "We need someone now, and I don't mean a physician."

"But who then?" asked Raglan.

Charles gently laid Elsea in Dorianne's lap and stood up. "Has anyone seen Antonie?"

Word of the duchess's fall spread quickly, and a group of peasants had gathered nearby. "I've seen him, My Lord," said one of them. "I'm from Longwood, and Antonie is our steward. He rode up the hill a few minutes ago."

Charles leapt onto his saddle and gave his horse a lash without looking back.

After he left, Lord Raglan directed several knights to lash together two Styrian shields with pikes and cords. They carefully placed Elsea on the crude litter and carried her up the hill toward the camp beyond the wall. Bishop Prochaska led the solemn procession through the wreckage of the battlefield. They passed knights who saluted with their swords, and peasants who knelt in the grass and crossed themselves as they bore the stricken duchess to the rear.

Charles crossed the wall through the opening the peasants had made, and headed for the main camp. He noticed an increasing number of women moving among the grisly dead and near dead scattered along the barricade. Streaming in from the surrounding villages were the wives, mothers, sisters, and daughters of the combatants who now stoically searched the field for their loved ones.

He crested the hill and encountered yet more misery. During the fight for the wall, most of the walking wounded had resorted here for safety. Charles saw hundreds of injured spread throughout the camp. The men that had laughed and joked confidently the night before around the warm light of their fires now lay moaning in pain by the cold ashes. The fortunate ones had friends or family to tend their wounds and comfort them. The less fortunate suffered alone.

Charles scanned the camp up and down until he at last saw the big man. He rode over to find him leaning over a motionless peasant stretched out on the ground.

"You're alive!" marveled Antonie.

"Somehow, I made it through the whole battle without a scratch," said Charles as he slid from his horse.

"I lost sight of you when you disappeared in the middle of all those Styrians," said Antonie. "I told that captain fellow of yours, but he didn't seem in too big a hurry. I didn't think he would ever get his people into the battle."

Charles nodded toward the man lying in the grass. "Do you know him?"

"He isn't much older than my Andre," answered Antonie somberly. "His father told him this wasn't a peasant's war and tried to talk him out of volunteering. The boy said that after the battle he wouldn't be a peasant anymore; he'd be free." Antonie shook his head. "I guess he's free now."

A pang of guilt swept over Charles for having encouraged the recruitment of the serfs, but he recalled the urgency of his mission and quickly swept it aside. "I am on my way to Longwood," he said. "I need to know where Sarah lives."

"What do you want with the old witch?"

"The duchess is injured."

"Doesn't she have her own physicians?"

"I don't want a physician," answered Charles with growing impatience. "I want Sarah. Please tell me where I can find her."

"Have it your way," shrugged Antonie, "but you won't have to go to Longwood."

"Why not?"

"The woman can smell death from ten leagues away, and she's drawn to it like a moth to a flame. She's already here."

"Where?" pleaded Charles.

"I last saw her over there," answered Antonie, pointing to a place in the distance.

Charles swung himself onto his horse and cantered away.

He found her kneeling by a man suffering from a wound to his stomach. Cradling his head in her lap was the man's wife. Sarah stuffed some rags into the bleeding gash, looked over at the young priest who stood nearby, and shook her head. The man moaned and begged his wife for water. She reached for an animal skin and started to put it to his lips, but Sarah stopped her.

"Don't give him anything to drink," she warned her.

"But he's thirsty," replied the anxious woman.

"Your husband's wound is mortal," said Sarah, "and there's nothing more I can do for him. If you do what you can to keep him comfortable, he might die peacefully. But if you give him that water, he'll die in a painful agony that will break your heart."

She laid a bloody hand on her arm and added softly, "If you love him, you'll ignore his pleadings."

Sarah stood to move on to the next sufferer, and the young priest stepped in to pray for the dying man.

Charles walked into her path. "Hello, Sarah, do you remember me?"

She stepped back and looked over the young bloodstained knight who stood before her. "The mysterious man who came back from the dead," she said without emotion. "I see the experience hasn't diminished your appetite for blood."

"Sarah, I need your help," he said, ignoring her comment. "There is someone who is badly wounded."

"Look around you," she said, throwing her arms out wide. "There are enough here to keep me busy for a week."

"You don't understand," he replied. "This is someone very important."

She glanced at the young couple on the ground. "More important than he is to his wife?"

"It is the duchess!" he blurted, certain that mentioning Elsea would end all debate.

"So it is the duchess," she said without changing her expression. She held up her hands. "She's the reason my hands are covered in blood. She's the reason that woman must watch her husband die in her lap." She waved an arm toward the center of the camp. "Why should I leave them to help her?"

Charles had no answer. He realized that his bloodstains came from those he had tried to kill, while hers were from those she had tried to save. Maybe those responsible for all the suffering around them did not deserve to be comforted. Yet the vision of Elsea lying injured on that field would not leave his mind. In desperation, he stepped closer. "Sarah," he begged, "I don't know if she deserves your help. I don't know if I deserved it when you saved my life. All I know is that she means very much to me and that if she dies all this suffering will have been for nothing. Please help her Sarah; there is no one else I trust."

She held his gaze for a long moment, gave a grunt, and slung her brown bag over her shoulder. "Take me to her," she sighed.

CHAPTER SIXTY-TWO

Seclusion

The injured duchess needed shelter. Normally, she would have traveled with enough tenting and provisions to house even the most discriminating in high style. Their hasty departure from Vienna had prevented them from bringing such portable comfort however. Raglan solved that problem by appropriating Eldridge's oversized royal tent from his abandoned camp, already crawling with peasants zealously hauling away armloads of precious spoil. His knights wasted no time tearing it down and dragging it up the hill.

While they hurriedly erected the tent, Sarah examined Elsea as she lay on her makeshift stretcher. She held her hand, looked in her eyes, and listened to her breathe, but made no comments beyond her habitual grunting. Charles studied her in vain for a clue to her thoughts. Once the tent was finished, she and Dorianne disappeared inside with the duchess.

Duke Eldridge had no shelter. He sat on a horse blanket spread out on the ground, ignominiously bound hand and foot and closely watched by a half dozen knights. The peasants who mocked him as they passed by did little to dampen his brooding.

The tireless Prochaska put his peasant army to work bringing the injured to a central area. Many of the wounded were Styrians, but the bishop insisted they receive the same treatment as the Austrians. "We are all God's children now," he declared.

Unlike the dead Austrians, whose friends and loved ones were coming to carry their bodies home, the Styrians needed burying. Prochaska ordered them laid out in the ditch before the wall. Many of the same peasants who just hours before had caused the death of these men now covered them with the very dirt they had sheltered behind.

It was important that Duke Otto hear a report of the battle from someone he trusted. Raglan decided to send William and his remaining Bavarians to find him.

"I've written the duke a letter," he said, handing him a small pouch. "In view of Her Lady's health, I recommend that we meet here to discuss the details of his proposal." He placed a hand on the big knight's shoulder. "I told him how much we are indebted to you."

"It's Charles you should thank," replied William. "He's the one who convinced the duke to help Her Grace in a war she had no hope of winning."

"Your friend has many qualities," admitted Raglan. "He is well deserving of your lord's confidence."

William pulled himself onto his horse. "Charles believes I'll find Duke Otto on the road west of Vienna. If that's true, you may expect to hear from him within a week."

Raglan watched them disappear down the road and then went looking for Charles whom he had not seen since he left in search of Antonie.

He found him sitting in the grass a few yards from Elsea's new tent agonizing over what to make of Sarah's long visit. Before he could speak, however, the flap of the tent door flew up and Sarah walked out. Charles leapt to his feet, and the two men rushed up to her.

"How is she?" blurted Charles.

Sarah stretched her arms toward the sun and let out a groaning yawn.

"The wound is serious," she announced matter-of-factly. "Were it not for her mail shirt, she might already be dead." She readjusted the bag around her neck and began walking to where Father Prochaska had been bringing the wounded.

The two men exchanged fearful glances. Charles ran after her and grabbed her by the arm. "Is that all?"

"I've explained everything to the girl," she moaned. "She will answer all your questions."

Charles continued to hold her arm.

"She probably has some broken ribs," she relented after a sigh, "but she isn't coughing up blood yet, and that's always a good sign. The pain from her injury is making it difficult for her to breathe. She will have that pain for many days, and I told her she must get used to it and try to breathe normally. It'll be at least a month before she can return to Vienna. Until then, keep those fools who call themselves physicians away from her. They will try to cure her with their poisonous potions or noxious fumes or something worse. If she gets sick and develops a cough, she will die."

Charles could not decide if the old woman's findings were good or bad. The only words he understood clearly were, 'she will die.'

"Her wound is grave," she explained in a softer tone after seeing the worry in his face, "but she is strong and seems to have a reason to live." Looking him in the eyes, she added, "She is asking for you."

Raglan stepped forward. "Is Her Grace awake?"

"Who are you?"

"I am Lord Raglan," he answered, placing a hand on his hip, "the Count of Hohenberg."

Sarah fought off another yawn. "I see, well, I don't recall her making mention of any Lord Counts." She spun on her heel and resumed her previous course. "Don't disturb her, and don't let those buffoons near her," she warned loudly without looking back. "I'll visit her again in a day or two."

"When you see the duchess," said Raglan, "be sure to tell her that Duke Otto may be here in a few days. There are many things we need to discuss before he arrives."

"I am not going to see the duchess," said Charles.

"What!"

"You heard Sarah—she must not be disturbed."

"But the old woman said she was asking for you."

"Look at me," replied Charles. "I am covered in blood. Now is not a good time."

"Well, I guess what I have to say can wait a day longer," thought Raglan out loud. "Anyway, I need to prepare the camp and send for Her Lady's tents. We must make ourselves present-able for the Duke."

After Raglan left, Charles returned to where he had left his saddle and armor. Without the company of his friend, or import-ant tasks to perform like Prochaska and Raglan, he felt unneeded and alone. He looked back at the tent door and thought over the real reason he did not go in. When he held her in his arms after the battle he had lost control of his emotions. Last night he told her they must stop thinking of each other lest they go mad. What if he had already gone mad? He dared not go in that tent because he did not trust himself.

He picked up his equipment and walked to the edge of the camp. Spreading his blanket in the shade of a small tree, he col-lapsed to the ground from sheer exhaustion and was asleep in seconds.

Apart from a trip to the river to wash the blood from his body and clothes, Charles did not leave his one-man encampment for the next three days. Assuming he needed rest, they at first left the weary knight alone. By the second day, however, Prochaska and Raglan began to urge him to join them at their fires or at least eat a proper meal. Charles refused both. When he was not sleeping, he sat and stared at the door of Elsea's tent from a distance, but would not venture near it.

On the morning of the fourth day, the vanguard of the Bavarian army arrived. Lord Raglan and Bishop Prochaska welcomed them with as much pomp and ceremony as their primitive conditions would allow. Duke Otto was impatient to see Charles, who now reluctantly left his self-imposed seclusion.

Otto's excitement turned to alarm as he approached him. "What is wrong?"

"Nothing," shrugged Charles.

Otto gave him a long embrace before studying him at arm's length. "You look so pale," he observed. "Are you ill, have you been injured?"

"I am fine, My Lord," was all Charles would offer.

Prince John insisted on a tour of the battlefield. Thankful for any excuse to get away from Otto and the others, Charles quickly volunteered. He soon discovered that the prince had already squeezed William thoroughly for every detail of the battle. Charles shuffled along behind as the prince provided all the commentary and pointed out landmarks as if he had known them all his life. Although fascinated with the broken weapons and fragments of discarded armor still littering the battlefield, the prince was immensely disappointed to find that all the bodies had been removed and had to content himself with the fresh Styrian graves laid out before what had once been the wall.

He clambered to the top of a still intact section of the barricade. "This is the wall the peasants built," he proclaimed excitedly. "And down there is where the Styrians made their camp on the eve of battle. Over here must be the place where William and our Bavarians drove the enemy back and saved the day."

He poured out a stream of questions. Where was the line of archers? What part of the woods did he charge from? Where did Eldridge surrender? He begged to be shown the exact spot where the duchess had fallen, but Charles pretended he could not remember.

After covering nearly every square yard between the river and the forest, they headed back to the main camp.

"I envy you Charles," said the prince as they walked along. "You and William got to fight a magnificent battle and have covered yourselves in glory. All we have done since crossing the frontier is chase cattle and scare peasants. Why, I did not draw my sword a single time. I cannot tell you how discouraging it was."

"Trust me, Your Highness," replied Charles without looking up, "the less you draw your sword the happier you will be in this life."

"But I'll soon be duke, and a duke must know how to lead men in battle."

Charles thought it best not to reply.

The two men returned to find the simple Austrian camp had been transformed into a small Bavarian town complete with a broad avenue and side streets. Banners and pennants fluttered above every tent, and knights and nobles from both armies exchanged greetings as they intermingled between the two camps.

Prince John complained he was hungry and went off in search of a hot meal. A relieved Charles headed back to his solitary outpost.

Waiting for him was William.

"There you are," said his big friend. "They told me you'd show up here eventually. Did the prince get his fill of glory?"

Charles dropped down on his blanket with a sigh. "He knew more about the battle than I did," he frowned. "Remember, I spent half the day lost in that forest."

"And how is the duchess?" asked William as he sat down alongside.

"Lord Raglan tells me she is doing better."

"What do you mean *Lord Raglan* tells you? Haven't you seen her?"

"Not since the battle," returned Charles without emotion.

William pointed to Elsea's tent. "She's right over there," he said. "What's keeping you?"

"Why do I need to see her?" asked Charles. "We have accomplished what we came for: her war is won, and she is safe. I am only waiting for the duke to fulfill his promise so we can go home."

"I see…" observed the skeptical William.

"There is nothing to see," declared Charles. "I have taken your advice and put her out of my mind."

"If that's so, then why are you so unhappy?"

"Who says I am unhappy?"

"I've got eyes, my friend." Tapping his forehead with a finger he added, "You can't get that woman out of your head. Why else would you sit here all day staring at her tent?"

"Sarah said not to allow the doctors near her," explained Charles. "I'm making sure they stay away."

William looked over at the door of the tent flanked by two of Raglan's knights. "No doubt that assignment is beyond their ability."

"I should have stayed with the prince," moaned Charles. "His conversation is less annoying."

William stretched out and propped himself up on one elbow. "Since I've nothing better to do, I think I'll join your vigil. Perhaps I'll even catch a glimpse of that Dorianne creature. I confess that there is something about her very pleasing to the eye. While we wait, allow me to annoy you further with the parts of the battle you missed. Let's begin with how your old friend upheld the honor of all Bavaria while you were lost in the woods."

Charles leaned back on his saddle. "Have mercy," he groaned.

CHAPTER SIXTY-THREE

Revelation

Otto, Raglan, and Savoyen relaxed in the duke's tent recalling their days of service in the endless wars of Emperor Frederick II. The three friends waxed nostalgic about those heady times and agreed that the world had changed much, though little for the better, since they were young men.

At last, the duke brought the conversation around to the real reason for Lord Raglan's visit. "I have read your letter," he said to him, "and I commend you on your brilliant victory."

"I have written quite poorly if His Grace believes I deserve any commendation," replied Raglan. "Whatever laurels are due belong solely to the young people, especially Charles. That one knight possesses more wisdom and bravery than half the crowned heads of Europe put together. I wish I knew where you found him; we could do with a few of his kind in Austria."

"I am pleased his service was useful," replied Otto after a glance at Savoyen. "It may interest you to know I was completely against this venture, but he pressed me so sorely on the matter that I relented." Otto forced himself to laugh. "He seems to believe he has some sort of feelings for this duchess of yours. A passing whimsy, I am sure."

"I think you underestimate the young man's sentiments," said Raglan. "I can assure you that his concern for Her Grace is quite genuine."

"You are mistaken," replied Otto with a shake of his head. "I have known Charles since he was a mere boy. He is concerned for her wellbeing, naturally, but only out of a noble sense of duty."

"I have made many mistakes in my life," conceded Raglan, "but in this case I trust my own eyes. That those two are smitten with each other is the worst kept secret in all Vienna. Why, just look at them now. They risked their lives to win a great victory they cannot enjoy. He sits day and night brooding under his tree, and since we got word you were coming, she has stopped eating."

"How am I to blame for the duchess's appetite?"

"You are in an unenviable position, My Lord. You are both the answer to her dilemma and the cause of their heartache. Your gracious intervention has saved her throne at the cost of separating them forever. The two of them can be trusted to do their duty, but you may be certain it is a duty they do not relish."

"I only agreed to this marriage out of pity for the poor wretch," confessed Otto. "Surely, you are not saying that a man like Charles would of his own volition choose to waste his affections on such a villainess."

"I will let Sir Charles answer that question," returned Raglan.

"But what hold does she have over him?" pressed the flabbergasted duke.

"I could as well ask you what hold he has over her. No one knows better than I how arrogant the woman could be. Until now, her greatest attribute was the ease with which she heaped disgrace upon herself. Your Charles has awakened something in her. It is something I had given up hoping she possessed. Four days ago, I watched her lead an army with a dignity and courage that reminded me of her grandfather. When it looked as if the battle was lost, I advised her to flee. I know of few kings in such circumstances who would have hesitated. Instead, she insisted on leading a charge that turned the tide of battle though it nearly cost her life. There is no disputing she has given you ample reasons to disparage her, My Lord, but people sometimes change. I am not ashamed to confess my pride in the young woman. I hope, for her sake, this Kendrick fellow is not too odious. After all she has undergone, she deserves at least that."

Duke Otto sat back in his chair, mouth agape. "This is a startling revelation, my friend. I could not be more astounded if you told me the Danube had just run dry."

"Perhaps we are getting too old," smiled Raglan. "We have forgotten how deep our passions ran when we were in our own youth. This calm wisdom we now enjoy came much later in life than we care to admit."

Otto got up from his chair and walked to the entrance of his tent. He stared out at the flurry of activity in the camp for a moment, and then turned to face Raglan. "I had intended to meet with Her Grace on the morrow," he said, "but I wonder— is it possible to meet with her today?"

"She is still confined to her bed," noted Raglan, "but I believe a brief audience can be arranged, if that is your wish."

"If it is agreeable to Her Grace," said Otto, "I shall come to her tent this afternoon."

Raglan stood, and the two men embraced. "I will inform the duchess of your wish," said Raglan. Before he left the tent, he stopped to add, "For my sake, old friend, don't be too harsh with her."

"What do you make of this?" Otto asked Savoyen after he was gone.

"It is most baffling, My Lord. I think you should meet this extraordinary woman without delay and end all doubt."

CHAPTER SIXTY-FOUR

Visitor

As soon as Lord Raglan left the tent, Dorianne rushed up to Elsea. "My Lady," she gushed, "what should we do?"

Propped up by pillows on all sides, Elsea sat on her bed wrapped in a blanket and dressed only in her underclothes. She quickly looked around the tent. "Hurry, Dori, bring me my new robe. He must not see me in this sick bed."

While Dorianne was retrieving the robe, Elsea swung her legs out over the edge of the bed and placed her feet on the soft fur of the animal hides lining the floor.

"What are you doing?" exclaimed Dorianne. "You know Sarah said you must not leave your bed for at least another week."

"Hush, Dori," replied Elsea through a pain induced grimace. "Help me to that chair."

Dorianne reluctantly led her the few feet to the chair, and then draped the long robe of black sable fur over her shoulders. The expensive garment was a gift from Lord Raglan to commemorate her victory. Because moving her right arm gave her sharp pains, Sarah had placed it in a sling. Elsea slid her left arm into the sleeve, but the other one hung empty at her side. Dorianne tied all the fasteners in front and hastily arranged her hair which spilled onto her fur-covered shoulders.

Elsea cautiously eased herself into the chair. "How do I look?"

"Like your mother come back to life," whispered Dorianne.

She sat up and took as deep a breath as her broken ribs would allow. "You may show him in now."

Duke Otto entered the tent and stopped abruptly at the sight of the young duchess sitting calmly on her improvised throne.

"Your Grace," he began after a pause, "I hope I have not come at an inconvenient time."

"You honor me with your presence, Duke Otto," she answered politely. She pointed at a nearby stool. "I regret I have nothing more comfortable to offer you."

Otto pulled the stool a little closer and sat down. "I congratulate you on your remarkable triumph over Duke Eldridge. Lord Raglan tells me you acquitted yourself nobly."

"I believe you have the greater share in the victory, My Lord. If you had not sent Sir Charles to my aid I would not be alive today."

"You are welcome," he replied coolly, "but as you know, I was never in favor of sending him."

"Yes, My Lord," was all she said.

"However," he continued, "I am a man of my word, and I am prepared to make good my offer of an alliance."

"Thank you, My Lord," she replied, but her gratitude lacked energy.

"You seem disappointed," he observed. "Certainly you know that a marriage into my family is better than anything a simple Bavarian knight could offer you."

"What does My Lord mean?"

"I understand you are purported to have feelings for Sir Charles," he answered bluntly.

"I was not aware this was common knowledge."

"Indeed, according to Lord Raglan, I must be the only man in Germany who does not know."

Elsea looked down briefly at the floor beneath her feet before looking up at Otto again. "I see Your Grace wishes to be straightforward in this matter," she said. "I shall be as candid and not deny my feelings for him."

"It seems these feeling of yours are rather capricious," he noted, "one might even say convenient."

"I do not understand His Grace."

"Come now; I am only giving voice to what even a blind man could see. You were fond of Charles when you thought he was my son, but once you learned the truth you cast him aside—and nearly to his death—without a second thought. Now you have a new opportunity before you, and to him you have assented without ever having seen his face."

Elsea forced herself to sit up a little more in her chair. "Duke Otto," she said calmly, "I see the point you are not so delicately hinting at. You think me calculating and mercenary. You believe I used Charles to gain an advantage with you. We are both well aware of my former behavior, and it shames me to admit I deserve the low opinion you have of me. However, My Lord, in this instance you are most assuredly wrong. Charles interceded for me in this affair without my knowledge. He is convinced it is for my best and has risked his life a dozen times over to make it possible. For me to refuse your offer now would make a mockery of all he has done for me, and I will not so dishonor him."

"You of all people will understand my skepticism," returned Otto. "You've given me no reason to trust the genuineness of these virtuous sentiments you now express."

An awkward moment passed before Elsea continued in a softer voice. "I know my conduct toward you has been shameful, My Lord. If it was possible, I would take back every disgraceful word and deed, but some things can never be undone. I only wish I could find the words now to convince you of my sincerity. For Charles's sake, I will marry whomever you wish and agree to any terms you impose, but I would rather be bound in irons and thrown into the river at the bottom of this hill than to live without him."

Otto studied her a long moment. "Is Lord Raglan correct?" he asked. "Have you indeed changed?"

"Whether I have changed or not is for others to judge," she replied. "Charles has given me a desire to be better, and his opinion is the only one that matters to me."

"As you certainly know, Charles speaks well of you."

"Yes, My Lord."

"Your problem has always been your excessive pride," declared Otto. "You must master it, or it will master you."

"Yes, My Lord. I know that only too well."

Another long pause followed Elsea's admission.

"Well, I suppose in that regard you will have no lack of comrades among the nobles of Germany," conceded Otto at last. "It is because I too struggle against that greatest of all sins that I am able to recognize it so easily in another."

Elsea relaxed into her chair and her features softened. "My Lord is being gracious."

Otto folded his arms across his chest and stroked his beard a moment. "Is it still your wish to marry my nephew Kendrick?"

"You know my predicament," she replied. "Everyone tells me I must make a suitable marriage or see the end of my family's rule. If you know of another way, I beseech you to tell me."

"Your quandary is a difficult one," he admitted. "Lord Savoyen has great wisdom in such matters. If you wish, I will seek his opinion."

"You have already done so much for me, My Lord, and I am truly grateful, but if you can find a way to help me I will be in your debt the rest of my life."

Otto stood up. "I have imposed on you long enough, Your

Grace," he said with a bow. "I beg your leave and ask permission to speak with you again when I have an answer for you."

"You will be welcomed at any time, My Lord."

Savoyen was waiting for the duke when he came through the door of his tent. "Well?"

"She is a stunning sight, Savoy," replied Otto as he flopped down in his chair. "The instant I saw her, I was convinced she was the ghost of her dear mother."

"Beauty is but skin deep, My Lord, but has the leopard indeed changed her spots?"

"Lord Raglan was right," confessed Otto, "she is not the spoiled child I remember."

"Don't tell me the vixen of Vienna has beguiled you as well!"

"It is worse than that, my friend: I think I know what Charles sees in her, and try as I might, I can find no fault in his taste."

"What will you do?"

There was a long silence as Otto considered Savoyen's simple question.

"I feel compelled to help her somehow," replied the Duke at last.

"Help her!" exclaimed Savoyen. "You have already given her far more help than she could ever have imagined. What more could you possibly do for her?"

"Did I say help her?" asked Otto. "I should have said help *them*. And you will show me how."

CHAPTER SIXTY-FIVE

Proposal

"But there is no precedent for this," argued Lord Savoyen from across the table.

"Then I shall make one by doing as I please," Otto argued back.

"I beg you to consider the consequences, My Lord."

"There you go again, Savoy. If there was a city called Discouragement, you would be its lord and master."

"You know I have always advised you based on the way things are, not on how you wish them to be. To abandon your aspirations is one thing, but what you are proposing is beyond irrational. What will the princes of Germany think?"

"Let those empty-headed peacocks think what they like!" exclaimed the duke. "I cannot be rid of their wearisome sanctimony soon enough. Charles's happiness is all that concerns me now. Can't you see? This will let me satisfy my wife's greedy brothers and guarantee the security of both my sons. I can go to my grave in peace!"

"You might live to be one hundred, My Lord. What about the throne of Germany? The crown is as good as in your grasp. Will you throw it all away when we are so close?"

"Ha!" snorted Otto. "I have spent a lifetime clawing my way to that throne. The older I get, the less it appeals to me. The very mention of it sours my stomach."

Savoyen let out a low sigh. "Will you not be dissuaded?" he tried one last time.

"My mind is set," answered the duke. "All I ask from you is your help to arrange it."

A long silence followed the Duke's declaration.

"They will not have an easy life, my friend," predicted Savoyen at last.

"You of all people should know there is no easy life in this world," noted Otto. "They are wiser than their years and will face their difficulties as we did: one day at a time."

"And you want to do this today?"

"As soon as I speak with John, I will go directly to the duchess."

"Lord Raglan should be informed as well," advised Savoyen.

"Of course," agreed Otto. "But after you finish talking with Raglan, bring Charles to her tent."

"Yes, My Lord."

Lord Savoyen stood over the two sleeping men and cleared his throat several times. Charles sat up and rubbed his eyes. William stretched himself out full length on the ground and let out a groaning yawn.

"You will forgive me for disturbing your repose," said Savoyen looking down on them, "but while you young men were napping, we old men were busy solving the problems of the realm. The duke is on his way to meet with the duchess. He is going to formalize their alliance."

"So soon?" asked the suddenly alert Charles.

"You know His Grace is not one to dawdle in matters of significance," replied Savoyen. "He sent me to find you. Since this whole affair is your doing, he wants you to be present."

Charles hurriedly brushed the dust from his clothing and ran his fingers through his hair a few times before following Savoyen to Elsea's tent. They found her sitting calmly in her chair, cloaked in her victory sable. Though it was the first time he had seen her since the day of the battle, he quickly detected that she was still in pain and that her composed demeanor was only a brave show.

They stared at each other from across the tent. Charles had convinced himself that his self-imposed separation would cure him of his desire for her, but the instant his eyes met hers his passion redoubled. He did not know how, but she seemed to have grown even more beautiful, and he had to avert his eyes to hide his despair.

"I am glad you are here, Sir Charles," she said. "I have not had opportunity to thank you for all you did to make our victory possible."

"My role was a minor one, Your Grace," he said, looking down at his feet. "Lord Raglan and Bishop Prochaska are more worthy of your gratitude."

"Your humility does you a disservice, Sir Charles," she smiled faintly. "I would not be sitting here today if not for you, and I am grateful for the risks you took on my behalf."

He ventured a glance to offer a reluctant, "Thank you," but looked away quickly when he met her eyes again.

The arrival of the duke rescued them from the uneasy silence that followed.

"Your Grace, I apologize for the inconvenience I am no doubt causing," said Otto, as he swept back the tent door's flap, "but there is a pressing matter I wish to resolve."

"You owe me no apology, My Lord. If the matter you speak of is the one I think it is, I am just as eager to get it behind us."

"Perhaps this is a topic better discussed in private, Your Highness," suggested Lord Savoyen.

Elsea gave Dorianne a nod, and she followed Savoyen out of the tent. Otto and Charles grabbed the only stools and sat down before the duchess.

"We are alone now, My Lord," noted Elsea. "Please feel free to speak frankly."

"I have thought much about our earlier conversation," began Otto. "You need an alliance and yet you do not wish to marry my nephew Kendrick."

Elsea looked at Charles briefly as she hesitated to reply. "My Lord knows the House of Babenberg is in peril. I am told that unless I make a proper marriage, my family's rule will end. Regrettably, my wishes in this matter are of no consequence, and it is my duty to preserve that legacy however unpleasant the task might be."

"And that is your dilemma," noted Otto. "You wish to honor your family, but not marry my nephew."

"Yes," confessed Elsea. "It was my hope that My Lord could find another way to help me."

"I regret that I have failed to find an alternative," admitted Otto. "Even Lord Savoyen, whose opinion I trust above all others in these matters, says you have no other options, and that a suitable marriage is your only solution." He paused to look into their dejected faces before adding, "Nevertheless, I have decided that you should not marry my nephew."

Charles leapt up from his stool. "But you gave your word!" he blurted.

"This decision is most unexpected, My Lord," interjected a calmer Elsea before Charles could continue. "Charles has hazarded his life, and many have died, because we trusted in your promise."

"Charles," smiled Otto, "I have no intention of breaking my promise. Please sit down and allow me to tell you a story. It is a story that will no doubt cause you to think less of me, but it is a story you should have heard long ago."

He waited for Charles to return to his seat alongside Elsea, and began, "Before I became duke, I met a girl in my father's castle. Although she was a peasant's daughter, and many years younger, she was the kindest, gentlest, most beautiful woman I had ever seen. Despite the differences in our age and class, we fell in love. I suppose we were no different from other lovers who let themselves believe theirs is the one true love strong enough to overcome all obstacles. Ours was a love that did not need to obey rules or fear their consequences. We both rejoiced the day she told me she was carrying my child. I went straight to my father and told him how much I desperately wanted to marry her. But instead of getting his blessing, my father flew into a rage and vehemently forbade it. He insisted I tell no one of our affair and ordered the girl sent away to be kept in secret. At first I thought he opposed our marriage because of her bloodline, but I soon learned he had another motive.

"Bavaria was on the verge of a civil war, and it was not certain that my family would prevail. We needed the support of the wealthy Lords Hechten and Lichten to gain the advantage and quell the rebellion. But they would not agree to an alliance unless I married their sister Agnes. For an entire month, every relative I had pleaded with me to accept the proposal and save our family. Every day since then I have regretted that I was not strong enough to refuse. The peace was settled the day I married Agnes. A week later my son was born in secrecy under a peasant's roof.

"My father did not get to enjoy his diplomatic triumph for long, for he died two years later. Once I became duke, I had the boy and his mother moved closer to the castle where I could ensure they were well cared for. But despite how much it galled me, I had to admit that the stability of my rule depended on the backing of my brothers-in-law. It was for fear of losing their support that the woman and our son had to remain a secret. However, as soon as the boy was old enough I had him brought into the castle. As far as anyone knew, he was just another young page with dreams of becoming a knight. I put him in the care of Sir William, and reared him beside my John."

Charles's eyes widened as the implications of this last information began to sink in.

"Yes," answered Otto to his unspoken question. "You were that boy. You are my son. Your dear mother wanted to tell you the truth many times, but her love for me was too great. It shames me to admit that I took advantage of that love. She endured the shame that should have been mine and protected my secret all these years. And so you have it, my son. It is a story that reflects as well upon your mother as it reflects poorly upon me. But it is the truth, nonetheless."

During the long silence that followed Otto's confession, Elsea reached over and put a hand on Charles's shoulder, but said nothing.

"This is much to take in," said Charles at last. "All my life I felt like I was missing something because I never knew my father, and yet you were there all along."

"It is true," admitted Otto. "Although you could never love me as a father, I could love you as a son. And I gave you everything a father who loves his son can give."

"Yes you did," agreed Charles. "And I suppose it all makes sense now. I hope you know how grateful I was that you took care of my mother and provided for me all those years. But, My Lord, I did not come here today to seek my own welfare, but that of Her Grace. I do not understand how what you have told me helps her."

416

"Come now, Charles, you are too clever not to understand. I promised that Her Grace would marry into my family. She will do so by marrying you!" Otto clapped his hands together on the last word and waited for Charles to gush with appreciation.

Instead, Charles seemed even more dejected. "Even if you are my father," he began, "I cannot marry Her Grace. She needs a marriage that will bring her honor, not reproach. There is a name for what I am, My Lord."

"Do not think such thoughts, Charles. You are my son, and soon the whole Empire will know it. From this day forward you will have the name that was your birthright. Her Grace will indeed marry into my family!"

"But what about Hechten and Lichten?" inserted Elsea. "Naming Charles as your firstborn would certainly alienate them as they will surely see him as a rival to their nephew."

"That is precisely what Lord Savoyen kept saying," replied Otto. "But all Hechten and Lichten have ever wanted is to see their nephew John inherit my duchy. They have been waiting patiently, one might say impatiently, these many years for me to die. Well, they will not need to wait any longer. I will abdicate and give the coronet to John *now*."

"This is too rash, My Lord!" objected Charles. "Everyone knows how close you are to the throne of all Germany!"

"Ha!" laughed Otto. "The two of you sound more like Savoyen then Savoyen himself." He reached over and took Charles by the hand. "Do you remember that morning you begged me to let you return to Austria? You told me sometimes being wise is the best thing, but not the right thing. Well, I want to do what is both right and best. I do not abdicate for Charles the knight; I do this for Charles my son. John will be the Duke of Bavaria, and you and Her Grace will reign over Austria. By this one act I will provide for both my sons while I still have life left to enjoy it.

417

My desire is that you marry Her Grace as soon as she has recovered. Lord Raglan has given his permission, and Bishop Prochaska has already agreed to perform the wedding." He looked from Charles to Elsea and back again. "I had hoped this would make you both happy."

"It would make me very happy indeed," said Elsea, now looking at Charles, "but I can only speak for myself."

Charles was overwhelmed by how quickly his life had changed in the last few moments. He had come into the tent anticipating the final breaking of what was left of his heart, but had instead learned something too wonderful to imagine. He thought of all that the man he now knew was his father was about to give up for him. Would not honor demand that he refuse his sacrifice? Yet as he looked into Elsea's imploring eyes, all nobility deserted him.

Dropping to one knee, he took her left hand and placed it on his heart. "Elsea," he said softly, "what you feel beating beneath your hand belongs to you and always will. Marry me, and let me spend the rest of my life proving it."

"There is nothing in this world I want more," she whispered back.

Otto stood and placed a hand on each of them like a priest bestowing a blessing. "You have made this old man happier than words can express," he laughed. "I would not trade this moment for all the kingdoms of the world."

By order of Duke Otto, a banquet was arranged to celebrate the announcement of their betrothal, and for three days the soldiers of Bavaria and Austria made preparations. Elsea insisted that Lord Raglan invite the families of the peasants who fought in the battle. When the day finally arrived, farmers garbed in homespun and plain clothed villagers mingled with the lavishly dressed knights and nobles in an excited anticipation.

Charles was waiting for Elsea when she stepped from her tent into the bright sunshine wearing a long dress of Bavarian blue in honor of Duke Otto. She took him by the arm, and he escorted her across the camp through the crowd of peasants and knights cheering themselves hoarse at the sight of the beautiful duchess and her handsome prince. Elsea's smile was never brighter, and Charles was never prouder.

Waiting for them on the dais were Otto, Prince John, Lords Hechten, Lichten, Savoyen, and Raglan. Her wound still caused her pain, and Charles held her arm tightly as she ascended the steps of the platform. At the top, she offered her hand to each of the lords as they bowed respectfully and kissed her hand lightly. When Duke Otto stepped up, however, she unexpectedly knelt at his feet.

"Thank you for your kindness," she said with head bowed. "I pray that I will be worthy of your faith in me."

"You have already shown yourself worthy," smiled Otto. "Now stand, my daughter, and take your place next to me. This day is in your honor, and there is only one person I will permit to bow the knee."

Duke Otto guided her to a seat at his right. After she sat down, he nodded to Lord Savoyen. From a small tent near the dais, Duke Eldridge emerged, and the cheering of the throng turned to derision. With an Austrian and Bavarian knight at each elbow, he approached the platform. After struggling up the steps, the large man knelt before the seated duchess. The crowd went quiet as Eldridge placed his hand on the small wooden box Bishop Prochaska held out for him.

"My Lady," he began, "I am your humble servant. From this day forth I solemnly pledge my faithful service. Whether in war or in peace, I will obey you in all things. Your friends will be my friends, and your enemies will be my enemies. I swear to you my fealty on these very bones of the Holy Saints, in the presence of these your honored guests, and in the sight of Almighty God."

"I accept your oath, Duke Eldridge," said Elsea. "Now rise as my vassal."

The assembled guests erupted into their loudest cheering yet.

At a signal from Duke Otto, the guests began lining up at the food tables. While the musicians played, the people danced, sang, and laughed well into the moon lit night in one continuous blur of merrymaking. No one could recall a day filled with more honest joy.

CHAPTER SIXTY-SIX

New Home

Two months later, in a crowded Vienna cathedral, Charles, son of Otto Wittelsbach, married Elsea, daughter of Frederick Babenberg. Excited well-wishers, unable to find a seat in the tightly packed sanctuary, thronged the doors, spilling down the steps and into the street. Out of respect for Otto, many of the princes from the surrounding German states were in attendance. Among the prestigious wedding guests were the Dukes of Saxony, Carinthia, Carniola, and Moravia. Eldridge, whose request to be excused from the ceremony was denied by Otto, sat sulking in a corner pew. Lord Raglan and Duke Otto sat side by side, neither able to conceal their overwhelming pride. William stood with Charles before the altar, and Dorianne wept silently at Elsea's elbow.

When Father Prochaska finally pronounced them husband and wife, Charles kissed his bride, and the church bells erupted in a joyous melody. An Austrian and Bavarian honor guard ushered the newlyweds from the church and through the cheering townspeople jostling to catch a glimpse of the happy bride and groom. Giggling girls cast flowers at the young couple's feet, and the sweet fragrance of the crushed petals filled the air.

The honor guard escorted them through the press of people to the open carriage Lord Raglan had provided. Charles climbed in first and reached down to pull the laughing Elsea in with him.

The driver gave the team of horses a light lash, and the carriage lurched forward. Charles and Elsea stood up looking back, waving to the crowd who at first tried to follow them, until they disappeared down the cobblestone street with a column of colorfully dressed knights trailing behind. The clacking of the horses' hooves echoed off the buildings and followed them out of the city.

Elsea rested her head on Charles's shoulder as they rode into the countryside. "Is this really happening?" she cooed.

"It is a dream," he laughed, as he tightened his arm around her shoulders, "and if we are very careful, we shall never wake from it."

They came to the fork in the road that would take them to the castle, but Charles tapped the driver on the shoulder, and they continued going straight.

"We've missed the turn," she said.

"I know."

"But what about our wedding banquet in the great hall? Lord Raglan will be upset if we are late."

"We have plenty of time," he assured her. "There is something I want to show you first."

"What is so important that it cannot wait?"

"I am the one who cannot wait," he smiled.

"Hmmm, sounds secretive. Can you give me a hint?"

"Patience, my wife. We are almost there."

They soon reached the place where Raglan held the tournament that day in early spring. Charles directed the driver to turn onto a road that led into the woods.

"I don't remember this road," said Elsea.

"That's because it was only finished yesterday."

"Is this the surprise?"

"I hardly think a new road is worth getting excited over," he answered.

Just then, they broke out into a clearing. "I know this place," said Elsea. "It's where the old ruins are."

"They are not ruins anymore," beamed Charles.

A large stone house rose up from the ground where the vestiges of the ancient building once stood. The carriage brought them right up to the front door.

"Your Grace," said Charles with a dramatic sweep of his arm, "welcome to your new summer home."

Elsea climbed down from the carriage and gazed in awe at the tightly-fitted grey fieldstone walls and the black slate roof. "It's beautiful," she gushed. "How did you do it?"

"My father wanted to give you a wedding gift," he explained. "I provided the inspiration, and he provided the money."

"Who would have guessed that beneath all that bluster, your father has such a soft heart?" she said.

"He certainly has a soft heart for you," agreed Charles. "After all, this is *your* wedding present."

Leaving their escort behind, Charles led her by the hand into the house. They walked across a floor of smooth oaken boards and ran their hands over the finely hewn cedar planking covering the walls. Elsea's laughter echoed within the yet barren rooms as she rushed down halls and through doorways as if discovering hidden treasure. Together, they explored sitting rooms, servants' quarters, a kitchen, a dining room, a modest hall, and a small library.

Charles pointed proudly at the large stained glass windows. "The glass panes came all the way from Venice."

They stopped before one last closed door. "I saved the best for last," he said.

He opened the door and brought her into another empty

room with its own fireplace. A tall southern facing window let in the sunshine, and they stood in the center of its warm light. Next to the hall, it was the largest room in the house.

"Welcome to our bedroom," he announced proudly.

Elsea brought her hands to her mouth as she looked from wall to wall. "Charles, it really is too marvelous. Now I know I am dreaming."

"I am glad you like it," he said.

"It is more than just this house, Charles. I am overwhelmed by all that has happened. Just a few months ago I was a miserable wretch. I was alone and without hope, and everyday brought more despair than the day before. But God saw me even when I did not know how to call on His name. He rooted out my bitterness and gave me in its place a contentment I did not know was possible. And most of all, He gave me you."

He pulled her to him, and she laid her head on his shoulder. "Seeing you happy is what makes me happy," he whispered in her ear.

"Oh, my love, is it too much to hope we will always be this happy?" she asked, looking up at him. "There will be more to ruling Austria than pleasant rides in an open carriage. Kirchenbetter and Keinmeyer still refuse to submit, and God only knows what malice Lord Eugene is up to in Bohemia. I fear the time may come when you will regret the vows you made this day, my husband."

"We will have our share of life's sorrows," he said, as he ran his fingertips through the hair above her eyes. "Some of them may even break our hearts and seem beyond our endurance, but with God's help we will face them together. This house and its walls will be our refuge from the rogues and ravages of life. Let the whole world turn against us, we must never let anything come between us here. You will always be my Austrian duchess, and I will always be your Bavarian knight. That is all the happiness anyone has a right to hope for in this world."

"You are wrong," she smiled. "You will always be my Viking King."

"Always," he promised.

Standing over the very spot where they first met as children, Charles kissed his wife.

THE END

ABOUT THE AUTHOR

J.C. Wilson is a Christian educator, teacher, and public speaker. He enjoys reading, writing, studying the Bible, playing sports, hunting, camping, and spending time with his sons, daughters-in-law, and grandchildren. He lives in Maryland with his lovely wife, and they are the proud parents of two sons and seven grandchildren. *Love's Orphan* is his first novel.

45260550R00257

Made in the USA
Middletown, DE
14 May 2019